Cover design by Taylor Thomas Smythe
Interior illustrations by Alice Waller

Independently published.
ISBN: 978-1-087-94665-8

Taylor Thomas Smythe / TTS
West Palm Beach, FL

www.kingdomofflorida.com
www.ttsmythe.com

KINGDOM *of* FLORIDA

VOLUME I

Stories from the Kingdom of Florida:
I. The Golden Alligator
II. The Lamplight Society
III. The Place Beyond the Sea
IV. The Fountain of Youth
V. The Curse of Coronado
VI. Coral and the Treasure Hunters
VII. (To be announced)

Visit *KingdomOfFlorida.com* for more!

Table of Contents

Book 1: The Golden Alligator   7

Book 2: The Lamplight Society   189

Book 3: The Place Beyond the Sea   357

Book 4: The Fountain of Youth   535

Kingdom of Florida
The Golden Alligator

Written by
Taylor Thomas Smythe

Illustrated by
Alice Waller

OLIVER

CHAPTER ONE
What Happened When the House Went Dark

Oliver had never been out of the state of Florida; it was the only home he had ever known. That vast, humid peninsula was full of sunshine on most days—perfect for enjoying a nice trip to the beach like the one Oliver had planned with two of his neighbors that particular afternoon. But something seemed to be stirring as the boy looked out the window toward the sky up above, and the clouds were not their usual cotton white.

"So much for our beach day," Oliver sulked to his friends as he straightened his glasses. The two had just shown up on the doorstep in full summer swim gear, and he hated to be the bearer of bad news.

"Maybe it will just rain a little," said Ellie hopefully as a smile flashed across her freckled face. She was the youngest of the group.

Her brother Ben, older by a year, chimed in: "It's summertime in Florida, Ellie. It'll be raining the whole afternoon."

"Then maybe we can have a rain day instead," she said as she stuck out her hand to see if she could feel any drops. A cacophonous crack split through the air and sent the children scurrying into a frightened clump. Seconds later, the calming pitter-patter faded in as the waves of rain swept up their tree-lined street.

"We'd better get inside," Ben said. "I'd rather *not* get struck by lightning."

Oliver ushered his friends through the doorway and into the living room. It had a simple and utilitarian feel, with a pair of mismatched sofas, a leather recliner, a few framed photos and some artwork from a thrift store. The house, made in the mid-century era, had small windows that let in minimal amounts of light in conjunction with the storm's present cloud-cover.

"Wanna play a game?" Oliver asked as he moved toward a cabinet.

"Sure," said Ellie, ever-ready for an amusing experience.

"Anything to pass the time," said Ben. "This storm's a bad one—there'll be no walking home until it's over." They only lived a few houses down, but Ben knew his parents would object to him endangering the life of his little sister to brave the rain and lightning. "What games have you got in there?"

Digging through the haphazardly organized stack of board games, Oliver tugged delicately on a dusty container he recognized as *Risk*. "How about this one?" He pulled out the fading teal case with its barely-readable red lettering. "It has lots of little pieces in different colors, and you try to make your color cover over the whole map."

As the oldest of the three, Oliver was used to being the one to make up the rules to the many games in the cabinet. His willing subjects never suspected that their gameplay was primarily crafted by Oliver's improvisations. But then again, they were all somewhat impressionable as Ben and Ellie could still count their ages on two hands.

As the rain continued to dance down the glass of the front windows, Ellie grabbed the box, removed the lid, and spilled its contents over the rug in the center of the room. Tiny colored soldiers and cannons amassed on the fuzzy rug, which the children quickly began to push into separate piles.

"Is your grandpa home?" Ben asked the game-master.

"He had to work today," replied Oliver. He was Oliver's caretaker, and the boy had lived with his grandfather since he was very young. Though he was old enough for his memory to begin fading, the man still worked at a bank to provide for his grandson, whom he often left at home alone. Oliver had always been a responsible and helpful child and he delighted in the freedom that this solitude afforded him. "He'll be home around dinner-time, I think."

As they sat on the rug, the room became darker. The winds had picked up and the rain on the windows now sounded more like a thousand tiny fingers tapping Morse-coded messages in unison. A rumble of thunder rattled the windows and the lights flickered. Ellie looked scared.

"Sometimes the power goes in and out when the storm is really bad," Oliver muttered. The lights flickered again.

A sudden strobe of light entered the room, followed by another peal of thunder that vibrated the whole house. The lamps in the living room went dark. A few seconds passed as the children waited for the light to return.

"The power's out," said Oliver in defeat.

Ellie shimmied a few inches further from the windows. "When will it come back on?"

"I'm not sure." Oliver told the truth, but hoped it would return soon. "I think we have some flashlights in the garage, though, if anyone wants to help me look for them in the dark."

"I'll come," said Ellie, eager to move further away from the windows that flashed monochromatic scenes of the tempest outside.

The two had already started toward the hall when Ben chimed in. "I won't let you two wander alone in this dark house in the middle of a blackout. I'm right behind you." Ben was ten and he was quite afraid of the dark.

The hallway had no windows, so the children did their best to find the door to the garage in the dim light leaking in from the living room. When Oliver's hand found the knob, he turned it and pushed in. Musty, humid air filled the hall as the children filed down the two steps into the garage. Out of habit, Oliver felt his hand up the wall to find the light switch, and was disappointed when he remembered it was not operational.

The rain sounded louder as it beat on the garage door. "Do you know where the flashlights are, Oliver?" asked Ben. He hoped they were easily accessible so they could get back into the house as quickly as possible.

"I thought we kept them on the workbench," replied Oliver. "But grandpa may have moved them to clear up some space." He pointed to a pile of cardboard boxes with scribbles of permanent marker on their sides. "Maybe they're in one of those boxes."

Carefully, they moved through the dark garage toward the chunky pyramid of cardboard boxes in the corner. It was so murky that Oliver—whose skin was several shades darker than his friends'—could barely see his own hands feeling out in front of him. His outstretched fingers made contact with one of the boxes, and he slid them along the surface until he found a corner. With both hands he lifted the box off the top of the stack and set it on the painted concrete floor. He remembered that there was a window in the garage, but a thick old sheet draped over a curtain rod typically covered it.

"Ben, can you open that curtain?" asked Oliver. "We can let a little light in."

Ben complied and moved toward the sliver of dim light behind him and his sister. A shaft of dusty grayish light illuminated Oliver and the cardboard box in front of him. The side of the box read: *Memorabilia.*

"Oh," Oliver said, realizing the box of mementos was not the most likely place for a flashlight. "Maybe it's in another one of those boxes." He moved toward the stack a second time.

Leaning in, Ellie tried to read the side of the box.

"What's *memora—memorabil—*?"

"Memorabilia," her brother finished. "Is that stuff from your parents?" Curious, Ben reached down to open the top of the box.

Oliver tried to read the sides of the other boxes as he responded to his neighbor's inquiry. "I guess so," he said. "I never really looked in there. It's just dusty old books and letters, I think. And probably some pictures of me as a baby."

"Aww," said Ellie as she pulled out one of the photographs. "You were chubby."

Oliver abandoned his survey of the box pyramid and joined his friends in sifting through the artifacts of his personal family history. Grabbing the tiny picture from Ellie, Oliver strained to see its details and moved toward the window. On the faded sepia square, his mother carried a chunky baby boy in a diaper and smiled for the camera. "Her name was Vera." Vera held herself in a regal manner, and her dark complexion was pretty and plain.

"She looks like a princess," said Ellie, peering around his shoulder. She tried to emulate the slight tilt of Vera's head and her soft smile.

"What's this?" Ben spoke up with curiosity. The others rushed over as he lifted a large, yellowed envelope from inside the trove of heirlooms and pulled what looked like thick, leathery paper out of it. Unfolding it, he could see lines, markings, and scribbles in a deep black ink. Smudges at the edges betrayed the slightest water damage on the otherwise pristine document. Realizing the object was upside-down, Ben rotated it to get a more accurate view and stated in wonder to the other two: "It's a map!"

CHAPTER TWO
The Map

The children had all seen maps of the world during their years in school—the kind on large pull-strings that teachers could never seem to get to retract back up without considerable effort—but this map was quite unique.

"What's it a map of?" inquired Ellie, the least familiar with geographical matters.

"It looks like a map of the state of Florida," said Ben. "And you know you shouldn't end a sentence with a preposition, Ellie."

"What's a *proposition?*" she inquired in an attempt to repeat a word that was new to her, and then walked back over to the box and dug around some more.

"Never mind that," said Oliver as he looked more closely at the map with Ben. Indeed, the inky lines on the thick parchment formed an outline akin to an early map of the oddly shaped state of Florida. However, the map had no visible writing or words to grant the children certainty about its contents.

Ben reviewed the map himself. "It's strange that there's no writing or labels on it. It looks hand-drawn."

"Found it!" Ellie exclaimed. She held up a tiny flashlight and clicked it on, shining it directly into the boys' eyes. "A flashlight!" The boys covered their faces with open hands and squinted toward Ellie.

"Good job," said Oliver. "Can you maybe shine it on the map and not in our eyes?" He used the map to shield his eyes from the bright light.

Ellie waved the light away from them as she walked over. As Ellie shone the light on the front of the map, other markings and symbols began to appear—markings that had not been visible without the light shining. The new ink formed a number of lakes dotting the mainland, with other lines indicating higher elevations and a shape jutting out from the peninsula in a slight variation on the maps they knew of Florida. Foreign symbols and lettering spread out across the ancient cartograph in a number of differing inks and colors.

"It looks like Florida," said Ben, nudging Ellie to move the flashlight closer. Pointing to the markings visible in the middle of the map, he continued, "But what are these? Mountains?"

"That's curious," chimed Oliver.

"Isn't it?" Ben repeated, gesturing to the bottom of the map. "Florida doesn't have any mountains—or even many hills, for that matter." The illuminated map now included a host of other dissimilarities from the usual images of the state in which they resided.

"Is it a treasure map?" Ellie wondered, shifting a bit

so that the beam of light drifted off the map. The new markings suddenly vanished from sight.

"It's certainly an *old* map," said Oliver feeling the aged paper. "But where did the markings go?"

"It appears that these symbols are only visible in the light," said Ben. "Point that light over here again, Ellie."

Ellie shone the light on the surface of the map again. A giant red X was now visible, struck over a spot on the southeastern coast of the mainland. "See," she said. "It *is* a treasure map!"

The boys couldn't argue with her, so they looked closer. "But a map to what treasure? And *where* does it lead?" Oliver wondered.

"If this was a map of Florida, I'd say that X was right near our town," posited Ben. "But we still haven't established if that's what this is a map of."

"Prepositions," chided Oliver.

Ben glared at him and shook his head at his friend's correction of his grammar. Then the word gave him an idea. "Positions!"

"Huh?" Oliver was confused, and Ellie's face echoed the sentiment.

"If this *is* a map of Florida, then maybe we can see if the *positions* of things in our town match up with the maps somehow. And these weird markings."

"And what if they don't match up?" Oliver asked.

Ben smiled. "What if they *do*?"

Oliver was accustomed to Ben's thoughtfulness so he waited for him to elaborate, but Ellie spoke up: "Treasure!"

They went silent and looked at the map again. The

sound of the rain continued outside with no signs of ceasing. There was no mistaking that the placement of the red X lined up with their town.

"If this rain ever stops, we have to follow the map to that treasure—or whatever it happens to be," said Oliver.

"It's getting darker out there," said Ellie. "Maybe we should go back in the house and play games."

"Ellie's right," said Ben. "We'll begin the treasure hunt first thing tomorrow."

With everyone in agreement, the three friends left the dank, musty garage and returned to the living room to enjoy a game of *Risk* by flashlight and Oliver's house rules. The rain eventually lessened to a drizzle just in time for Ben and Ellie to return home for supper. And as they could not stop thinking about their impending adventure, none of the children obtained much sleep that night.

CHAPTER THREE
A Harrowing Bicycle Ride

The next morning, the sky was clear and the rain had stopped. Before the summertime heat wave had time to creep above the horizon, Ben, Ellie, and Oliver wheeled up to the corner of their shady street on their bicycles. Since it was among his family's belongings, Oliver became de facto keeper of the ancient map, and he pulled it out of his backpack as he unzipped it.

"Which way do we go?" asked Ellie as her neighbor looked closely at the huge, unfolded map to chart their course.

"Let's see," said Oliver. He held the map out to allow some sunlight to illuminate it beneath the dappled shadows of the trees. The red X reappeared, along with some quickly-scratched words in dark ink. Oliver leaned in closer to read the markings. "I think this is an address: 505 Azalea Drive."

Ben thought for a moment. "That must be over

in Flamingo Park," he said, pointing down the street. "Let's go!"

No sooner had Oliver folded the map and returned it to his book bag than Ellie and Ben took off pedaling down the road. A gentle breeze filled his hair as Oliver caught up with his friends, passing large banyan and mango trees, and they made their way to the first stop sign. Rolling through the intersection, the posse veered right and approached a busier street. They wheeled past a woman pushing a baby carriage, a group of boys and men playing soccer outside a church, and then made another sharp turn.

As it was late morning, traffic was light, and the children looked all ways before crossing the next wide intersection without waiting for a signal. The sun was starting to warm up the asphalt, and they were relieved when they returned to a quiet street on the other side with massive oak branches spreading overhead.

"Almost there," said Ben as they passed through Pineapple Park and into the next neighborhood. "This is Azalea Drive."

Ben didn't mention that "almost there" meant that they were about to start pedaling up one of the highest points in their seaside town. He figured it was for the best, and he was fairly certain this mysterious address was just on the other side.

The three friends struggled to scale the slope, inching their way past stucco-covered mansions, coconut palms, and redbrick roundabouts. This particular neighborhood had once fallen into disrepair as many of its homeowners fled to the newer suburban communities to the west, but these historic homes were being renovated and flipped by the day now. A few houses still had the signs of that blighted era—overgrown front yards that looked more like jungles and sheets of ply-wood obscuring broken windows—but, on the whole, Flamingo Park was turning itself around.

As they reached the top of the coastal ridge, the chil-dren let out a sigh of relief and allowed their tensed-up muscles to loosen. There was a brief lull as they drifted at the hill's peak. Then the force of the downward slope propelled them, each bike picking up speed in exponen-tial increments as they descended back toward sea level.

"Be careful, Ellie!" shouted her concerned older brother. He knew she had only recently graduated from having training wheels on her bike, and this was a much greater incline than any she'd ridden on their street.

Ellie's eyes widened as she neared the base of the hill. Ahead of her, the road intersected with a set of train tracks, and its long, thin safety gates had just begun to blink their flashing red lights. As the gates lowered slowly, Ellie tried to pedal backwards to slow herself, but her leg slipped. The pedals kept spinning, faster, and Ellie's legs were now spread to either side of the bike to avoid the rapidly rotating metal bars. She couldn't synchronize her feet with the swift motion of the bike's speed-regulating mechanisms.

"Ellie!" Ben yelled from mid-way down the hill.

The safety gates reached their lowest position and continued to flash. The sound of a freight train barrel-ing from the north cut through the dinging bells of the gates and grew louder. Ellie was just feet from the gates and the tracks when the hulking train engine entered her view. The weight of it displaced warm air that Ellie could feel surrounding her. The boys screamed from behind. With desperation, Ellie swerved to the right, sending her tiny body and her brand new bicycle sailing over a curb and into a patch of two-foot-tall weeds in a nearby lot.

Oliver and Ben reached the foot of the hill seconds later and threw their bikes to the ground. Fearing the worst, Ben began to cry as he approached the scene. He couldn't see Ellie through the tall overgrowth and the mystery frightened him even more.

The sound of the long, passing train muffled their calls, and they couldn't make out if Ellie was respond-ing back to them. Then they saw a hand waving just above the long grass. Drawing nearer quickly, the boys found Ellie lying on the ground. Her eyes were open and she had enough strength to wave, and this immedi-ately brought relief to Ben.

"Are you hurt?" shouted Ben, hoping his sister could hear above the din. She shouted something back, but Ben could neither hear her nor read her lips as she had landed on her back facing away from the street, and the long freight train continued to barrel past them.

She spoke again, and Ben pivoted himself to get a better view to read her lips. He couldn't understand. It looked to him that she was quoting a phrase—"*fee-fi-fo-fum*"— from one of their family's bedtime stories, but that was most certainly a mistake.

Ben leaned closer as Ellie pointed a finger beyond him. It was an old house, with boards over the windows.

This time Ben could make out *five-oh-five* floating from his sister's lips. He looked at the house again. There was a set of chipped brass numbers above the door, painted the same color as the outside wall of the house. Sure enough, he had heard correctly this time. The sound of the train faded away as the gates were raised and the locomotive continued on its journey south to Miami.

"Five-oh-five," said Oliver. "Five-oh-five Azalea Drive!" Ellie's narrow escape from collision with a freight train had flipped her off her bike and right into the front yard of the house they were searching for.

"I don't think anybody's home, though," Oliver added while he aided Ben in getting Ellie to stand up. The house was painted a fading white with dirt stains around its base. Stucco covered it from the ground up to the roof of its second story, where it terminated in a row of mostly-cracked terracotta roof tiles. The house had to be around a hundred years old.

Ben, relieved that his sister had sustained no more than a few scrapes, craned back his head to take in the sight of the tall house himself. "Doesn't look like anybody's been home in quite some time," he said.

Oliver took off his backpack and withdrew the fragile map. He looked closely at the drawings and lines, held it up to the light of the summer sun, squinted, and looked at the numbers on the house. "Yep," he said, tucking the map back away. "This is it."

None of the three small children wanted to take the first step toward the house, but Ellie chimed in, "Should we knock?" Without waiting for a response, she glided up the tile front steps and held out her tiny fist to knock

on the massive wooden door. *Tap tap tap.* She waited a moment and the boys held their breath in suspense.

No answer. "It's like we said," chimed Ben. "No one's home. I guess we'd better get off the property before one of the neighbors calls—"

Before her brother could finish, Ellie had reached for the wrought-iron door handle and, sure enough, the door was unlocked. As the door creaked open, she turned back toward the boys, half-frightened and half-ready to find this mysterious potential treasure.

"Are you crazy?" Ben whispered loudly, moving toward his sister and the door.

"Hello?" shouted Ellie into the house. No answer.

"This is what we came here for," said Oliver. "The treasure could be inside." He joined Ellie on the steps and they peered into the dark innards of the house's foyer together. They couldn't see much beyond the layers of cobwebs and floating clouds of dust so, reaching a hand into his backpack again, Oliver produced the flashlight they had used the previous night in the garage. He clicked it on, took a deep breath, and pushed the door open all the way.

"I'm right behind you," said Ben as he hesitantly took his place at the back of the pack. With obvious trepidation, Oliver and Ellie led the way into the dark and dilapidated house on Azalea Drive, and they all stepped as quietly as could be.

CHAPTER FOUR
The House on Azalea Drive

There was a stench to the place—the sort of smell that lingers when the sunlight and fresh air haven't been allowed into a house in decades. One could easily make out the telltale fragrances of the pecky cypress rafters or the cracked Dade pine wood floors, aged to perfection and untouched by humans for quite some time. In a word, it smelled *old*—ancient, even.

Guiding the group of children with his flashlight far ahead of him, Oliver leaned around a corner. The floorboards below him creaked lightly under his meager body mass, but the children were silent. The beam emanating from the flashlight looked almost solid as it met the decades of dust that they had disturbed, but it faintly illuminated the other side of the room they now entered.

The living room, absent any signs of living, was expansive. On the wall to their left, the children could make out an old fireplace made of brick. (Why someone would install a fireplace in South Florida was another mystery for another time.) To the right was the dining room, in which a massive, hand-carved wooden table sat covered in a sheet of white fabric, along with six mismatched chairs. Straight ahead, Oliver's light revealed a staircase. The younglings could see light coming from the top of the stairs, presumably from a bedroom window that was too far out of reach to receive the customary plywood covering.

"Do you think the treasure is upstairs?" asked Ellie, pointing even though it was too dark for the boys to see the gesture.

Ben had doubts that a place like this decrepit house could hold anything of value. Before he could suggest they turn back, Oliver moved swiftly forward, with Ellie trailing closely behind him. The spill of the light illuminated the ground just enough for her to see a step or two ahead.

Oliver reached the bottom of the staircase and looked to the top. "Careful," he warned. "These steps don't look entirely stable." Ellie and Ben heeded his advice, waiting for Oliver to go first. One step. Two steps. Three.

As Oliver allowed the weight of his foot to settle on the fourth step, he heard a light cracking noise and quickly raised his leg. He tried setting his foot on another spot on the fourth step and was able to avoid such a noise this time. He pointed to the spot with the flashlight and Ellie and Ben nodded in affirmation as they carefully scaled the prior steps and skirted around the precarious one.

The rest of the flight was scaled with less excitement, and the troupe reached the second-floor landing. To their immediate left was the bedroom with light spilling in. A couple of them poked their heads through the doorway. It was empty except for a pile of dead leaves that had blown in through a hole in the window. Tiny glass shards like diamonds laced the windowsill.

Turning toward the opposite end of the hall, the children noticed a closed door. They could not see any light sneaking through the gaps above or beneath the door, which they assumed meant that the room's windows had been covered like the others on the ground floor. As they approached the darkened portal, Oliver focused the light's rays on the handle. This door had a crystal knob with a keyhole below it that reminded him of the kind he had seen in fairy tale stories.

Even more curious was the fact that, as they approached the sealed room, they heard a faint, tinny ringing.

"Do you hear that?" muttered Ellie, whispering so as not to overpower the almost imperceptible sound.

"What is it?" Ben wondered aloud. The pale jingle persisted, and even grew louder as they neared the door. "I think it's coming from inside that room."

Oliver, still at the front of the pack, reached toward the door's handle.

"What are you doing?" shouted Ben in a frantic but hushed tone.

"I think that sound means we're headed in the right direction," he replied. "It seems... familiar." He turned to try the knob but discovered that it was locked. He could hear the shimmery ring continue, as if it was coming from within his own ears. "We've got to unlock this door."

"How?" asked Ben. "We haven't got the key."

Ellie ignored her brother's usual cynicism and began to carefully run her hands along the wall to guide her back toward the stairs. She peeked into an open door—a small bathroom—and felt her fingers along the inside of the wall until they came to a switch. A warm, yellow light spilled out into the hallway, frightening the boys. Ellie smiled and tried to ignore the concurrent sound of a dozen tiny roaches scuttling into hiding.

"Well, I sure feel foolish," muttered Oliver under his breath. With the revelation that the house had functioning electricity, the three began to search the house, flipping on more lights as they went. Ellie finished her survey of the bathroom, finding only the remnants of a cardboard toilet paper roll that had become fodder for rodents.

Oliver headed back down the steps and through the living room, followed closely by Ben, and then ventured into the kitchen where he began to methodically open and close every cabinet and drawer. Ben was intrigued by the geographically out-of-place inclusion of the fireplace in the house and began testing the integrity of each brick in hopes of discovering some sort of clandestine hiding place.

In the kitchen, Oliver thrust his arm into the deepest parts of each compartment to feel for anything that might resemble a key. As he opened a tiny drawer near the oven, Oliver heard something small and round roll along the wood. He reached his hand under the counter and into the space and retrieved a small metallic piece of jewelry. He turned it in his fingers.

It was a simple ring with the etched image of a lamp emitting stylized beams of light on its largest surface. *Curious*, he thought.

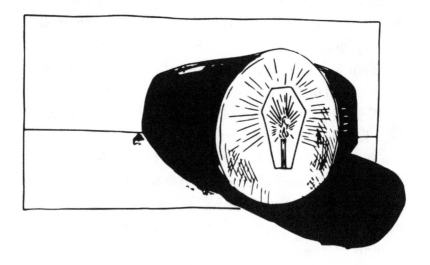

As Ellie made her way downstairs to join them, her foot landed on the brittle surface of the fourth step. The boys heard the loud crunch and Ben turned quickly to see Ellie's legs disappear into the newly-formed hole in the step. She caught herself on the railing and held on tight as Oliver re-emerged from the kitchen.

"Hold on," he shouted to Ellie as he and the girl's brother ran to her side. With the boys at either side of her, Ellie daintily shifted her weight and allowed them to hold on to her arms. They mustered their strength and lifted her to a secure and solid position. She sat down at the foot of the steps. Her brother followed suit. Oliver remained on the fifth step, staring into the hole. Something in the crevice caught his eye.

"Hey, Ben," he said. "Can you grab the flashlight? I think I left it on the kitchen counter."

Still catching his breath, Ben shot his friend an irritated glance and then reluctantly picked himself up. He slumped into the kitchen, grabbed the light from the tile counter, and reappeared in the living room. "What do you see?" he asked as he handed the light over his sister's head.

Oliver clicked the light on and shone it past the splintered wood boards. The reflective glint of the light on something shiny spurred him to kneel and look closer. In the brilliance and dust, Oliver attempted to interpret the shape of a small object. He leaned lower and reached out his free hand into the tiny cavern, which gradually swallowed his whole arm.

His fingers danced in the dark and dirt until they alighted on the enigmatic item. The gaping splintered jaws of the step released Oliver's arm and revealed his clenched fist. He held it out toward the siblings below and opened his fingers to reveal a small bronze key. Its ancient oxidized filigree consisted of three ornate circles joined together in a triangular formation. Each circle was filled with a small green gemstone, and the side of the key consisted of a set of teeth that looked to belong to a lock from a different time and place than their own.

"The key!" Ellie's eyes widened and she forgot about

her recent plight with the faulty step. She and Ben ascended to Oliver's level and observed the object more scrupulously. It was a beautiful key, she thought as she inspected it. "It must have fallen through a crack in the floorboards."

"It's got to be the key to that door," suggested Oliver. Everyone agreed and followed as he returned to the second-floor hallway. Once again, the party began to discern the faint ringing as they approached the locked door. It seemed to be like the sound of hundreds of tiny bells rung in unison, muted as though locked inside a thick wooden box.

Ever the fearless leader, Oliver carefully placed the antique and otherworldly key into the tiny slot. It was a perfect fit. He turned it a slow, full turn, listening as the locking mechanisms clicked along with the soft chimes. The door didn't open on its own, so the boy handed the flashlight to Ben and leaned his shoulder into the door. As the door's old paint became unstuck from that of its frame, it creaked open with a sharp jolt. Oliver fell into the dark void of the room and into a palpable wall of moist air. He noticed that the light from the hallway didn't spill into the room the way he expected it to and the ground didn't feel like wood flooring. The room remained mostly dark.

"Shine that flashlight in here," Oliver called from within the unlit room. His voice didn't have the typical echo of an empty room—it sounded larger—so Oliver felt around for whatever objects might be near. Ben and Ellie tiptoed through the pitch-black bedroom door and toward their neighbor's voice. The flashlight beam wandered from side to side before it alighted on Oliver. They walked over to check on him.

Suddenly, a sharp draft filled the room and the children were caught off guard. The door to the room slammed shut behind them and Ben jumped. Flashlight in hand, he ran toward the closed door. His hand grasped the old knob and tried to open it. It was locked. The boy reached his hand to feel along the wall in hopes of finding a light switch, but his hands waved in empty space. The wall had vanished. Working his fingers around the doorframe, Ben reached around to its backside. The door was locked from that side, as well, and there was no tiny, ancient key in the hole. They were now trapped in an unlit, humid space with no apparent way out.

CHAPTER FIVE
What They Found Through the Door

"The door is locked and the key is gone," Ben stated. "And, in fact, I think the entire wall has vanished."

The ten-year-old boy was baffled. He had never heard of anything like this happening. How would they get home for supper if they couldn't open the door out of this dark, damp room?

"Well, it can't have gone far," piped Oliver optimistically. *Walls don't just grow legs and walk off,* he thought to himself. But sure enough, shining a light on the doorframe and the areas near it revealed that the other three walls of the room were missing, too.

"Where are we?" Ellie was frightened, and it was clear she wasn't the only one. She noticed that the flashlight in her brother's hand was shaking.

They fell silent, unsure of their next course of action. Oliver noticed that the light ringing sound had ceased, and he could now hear the intermittent sound of water droplets falling from above into what he assumed to be a shallow puddle on the floor. The gentle echo of the drops seemed to extend far into the distance. Wherever they had ended up, it was large.

Ben shone the flashlight above in the direction from which the drips seemed to be originating and revealed a set of sharp, jagged stones that looked like teeth about to chomp down on them. With a start, he stepped back, and then realized he was looking at a set of stalactites. "It's a cave," he said.

"How did we end up in a cave?" Oliver asked it more hypothetically, but the question still stood. There was no logical explanation for this kind of happening.

"I think it's some sort of strange magic," suggested Ellie. She was the youngest of the bunch and was accustomed to dreaming and reading stories of strange and enchanted places.

"Magic?" Ben repeated dismissively.

"It's the only explanation that makes sense," his sister continued. "An enchanted treasure map, a curious jingle, an ancient key, and a portal to a dark cave. Think about it, Ben."

"If this is an enchantment of some kind, what do we do next?" Oliver wasn't interested in an argument over how they got to the cave; his primary concern was figuring out a way for them to get out of it and find their way back home.

The slow drips continued. Ben pivoted and cast the light in a clockwise motion to get a better idea of their surroundings. It appeared that they were in the middle of a tunnel that stretched in opposite directions. The walls of the tunnel were about the width of the other upstairs bedroom in the old house from which they'd just come. There was no light or endpoint to discern in either direction.

"Which way do we go?" asked Oliver.

"Perhaps we just choose one," Ellie said. "And we can turn around if it doesn't lead us to the outside."

It sounded like a good enough plan to the boys. They spent a few moments looking back and forth between the two routes, unable to garner any clues as to which might be a more probable path to the exit.

Finally, Ellie pointed—though no one could see her finger in the dark—and said, "I choose this path." The others had no reason to disagree, so the group set off down the tunnel slowly, carefully treading over the uneven and rocky surfaces beneath them.

They had not been traveling for long when Ben spoke up: "What if the cave goes on forever, deeper into the ground? Then we might die of starvation and never reach the surface."

"I suppose that we'll just have to hope this tunnel doesn't go on forever, then," said Oliver. Ben made a valid point; they did not have much in the way of rations, and now that it was mentioned, Oliver felt a little hungry.

When they had walked down the tunnel for another hour or so, Oliver could hear his stomach rumbling. He almost spoke up to ask if anyone had any food when a tiny speck of light caught his eye. He stopped walking and squinted. There, far ahead of them, was a light at the end of the tunnel. "I think we're almost to the

surface," he shouted, his voice bouncing off beyond their position.

With energy momentarily regained, Ellie, Ben, and Oliver intensified their pace and made headway toward the light. The speck seemed to double in size with every few steps they took forward. They were moving uphill now, so they began to slow again. A crisp air wafted at their faces and ankles as they drew nearer to the bright opening.

It feels like spring, thought Oliver.

Presently he arrived at the mouth of the cave, and Ellie and Ben joined at his sides. They looked in awe at the sight before them: a verdant forest with clumps of tall, tropical trees and a ground covering of thick, leafy ferns. They could see no buildings or structures in sight, and the wood looked as if it had remained untouched and undiscovered by humankind until that very moment.

As the trio of explorers observed the natural beauty of the scene, they heard a rustling in the undergrowth. Something was approaching, and they could tell two things: it was large and it was headed right toward them.

CHAPTER SIX
Tazmo the Snifflack

The three friends huddled close together at the mouth of the cave. A low growl rumbled from the bushes, moving nearer and nearer to them. It was now close enough for them to see a large patch of thick fur above the tall underbrush.

The creature leaped and disappeared again behind the plentiful shrubbery. The rustling stopped and was replaced by a sharp squeal. Seconds later, a tiny rodent emerged at the children's feet, brushing past Ellie's leg as it burrowed itself away in the cave. Ben cupped his hand over his sister's mouth to stop her from screaming. The rodent's hunter was still crouched in the bushes adjacent to them.

The children stood motionless. Then, a deep voice sulked from behind the greenery: "Oh, goodness. They always seem to get away!" Exchanging confused glances with his friends, Oliver made a step toward the voice as it was replaced with the mellow sound of sobbing.

"You can come out now," he said to the voice of the beast. The whimper turned to silence.

"I think I'd rather stay here and cry awhile, thank you very much," replied the beast.

"You're not going to eat us, are you?" asked Ellie.

"Well, that depends on how good you taste," the beast responded. Ellie shuddered and took a step back. "But I'm sure you'd get away before I could even have a bite. I'm not much of a hunter."

"Then what are you?" Ben chimed in.

There was a brief pause, then the bushes started to rustle again as the beast moved. As it stood on its hind legs, the beast rose above the underbrush and towered over the children. It had the form of a bear, but with a much rounder, kinder countenance with a distinctively prominent nose. Two tiny ears drooped on either side of its head, buried in a shaggy mane like a lion's that encircled his face.

"I'm a snifflack, of course," the beast replied with a smile.

"If you please, what's a snifflack?" Ellie asked.

"Why, it's me," the snifflack retorted.

"I'm sorry, Mr. Snifflack," said Ellie apologetically. "I've never seen anything like you, so I do hope you'll excuse me for not knowing."

"Please," responded the creature. "You can call me Tazmo."

"Pleased to meet you, Tazmo," said Oliver with a slight nod in his direction. "My name is Oliver, and these are my friends Ellie and Ben."

TAZMO THE SNIFFLACK

The others followed suit with nods of their own. The four exchanged a moment of silence as they continued to acclimate to the strangeness of their present circumstance. While the sudden appearance of a talking bear-like creature in a magical jungle was enough to baffle the children, the snifflack himself was unaccustomed to seeing children alone in this secluded domain.

"Pardon me, Tazmo," Ben spoke up. "Where are we?"

"You're right here, of course," was Tazmo's response.

"Of course we're here," said Ben, irritated. "But where exactly is *here*?"

"This is a stretch of the Granada Jungle." Tazmo elaborated, "We're not far from the coast or the Eastern trade routes—though I try to stay away from them, myself."

Confusion continued to run its course with the children. They were most certainly far from home, for even the most educated of the children had never heard of a jungle or trade routes near their town. It sounded like something out of a history book, or a geography book detailing a far-off country.

"Could you be so kind as to point us in the direction of Palm Beach?" inquired Oliver, remembering their predicament.

"I've never heard of any Palm Beach," replied Tazmo. "But there's plenty of coconut palms down by the ocean that way." He pointed east with the fingers on his furry paws.

"How about Flamingo Park?" asked Ellie.

"Never heard of that, either," said Tazmo. "The Prince keeps some of the pink birds on the palace grounds, though, if you're hoping to see some. That'll be down south, at least a full day's journey."

Ben was starting to get worried. "What do you mean you've never heard of them? We can't have traveled that far in such a short time."

"I don't know what to tell you," Tazmo shrugged. "This jungle is my home, and I can tell you it'd be a rare sight to see a flamingo or a beach this deep into it."

"You mentioned a prince," observed Oliver. "Is he the ruler of this place?"

"Oh, he'd like to think so," replied Tazmo with a scoff. "Prince Florian is a wicked man and a usurper."

"What's *usurper* mean?" asked Ellie.

"It means he took the throne when it was supposed to be given to someone else," said Tazmo. "For the longest of times, the Kingdom had three good kings that ruled in unison—they called them The Triumvirate. Whenever one would grow too old to rule, one of his own kin would be chosen to take his place. It was always like this. Until Florian."

"What did he do?" Ben asked.

"Well, typically the chosen new king or queen is the oldest of the family members. But Florian's ailing father King Fernando chose his younger brother, Ronaldo, to be the next king instead. The Prince didn't like this one bit, and his jealousy got the better of him. At the inauguration banquet for his brother, the Prince poisoned the entirety of the royal family—all three lineages—in a toast to the imminent king. This left Prince Florian as the only surviving member of the royal family in the Kingdom, and therefore its lone ruler. There's no more

Triumvirate. Florian sees himself as our king, but he never had a proper ceremony to make it official, so he's still just a wicked Prince."

The children sat in silence for a moment, thinking about what they had just heard from their new friend. "He sounds like a horrible man," shuddered Ellie. "We shall be sure to steer clear of this Prince and his palace."

"That would do you good," said Tazmo.

Oliver remembered he was hungry, and asked the beast, "Do you know where we can find something to eat? I'm dreadfully hungry."

"Well, that fern mouse that got away was supposed to be my lunch," he said. "I know where we can find some good mangos and citrus, though."

"That should do the trick," replied Oliver.

"Then follow me." Tazmo returned to walking on all fours and began to plod his way back in the direction from which he had emerged. The three hungry children assumed a single-file line behind him, with Oliver taking up the rear to keep watch for any other potential predators that might be lurking in the jungle.

CHAPTER SEVEN
An Irritable Ibis

A brief time later, the undernourished children and their new furry friend arrived in a shady grove in which a shallow brook babbled. The afternoon sun slanted into the clearing through pockets in the canopy and illuminated the red, orange and yellow spheres hanging from the smaller trees below. Oranges, mangos, lemons, and grapefruits the size of Ellie's head hung lazily from the sagging, leafy branches, bringing a gleam to the children's weary faces.

"My, they look delightful," Ellie shouted as she ran toward one of the lower-hanging limbs. Before her fingers could reach the sumptuous citrus, she heard a piercing shriek from above. She glanced upward in time to see a giant white bird with a long pink beak diving right at her. With another scream, Ellie ducked and covered her upper half with her arms.

A large flock of a dozen or more of the ivory birds

followed in the path of their leader and swarmed toward the helpless girl. Tazmo let out a growl, which frightened the birds enough to distract them from their initial target and turn them toward him. He swatted at the birds with a large paw, but the birds pecked at him from all sides. "Find cover," he hollered to the children, who obediently sprinted behind a thick patch of tall waxy bushes.

Tazmo—his fur now mangled in tiny tufts—was able to scare the birds away from himself momentarily as he ran to find his own cover away from the fruit trees. The birds quickly flitted up to new perches atop the boughs of citrus and drupe, guarding their colorful bounty from the hungry interlopers.

"What do we do now?" whispered Ben to his friends. "These birds won't let us get at the fruit."

"Maybe we just need to ask them nicely," Oliver offered. "Maybe these birds can speak like our furry friend Tazmo."

"It's possible," Ben admitted. "But they may not let us get close enough for a conversation."

"It's worth a try," said Ellie. She was not about to volunteer, given the recent attack that had caught her off guard.

"Alright," said Oliver. "I'll give it a shot." He edged his way from their hiding place and back toward the clearing. With a deep breath, he shouted to their assailants, "Dearest feathered associates, would you kindly allow us to partake in a small share of the fruit that grows on those fair trees?"

They waited for a response, noticing that the birds

had turned in their general direction when Oliver began to speak. Were these angry avian guardians able to use words in the same way the sentient snifflack could?

After another moment of silence and muffled squawking, the bird that had led the flock in its strike on the young girl flapped its wings and then opened its beak to speak: "These are sacred trees and you may not partake. These fruits may only be tasted by the ibises of our flock."

Still shocked that apparently many animals in this land could use words, the children looked at each other in disbelief.

Oliver tried again: "Are you sure you can't spare just a few? We've been traveling all day through caves and jungle trails and we are quite famished."

Again the lead ibis spoke. "You may not partake," it said. "Unless you can make us a fair trade for something of equal or greater value."

Confounded, Oliver returned again to his friends. "Have we got anything we can trade?"

Ben held out his hand. "All I have is this flashlight."

Ellie shrugged her shoulders and held out her empty hands.

"I suppose the light will have to do," Oliver said as his neighbor handed the apparatus to him. He approached the grove clearing once more and presented the offering of the flashlight to the aristocratic flock. "We present to you this gift, the most magical contraption that is able to illuminate even the darkest corners of the world with the press of a button." At this, Oliver flipped the power switch on the flashlight. To his dismay, the lamp did not activate. *The battery must be dead,* he thought.

"This contraption has no value to us," said the ibis leader. "If you have nothing else of value to trade with us, you should be on your way swiftly, or we shall peck out your ears and eyes."

"I've got nothing else," said Ben, emptying out his pockets. Oliver went to do the same and remembered a tiny item that he had slipped into his pocket in the old house.

"Wait," said Oliver. "Before you jab your sharpened beaks into our tiny human bodies, I will offer you a very fair trade." He reached into the pocket of his pants and withdrew a small, shiny piece of metal that glinted in the dappled sunbeams. It was the ring he had found in the kitchen.

"Where did you get that?" wondered Ellie aloud.

"I found it in the kitchen of the old house," answered Oliver quietly.

At the sight of the shiny object, the entire flock craned their long necks toward the boy and began to ruffle their feathers. "This ring looks to be a fair trade, indeed," said the leader. "Describe to me, if you will, what is engraved on this piece of precious jewelry."

Oliver examined the piece closely to ensure his account would be accurate. "It's the image of a lamp, with beams of light shining out from it. It's carved simply, and looks to be one-of-a-kind and hand-crafted." He added the last bit to seal the deal.

The flock formed a small huddle to discuss the merits of the trade, and the children waited for the lead ibis to respond. Then the bird turned back toward Tazmo and the youngsters.

"As leader of our flock, I will accept this trade of our fruit for your ring," the leader said. "For I have always wanted to be a ring-leader, and now my wish has been granted."

The boy approached the fruit trees and set the ring on the grass. No sooner had the ring touched the turf than the chief ibis swooped from its perch and snatched the ring in its bill. The rest of the flock followed suit in the same path, and they proceeded to take flight in single-file out through an opening in the tall trees that shielded the grove from the sunlight. Within seconds, the birds were gone, leaving only a few loose down feathers and a grove full of delectable fruits ripe for the taking.

"Let's eat," shouted Tazmo, who had remained in hiding during the prior exchange. The children took to his declaration with delight and made their way to the foot of the nearest tree.

Ellie once again reached for a low-hanging mango and this time was able to grab it without being attacked. She dug her teeth into the juicy meat of the red and purple fruit and immediately felt her hunger begin to subside. The boys and Tazmo did the same. Everyone ate their fill of the tropical delicacies and soon decided it was time for a short nap in the shade and breeze of the now birdless grove.

CHAPTER EIGHT
Onward to the Ferry

A soft breeze drifted through the grove, and a beam of bright horizontal light fell on Oliver's face. The warmth of the strong golden ray woke him up gradually. His eyes blinked heavy and slow as he regained his bearings and returned to a wakeful state. The sight of his friends fast asleep on a swath of soft turf brought him a quiet satisfaction and peace after a somewhat tumultuous morning.

One by one, the others awoke from their own naps, yawning and sprawling. Tazmo's stretching revealed a display of fearsome and sharpened teeth, with threads of saliva dripping from the upper layer. Ellie shuddered slightly when she saw the creature's capabilities, but her memories of the kindness he had shown them in leading them to food and water put her mind at ease.

"Now that we've had our fill of fruit and rest," said Oliver, "I suppose we should think about how we might

get back home." The other children nodded in agreement. "Tazmo, do you know anywhere we might find directions back to the world we came from?"

"I don't know of any other worlds," said Tazmo. "But I have heard of an old woman who lives in a village up the river. The village is built on a lagoon deep in the mangrove forests, and is only accessible by boat."

"And this woman," Ben said. "She can help us to get home?"

"She's quite a wise woman," responded Tazmo. "And she's been around far longer than any of us."

"How do we find her?" asked Ellie.

"You will need a vessel of some sort," replied Tazmo, "to venture up the river."

The children looked at each other, discouraged and dejected. "Where are we to find a boat in the middle of the jungle?" asked Ben, ever practical.

"You could take the ferry," responded Tazmo matter-of-factly. "We're not far from one of its docks at present."

"But we haven't got any money to pay our way," Ben said.

"Perhaps the ferry-captain will take sympathy on three helpless children who are trying to return to their home," Tazmo offered. His optimism was reassuring to the children.

"Well," said Oliver. "It appears to be our only course of action. Tazmo, can you show us the way to this dock?"

"Most certainly," Tazmo replied and began to walk on all fours away from the grove. The three children followed, once again assuming a single-file line through the narrow jungle pathways.

As they made their way through the verdant jungle, the sun continued its descent. The expanse of foliage and ferns and vines beyond them seemed to come alive as the light faded in the distance. New noises began to materialize in the thicket, along with pairs of blinking eyes of all sizes, and Ellie clung a little closer to her older brother.

"It's beginning to get dark," stated Oliver. "How much farther until we reach the ferry?"

Tazmo paused in his plodding and looked around. He took a sniff of the breeze, and then made a glance at the tiny slits of sky through the tree canopy above. "Not far," was his simple reply.

They kept on for a few more minutes, in which the light seemed to fade even quicker. Their steps continued, treading over moist soil and crackling leaves. Tazmo held up a paw, which the children correctly interpreted as a signal for them to stand still. Oliver tensed up and whispered, "What is it?"

Tazmo allowed the silence to persist for another moment as the darkness of evening set in. It was just long enough for their child-ears to soak in a quiet, melodic chirping that seemed to sweep over the jungle in a sonic wave. Their guide pointed his paw toward the clearing at their side, directing the children's attention toward the source of the soothing sounds.

The entire clearing began to fill slowly with a luminescent twinkling, a sea of tiny lights drifting upward in every color imaginable. Ellie covered her gaping mouth with both hands, awe-stricken at the anomalous sight.

Soon, the entire space around them was embellished with a prismatic and scintillating glow, and the four travelers stood mesmerized.

When the children had observed the mystifying light show for a few more minutes, the tiny bulbs began to go out one-by-one. The swarm of alluring fireflies slowly returned to the other parts of the forest from which they had come, and the children once again focused their attention on their journey.

Tazmo sauntered a few more steps along the overgrown path and pushed aside a pair of gigantic, leathery monstera leaves, revealing a slow-moving river illuminated by the moonlight. A rickety wooden dock hovered above the water's surface, lashed with thick grayish ropes to keep it from falling apart.

"I do hope we won't have to wait long for the ferry-driver to arrive," said Ben as they emerged from the undergrowth.

"The ferryman will be making his last trip of the day," said Tazmo. "Always comes during the first light of the moonrise."

The children had grown tired. They were not accustomed to such strenuous activity in the course of a single day, and they had begun to lose hope that they would ever return to their home. As visions of his mother's home-cooked chicken dinners meandered into his mind, Ben began to feel his eyes droop. Before he could drift to sleep, though, he was startled by the sound of a light splash. Opening his eyes abruptly, he caught sight of a small raft floating up the stream. A tiny, weathered man stood atop the craft with a long, thin oar dipping in and out of the water in a leisurely rhythm.

"Ho, there," shouted the man at the sight of the four curious strangers on the dock. "I don't reckon you all would be waiting for a ride on this 'ere ferry?" A long and scraggly beard spread from his chin, and dirt and soot stained his simple, threadbare garments. He had a kind smile, though, which caught Oliver by surprise.

"Yes, sir," Oliver responded. "We'd like a ride, very much. Only we haven't got anything by which to pay our way. We're lost here, you see?"

The small-framed man leaned in, pulling himself and the raft in to make berth on the dock. "Lost, eh? Where might you be heading?" The man threw a rope around a wooden post.

"Just up the river," said Ben. "We're looking for a woman who can help us find our way back to our home."

"A woman, eh," the man said with a clear curiosity. "A wise, old guide, is she?"

"You know her?" asked Tazmo with surprise.

"Why, yes," replied the ferryman. "Matter of fact, that'll be my last stop on my route this very evening. Wouldn't hurt me to give you all a ride with me there for no charge. We'll be going upstream with the current, so the extra weight might even expedite the journey."

"Thank you, mister," said Ellie with a relief that was felt by all three children.

"You think you three can manage without me?" said Tazmo.

They were surprised. "You aren't coming with us?" asked Oliver.

"I've got to get back to my home for the night," he said. "I've got a litter of my own to take care of."

"But how will we find this wise woman?" Ben interjected.

"Oh, you'll know when you've found her," said Tazmo. "Look for the lamp."

The children were slightly confused by this statement from Tazmo, but decided not to press the matter any longer.

"Well, it's clear there's no convincing you to come along with us for the rest of the journey," said Oliver. The children, eager to get to their destination before the night grew darker, agreed and said their goodbyes to their new friend Tazmo.

"We'll see each other again," said Tazmo. "Make sure of it, little Ellie." He tousled her hair as she smiled shyly then threw herself at the furry beast, burying herself in his bosom with a hug.

"Thank you for everything," said Oliver. The boys gave their own hugs to the friendly creature and then they hopped aboard, holding Ellie's hand as she jumped over the tiny gap between the raft and the dock. The little ferry-captain untied the thin line and pushed off with his long oar as the children waved in unison and watched Tazmo disappear into the moonlit haze of the jungle. They laid themselves across a pile of soft burlap sacks while the slow babble of the river rocked them into a deep slumber.

CHAPTER NINE
"Look for the Lamp"

A swath of thick Spanish moss brushed across Oliver's face, startling him awake. Tufts of it hung droopily from the huge mangroves and oaks that lined the sides of the river. It was still dark, but he couldn't tell how long he had been asleep. Above the rhythmic rowing of the ferryman, Oliver could hear the sounds of the jungle—foreign animal tongues shouting back and forth in their own ways. Though his imagination conjured images of the creatures that might be making these sounds, the boy was not afraid. He felt safe as long as he was on the raft with his two closest friends.

As he sat up, Oliver's eyes adjusted to the dim light and he was able to see just beyond the edge of the river and into the thick of trees. He caught a glimpse of a creature poised atop a log, perfectly framed by the branches and the patches of hanging moss. The majestic sight of a regal stag, silently staring directly at the boy on the

raft, seemed to freeze in time for a moment. The moonlight accentuated its dappled brown coat and intricately braided antlers. Then the raft continued to drift and the deer receded from view.

Oliver now turned his gaze to the rippling water below him and edged his way to the side of the raft. He lowered his hand into the water and began to splash it around lightly.

Suddenly, he found himself being yanked backward onto his back on the floorboards of the raft. The tiny ferryman released his grip and pointed a finger in the boy's face. "Best to keep your limbs out of the water," he said. "Unless you don't mind saying goodbye to 'em."

The child was confused but allowed his focus to turn to the rippling wake behind the raft. Dozens of pairs of glowing lights followed the boat slowly. When he looked closer, he realized they were sets of eyes reflecting the moonlight, hiding the rest of their bodies underneath the surface.

"'Gators," said the ferryman. "Razor-sharp teeth. Vice-tight grip." He held up his left hand, which was covered in a dark brown glove. As he pulled the glove off with his free hand, Oliver counted the ferryman's fingers; one was missing.

Oliver took a gulp and was thankful for the quick and abrupt yank from his new companion. He tried not to make eye contact with the alligators but found himself drawn to their mesmerizing gaze. Several ducked their heads under the surface when they realized they were being watched, and this created even more unease in Oliver's mind as he could no longer see how close they were to the raft.

Presently, the raft slowed and the river widened. Ahead was what appeared to be a small island in the middle of a lagoon. They floated into the clearing, toward the island. Old shacks and canvas tents built on stilts around the mangroves created a haphazard look to the place, which Oliver squinted to observe in the dim moonlight. As they drew nearer, a soft, warm light emanated from the tiny town. The ferry captain fixed his long oar further into the water until it stuck in the muck below the river, anchoring the vessel just enough to pivot over to a small dock that had come into view. The change of pace jarred the children and caused the siblings to wake up. Ben and Ellie looked around, remembering that they were in a strange new land far from home, while Oliver helped pass a rope to the ferryman.

"Last stop," said the captain as he jumped to the dock and tied the raft to it tightly. The children hopped onto the shore one-by-one, following his lead.

Gathering their bearings, the children's eyes wandered around the man-made island. Faces peered between tent flaps and through curtains in upstairs windows. *This must be the village*, thought Oliver.

The ferryman now began to walk down a narrow alley between the shacks and the children tailed him for fear of getting left behind in this strange and eerie place. It seemed the entire island was built precariously on a combination of wooden stilts and mangrove roots, and the party navigated their way throughout its maze of makeshift wooden walkways. A baby cried through one cracked-open door, and the sound of a boiling kettle slipped through another.

Their guide led them around a sharp corner, which opened into a small town square. The clear focal point of this courtyard was a house with a small, carved wooden sign hanging over its door. There were no words on the sign, just the etched symbol of a lamp with emanating rays.

"Look for the *lamp*," muttered Oliver to himself as he saw the marker.

"What was that?" Ben asked.

"Tazmo told us to look for the lamp," Oliver explained. "And that's the same symbol as the one on the ring I traded to those birds." He pointed up to the sign.

"You'll find your wise lady in there, alright," said the ferryman. "Now, if you'll excuse me, I've got to get me some rest before I head back down the river tomorrow."

The children thanked their new friend for his kindness, and he disappeared quickly down another alley of planks and tents. The sound of crickets chirping in the jungle beyond reached their ears as they stood before the rickety house. Ellie approached the door, made of red-painted timber, and gave it a firm knock.

Seconds later, they heard the sound of padded footsteps creaking on the floorboards inside, followed by the unlatching of a lock. The door slowly creaked open and a hunched old woman stood before them. A shock of gray hair atop her head was tied loosely in a bun, while a patchwork of rustic shades and textures made up her garb. She held a candlestick toward them to get a closer look at their faces and smiled softly when she realized they were young children.

"Well, hello there," the woman said. "Isn't it a bit late for children like you to be out and about? You must be far from home."

"Yes, ma'am," replied Ellie. "That's why we're here. We are dreadfully far from our home and we don't know the way to get back."

The woman looked at them, a sparkle in her eye, and then opened the door wider. "You'd better come inside, then," she said and motioned for them to enter her home. The children knew they shouldn't normally enter the house of a stranger, but at the moment they believed they would fare better inside this woman's home than out in the unpredictable alley at night. Oliver led the way as they stepped over the threshold and into the wise woman's house.

LADY JUNIPER

CHAPTER TEN
Lady Juniper Speaks of Magic

Her living quarters were small and simple, but every inch of the room seemed to be filled to the brim with eccentricities. The old woman motioned toward a pair of wooden benches in the corner and the children sat down, shuffling a stack of crinkled papers to the side. The hostess waddled over toward a stove and removed a cast-iron teapot, which she brought over and set on a low table in front of the benches. A floral aroma drifted through the room.

"Tea?" asked the woman.

All three children nodded, catching whiffs of the pleasant scent.

"It smells delightful," said Ellie as the woman began to pour the tea into four tiny earthenware cups. "What type of tea is it?"

"I call it my 'everglade blend,'" she answered. "There are hints of lily pad, mangrove, licorice, and lavender.

I made it myself." The children took their first sips and were surprised to find that they rather enjoyed the taste in spite of the curious mix of ingredients. Sipping from her own cup, the wise woman added: "It just occurred to me that we haven't given proper introductions. I am Lady Juniper, and I serve as the leader of this small island."

"Pleased to meet you, Lady Juniper," said Ellie with a nod. "My name is Ellie, and this is my big brother Ben."

Ben nodded to Juniper. "Thank you for your hospitality, m'lady."

Just then, they heard a rustling of some of the papers in the corner. The children craned their necks toward the sound as a tiny reptilian creature scampered out from under the pile, scurried across the room, and leaped into Lady Juniper's lap.

"And this," she said, "is my pet Kiwi. He keeps me company here in this big house." The creature resembled a plump turtle, only without the shell. Its greenish body was covered in a scaly skin.

"He's so cute," said Ellie, leaning in to pet it.

"Now, where were we?" asked Juniper.

The third child finally introduced himself. "I'm Oliver," he said while the lady tilted her head slightly to get a better look at the child. "As my friends mentioned earlier, we were hoping you might be able to help us find our way home. You see, we came here through a curious turn of events, but we haven't got the slightest clue as to how to return to the world we belong to."

Lady Juniper smiled and nodded. "And what world do you belong to, child?"

"It's the world we left when he stepped through a curious door in an old house," explained the boy. "Only we haven't got a way to open the door back up again."

The lady paused as she soaked in the new information. "And what—or who—led you to this door in this old house in the first place?"

"Well, we were following a treasure map—" Oliver stopped and remembered he still had the ancient document in his backpack. "I'd almost forgotten about it," he said as he pulled the folded map out of the bag.

Lady Juniper's eyes widened as the boy unfolded the old map. It was a look of recognition. "Where did you get this?" she asked.

"I think it belonged to my mother," the boy responded. "We found it in a box of old things. I don't remember much about her."

"I see," said Juniper, stroking Kiwi's scale-covered back and leaning over the massive map. "Was there anything unusual about the door that brought you here?"

The children thought for a moment, then Ben spoke up. "There was a sound that we heard as we approached it, like a faint ringing—a shimmer, really."

"*Las Puertas*," Lady Juniper nodded slowly. "You found one of the Gates," she said definitively.

"Gates?" asked Ellie. "What does that mean?"

Juniper settled herself more comfortably into her seat, knowing that there was much about to be explained. "The Gates—or *las Puertas*, as the people of this region refer to them—are spaces that connect our world with your world. There were many gates at one time, and our worlds were much more seamless back then."

"Are all of the Gates like that door in the old house?" asked Ben.

"Oh, no," said Juniper. "Many are, but some are simply thin places through which one can pass without lock or key."

"Can you take us to one of these 'thin places' so we can get home?" Ellie asked.

"I'm afraid not, my dear," she replied. "Most of them are long gone now, and I wouldn't know where to look for one."

"How about one of the other doors, er, Gates?" asked the girl's brother.

"There are some," Juniper said. "But all of the Gates I know about are heavily guarded—or worse; they've been sealed shut or destroyed! This door you three came through might be your best chance of returning home."

"I think it may have been sealed, too," said Oliver. "And the key was left on the other side."

"Curious," said their hostess. "Magic has a strange way of doing the unpredictable."

"Do you know how we can open it again?" Ellie pleaded.

Lady Juniper let out a long sigh and then said, "I do. But it won't be simple. Or easy." The woman paused as if deep in thought or remembering something that saddened her.

"What is it, Lady Juniper?" asked Ellie.

"The keys to the Gates," said Juniper. "They're all kept in a vault in the royal palace."

"Is that where Prince Florian lives?" Oliver inquired, recalling their conversation with Tazmo earlier in the day.

"So you've heard of him," Lady Juniper said. "Yes, that's where he lives—in the palace to the south of us—Castillo Rosa. It's heavily guarded and the wicked man will see you coming, so we'll have to be clever. But we can discuss that tomorrow." At this, she rose. "You three look exhausted. Let me prepare a place for you to get some rest."

The children had no desire to refuse the kindness of Lady Juniper, so they helped her unpack and arrange a stack of blankets into makeshift beds on the floor. She set Kiwi down and he immediately let out a small bark and scurried back into hiding, while Juniper moved a box full of old envelopes and letters out of the way. She then handed them each a small pillow that consisted of a burlap bag stuffed with soft straw. As the woman proceeded to snuff out the candles that illuminated the varying corners of her living space, the children settled into their beds and tucked themselves underneath the cozy, thick blankets. Lady Juniper disappeared behind a drawn curtain and they all fell fast asleep to the sounds of crickets humming their natural lullabies in the distant jungle canopy.

CHAPTER ELEVEN
The Children Search for a Solution

The soft morning sunbeams danced through the textured curtains of Lady Juniper's humble home. The three children awoke to the aroma of fresh tea steeping and sweet pastries baking in the oven. Kiwi jumped on Ellie and began to lick her face, prompting her to let out a chuckle. As they rolled out of their improvised beds, the woman sliced a half-dozen miniature oranges into wedges and arranged them in a pleasing pattern on a ceramic serving dish, which she placed at a round table. She pulled the oven open a crack, peering in, then opened it all the way. Juniper withdrew a pan covered in golden muffins dotted with powdered spices that had been baked into them.

"Good morning, children," Lady Juniper said softly. "Breakfast is ready."

The children, still a bit famished from the previous day's excursion, wasted no time in gathering around the dining table, taking seats in front of already-prepared place settings.

"Don't be shy," said Juniper as she plopped one of the spiced muffins onto each of the children's plates then, lastly, on her own. The children heeded her instruction and filled their plates with an assortment of the delicacies that sat in front of them.

With his teeth digging into the juicy flesh of a citrus slice, Oliver decided to resume the conversation that had been cut short the previous night. "Lady Juniper," he began. "What did you mean when you said the Prince would see us coming? Does he have a lookout or a lighthouse at his palace?"

"If only it were that simple," she replied. "No, the Prince has a group of special advisors who are under some kind of dark enchantment. They're called Seers, and they can envision what anyone is doing at a given time, though they can't see *where* a subject is. And with our luck, he probably already knows you're here."

"Why would he be concerned with children being here?" asked Ellie. "We just want to find our way home."

"He's not concerned with you, per se. The Prince has a special interest in finding those Gates, like the door you used to get into the Kingdom." Juniper sipped her tea. "You see, the Prince has made it his mission to find and seal off any and all Gates so that a true heir to the Triumvirate can never return. And you can bet he'll treat anyone who passes through a Gate as a threat—including you."

"But I thought the Prince poisoned the entire royal family," Ben pointed out. He brushed some crumbs off his shirt, which Kiwi promptly licked off the floor around his chair.

"That's what many thought," said Lady Juniper. "But he knows that at least one heir from one of the three bloodlines made it out of the Kingdom prior to the unfortunate incident."

"So there is someone who could still return and reclaim the throne from Prince Florian?" Ellie said with hope.

"Not if he seals off all of those Gates first," Juniper said as she lowered her head.

Ben spoke up again. "How might we find the key to open our own door again, Lady Juniper?"

"As I said, it won't be easy. If you can make it into Castillo Rosa without those Seers knowing (which will take a miracle), you'll have to find a way into the vault.

That's where all of the keys to the Gates are kept—even those to the Gates that have been destroyed."

The children had almost finished their breakfast at this point, and they remained silent as they made the last few muffins disappear. Ellie slurped down the final drops in her cup of tea, while her brother squeezed the juice of an orange slice directly into his mouth.

Lady Juniper rose from her seat and began to clear the table. "Well, we've got a lot of thinking to do," she said. "How about you three take a walk through the village to get your imaginations working. Perhaps something will inspire you with a solution to the present predicament."

The children handed their dishes to Juniper in a precarious stack and then went to fold up the blankets they had left on the floor while Kiwi ran in circles around them. When they were ready to go, Lady Juniper produced a small slip of paper and handed it to Oliver. "These are a few things I need from the market. Can you all bring these back with you?"

"Certainly," Oliver replied. "But we haven't got any money."

"That's alright," Juniper said. "Just tell them it's for Lady Juniper and you shouldn't have any problems."

With this reassurance, Oliver slung his backpack over his shoulder and the children made their way out the door and into the now-crowded town square. Kiwi barked after them but didn't cross the threshold. The cool air from the shaded marketplace was a welcome change from the summer heat in their own world, and a light morning mist hovered all around them. The eldest child glanced down at Lady Juniper's handwritten list:

Elderflower extract
Banyan berries, one bunch
A stalk of aloe vera

Oliver hoped he and his friends would be able to identify these items in the congested market. So they began their search, weaving in and out of the throngs of people, to try and get closer glimpses at the wares and goods for sale.

The sun had not yet crept over the height of the village, but the square was aflutter with activity. A handful of the kiosks sat underneath canvas tents, similar to those that some of the homes and shops were made of in the alley, while the rest exposed tables and shelves of merchandise to the open air.

Ellie found herself pushed up against a booth with an assortment of crates made of wood, metal, and sticks. Upon closer inspection, she realized they were cages housing a variety of creatures, large and small. There were miniature monkeys, furry kittens, ducks, and toucans, as well as some animals she had never seen before, all contributing to the raucous noise of the town square. The boys appeared on either side of her, amazed at these novelties.

Ellie poked her tiny finger through one of the cages to try and feel the coat of a fluffy rodent, and the vendor shouted, "Careful!" She yanked her finger back just in time to avoid a set of sharp incisors clamping at the air.

"What is it?" she inquired of the animal keeper.

"That's a carnivorous capybara," he said. "Very rare. Very dangerous. They make excellent hunters of pests that may creep into your home."

The little girl backed away from the cage, frightened by the beast, and the group continued their search for the items on Lady Juniper's list.

Their next stop was a less-threatening stall, which contained a variety of fruits, vegetables, and other fresh produce. Oliver looked back at the list, and then up at the baskets of loose produce. His eyes alighted on some smaller containers of berries, ranging in color from deep blue and purple to bright red-orange.

"Pardon me," he spoke to the shopkeeper. "Do you have any banyan berries?" Oliver did not know how to identify the item himself.

"Certainly," she replied. "As a matter-of-fact, we just harvested a brand-new batch this morning. How much do you need?"

"Just one bunch," Oliver replied. "It's for Lady Juniper."

The vendor's face lit up with a wide smile. "Well, why didn't you say so in the first place?" She grabbed a few strands of the red-orange berries, with some of the thick leaves still attached, and put them in a loosely-woven cloth bag. "There's one bunch, and a couple extra for the good Lady. Anything else I can help you with?"

The children took the bag and thanked the saleswoman, and Oliver again looked at the list. "You wouldn't happen to have a stalk of aloe vera or some elderflower extract, would you?"

She reached into a stack of greenery and produced

a thick and jagged leaf, covered in a waxy outer layer. "Here's the aloe," she said, handing it to them. "Mr. Otterman down the way has all sorts of juices and extracts. Should be able to find the elderflower over there." She pointed toward the narrow alley they had traveled through the prior night.

Ben took the aloe stalk and placed it in the bag with the berries, and then the group proceeded to wander the tightly crowded square toward the alley.

An exquisite, savory aroma wafted into their nostrils as they moved past a series of stalls selling loaves of bread and warm, spicy dishes covered in oozing sauces. One of the cooks flipped fillets of fish on a smoky grill, while another used a cast-iron pan and a wooden spatula to transfer a perfectly-seared slice of tilapia onto a plate, handing it across the booth's counter and over to a satisfied customer. If they hadn't just received a filling breakfast from their generous hostess, the children would have stopped to try a sampling of the delicacies being served.

As they rounded the bend into the cramped alleyway, they squeezed single-file past the other shoppers and tables. Ben's eyes alighted on a sign over a doorway that indicated the entrance to Mr. Otterman's shop. They proceeded through the open door.

The small storefront had walls that were made of a wood frame and canvas, and the interior was lined with rows of mismatched shelves covered in a variety of glass bottles. A disheveled man organized a series of vials on the wall farthest from them. As he was the only person in the shop, they presumed this was Mr. Otterman himself.

"Excuse me," spoke Oliver, prompting the man to turn toward them. "Are you Mr. Otterman?"

"Naturally, and I'm pleased to make your acquaintance," he said rushing toward them with an outstretched hand, which he extended to each of them one-by-one. "What are you looking for today? Can I interest you in some fresh mango juice? Or perhaps something more rare—a pomegranate essence?"

"Actually we're looking for an elderflower extract for Lady Juniper," Ben chimed in.

"Ah, yes," the quirky man said. "I have it prepared and ready for her, as usual." He disappeared behind a tall wooden counter and then re-emerged with a glass bottle filled with a clear, syrupy liquid. "One bottle of elderflower extract, for our benevolent leader."

The children were beginning to grow accustomed to the citizens of this small island town singing high praises for Lady Juniper. Apparently, her hospitality had created quite the impression on the villagers, for they all seemed to fawn over any opportunity to return the favor with service to their benefactor.

The three friends took the glass vessel, thanked Mr. Otterman, and left the shop.

Having acquired all of the items on the list, they shuffled back through the alley in order to return to the house. As they avoided a large wooden cart drawn by a large ostrich-like bird, the children passed by a man holding out a metal mug, which jingled with a few coins.

"Spare a doubloon for a poor man," he shouted. "Every doubloon helps." A couple of townspeople wandered by, and one dropped a coin into the cup with a clink. "Thank you for your kindness, madam," the beggar said, though it had clearly been a man who donated the coin. The children, watching closely, realized that the beggar was blind.

Oliver stopped walking while the siblings continued. An idea had just come over him.

"What is it?" asked Ben, noticing his friend had fallen behind.

"I think I may have an idea that could get us into the palace without being seen," he said excitedly, as they began to quicken their pace back to Lady Juniper's house.

CHAPTER TWELVE
Oliver's Dangerous Idea

Kiwi greeted Ellie and the boys with a slobbery kiss when they arrived at the house. Oliver handed over the bag of the items they'd acquired at the market, which Lady Juniper promptly unpacked onto the dining table.

"That was quick," she said, inspecting the stalk of aloe and the bunches of berries. "And you picked the cream of the crop, it seems."

"You have your loyal citizens to thank for that," said Ben. "Everyone here is so kind and generous."

"It is true," said Juniper. "I love my people well and they love me in return. Their gratitude is truly a beautiful thing." At this, she began to mash the banyan berries into a pulp on a small cedar cutting board. She then produced a clear glass pitcher from a cabinet and scraped the pulp into it. Next, Juniper poured in a thick, lightly-colored liquid out of an earthen bowl. "Lemon juice," she said. Finally, she pulled the cork off

ELLIE

the vial of elderflower extract and poured a couple splashes into the mixture.

She handed a wooden spoon to Ellie. "Care to stir?" The little girl eagerly took the instrument and began to stir the fruit and juices until they were well-blended to an appealing peach-pink color. Lady Juniper then took up the pitcher and poured each of the children a glass.

"Elderflower lemonade," Juniper said, satisfied with the work of their hands. "It's a favorite of mine on a beautiful day like today."

The children sipped it cautiously but, like everything else the woman had prepared for them since their arrival the previous day, they found it to be extremely pleasing to the taste. Oliver drank his quickly so Juniper poured him another cup-full. She then lowered her own glass to the floor so Kiwi could take a few licks.

"Now," she said as they continued to sip on the cool, refreshing beverage. "We must still discuss the matter of how to get you into the palace vault without being seen."

"Actually," said Ellie. "Oliver's got an idea—or so he says."

"Let's hear it then," Juniper said to the boy.

"Well, I was thinking," began Oliver. "You mentioned that these Seers can tell *what* a person is doing, but not *where* they are, right?"

"That's correct," affirmed the wise woman.

"Then perhaps we can simply fool the Seers," he said matter-of-factly.

"These Seers are wise and powerful," said Lady Juniper. "How do you figure you'll fool them?"

"Well, if we can convince them that we're doing something other than what we actually are, perhaps they will be distracted enough for us to infiltrate the palace."

"Go on," said Ben. He wasn't sure he understood where Oliver was going with this idea.

"Have you ever heard the story of the Trojan Horse?" asked Oliver.

"What's that?" Ellie wondered aloud.

"It was a giant wooden horse," the boy said. "For years, the Greeks had tried to conquer the people of the city of Troy, but they could never get inside its walls. So the Greeks built the horse and gave it as a gift to the Trojans, which they brought into the city. But the Greeks had hidden some of their best soldiers inside the wooden sculpture and one night, when everyone else in the city was sleeping, the soldiers snuck out of a small hatch in the horse and conquered the city."

"So what's your plan?" asked Ben after Oliver finished the story.

"We fool the Seers into thinking we're asleep. They'll think we are somewhere safe in our beds, but we'll really be inside our own 'Trojan Horse.' And then when they wheel us into the palace, we'll sneak out and make our way into the vault. By the time they realize what we're doing, we'll have the key and be on our way back home."

The plan sounded good, but Ellie asked, "Where are we going to get a big wooden horse?"

"That's the part I still haven't figured out yet," Oliver replied.

"And how will we stay asleep long enough to trick the Seers?" Ben added to the list of questions still remaining. Oliver realized he hadn't thought through a solution to that, either.

Lady Juniper tapped a finger on the table slowly, deep in thought. "Prince Florian is always collecting rare art for the palace grounds," she said finally. "Perhaps we can find a craftsman in one of the villages near the palace who can help us. As for the question of sleeping, leave that to me."

At this, Lady Juniper rose from her seat and walked over to a basket of strange and colorful fruits. She held up one with a smooth exterior. "This should do the trick," she said.

"What is it?" asked Ben.

"It doesn't really have a name," was the woman's reply. "But it tastes like guava and will sedate a person for almost a full day. For children your size, probably even longer. As long as the Seers see you're asleep, they won't pay you any mind." She handed a few of the fruits to Oliver, who put them in his backpack. "Take a few bites just before you want to fall asleep. It acts quick—in a matter of minutes—so use it wisely."

At this, Juniper produced three small burlap bags. "I figured you'd be off soon, so I went ahead and packed you each a sack full of rations for lunch and dinner." The children accepted the gifts readily.

"How will we know where to go?" asked Oliver.

"I think I know a way," said Juniper. "Do you still have that old map?"

Oliver nodded and withdrew the map once again

from his backpack. Unfolding it, he placed it on the table. As the children looked at it in the morning sunlight, a dashed line began to appear. It originated at their current location and terminated at a place down the river. All three children stared in wonder at the strange enchantment before them.

"How is that possible?" Ben wondered aloud.

"Magic," said Juniper matter-of-factly. "When you first showed me this map, I thought it looked familiar. I know this map and its ways—or one very much like it. When viewed in the light, it will show you how to find what you seek."

The children had many questions but kept silent as the woman continued with her instructions.

"Our ferry captain can get you most of the way," Juniper said, pointing along the lines that had just become visible. "Then it's a pretty short walk to the artisans' village. Now you'd better get going. The ferry's about to leave."

The children thanked her once again and gathered their belongings. Ellie knelt down to give Kiwi a goodbye squeeze, and then they departed from the cozy house. Lady Juniper waved to them, smiling from her front step as they disappeared through the crowded alley and back toward the docks.

CHAPTER THIRTEEN
At the Mercy of the River Dragon

The air on the river was crisp and cool as the afternoon sun hid behind the thick covering of the oak canopy. Every once in a while the sunbeams would break through a gap in the overbrush and hit the water just right so that one could see the fish and foliage below the dark surface. The ferry moved against the gentle current on its present journey, so the captain and a single crewman paddled the long oars on either side of the raft—the extra crewmember often came along when the ferryman anticipated a larger pickup. The children and their belongings sat in the center of the raft, nestled against empty crates that would be filled with wares upon the ferry's arrival at its southernmost destination.

The river seemed less eerie by day, and the trade route seemed surprisingly lively on this particular day. Every couple miles, the party would pass another raft or boat headed in the opposite direction. The captains would wave to each other and smile and, if the current allowed their boats to drift beside each other long enough, carry on an amicable conversation. The ferryman appeared to know all of the other boat captains, and it became clear to the children that he had served in his role aboard the river for many years.

As they drifted and paddled, the ferryman told the children stories of the interesting characters and exciting places he'd encountered aboard his river craft. The other crewman with the oar would occasionally chime in, correcting the ferryman's hyperbolic claims with a measure of truth.

At one point, the river bent slightly inland. The raft rounded the corner slowly, revealing an inlet that was no longer shaded by the tall gnarly trees. Instead, the sun filled the entire area brightly. The low-growing mangrove trees leaned their branches over the river's brackish water, which was fully covered in a layer of blossoming lily pads. Atop each pad grew a single yellow bloom, and the raft slowly drifted through them.

The ferry-drivers had to slow the raft considerably in order to navigate the thick growth in front of them, and Oliver caught a glimpse of the captain's expression as he turned to alter his footing. It was the look of *fear*.

"What's wrong?" said Oliver.

"Best to keep quiet," said the ferry-captain, placing his forefinger in front of his lips.

Ellie nudged closer to her brother and looked around, trying to discern what was the matter. Oliver leaned to look over the side of the raft and thought he saw a row of lily pads move—or was that just his imagination?

The crewman stopped paddling and stuck his oar down into the water to get a reading of the depth. As he stood at the side of the vessel, something large scraped the underside of the raft, causing it to shift and sway sharply in the thick patch of water shrubs. In the commotion, the crewman lost his balance and slipped on the edge of the raft, tumbling into the river with a splash. He disappeared under the water and the lily pads quickly covered over the place, while the oar floated at the surface.

The next several seconds passed slowly while the children waited for the man to come up for air. Oliver counted: *One-Mississippi. Two-Mississippi. Three-Mississippi. Nothing. Four-Mississippi. Five-Mississippi. Six-Missi–*

Splash! Instead of the man, a massive scaly tail slid out of the river and then quickly returned to obscurity. The children gasped and grabbed each other tightly, moving as close to the center of the boat as they could.

"What was that?" whispered Ben shakily.

"River dragon," said the ferry-captain with a breathy tone. "Stay still, and as quiet as you can."

"Will it hurt us?" asked Ellie.

"River dragons have horrible eyesight and dreadful hearing," he continued. "Any sudden motion will give us away. But we've got to get out of this thicket if we want to escape with our lives." He began to slowly attempt to row the raft forward, but his single oar was no match for the thicket.

Oliver glanced at the oar that floated next to the raft. He was the closest one to it, as he had sat next to the unfortunate crewmember that had rowed them this far on their journey. Holding on to a piece of wood attached to the boat's frame, he extended his arm and tried to reach the wooden paddle. *Almost*, he thought. His fingers stopped short just inches away from the object.

A series of large bubbles drifted to the surface of the water just beyond the oar. They moved slowly, creating a trail that gurgled its way around the raft in a circle. Like a hungry shark, the beast hovered below them, orbiting the raft in wait of its next meal.

Just then, Ben remembered the contents of a crate at the back of the raft. Inside the wooden container were three small burlap bags, each full of delicious lunches and snacks from Lady Juniper. Reaching for one of the bags, Ben pulled its drawstring loose and looked inside. He reached in and produced a plump apple-sized fruit.

The boy stood up, wound back his arm, and tossed

the fruit toward the direction from which they had drifted. With a tiny splash, the fruit displaced the water and then began to bob at the surface. The bubbling circle ceased as the creature dove deeper under the surface. Suddenly, a set of huge, long jaws emerged from the river, engulfing the tiny fruit, and then dove back under the river.

As the creature devoured its snack, Oliver grabbed Ellie's hand and leaned over the side of the raft, which allowed him to reach just a few inches farther. His hands alighted on the wooden oar and he quickly wrapped the rest of his hand around it and pulled it to the raft. He stood across from the ferry-captain and began to help him slowly and cautiously row away from where the creature was last seen.

"Do that again," Oliver said to Ben, who reached into the bag once more and pulled out a slice of a sandwich. He tossed it behind the raft, this time further away, where it was again swiftly digested. He continued this process as Oliver and the captain quickened the pace of their rowing.

It was a few more moments before they had passed through the remainder of the lily pad thicket, and then the river began to narrow once more. The shady canopy returned and the ferry-captain slowed his pace.

"We're safe from the river dragon now," the captain said, taking a deep breath.

The children allowed the tension in their hands and bodies to release at the news that danger had passed, and Ben spoke up. "We may be safe from the river dragon, but not from hunger. I think I just fed all of our lunch to that beast!"

Ellie giggled a little at this last statement, then sobered up as she realized their predicament and said, "Did you really feed it all *three* of our lunches?"

"All but one sandwich," he said, lifting it up to show them. "And the magical sleeping fruit, but we've got to save that for the final leg of our trip to the palace."

"Now that you mention it," said Oliver. "I am a bit hungry. Shall we divvy up the leftover sandwich?"

Ben began to split the tiny sandwich into four equal pieces. "Three pieces will do just fine," said the captain. "I'm not hungry. You three eat your fill." So they did.

"I'm sorry about your friend," Oliver said, lamenting the loss of the faithful crewman as he took a bite of his portion of the sandwich.

The ferry-captain nodded and lowered his head, then turned away as he continued rowing. He began to whistle a melancholy folk tune and the party drifted slowly down the shaded river.

CHAPTER FOURTEEN
A Reunion for Henry and Barnaby

It was golden hour on the river. The stream of boaters had steadily decreased as the day went on, and nearly an hour had gone by since the last of the friendly crews had passed. The ferry-captain clutched his trusty oar with all nine of his fingers and continued to whistle and hum, while Oliver mirrored him on the other side of the raft.

"Captain," said Ellie, breaking the quiet.

"Yes, m'dear," he acknowledged her softly.

"Do you remember the time before the Prince took the throne?" She continued, "That is, the time when the Triumvirate ruled?"

"I remember it," he replied. "It's the faintest of memories, but I remember."

"What was it like?" the girl inquired.

"The three kings were good to us," he said, his focus ahead down the river. "They were wise and kind and cared for this land and its people. They worked hard to keep the Kingdom united—unified under a common banner. They taught us to love our neighbor, to give generously to the traveler, and to hope."

"It must be hard to see all of that go away," the little child said. The nine-fingered man sighed at the young girl's comment and kept paddling.

"It didn't *all* go away," chimed Oliver optimistically.

"How do you figure?" questioned the ferryman.

"Why, your people are some of the kindest I've ever met," Oliver said. "Tazmo guided us through the jungle, Lady Juniper fed us breakfast and put a roof over our heads, and you—you've not only taken us on your ferry route but saved our lives as well! And I'm forever grateful."

The man contemplated the things his youthful new companion said. "I suppose you're right," he said. "Things aren't *all* bad. The Prince may be on the throne, but he can never take away what we've got."

They continued rowing as the sun continued to descend. The ferry-captain added, "Doesn't make it any easier to keep hoping, though."

"What've you got to hope for?" Ben asked from his seat in the middle of the raft.

"The Triumvirate," he said. "They can still return. They have to."

The somber conversation came to a lull as their raft drifted around another bend under the now-dark canopy of night and banyans and mangrove knobs. A series of vertical wooden beams stuck out from the water at either side of the river, spaced out in semi-regular increments toward a dock at what appeared to be the end of the river. Rusty lanterns were strapped to the tops of the beams to guide boats as they made berth in the quay, and strings of colorful strips and clippings of fabric hung across the water from tall branches.

A pair of weathered attendants helped to pull the raft into its mooring and lash ropes to the dock to prevent the craft from drifting as they disembarked. The children stepped over onto the dock with their few possessions, and the ferryman followed closely behind.

The children caught a whiff of smoke and realized that the entrance to the village was just ahead of them. A villager stood rotating a small boar on a turnspit over an open flame. The piquant smell whetted the appetite of the weary travelers, and they found themselves drawn toward the glow.

"Hungry?" asked the ferryman. The children nodded rapidly in the affirmative, and he motioned for them to continue on the path toward the roasting pig.

A woman holding two small toddlers accompanied the man at the spit. When they approached the warmth of the area around the flame, the woman looked up, greeted the children with a smile, and set the toddlers down. She picked up a stack of small hand-carved bowls and wooden spoons and handed one to each of the visitors, which she promptly filled with a mixture of rice and beans from a large pot. The man placed a slice of soft meat on top of each of their portions with a long metal spike. The children and the ferryman began to devour the food promptly and were soon full. They washed down the dense meal with a drink from a shared clay jug, which was passed from person to person.

"Thank you, kindly," said Ben to their new hosts.

The woman and man nodded without saying a word.

"Our language doesn't come easy to them," said the ferryman in explanation of their silence. "But they understand the language of our stomachs." He chuckled a little, and their hosts also flashed back wide grins revealing stained, innocent smiles. Their toddlers waddled over to the children and began to inspect the strangers with curious fingers and copious amounts of slobber, prompting more smiles from the children.

As Oliver allowed one of the toddlers to climb over his legs while he examined their place on his map, he looked up and caught a glimpse of what he thought to be a figure further up the path in the village. The figure appeared to be standing still, clothed in deep brown, watching them from within the shadow of a small house. A light breeze fluttered its flowing garments, obscuring the person's true shape. When it realized it had been seen, the form vanished behind a wall. Oliver craned his neck to try and keep his vision locked on the stranger, but it was to no avail.

"Did you see that?" he said quietly to the ferry-captain, nodding toward the place he had last seen the enigma. "I think someone is watching us."

"Nay," replied the ferryman. "But I think it might be best if I stay in the village for the night to keep watch over you three."

When they had said their goodbyes to the hospitable family who fed them dinner, the party of four trudged up the hilly path into the more densely-populated areas of the village. On either side of them were rows of cottages and small shops, made of sturdy cedar planks and mud daubing with roofs of dried palmetto thatching. The ferryman studied the signage above the buildings until they stopped in front of a quaint, two-storied structure with milky glass windows.

"This should do," he said as he guided them through the squeaky front door, sounding a small silver bell as the entered.

The lobby of the inn was cramped, and the children stood shoulder-to-shoulder as their guide approached the counter. A massive, bearded man emerged from a door behind the desk and looked at the children with curiosity. He then produced a smile of recognition when his eyes alighted on the ferryman.

"Henry," he exclaimed. "Wasn't sure when I'd see you next, but it looks like today's my lucky day!"

"Hello, Barnaby," said the ferryman. "You know I only stay in the village if my route runs too long, and you know I *never* let that happen."

"It seems 'never' has got an exception clause, friend," the innkeeper said. "Seeing as you're standing here, and all."

Henry the ferry-captain laughed, and then said, "Actually, we need a place to lay our heads for a few days—well, I'll just be a night, but my friends will be in the village for a bit longer." He fished around in his pocket and produced several small doubloons, which he placed on the countertop. Barnaby counted the coins and then brushed them off into his other hand and then into his own pocket.

HENRY THE FERRY-CAPTAIN

"I've got just the thing," said Barnaby. He grabbed a set of jingling keys from beneath the counter and then ushered the guests around an even tighter corner toward the stairs.

The children followed the large man up the narrow staircase with Henry taking up the rear. Their host barely fit through the doorway onto the second floor, but finally tucked himself into a hallway alcove, where he unlocked a door.

The door swung open into a spacious room with three little beds, clothed in dark, thick sheets and blankets. On one side of the room was a small settee, embroidered in a faded banana leaf pattern. Henry moved toward the sofa, while the children piled onto the beds. Their host set the keys on an end table beside the door.

"Breakfast will be served at sun-up," said Barnaby. "Sleep tight." The innkeeper closed the door behind him and creaked back down the stairs.

Henry kicked off his boots and set his leathery gloves beside them and stretched his aching body across the sofa. "Now, get some good sleep," he began to say to the children. "Don't you worry 'bout a thing—" As he said this, he leaned over to see that all three children had already fallen fast asleep under the knitted blankets, peacefully drifting into what he hoped were pleasant dreams and restful slumber.

CHAPTER FIFTEEN
A Stranger and a Change of Clothes

The children awoke to the sound of sizzling coming from downstairs. The sun was peeking through their curtains just above the little sofa, which was empty except for a folded blanket and a small piece of paper. Oliver threw off the covers of his own bed and stepped onto the cool hardwood floor, while Ben and Ellie turned in their own beds, yawning and blinking to welcome the morning.

The piece of paper was folded and matched a stack of identical sheets on the end table. Oliver picked it up and unfolded it. A message was scrawled in black ink:

Gone back to work.
Stay together and don't go out after dark.
Find B. Baron.
- Henry

Oliver read the handwritten note to his friends, and they collectively agreed they would miss the ferryman's company as they continued on their journey.

"I suppose this 'B. Baron' is the one who can help us get into the palace?" said Ben.

"I suppose so," Oliver replied and tucked the note into his pocket for safekeeping. "We'll begin our search after we've had a bite to eat. Something downstairs smells delicious and it's making me hungry."

The children proceeded to file down the narrow staircase toward the area where they had entered the building the previous night. They found that the scent and the sound of frying grew stronger, which signaled that they were headed in the right direction. An open doorway off the lobby of the inn revealed a sunroom filled with an assortment of tables and chairs. A cloud of wispy smoke hung in the room, the smell of fresh bacon filling the entire house, and the children quickened their steps toward it.

When they entered the space, they witnessed Barnaby flipping strips of crispy meat in an iron pan. He turned when he heard their steps.

"Good morning to ya," he said with a jovial smile. "Make yourselves at home." He motioned to one of the tables, set with care, and the children took their seats. Barnaby slid a few strips of bacon off the pan and on to each of their plates, and then he proceeded to pour each of them a mug of warm, dark tea. Ellie promptly reached for the sugar bowl and shoveled three heaping spoonfuls into her cup. They added other delicacies to their plates from a number of serving dishes in the center of the table—warm croissants from a local bakery, baked beans, and a plethora of fresh fruit.

"And how did you sleep?" asked the host.

"I think I was asleep before my head met the pillow," said Ben with a grin. "Thank you for your hospitality, Mr. Barnaby."

"Don't mention it," was the reply as Barnaby prepared a plate of his own and sat down at the table with them.

For a while, the only sounds were the scraping of forks and knives on their plates as the children devoured their hearty breakfast with delight.

Then, Oliver spoke up. "Barnaby," he began with his mouth full despite the constant admonitions of his grandfather. "We may be in town for a few days, and we need to do our best to go unnoticed by the—the—" He chewed a large piece of bacon for a second, swallowed it with a gulp, then continued, "by the Prince and his men, or anyone who might want to hurt us or find us. Would you happen to know where we might be able to find some old clothes that would help us blend in here? As we weren't planning for a several-day excursion when we accidentally stepped into this world, all we've got are the clothes on our backs."

Barnaby thought for a moment, then said: "Why, I think there's an old charitable house just down the avenue. Perhaps you can find yourselves new attire by sifting through the donations. When you're ready to go, I'll point you in that direction."

"Thank you, Barnaby," Oliver said. "We'd greatly appreciate it."

They all finished their meals, and the children offered to help clear and clean the dishes while Barnaby continued to cook for a few more of the innkeeper's guests that had just arrived at the dining room. When the children were done, they returned upstairs where they were able to wash and freshen up. Oliver grabbed his backpack and they proceeded back down the rickety stairs.

When Barnaby saw them return, he walked them out the front door and offered them instructions on where they could look for their change of clothes. He gave each of the tiny children a bear hug in his massive arms and then watched and waved as they walked away down the avenue.

Oliver, Ellie, and Ben walked briskly at first, but then slowed as they began to pass a number of curious and interesting shops with extravagant displays in their front windows. As they stared into one of these windows, Oliver's eyes were drawn to the reflection on the glass. Behind them, across the street, was the same dark figure from the night before, and the boy turned quickly to catch a better look at the character. But when he had turned to face the other side of the street, the shadowy persona was gone.

"Let's stay close together," said Oliver, ushering his friends to continue down the street toward their destination. "Like Henry said in his note."

The trio resumed their stroll down the avenue, Oliver leading them to pick up a brisker pace subsequent to his glimpse of the dark figure. This individual appeared to be following them, but Oliver couldn't be

sure, so they'd have to take every precaution for the present time.

At the sign of a crudely painted cross on a large rounded door, the children stopped, realizing they had arrived at the charity's gates. One half of the two-piece door was propped fully open, so the children proceeded to enter into a brief, arched breezeway. The arcade terminated in a small, grassy courtyard where a group of women dressed in black slowly processed.

One of the sisters approached the children and gently asked if they sought assistance. Her kind, tanned complexion put them all at ease.

"We were hoping you might have a few garments to spare for three poor children with no money," said Ellie to the woman.

"Of course," she replied. "Right his way." She led the children to a compartment just off the courtyard. Inside, crates filled the room from floor to ceiling, with heaps of old, faded clothing spilling out of them. "Please take what you need," the sister said and unhurriedly returned to her prayers with the other women.

The crates of clothing lacked any semblance of organization, so it was some time before the children were able to locate outfits that fit them. But when they had each picked out a set of garments and footwear that would help them blend in as citizens of the Kingdom, they returned to the courtyard and thanked the woman who had helped them. They then returned through the arcade and found themselves back on the crowded avenue.

"Now," said Oliver. "Time to find this 'Baron' that

Henry told us about."

They approached a man with a friendly appearance on the street and inquired where they could find Baron's shop.

"Oh yes," said the man. "To get to Baron's workshop, just continue down our main street here, then take a right just before the little park. You can't miss it!"

The children thanked the man and took off down the street. They passed by a sweet-scented bakery, a shop selling houseplants, and an assortment of high-end clothiers. Eventually, they spied the park their guide had indicated as a landmark.

Turning down a smaller street to the right, the children found themselves in a generously-decorated thoroughfare. All of the buildings were painted in brighter colors, with mesmerizing patterns and inscriptions on many of the walls. Thin ropes hung above the buildings with strips of dyed fabric hanging to dry, much like those the children saw upon their arrival to the docks the previous night. The sound of guitars and singing caught their attention and the children noticed that there were a number of musicians playing at various points down the street.

Ben spoke up: "I think we found the artisans' village."

CHAPTER SIXTEEN
B. Baron

The children, in wide-eyed wonder, proceeded down the eclectic avenue. Every corner of the street seemed to be alive with energy and innovation, and every person conveyed a jovial and unhurried disposition. Stray cats and dogs roamed the streets with braids of colorful yarn woven into their shaggy coats. Pleasant aromas captivated passersby at a tiny outdoor restaurant that sold tortillas, where a large woman—presumably the cook and owner—embraced long-time patrons upon their arrival.

A lone, graying guitarist leaned against an uneven wall and plucked in double-time. The impressive feat captured the attention of the three youngsters, who stopped to watch and listen to the beautiful tune.

When he had finished, the man flashed a wide, toothless smile that mostly obscured his eyes. Ellie clapped rapidly with a smile of her own, and the children continued on their way.

Their senses continued to take in the amusements of the street, and at one point they realized they were nearing the end of the main thoroughfare. Ben and Oliver had taken to glancing at the signage that was displayed at each of the storefronts, but the task was made difficult by the sheer overwhelming variety of color and pattern that filled the village. However, the visual cacophony did not prevent them from noticing a stark storefront at the farthest corner of the street. The facade was painted a solid black, and stenciled in white seriffed lettering was the inscription:

B. Baron
Sculpture & Fine Art

This was most certainly the place they had been looking for. The party approached the door to the small studio and knocked on the door. After a moment, the door was unlatched from the inside and swung open to reveal a frazzled woman in a paint-soaked apron.

"Didn't you read the sign?" she said in a tone that emphasized her irritation.

"What sign, ma'am?" replied Oliver, looking around to see if he'd missed it.

"The sign!" the woman said with greater frustration, this time leaning her body out of the doorway to look for the sign herself. There was no sign to be seen, so she huffed, lunged back into the studio, and then reappeared quickly with a small rectangular wooden sign that she hung on a small hook near the door. "*That* sign," she said.

Oliver leaned toward it to read the sign. It said:

No inquiries until after the festival.

"Read it?" the disheveled woman asked.

"Yes," said the boy.

"Good," said the woman sternly as she began to close the door on them.

Oliver shoved his hand and foot between the gap to keep the door open as he appealed: "Please, miss. We aren't looking to make an inquiry. At least, not the kind I think you're trying to prevent."

"Well," she said. "Then what are you here for?"

"We need help," Oliver pleaded.

"The charity is down the street," the woman said. "I have a lot of work to get to before the festival, so if you'll run along, that'll be all."

The woman had nearly closed the door once more when Ellie piped up: "Lady Juniper sent us."

At this, the frazzled artist re-opened the door and her countenance changed. "Juniper? *She* sent *you?* To *me?*"

"Are you B. Baron?" asked Ben.

"I am," she replied and, holding out her hand, introduced herself. "Bevelle Baron: sculptor and artist."

"Lady Juniper and our friend Henry the ferry-captain sent us here because they think you can help us get back to our home," Ben said.

"Any friend of Juniper's is a friend of mine," Bevelle replied. "Come inside."

Bevelle Baron ushered the children into the studio

and closed the door behind them. They walked past wooden shelves full of wire models and carvings, and then down a narrow hallway covered in a giant abstract painted mural. At the far end of the hallway, they arrived in a large open room where gigantic sculptures stood in varying materials and states of completion. Some reached up to the high-beamed ceilings, while others took up considerable horizontal space. One such sculpture caught Ellie's eye—a hollow sculpture of a fearsome reptile that stood taller than any of the children, with two round eyes made of greenish glass.

The children relayed their predicament to the artist. Oliver explained the proposal to breach the gates of the palace and how they would use the magic fruit to fall asleep until they were safely inside.

"So you want to hide on the inside of one of my sculptures?" Bevelle clarified.

"That's the idea," said Oliver. "And then we find a way to get it into the palace, and we'll handle it from there. Do you think it will work?"

Miss Baron thought for a moment, pacing across the studio floor. "I've got one of my pieces that could work, with a few minor modifications."

"Is it the crocodile statue?" asked Ellie eagerly.

"It's an alligator," corrected Bevelle. "But I think it could fit all three of you laying down. I'll need to fashion an escape hatch and finish its coat—I've got a mind to cover it in gold leaf if I can get enough of it."

Her eyes glimmered as she imagined the finished piece, and she walked over to the nearly-complete wooden frame of the alligator sculpture. The artist showed them where the hatch would be and the space where the three children would sleep while it was transported to the palace.

"I only hope that I can finish it in time," said Bevelle. "There's only three days until the annual festival. The Prince will most certainly send delegates to scout new pieces for the palace—he always does."

"How can we help?" asked Oliver.

"If you can get me all of the gold leaf we need," said Bevelle. "That will give me time to work around the clock in the studio to finish the sculpture itself."

"Gold leaf sounds expensive," Ben remarked.

"Nonsense," retorted Bevelle. "If we can find a gold-leafed fern it won't set us back at all. Its fronds are pure gold!"

The children had never heard of such a plant existing in their world, but they listened as the artist explained how to identify the plant and where they could find it. When they had solidified their plan, the children said their goodbyes and left the artist in her studio to continue her work. With the knowledge that they now had several days to spend in the village, the children decided to take the rest of the day to familiarize themselves with their new surroundings. They returned to the inn for a brief and hearty lunch with Barnaby before departing again on their exploration.

CHAPTER SEVENTEEN
The Search for the Gold-Leafed Fern

The next morning, Barnaby packed each of the children a lunch, which they put into Oliver's backpack. They were headed into the forests just beyond the village to search for the rare and valuable gold-leafed fern—the crucial final element to Bevelle Baron's alligator sculpture. She believed this was necessary to entice the Prince's delegates to purchase the piece on their visit during the upcoming festival, and they couldn't take the risk of attempting a sale without it.

The artist had given them instructions on how to find and identify the plant, along with a hand-drawn sketch of the fern, but to their untrained eyes, it would be a time-consuming task. Thus, the children left as early as possible to ensure that they had a full day's light with which to search the thick jungle.

In the radiant light of dawn, the three children arrived at the edge of the jungle. Still a bit groggy, Ben

BEN

suggested they split up the surrounding area and tackle it in three sections. In a few hours, he suggested, they could reunite to eat their lunches and then canvas another region of the forest. So each of the children picked a segment of the dense jungle and began their hunt for the exotic plant. Ben suggested for Ellie to take the middle section so one of the boys would run into her if she drifted too far.

Oliver took the southernmost segment, along with the backpack full of their meals and his other items. The land was rather rocky, so he found himself engaging in a significant amount of climbing. When he would reach the height of a particular mound, the boy would survey the surrounding area to see if he could glimpse the shiny fronds that made the plant distinct. Then he would descend into a fissure between two rock formations and begin the process all over again.

On one such occasion, as Oliver stood atop a stone-covered hill, the boy caught a swift, dark motion at the mound behind him out of the corner of his eye. Turning quickly, he scanned the area, but his eyes could not discern what had caused the commotion.

Perhaps, he thought, *I'm simply getting hungry and my mind is playing tricks on me.*

This thought reminded him that it was nearly time for the party to reconvene at the location they'd started from, so Oliver began to trudge back through the jungle and over the rocks at a brisker pace.

Oliver spotted Ben as he skirted the final mound. While the two boys exchanged similar stories of fruit-less searches, they waited for little Ellie to join them. After a few moments, Oliver removed two lunches from his pack and they began to eat.

Nearly half an hour passed and they still had not heard from Ben's little sister.

"Do you think something's happened to her?" Ben worried.

Oliver assured him that his sister was likely on her way to meet them, though this did little to comfort the boy.

"Ellie!" Ben shouted in the direction she had last been seen. "You can come back now!"

The boys did not hear a response.

"I knew I shouldn't have let her go out there alone," muttered her brother under his breath.

"I'm sure she's just lost track of time," Oliver said as a consolation to his anxious friend.

"It's been too long," he replied. "We need to go and find her."

"And what if she returns to the clearing while we're gone?" It was a valid question. "Henry was right," Oliver continued. "We should have stayed together." He decided not to worry Ben further by telling him about the phantom motion he had seen flash by him in the jungle. But the thought of it did worry Oliver.

"I have a bad feeling about this," said Ben, pacing and wringing sweaty hands in front of him.

The boys decided that it would be best to wait at the clearing until nightfall. If Ellie had still not returned by that time, suggested Oliver, they would embark on a search. So the two young boys sat and waited.

And waited.

CHAPTER EIGHTEEN
Ellie Finds a Fern

For the first hour of their exploration, all three children had stayed within earshot of one another. Every few minutes, Ellie would look behind to orient herself to the village and ensure that she hadn't drifted too far into one of the boys' territory. She searched meticulously under mammoth monstera leaves, for Bevelle had taught them that gold-leafed ferns often grew in cool, shaded places in the underbrush of the jungle. She also informed them that the plants propagated considerably when they were rooted near bodies of water.

Remembering this fact, Ellie turned her attention to a babbling brook that wound its way toward the village at one end and deeper into the jungle at the other. Kneeling, the girl inspected a thicket of bushes with large, waxy leaves. No sign of the shimmering leaves. She continued to follow the brook into an area where the trees grew closer together and formed a sort of wall.

Ellie tried to catch a glimpse of her brother or Oliver beyond the tree line but found that the trunks obscured her line of sight. She called out to Ben and waited to hear him shout back. The stream muffled sound such that she wasn't quite sure if she heard him respond with his own call.

We'll be meeting up at the designated time, anyhow, she thought. *No use in worrying.* The little girl continued to turn over every patch of low-growing shrubs along the stream's edges as she followed it deeper and deeper into the thicket.

As with most young children, Ellie's sense of the passing of time had not yet matured, and neither did she possess a watch by which to tell the time. So she did not realize when the children's designated meeting time came and went. The little girl, focused on the task at hand, continued to follow the rivulet.

Soon, it grew dark in the forest, and the swells of sleepy crickets and hooting owls engulfed her ears. Ellie now realized that she had missed the rendezvous and began to call out into the darkness for her companions. There was no answer, except for the continued soft splashes of the stream.

Ellie sat down on a rock by the water and began to cry, for she was most certainly lost and alone in a strange jungle far from her home and her friends. Salty tears trickled down her cheeks and intermixed with the flowing brook, and she cupped her small round face in her two tiny hands.

Through the gaps between her fingers, something caught the girl's tear-blurred vision. It had a sparkle and glimmer to it in the moonlight. Ellie wiped her tears and snot away with a sleeve and stood up on the flat rock to see the spot on the opposite side of the rivulet. She could now see clearly enough to tell that what she observed was a patch of small plants with leaves of pure gold.

Elated, she leaped over to the other side of the stream and knelt beside the ferns. In this sudden stroke of good fortune, the girl had forgotten her fear of being lost in the jungle and now began to quickly pick from the minuscule branches to gather a sizeable load to bring back to their new friend the artist. When the space between her arms was filled to its capacity, Ellie stopped to think about how she might find her way home.

Hmm, she thought for a moment, looking all around. *If following this stream was what brought me to these ferns, then all I have to do is follow it back and I should arrive at the place where I started.* With resolve, Ellie began to do just that.

The journey back seemed to pass more quickly to the little girl, as she was no longer occupied with inspecting every patch of plants that she encountered. Before long, she could see the edge of the forest and hear the sounds of music coming from the village. She proceeded to make her way toward the sounds and soon was standing in the thoroughfare near Bevelle Baron's art studio.

When she came upon the entrance to Bevelle's place, Ellie found the front door ajar. Peering in through the crack, she heard voices. One voice was clearly that of Miss Baron, while the other was a lower, gruffer voice that, Ellie surmised, belonged to a man.

"Where are they?" asked the man's voice.

"I can't say," replied Bevelle.

"Where are the children, Baron?" the man asked again, this time more firmly.

Ellie could not hear a reply from Bevelle.

"Did they come to you or not?" The man seemed irritated now, but Bevelle remained silent. "Don't make me do this the hard way."

Frightened by the snippet of the conversation she had just heard, Ellie turned and began to run back into the woods. But as she turned, she collided with a couple of young children who were walking by the studio. The pile of golden fern leaves spilled all over the street and the girl immediately began to apologize and reach to pick them up. When she looked up, though, she realized the two boys she had just run into were her brother Ben and their good friend Oliver.

"Boy, am I glad to see you," she gushed as she embraced them one-at-a-time.

"Where have you been?" Ben asked sternly. "We were worried sick, and we searched for you for hours!"

"I'm sorry," said Ellie. "I lost track of time and, for a moment, lost my place in the jungle. But it was all worth it, for I found more than enough of the gold leaves that Miss Baron needs to finish the 'gator."

The boys inspected the scattered pieces that lay around them on the street and began to help the girl gather them up. "That you have," said Oliver.

"But, quick—" said Ellie in hushed tones. "We need to get into hiding, for there's a strange man who's just been talking with Miss Baron, and I think he is looking for us!"

The three children hurriedly collected the remaining, shimmery branches and began to take a few steps away from the studio entrance. Just then, a man's voice behind them called out.

"Well, there," he said. "I've been looking for you three."

The children stopped in their tracks and slowly turned toward the voice. There in the doorway was a man in a thick, brown hooded cloak—the same man that Oliver had caught glimpses of since their arrival in the village—and they did not know if he was friend or foe.

CHAPTER NINETEEN
The Man in the Hooded Cloak

Oliver, Ellie, and Ben stood motionless in front of the dark-garbed man, their hearts racing and their hands full of bushels of golden branches. As they waited to see who would make utterance next, Oliver ran through plans of possible escape in his mind. Finally, he decided to speak.

"You've been following us," he said.

The man in the brown cloak made no motion of acknowledgment.

"I saw you when we first entered the village," Oliver continued. "Lurking in the shadows."

The man now slipped off the hood of the overcoat and allowed the street lamps to illuminate his bearded face. "I promise," he said. "I mean you no harm."

"Is that supposed to assure us?" Ben said, eyeing the man with greater suspicion.

Around this time, Bevelle emerged from inside the

studio. "Please," she said. "Lower your voices and come inside." She waved her hands hastily for the four to enter the shop. The children cautiously followed the mysterious stranger in through the dark hallway and back to Miss Baron's eclectic primary workspace.

"I see you found what we were looking for," she said as she noticed the boughs of gold in the hands of the children. They handed the bunches to her and she immediately began to pick the leaves off one-by-one and drop them into a wooden bucket. Noticing that the children continued to eye the stranger with suspicion, she piped in, "He's alright. I promise."

Not satisfied with this testimony, the children kept their distance. The man walked over to a chair and took a seat.

"Well then," said Oliver, approaching the man soberly. "Tell us who you are and what you intended by following us at our every turn."

"Juniper sent him," explained Bevelle. "He's here to look after you."

"How can we know that for sure?" asked Ben skeptically. "She didn't say anything about a protector when we left her home."

The man sighed and then reached his hand under the half-buttoned opening at the top of his shirt. He revealed a thin golden chain around his neck, with a small, flattened charm hanging just below his sternum. Oliver leaned in for a closer look at the piece of jewelry and observed a familiar emblem—the etched symbol of a lamp. It was the exact same symbol they had seen on the ring found in the old house, as well as on the sign above Lady Juniper's doorframe.

The man nodded in agreement. "Bevelle's right," he said. "I received the message just after you left Juniper's island. I didn't want to draw any more attention to the three of you, so I waited and kept watch from a distance."

The children were silent as if deciding whether or not to believe the man.

"What's your name?" Oliver said finally.

"Marco," was the reply. He held out a hand to the oldest child, which was hesitantly reciprocated with a shake.

"I'm Oliver," he said. "These are my friends, Ben and Ellie."

"Pleased to meet you all," Marco said. "And it's a good thing I met you when I did, too; Prince Florian's men have already begun a search for a certain three younglings from another world."

The children shuddered at this news. While they had known he *could* be watching them with the help of his Seers, they had no idea if he actually *was* doing so until now.

"That's why Lady Juniper sent me," he continued. "She told me about your plan, and I'm here to make sure it goes off without any complications. We've got to get you into that palace if we're going to get you home safely."

"Will they find us here in the village?" inquired Ben.

"You blend in here for now," said Marco. "But before too long, the Prince will come looking for you."

While the reality of their dangerous predicament set

in, Ellie thought of the charm around Marco's neck. "What does the lamp mean?" she asked innocently.

"It means I'm a friend," he replied. "We are the ones who hope in a restoration of the Triumvirate, and who light the way for their return."

"You're going to help us open the Gate so that we can get home and then a true heir can return?" Ben wanted to be sure he understood the man's purpose and intent. The man nodded. "Will one true heir be enough to dethrone the Prince?"

"We are not sure, but there may be more," Marco said. "At least, we hope so."

The room had become somber and still with the conversation about the fate of the Kingdom. During this time, Bevelle had begun to meticulously apply the gold leaf to her alligator sculpture.

"For now," said Marco, speaking up again, "we're going to get you into that palace. Bevelle, how much more time will you need?"

"What I *need* is irrelevant," she said from her place across the room. "What I've *got* is one more night; the festival is tomorrow!"

"So," Ben asked. "Will the golden 'gator be ready?"

"I sure hope so," she said with little confidence. "But you three had better get some rest before—" Bevelle laughed to herself, then continued, "—before tomorrow, when you'll be getting *plenty* of rest inside my sculpture!"

The children laughed with her and agreed that it was far past their usual bedtime. Marco insisted on escorting the children down the darkened streets and back to Barnaby's inn, where he secured his own lodging.

That night, tucked cozily beneath the thick, hand-woven covers, the three friends slept soundly. Ellie dreamt of silver streams and golden leaves and drifted into a deep slumber in peace.

CHAPTER TWENTY
The Festival

On the day of the festival, the children were awakened by the sound of jingling tambourines and drums outside their window in the street below. Ellie groggily crept over to the window to view the spectacle, which consisted of a parade of citizens in colorful masks and costumes, with hand-made instruments and banners waving.

The troupe that passed the inn presently was comprised of a group of dainty dancers, with strips of dyed fabric hanging from their arms like wings that fluttered as they spun to the rhythm of the drums. Tiny silver bells were tied with twine around their waists, and these created a sound that mesmerized little Ellie.

As the dancers passed out of sight, the girl's brother joined her at the window in time to view a large display that rolled by with the aid of large wooden wheels and a small brown horse. Atop the float was an assortment of botanical delights: a sea of green and blue leaves and fronds peppered with pops of bright pink and yellow; a replica of a massive willow tree made from paper-mache hung with real, painted leaves; and three small boys sitting on a bench, waving to the crowd. The children wore soft golden crowns around their heads.

"I wonder if those boys are supposed to represent the three kings of old," said Oliver, now leaning between the siblings with his blanket wrapped around him.

No sooner had he said this than a platoon of soldiers appeared in glistening armor ahead of the wooden cart. One of the soldiers, an officer, made wide gestures to the man riding the horse and began to point toward the boys. From the window, the observers could not discern what was being said, but they could see enough to know that the officer was not pleased. Next, the soldier slowly removed a coiled leather whip from the side of his person and made sure the driver could see it clearly. But he did not move. The soldier began to walk toward him, closer to the horse.

After a few moments, the driver got off his horse, walked over to the children on the float, and motioned for two of them to step off. He took them in his arms and set their feet on the street while the third boy remained. The officer briskly walked over to the two boys and removed their crowns, which he promptly tossed into the mud and grime of the street. Speechless, the boys stared toward the crowns and began to cry. A woman from the crowd embraced and comforted them and led them away from the scene.

With a shrill whistle, the officer rejoined his men

in formation and the driver of the cart was allowed to continue along the parade route. The little boy atop the float seemed confused and could be seen craning his neck behind him to try and spot his missing counterparts.

As the cart rounded a bend in the street and disappeared from view, the three children in the window held their mouths agape.

"Those must be the Prince's men," said Ben.

"Is that what happens when people speak of the Triumvirate?" Ellie asked. "Those men gave me such a fright, and they looked as if they were about to do something dreadful."

"It seems that the people have only two options here," Oliver spoke. "Keep quiet about the truth or risk a perilous fate."

"Silence or punishment," Ben summarized in agreement.

The three watched a few more groups pass by the window before they began to ready themselves for the day. When they opened the door to go downstairs, the sweet smell of freshly baked cinnamon buns drifted into their room. As they arrived at the dining room, the pastries were stacked high on a three-tiered platter, steam still rising from the warm buns. All three of the children reached for the rolls and found them to be perfectly sweet and gooey. Within minutes, they had devoured a whole plate-full between them. They thanked Barnaby, who smiled widely through his beard, and Marco entered the room, looking refreshed and as if he'd been awake for some time.

Deciding it was time to check up on Miss Baron's progress on the sculpture, the four travelers made their way into the heavily-crowded streets. As he was more than a head taller than the rest of the group, Marco led the way so that the children could easily trail behind him.

As they rounded the street before the little park, the children could hardly recognize the artisans' village. There were even more shops set up than usual, with many playing hosts to large sculptures and tents full of canvases and oil paintings. A gaggle of finely-dressed individuals passed by the children, leaving a trail of perfume that seemed out of place in the crowded, humble streets. Indeed, the festival brought the wealthiest people who lived nearer to the palace, including owners of pineapple plantations and exquisite Spanish mansions. Marco explained this to the children as they walked.

The party reached the end of the street and moved toward Bevelle's sculpture studio. A flock of primly groomed women emerged from the doorway, gabbing about the works they had seen within. One woman praised the craftsmanship of Miss Baron's work, and another was fixated on a certain gold-coated reptile.

After the women passed, the children and Marco entered the studio and greeted Bevelle.

"Good news," said Bevelle with a smile. "People love the golden 'gator!" Her grin quickly sank.

"But...?" Marco tried to gather more from the woman.

"The Prince's personal art curator hasn't come through the studio yet," she said. "If he doesn't show,

I'm afraid I'll have to take the highest offer."

The children realized this could mean the failure of their plan. It was critical that the Prince's curator purchase the alligator sculpture for the palace grounds, or they would have no means of sneaking in to retrieve the key they needed to re-open the Gate to their world.

Marco could see the children starting to worry, so he tried to be optimistic: "It's not yet afternoon," he said. "There is still plenty of time for this curator to show up."

Just then, another group of wealthy prospective art collectors entered the studio with a pretentious laugh. The children followed Marco back out to the street, their heads down, and decided to explore the festival as they passed the time.

At the middle of the street, they came upon a small concert consisting of a variety of singers and performers playing stringed instruments. The troupe was lively and engaging and had drawn a significant crowd. The children inched their way through the throng to get a better view of the band and found themselves tapping and stomping their feet along to the tune in a matter of moments.

While the children enjoyed their front row seats to the performance, Marco stood behind the crowd. Around that time, he spotted a man in a white satin robe strolling slowly through the crowd. He was flanked by a couple of lightly-armored bodyguards and they were headed toward the main road that led out of the artists' village. Marco immediately recognized this as the Prince's art curator and slipped into the crowd to tail the man. He couldn't let the curator leave the festival without an attempt to get him into Bevelle's studio.

Dodging dozens of civilians, Marco found himself inching closer to the curator's location. His line of sight was obscured when a giant costume of a river dragon floated past him, its massive body obscuring all but the many legs of its operators beneath it. When the dragon had passed, Marco glanced around. The curator had disappeared. Marco frantically scanned the crowd again to look for the distinct white robes.

There! The curator and his entourage had nearly reached the end of the street. If Marco didn't act quickly, the man would be gone—along with any hope of getting the man to acquire the sculpture and allow the children to surreptitiously enter the palace.

He was just inches away from the man now. Marco reached out to the shoulder of the man, who turned, along with his two bodyguards, in a swift motion to confront him. Holding his hands up to indicate innocent intentions, Marco spoke up: "I'm sorry, I didn't mean to startle you."

"Then what are you doing soiling my robes?" was the curator's response.

"I didn't mean to, honestly. It just looked as if you were preparing to leave the festival."

"And so I was," the curator said curtly, as he began to turn his back to Marco.

"Well," said Marco. "I thought a man of your stature and means couldn't possibly be leaving without paying a visit to Bevelle Baron's sculpture shop."

"And why is that?" said the man. "I've never heard of

this Baron, and therefore I can't possibly imagine why I would have any interest."

"Oh," Marco said. "Well, I think I saw the Duchess of Vizcaya exiting the studio just moments ago. But I suppose if you're content to leave the festival empty-handed while they lay claim to the wonder that is 'The Golden Gator,' then be on your way."

While Marco feigned an exit from the conversation by taking a single step away, the curator's interest was piqued. The man's countenance shifted as he thought over his next move, and Marco waited.

"And where might one find the shop of this sculptor?" he asked finally.

"Why, that would be the shop all the way at the end of the street," said Marco, pointing. "You can't miss it."

Without a pause to thank Marco for the tip, the curator signaled for his guards to follow as he headed back down the crowded thoroughfare. Marco waited a few moments before he trailed behind, so as not to draw any suspicion.

When he returned to the place where he had left the children, he found that the musicians had just finished playing. The children immediately ran to him.

"Where have you been?" asked Ben.

"Yes, Marco" added Ellie. "You missed the most wonderful music!"

Marco smiled, and said, "That I did. But I think I may have found a way to keep our plan in motion."

CHAPTER TWENTY-ONE
Bevelle Strikes a Deal

Marco treated the children to a tasty dinner from one of the street vendors as the sun sank below the village. The Prince's art curator had been inside Bevelle Baron's studio for several hours, and Marco tried not to appear uneasy in front of the children.

Presently, as they sat at a small wooden table eating their delicacies, Oliver tapped Marco and motioned for him to turn around. The curator and his bodyguards emerged from the studio at long last, and the Prince's man had a smug look upon his face. The group watched as the dignitaries disappeared back down the street and left the festival. When they were sufficiently far from view, Marco and the children hurried into the studio.

Inside, they found Bevelle sweeping up the dust that had found its way into her shop via the heavy foot traffic of the day. She looked up and greeted them with a smile, setting down her broom.

"We did it!" she said enthusiastically. "The Prince's art curator purchased the golden alligator sculpture. His men will pick it up first thing in the morning."

The children and Marco rejoiced at the news and felt relief after their several days of preparation and worry.

"This couldn't have worked out more flawlessly," said Oliver. "The timing will be perfect if we eat the magic sleeping fruit tonight. That way the Prince's Seers will think we've only gone to rest in our beds, while we are actually being carried right into his own palace without him knowing it!"

All agreed that this would be the best course of action. Bevelle ushered the three children over to the alligator sculpture and showed them the secret hatch under its belly. This is where they would enter and then exit the sculpture when they were safely inside the palace. It was neatly masked by the pattern of the gold leaves that Miss Baron had applied somewhat hastily over the course of the past day.

When Bevelle had finished giving instructions to the children about the sculpture, Marco spoke up.

"Once you're inside," he said, "you will only have a few hours to find the key and get out."

"How will we escape from the palace once we've found the key to the Gate?" asked Oliver.

Marco explained that he would procure a small sailboat and meet them at a rendezvous point on the east side of the palace—once they found the key. The palace was built right on an ocean bay and thus had a series of docks where fishermen and famous dignitaries could drop off passengers and goods.

When they had worked through the details of this portion of the plan, the trio said their goodbyes to the artist and their protector. With this dangerous quest ahead of them, the children had no idea whether or not they would see Bevelle again.

"Thank you for everything," said Oliver to the two grown-ups. "We are truly indebted for your kindness to us."

"You need not mention it," said Marco. "Our only desire is that you make it home safely to the world where you belong."

Bevelle gave the children hugs, and then Oliver handed each of his counterparts one of the magical fruits from his backpack. The sculptor opened the hatch and helped tuck the children into the tight space. When they were all inside, Oliver used a small lever on the inside of the door to close it and then latch it so that it would stay shut during its transport to the palace.

The only source of light inside the body of the beast

was a faint glow that entered through the alligator's glass eyes. The green tint allowed just enough clarity in their vision for the children to make eye contact and view the fruit in their hands.

"Alright," said Oliver. "Here goes everything."

In unison, the children held the small, round fruits to their mouths. Taking deep breaths, they bit into the fruit. Remembering Lady Juniper's advice, Oliver took a few more bites. The others did the same and soon they could feel themselves getting extremely groggy. In a matter of seconds, each of the children had collapsed in a heap and they drifted off into the deepest and longest sleep any of them had ever had.

CHAPTER TWENTY-TWO
Journey of the Golden Alligator

As they slept, the children were unaware of what happened around them. The next morning, it began to rain just as the Prince's men arrived to deliver the sculpture to the palace. The golden alligator, with the three of them inside, was hoisted onto a long wooden cart by the help of about a dozen people and then covered with a large canvas drop cloth to protect it from the elements. The cart was then wheeled out through a large back door of the studio and attached to a pair of horses.

The horses carried the cart through the puddle-ridden streets of the village, which wound back and forth. Before long, they were passing through the large wooden gates that separated the town from a marshy plain.

It was from this plain that one could begin to catch a glimpse of the magnificent and towering royal palace where Prince Florian lived—Castillo Rosa. Even from far away, its distinctive blend of peach and blush paint made its stuccoed walls stand out amid the chartreuse of the verdant plains and foliage. The building's symmetrical silhouette consisted of three main rectangular sections in a row, with the center segment being the tallest. Two slender minarets rose from the center, with small tattered flags waving in the salty wet wind. Terracotta barrel tiles covered the lower-elevated roof sections.

As the cart approached the gates of the palace, it eventually settled onto a path paved with light, polished coral that bounced skewed reflections in the rain. The road was lined with tall and immaculately-trimmed palmetto trees and their minty fronds seemed to grant the cart a round of applause in the breeze as it passed.

The entrance to the palace itself was a large gate, set back underneath a vaulted colonnade that ran around the entire perimeter of the palace. It was preceded by a paved roundabout, in which the cart presently arrived, bringing its precious cargo out of the storm. As it pulled to a stop in front of the closed, double-doored gates, an attendant exchanged words with the cart-driver. When its contents had been verified, the massive gates were slowly swung open and the cart was wheeled through.

Inside, the cart crept through a dark and lofty arcade, which echoed eerily. The cart-driver glanced up at a row of dimly glowing lanterns that hung from the ceiling. They created just enough light to permit him to see where he was going but allowed just enough darkness to make him feel uneasy. Another member of the palace guard stopped the cart at the end of the arcade and guided its driver slowly around a corner, into a tall chamber where it would be stored until the rain passed. The driver unfastened the horses from the cart, walked them back out through the arched corridor, and disappeared toward the stables.

The harsh pitter-patter of the rain and the occasional sounds of thunder and lightning were amplified down the column-lined halls of the grand structure. It continued to rain throughout the remainder of the day and into nightfall, while the golden alligator sat covered by the canvas cloth inside the dark chamber, with three small children asleep within.

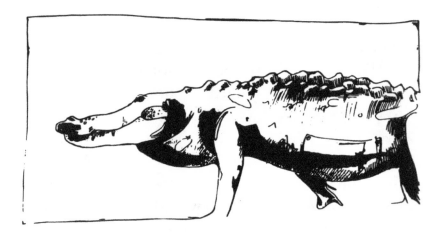

Oliver awoke first, and for a moment he forgot where he was. He could feel the warmth of his own breath as it bounced off the wooden interior frame of the gold-coated alligator sculpture in which he and his friends slept. The effect of the sleeping fruit had mostly worn off, so Oliver sat up quickly. He hit his head sharply on a thin wooden support, winced, and laid his head back down for a moment while he rubbed the growing welt on his forehead.

By the time the pain had subsided, he could hear Ellie beginning to move at the other end of the sculpture. As there was no light inside the alligator now, Oliver could not see the girl, but he did hear a shuffle, a *thud*, and a dainty groan.

"Ouch!" said Ellie, having repeated the same mistake as Oliver.

"It's a little tight in here," he whispered.

Continuing to rub her forehead, Ellie said, "Did we make it into the palace?"

"I think so," Oliver said softly. "But we'd better act quickly, for the Seers may begin watching us at any moment!"

They were quiet for a moment and listened to the sound of the rain continuing lightly.

"Ben," said Oliver. "Are you awake?"

There was no response. Oliver shifted himself so that he could try to get a view of his friend in the dark, and could hear the almost indistinguishable sound of snoring.

"He's still asleep!" Oliver said, slightly alarmed as their window of time to remain unseen was slowly shrinking.

"What do we do?" asked Ellie.

"Well, we can't leave him here. We have to take him with us and find the vault."

Ben slept directly over the escape hatch, so the two had to shuffle for quite some time to move his limp body out of the way. When they had finally accomplished this, Oliver twisted the latch and the small door swung open.

Oliver passed through the hole first, so that he could check to ensure that the coast was clear. Luckily, the canvas cloth covered the entire sculpture, so they were still guarded from view by the makeshift tent-like space beneath the alligator.

From inside the sculpture, Ellie helped to slowly and clumsily squeeze her brother through the hatch opening, headfirst. Oliver carefully lowered Ben's head and upper body to the ground while Ellie maintained a hold on his feet above.

"Okay," said Oliver. "You can let go now."

Hearing this, Ellie loosened her grip and the boy's body tumbled on top of Oliver, leaving them in a heap. Realizing that they appeared to be unharmed, the little girl chortled a bit, but quickly clasped her own hand over her mouth to muffle the sound. She then passed through the opening herself and sealed it back up behind her.

The children were able to fit the boy between them by throwing his arms over their shoulders. Lifting a flap of the canvas, Oliver subtly surveyed their surroundings. The room was unguarded, and the glow of shrinking candles cast shadows into its corners. Quickly, they wiggled out from under the cloth and headed for the single doorway out of the chamber. Before rounding the corner, the older of the children craned his neck to investigate.

To one side was the archway that led back to the entrance of the palace, and to the other was an open-air courtyard, a garden lined with tall green hedges of thick bougainvillea and sputtering fountains that were lightly

illuminated by the moon. A narrower, covered colonnade ran around the border of the courtyard. The rain
continued to pour into the courtyard, and there were
no guards in sight, presumably due to a lightly-staffed
night shift. Oliver motioned that they should make
their way around the edge of the courtyard and stay
under the slightly shaded areas.

The limp body of Ben slowed the children's pace
considerably, but they eventually developed a rhythm
that allowed them to make slow progress in their trek
through the palace. As they did not know the layout of
the massive structure, their task was made more difficult than they first imagined.

"How will we ever find the vault when the palace is
so big?" Ellie asked.

"We just have to keep searching," was Oliver's reply.
And search they did.

At one point, they came to another place where the
hall diverged into several paths. Before they could discuss which way to go, they heard the sound of footsteps
echoing through the corridor. In fear that they would
be discovered, Oliver dramatically nodded his head in
the opposite direction and guided Ellie and the body of
Ben into a hall with even larger ceilings.

Directly in front of them stood a tall wooden door,
inlaid with gold details that formed the shapes of palm
trees. The two children dragged Ben carefully as they
approached it. To the right of the exquisite door was a
much smaller, humbler door that was almost hidden in
the shadows cast by a set of candelabras.

"Do you think this could be the vault we're looking

for?" Ellie wondered aloud. The attention paid to the detail of the door suggested that it hid something of great value and importance.

The footsteps grew louder, and the children realized that the sound was coming from just outside the hall now. As they turned to try and enter through the wide gate, it began to open, pushed from inside slowly. Thinking quickly, the friends inched their way over to the small, narrow door in the wall and tried the handle. The door was unlocked, and the three disappeared into a darker space than the antechamber from which they had just departed. Oliver closed the door quickly but silently.

When they had caught their breath, the two children found that they were inside what appeared to be a narrow passage. There were few adornments, so they surmised this must be a servants' access tunnel. But to what was it giving access?

Just then, Ellie and Oliver heard the sound of a forceful exhale—Ben had finally awakened.

"Ben!" exclaimed Ellie quietly. "You're awake!"

"Where am I?" The groggy boy inquired.

"We made it," said Oliver. "We're inside the palace of Prince Florian!"

Ben smiled in delight and was about to speak when they all heard the faint sound of voices echoing from the far end of the access tunnel.

CHAPTER TWENTY-THREE
Prince Florian and the Seers

The voices continued, and the three children crept toward them to see if they might hear any information that would lead them closer to the vault. At the end of the hallway was another door, but just before the door was a small, steel grate in the wall. The three friends crouched to peer through its gaps discreetly.

Through the metal grate, the children could see into a majestic audience chamber. The walls were covered in golden ornamentations, which made the room look brighter and more open than the previous chambers they had passed through. The farthest wall featured a gigantic set of arched floor-to-ceiling glass windows, whose milky appearance allowed spurts of light in whenever the storm outside produced a flash of lightning.

In the center of the room was an ornate, rattan throne, upon which was featured the three-dimensional image of a pineapple carved out of a single piece of wood. It, like most other things in the room, was covered in gold. Several sturdy and strong menservants stood or sat on the steps at either side of the throne, a pair of them waving gargantuan fronds of palm. Atop the throne sat a captivating figure: Prince Florian.

For a person who was so universally despised by the denizens of the Kingdom, Florian was quite attractive in appearance. His thick, wavy black hair was trimmed neatly at the sides of his head, accentuating his naturally tan skin, and a light stubble grew upon his chiseled jawline. Florian was, in a word, handsome. He wore a lightweight, pink linen shirt, halfway unbuttoned and fitting loosely over his musculature. In his posture and poise was the evidence of his nobility, for he held himself with a sense of authority and pride that commanded the attention of all who entered his presence.

As the children watched, a man approached the throne, the large doors closing behind him with the aid of two quiet attendants. He was garbed in sharp boots, narrow trousers, and a voluminous shirt with puffy upper sleeves that terminated in a pair of forearm-length black gloves. A perfectly-hammered morion helmet was on his head, from which stuck a substantial, jaunty red plume.

"Your Excellency," said the man, making a dramatic bow.

"General Pompadour," said the Prince, casually waving for his menservants to cease their fanning of him. "What news do you bring me from your expeditions up the coast?"

"We searched the artisans' village thoroughly," the

PRINCE FLORIAN

general said as the children listened from behind the grate. "There was no trace of the children," he added reluctantly.

The Prince's fists clenched tight, and he began to breathe more heavily. "What do you mean, General?"

"My lord?" The general took a nervous gulp.

"How is it that there was no trace of the children, General," continued Florian, "if my Seers have told us that the children are still asleep, with their last known interactions taking place in that very village?"

"We searched every inn and every corner," the general added.

"Do you mean to tell me, General, that my Seers have lied to my face?"

"No, sir—"

Florian cut him off. "For you know, as well as I, that we have measures in place to prevent them—and their Mouthpiece—from speaking things that are not true."

The children watched in silence and fear as the Prince signaled to one of his attendants, who promptly appeared at his side. Whispering to the servant, the Prince then settled back into his throne as the attendant scurried off through a clandestine door in the wall that was disguised by the gold patterns inlaid upon it.

"We shall see if our Seers can corroborate your story," said Florian to the nervous general.

As they waited for the arrival of the Seers, General Pompadour shifted in his boots.

"In the meantime, please tell me you did not come here only to bring me bad news, General," said the Prince.

"I wouldn't dream of it, sire," said the man, still trembling slightly.

"Well, then," Florian said impatiently. "What is it?"

"Our men were able to take one prisoner," said the general, and the children leaned in. "One confirmed ally of the three fugitives that we found hiding in the jungle further north. A certain... creature—a snifflack."

Ellie covered her mouth to prevent a gasp from being heard. Could the general be referring to their new friend who had helped them on their journey? Could it be Tazmo?

"A snifflack, you say?" asked the Prince.

"Yes, sire. Its dreadful mane and beastly nature caused my men quite a fight, but it now sulks securely in a cell in the lower prison chambers."

"It shall make a fine addition to my menagerie," Florian said as he stroked his chin. "And has the creature given any information about the whereabouts of these deplorable children?"

From behind the grate, Ben shook his head in disgust at the Prince's unsavory description of them. They continued to observe the proceedings from behind the vent.

"Not yet, your Excellency," the general groveled. "But we shall break him in due time."

Ben pulled his little sister close, for he remembered how attached she had grown to the helpful and kindly creature. He only hoped that Tazmo would not break before they could find the key and the vault in which it was kept.

"We have to find Tazmo and get him out of here,"

whispered Ellie.

"We can try," said Oliver. "It may take a miracle for us to escape ourselves, but we'll do our best to find where he's being held."

Presently, the small door in the wall re-opened. From within emerged a train of several tall men and women in flowing robes—Oliver counted seven altogether. Each of their robes had a high, thick collar that masked his or her mouth from view, and their pupils were a foggy gray.

At the back of the train was an eighth individual: a small, short-haired child who wore a simple, neutral smock over his gaunt form. His feet were bare and generated a soft padding sound as he walked across the room's shiny tile floor, and Oliver presumed that the child must be around the same age as him and his friends.

When the seven Seers had gathered in a semicircle in front of the throne, the diminutive boy stood in the center, between them and the Prince. The children observed that the boy wore a necklace with a long, thin golden chain; at the end of it hung a single, multifaceted emerald.

"I received the impression from your last oracle," began Prince Florian, "that the three young children who entered my domain were soundly asleep in the village."

The Seers stared at the evil Prince blankly, awaiting his further admonition.

"Tell me, my Seers," he continued. "What are these children up to this very moment? For General Pompadour claims to me that they were nowhere to be found."

GENERAL POMPADOUR

While the Prince had begun to say these things, the children realized the predicament they were now in. Oliver motioned for the others to lie flat on the ground as if they were asleep, for they would have to do their best not to give away that they had been eavesdropping on the whole scene. If the Seers could only see *what* they were doing, rather than *where* they were, perhaps they had a chance of tricking them again—long enough to find the vault and rescue their friend.

Following the Prince's request, the Seers all closed their eyes in unison. General Pompadour stood to the side and watched in wonder and incertitude as they began to lean their heads in all different directions. It looked as if the Seers were craning their necks to look around, but their eyes remained shut. The thin child stood motionless facing the impatient Prince.

After a few moments, all seven of the Seers snapped their heads forward and opened their eyes suddenly. With a slow movement, each raised a hand and pointed a finger toward the humble boy in the center.

Finally, the boy spoke in a soft, innocent voice: "Three children lie down but do not sleep."

The Prince shifted in his throne. Unsatisfied with this response, he pried further: "Where are they? Are they still in the village?"

"The Seers cannot envision *where* anyone is in place or space," said their Mouthpiece, reminding the Prince of the rules that he knew well. "You must make your own conclusions of that based on their interactions and actions."

"Do not insult me, boy," said the Prince, growing

impatient with the child's vague and cryptic responses.

The child was trembling, shivering at the coldness of the strange magic that he was compelled to project.

"What else are they doing?" asked Florian. "What do they *feel?*"

The Mouthpiece moved his feet nervously as if he knew something that he dared not share. Then he spoke again: "They feel fear." The Prince gave him a look that suggested he was still not satisfied, so he continued. "They tremble."

"Tell me who else they have interacted with since we last spied upon them," said the Prince as the Seers continued to direct their pointer fingers at the boy.

"The children have interacted with no one," started the Mouthpiece, "as they are believed to have been in slumber until quite recently." At this, the boy's eyes drifted toward a vent in the wall that was right at his eye level, and he thought he perceived the slightest movement. *The children,* thought the Mouthpiece, for his intuition told him they had found a way inside the palace walls. But he dared not say a thing.

"Why have they entered my domain?" Florian inquired. "And do not dare lie to me, boy; for I shall know clearly if you lie by the color of that precious Gem of Truth you wear around your neck."

The boy wanted to find a way to help the children on their quest, for he empathized with their plight and knew of the Prince's evil ways. He looked down at the Gem of Truth, its green, translucent facets glinting in the candlelight. The Mouthpiece knew that if he were to lie, the gem would change from its usual emerald brilliance into a blood-red glow. This was a special enchantment the Prince had implemented to ensure that he could use the knowledge of the Seers to his own advantage without the fear of being hoodwinked by the boy who spoke on their behalf.

"They have entered your domain," the Mouthpiece spoke finally, telling the truth, "as they seek an item of great importance." The boy weighed whether he should continue, for there was more he knew but he felt a continued tug to help the children and loathed the idea of the Prince using this knowledge against them.

"There is something else," said the Prince. "I see it in your eyes. Tell me."

With a deep breath, the boy told him: "They seek an item that rests in this very palace." Then he added, slightly louder in hopes that the children would hear it, "In the vault in the northeast tower."

At this Florian began to laugh deviously. "What do you think, General Pompadour?" he said leaning toward the man with a smile. "Shall we reinforce your guard of the northeast tower?"

The man stood silently, not sure what the Prince was getting at.

"Perhaps," the Prince answered his own query. "It would be foolishness to think that mere children would even be able to get past the sight of my Seers *and* the might of our armed guards at the gate. But, as the Gem of Truth remains its beautiful emerald color, I suppose we shall take precautions. If they should arrive, they will be thrown into the dungeon. Add an extra round to the rotation in the northeast tower, beginning with the changing of the guard tomorrow morning."

The children, overhearing the evil man's intent, shuddered as they lay across the cold stone floor in the servants' hall.

"Insolent child," Prince Florian said, turning back to the Mouthpiece. "I should keep you locked away in the dungeon with that creature." Realizing their sorcery would bring him no more clarity on the whereabouts of the children, Prince Florian sent away the Seers and the Mouthpiece with a dismissive wave and they issued back through the secret door. The boy trailed behind, making a final glance toward the grate in the wall before he disappeared into the darkness.

CHAPTER TWENTY-FOUR
The Dungeon

When the Prince had retired from his throne room, the children finally sat upright. They were now more fearful than ever of the evil man and what he might do to them and those that had helped them along their journey.

"I don't want to be thrown into the dungeon," said Ben. "Let's get that key and get out of here as quickly as we can!"

"But we can't just leave Tazmo here to rot," Ellie pleaded.

"Perhaps we can find his prison cell while we make our way toward the vault," consoled Oliver. "Speaking of which, it seems we now know where to find it."

"The northeast tower," finished Ellie, repeating the words of the little child from the throne room. "It seemed to me as if that small, poor boy was trying to help us."

Ben nodded. "I believe he knows we're here in the palace, but we've got to be careful. Who knows if he's friend or foe."

The children thought about their next move for some time. At last, Ellie chimed in.

"The general said Tazmo is in the lower prison chambers," she said. "Perhaps the chambers run beneath the palace, and we can travel through them to the northeast tower without being detected."

"It's a good idea," said Oliver. "And it might be our best at this point."

Though still slightly hesitant, Ben agreed, and they crept back to the door to the servant's hall. Checking to ensure the area was clear of guards, the children opened the door and moved across the antechamber and back toward the courtyard.

Oliver pointed out an area where the wall dipped in a bit, and they discovered that it was a stairwell that led downward. Believing this to be the best route to the dungeon, the three children carefully descended into the dark lower levels of the palace.

The air was musty and dank, and the sounds of slowly dripping water reminded the children of the cave they had passed through upon first entering the Kingdom. Ahead of them was a long corridor that was dimly lit by small lamps set at wide intervals on one side of the tunnel. It was clear that very few people from the palace ever ventured down beneath its surface level, for cobwebs grew across the halls.

Seeing a series of doors with bars along the wall, the children correctly surmised that they had arrived at the dungeon. As they passed by, they noticed that most of the chambers were empty—except for a few rotting skeletons that gave the children a fright.

Eventually, they neared the end of the corridor. Beyond them, it bent at a right angle, creating another long hallway. Oliver calculated that they were directly underneath the center of the courtyard. The party rounded the corner and began the trek down another lifeless hallway.

As they crept slowly, they heard a noise. It sounded like a voice muttering in low, barely audible tones. Speeding their pace, the children moved toward it. There, in a cell at the end of this particular stretch of the corridor, was their dear friend Tazmo. The giant furry beast was curled up in a corner of the cell singing an old lullaby to himself.

"Tazmo!" squealed Ellie softly, so as not to be overheard.

Turning toward them, Tazmo realized where the voice had originated. "I thought I told you three to steer clear of the palace," he said with a smile.

"Are you alright?" Oliver asked their old friend.

"Just a few scuffs," said the beast. "But what are you doing here?"

Ben answered: "We're here to break into the vault and find a key so we can open the door back to our world. Lady Juniper said it's the only way to get back."

"And when we heard you were being kept here," said Ellie, "we just had to come and get you out of here."

"I appreciate the sentiments," said Tazmo. "But these cells are locked tight, and I don't see any keys in your hands." He lowered his head. "And I'm afraid if the Prince found that I had been set loose, he'd scour the entire palace—then you'd have no *chance* of getting into that vault!"

The children ingested this new information while Ellie pet Tazmo's fur coat through the bars. The boys looked around in the wide, dim hall. A pair of wooden benches was stacked in an open, empty cell next door. Oliver ran over to the stack and began to drag one of the benches out into the corridor.

"What's that for?" inquired the curious snifflack.

"I've got an idea," said Oliver as he slid the legs of the bench beneath a bar near the middle of the cell door. "Help me," he said to Ben and Ellie, and they ran over to where he stood holding the wooden bench.

"These bars are quite strong," said Tazmo, watching the proceedings in confusion.

When they had arranged a sort of makeshift lever with the bench propped under the bars, Oliver said, "Alright, now all together—push!" They pushed down on the wooden seat with all of their strength, and slowly the hinges on the metal door began to lift. With one last shove of force, the door fell off the hinges and clattered to the ground.

Tazmo stood in the now-open doorway of his cell, in disbelief over the ingenuity of the children. "I saw something like it in a motion picture once," said Oliver with a grin. "But quickly now. Someone will have heard that."

The four friends took off running down the corridor and continued in the direction they were headed before they found Tazmo. At one point, the winding dungeon hallways came to an end in another wide, stone staircase, and the children and the friendly beast followed it back up to the surface. They continued to climb the steps and found themselves in the base of the northeast tower.

Entering a vast chamber, the four were met with another sizable door. This one, however, was unique in that it featured a gigantic wooden wheel mechanism as its latch. Like much of the palace interior at night, this chamber was not guarded, so the children and Tazmo approached it easily.

"Do you think this is the vault?" asked Ben.

"It looks like a vault to me," was Tazmo's reply. "How do we open it?"

Inspecting the wheel, Oliver said, "Perhaps we're just supposed to turn this?" And as he did so, the apparatus creaked under its massive, shifting weight. When he had turned it further, the creaking stopped and a large click signaled they had completed a cycle. The door was now unlatched, and they pulled on it. It crept open, and the children were once again in another dark space.

When they had all stepped inside and closed the door, however, a series of torches seemed to light themselves. The torches illuminated the entirety of the chamber, which they could see now stretched up several stories to the top of the tower, where the light of the moon shone faintly through a series of large windows. In the middle of the room was a massive wooden structure—several levels of sturdy scaffolding around which a spiral staircase wound. Long wooden rafters stretched from the structure to the tower walls to support it, for it was quite tall and otherwise would have easily toppled over. It consisted of seven consecutive flights that also reached up into the expanse of the tower, and on which were built an assortment of shelves and compartments. Neither the children nor Tazmo could discern what was present on these shelves from their current position, so they moved toward the stairs.

Ben craned his neck to survey the scale of the series of stairs. "How are we supposed to find the key now?" he asked. "It could take us days to thoroughly search each level and every shelf."

"Perhaps there is a logic to it all," said Oliver. "Just like in a library."

They all agreed that there must be an order to the shelving of the items in the vault, and they hoped that they would be able to find the key easily once they discerned the pattern.

"Well, we had better get going," Tazmo said, leading the others toward the first level with confidence. The children peered through the doorway that led into the lowest level of the wooden tower. Inside were stacks of fine china and exquisite dishes—pieces that appeared to be antiques.

Ellie approached a row of dinner plates and examined them closely. Around the edges ran a single band of gold inlaid within the perfectly polished dishes. In the center of each was a tiny crest. Closer inspection revealed a coat of arms that featured the royal symbol of the kingdom—a pair of banana leaves arched into a circle with the symbol of a shield inside it.

Oliver discovered a shelf of crystal goblets, each tinted in the palace's signature rosy scheme. The light from the torches bounced off the facets of the vessels, creating a scintillating pattern that illuminated the rest of the dishes in that row.

Realizing that this first level did not appear to contain any keys, the children and their friend continued their trek up the stairs to the second level where they discovered old statues and dusty wooden chests. This level contained no keys either, though; nor did the third or fourth levels, which housed ceremonial robes, hand-drawn maps, leather-bound books, and an assortment of trinkets made of wood.

By the time they arrived at the fifth level, the party was growing discouraged. As they rounded the edge of the stairs and approached the doorway to this level, they found that the walls of this level were made of loose, black metal bars. Through the bars, the children witnessed one of the most fear-inducing sights of their journey yet: a giant, feathered dragon, asleep and filling up the entirety of the fifth floor.

When they saw it, the group stood motionless. Then, ever so slowly, they began to creep toward the stairs to continue to the sixth floor. As they passed by the dragon's head, one step released a loud *creak!* The sleeping dragon was roused. It blinked its massive eyes and focused in on the four tiny travelers. Then, it stuck out its long neck through the doorway, blocking their path. A heavy, metal chain allowed the creature to come within inches of the children's current position on the steps to the sixth floor.

"Where are you going in such a hurry?" said the imposing creature. "We have not yet been introduced."

The children shuddered in fear.

"Please, sir dragon," said Oliver. "We only wish to continue in peace."

"I suppose I can allow you to do so," the dragon said. "However, would you be so kind as to give me a morsel to eat upon your return?"

Looking at each other out of confusion, the children did not know how to respond.

Tazmo spoke up. "We haven't got anything for you to eat, dragon. We are only looking for a special key."

"Ah," said the dragon. "But those children look delightful. It has been some time since I have had any children to eat."

Ellie squealed and hid behind her brother as the dragon smelled them with its imposing nostrils.

"They are not for eating," said Tazmo. "Perhaps there's something else that would appease your appetite?"

The dragon, disappointed that they would not let him consume the younglings, thought for a moment, then said: "As I am a dragon, I am quite fond of treasure. In fact, it is truly my favorite meal."

"How can you eat treasure?" asked the little girl from behind Ben's back.

"Easily," the dragon retorted. "For when I devour treasure in my warm mouth, it is easily melted into a delectable juice which allows me to breathe fire. If you will find me some treasure, I will be much obliged and agree to not eat any of you. As it is, I am trapped behind these bars and must be content to eat those who come in my reach. But if I were to be fed some treasure, I should breathe fire and melt these bars and chains to make my escape from this terrible cavernous tower, where I can be free to forage for my own food."

"Do you know of any treasure on these higher levels?" asked Ben.

"Why, yes," said he. "While the sixth level contains only paper documents—and I'm not sure why one would feel the need to guard such things—the seventh level is filled with thousands of keys. Some of these keys are even made of pure gold or precious gems."

At this point, the children felt sympathy for the poor creature, confined to a life of solitude in order to guard the more precious contents of the vault on its upper levels.

"Then," said Oliver. "If you will allow us to pass back down upon our return, we shall make a promise to bring you back some of these precious keys for you to consume. But you must promise not to eat any of us!"

"This seems a fair trade," the dragon replied.

Having reached a deal with the fearsome creature, the children continued their ascent in hopes that they could find a swath of gold or silver to feed him and spare their own certain doom.

CHAPTER TWENTY-FIVE
The Mouthpiece Tells a Lie

Prince Florian reconvened his council with the Seers in his golden throne room, and the robed assembly gathered in their typical semi-circle formation. The frail child—the Mouthpiece—stood in front of them silently, while Florian's menservants stood at attention at either side of the throne.

"It is time," said the Prince. "We must make another attempt to locate the three children who came from another world. For if they can enter, that means others may enter—and we cannot allow another heir to return to this Kingdom, for it would mean my ruin. So, my Seers—tell me what the children are doing this very moment."

While the Seers closed their eyes and summoned their extraordinary powers of perception, the small boy in the center of the room shifted his weight from side to side. He was nervous, knowing that the children were loose in the palace, and he knew that he would have to share the truth with the Prince if the Seers observed them.

As was their routine when they were ready to share their vision, the Seers opened their eyes and pointed their fingers at the boy. The Mouthpiece shuddered.

"Well," said Florian. "What have they seen?"

"Three children," the Mouthpiece spoke slowly. "Walking."

"And?" the Prince inquired.

"Three children walk up a flight of stairs," he clarified. The boy knew it was vague enough so as not to give away their location, but hoped the Prince would not ask many follow-up questions.

"And at some point, they surely must stop their ascension, no?" asked Florian.

"They continue to climb," said the Mouthpiece.

Prince Florian waited, impatient at the limitations of his magical methods of espionage. "And now?"

"They continue to climb," the Mouthpiece said again.

"How long shall we wait?" shouted the Prince, before he added sarcastically: "Or have they found a stairway to the heavens?"

The boy closed his eyes to be able to focus on the images that filled his head by the magic of the Seers. The children had now stopped climbing, but he said nothing.

"What now?"

"They are tired," said the Mouthpiece. "And they are conversing."

THE MOUTHPIECE OF THE SEERS

"Conversing with whom?" asked the Prince.

"They are conversing with each other," the boy said, looking down at the Gem of Truth that hung on the chain around his neck. "And a friend," he added regretfully. The stone remained its usual emerald green.

"What friend?" the Prince questioned, his temper beginning to flare as he stared intently at the boy, his chest rising and lowering with quick breaths.

The boy did not know how to answer without revealing that the children had freed the furry snifflack, so he stood silently and did not answer.

"What. *Friend?*" repeated the Prince coldly.

With another large gulp, the boy said, "I do not know." As he spoke these words, the stone around his neck began to glow a bright, pulsing crimson. The Prince leaped from his throne and approached the boy suddenly.

"You lie!" he said, inches from the boy's face. The Mouthpiece closed his eyes and looked away, but the Prince grabbed his chin and turned the child's face toward his own. "You will tell me the truth," said Florian, "or I shall throw you in the dungeon."

The boy stared into the eyes of the fuming, wicked Prince and considered his options. At long last, he took a deep breath. "The snifflack," he said. "The children are conversing with the snifflack."

Baffled, the Prince replied, "The snifflack? Why, the snifflack is safely in the dungeon—"

Realizing what had happened at once, Florian summoned General Pompadour to his presence. "General," he shouted. "The children have infiltrated the palace, and I believe they may be inside the vault this very moment. Capture them!"

With a quick bow and a nod, General Pompadour disappeared through the huge main doors of the audience chamber to rally his men. Florian sat atop his throne, seething, while the Seers and their Mouthpiece stood by in fear and silence.

CHAPTER TWENTY-SIX
On the Seventh Floor

Because time was of the essence, the children did not stop to survey the contents of the sixth floor. At the top of the winding spiral staircase, the four adventurers finally arrived at the last landing. While they stopped to catch their breath, Ben surveyed the distance they had come. He leaned his head over the edge of the staircase and looked down. The dizzying height made the floor down below seem to disappear, and the boy pulled himself back away from the edge quickly when he thought of how far one could fall.

Oliver looked ahead at the maze of shelves that stood before them. Upon closer inspection, he could see that each shelf consisted of tons of tiny hooks from which hung thousands of keys of different colors, shapes, materials, and sizes.

"How are we going to find the key to our Gate back home?" asked Ellie in despair.

"We'll have to use our intuition," said Oliver with outward optimism. "We've come this far. Perhaps the key will make itself apparent to us."

He suggested that they split up to cover more ground, and off they went to search for the key—though they did not know exactly what kind of key they were looking for.

The children and the furry Tazmo filed up and down every row of shelves. Ben and Ellie passed by a row of huge, silver keys as big as the girl's arms, and they dazzled her with a shimmer. *Those are beautiful,* she thought, *but not the keys to our old door.* She kept looking.

Oliver surveyed his row of keys. They did not seem to be in any particular order, as one simple gold key was hung next to the most ornate key cut from a single ruby. His eyes began to grow weary of trying to take note of each distinctive key, but he grabbed a few keys made of precious metals that caught his eye and put them into his backpack as he continued to stroll through the rows.

They were all becoming quite disheartened as they failed to recognize a key that might correspond with their door in the cave when suddenly Oliver called out to the others. They ran to him, following his voice to navigate through the maze of aisles, and found him standing with a small key in his hands.

It was a small, bronze key with ancient teeth on one end. At the other end was a series of three circles, inlaid with vibrant emeralds in a triangular shape.

"This is the one!" said Oliver.

"How can you tell?" asked Tazmo.

"It's exactly like the one we found in the old house that led us *into* the door in the first place," he said enthusiastically.

"Hooray!" said Ellie as she clapped with glee.

"We'd better get out of here quick and find the docks," said Ben. "The Prince will be right on our tail if he uses the power of his Seers again, and we've got to get to Marco before he does."

"I just hope Marco was able to make it to the rendezvous point on time," Oliver added.

The children hustled down the steps until they came again to the giant, feathered dragon, which immediately stretched his neck to the full length his chain would allow. The dragon made a snap at the children with his enormous jaws.

Oliver, with a backpack full of gold and ruby keys, stood face-to-face with the giant, drowsy dragon, and as it blinked its eyes, they sparkled like sapphires and focused right on the boy.

"Excuse me," said Oliver, shaking. "Can you allow us to pass, sir dragon?"

The beast heaved and breathed a warm sigh, then replied: "I can allow you to pass only if you will help to feed me something delectable."

"Surely," Oliver said. "That is as we agreed."

"As I mentioned before, I am quite hungry," said the

dragon. "If you were not able to find any treasure, then I will have to eat you and *then* I will be able to allow you to pass."

"Of course you may not eat us," was the boy's response. "Then there would not be any 'us' left to pass!" Then, holding out the assortment of keys made of precious materials, he continued, "Perhaps you'd be interested in these, instead?"

The dragon licked its lips with a slithering tongue, and said, "Those will do fine."

Oliver handed them to the dragon to appease its appetite, then inquired: "Now for our request; would you please allow us to pass back down this scaffolding in peace?"

The beast thought about the request for a short while as it devoured the solid keys. They melted in its mouth like butter with a sizzle, and soon they were all gone. "That seems only fair," it said. "Since you fed me some of my favorite delicacies and now I can melt these bars and chains that have kept me trapped inside for so long."

The children and Tazmo cautiously inched their way down the steps past the fifth floor and down to the lower level. After they had passed safely, they looked up toward the dragon. With a fiery snort, the beast heaved a huge breath that filled the entire floor with a bright red glow. Flames engulfed the metal bars and chains at one side of the fifth floor and they melted quickly, allowing the beast to move freely. The creature had been coiled, wrapped and trapped tightly inside the tower for so long, but now looked massive when unfurled.

With a jolt, the creature leaped into the air and flew up through the space between the wall and the wooden scaffolding that made up the tower. It sailed toward the ceiling, and at the last minute burst through one of the large windows and into the humid, night sky in a shower of glass and rain.

The four, after witnessing this awe-inspiring sight, continued to quickly descend toward the base of the tower.

Just then, as they reached the second floor, the door into the vault began to creak open and footsteps could be heard echoing up the stone walls that surrounded the wooden tower of stairs and shelves. As they looked down, the children could see a group of Prince Florian's soldiers enter the room and begin to search the level below. When their search yielded no results, they began to ascend the staircase with purpose.

The children and Tazmo quickly motioned to one another to hide behind the towering and dirty statues of the second floor. As they held their breaths, Florian's soldiers ascended to their level. Peering into the shadows created by the wooden structure of the tower, the men stopped for a moment to survey the space.

When their initial pass did not reveal any of the intruders, the soldiers continued up the steps toward a higher level. The children and Tazmo waited until they had gone up another couple levels before they sprinted down the steps and out the door back into the cavernous halls of the palace.

CHAPTER TWENTY-SEVEN
The Rendezvous

As they moved from shadow to shadow, the four intruders avoided several platoons of guards who passed by them—presumably to provide backup to the search in the northeast tower from which they had just emerged. Tazmo and the children had become more familiar with the layout of the palace by this time and found their way to the east gates of the palace with little difficulty.

Tazmo heaved a large door open, revealing a set of wide steps and landings down toward the docks. It was still dark out and raining lightly, but the children could make out the form of several small boats lined up in the bay.

"Do any of you see Marco?" asked Oliver as they scanned the moorings.

When their initial observation did not reveal their friend and protector, Ben said, "What if he couldn't get here in time? The Prince's men are hot on our tail."

Before they could worry much longer, Ellie spotted the shape of a man waving at them from the far end of the dock.

"There!" she pointed, and the children and Tazmo took off running cautiously across the slippery stone steps.

As they came closer, Marco's face became distinguishable. He greeted the four travelers, introduced himself to the snifflack quickly, and then held out a hand to help each of them make the leap across the small gap between the dock and vessel. The children found a spot under a small covered area at the aft of the sailboat, which shielded them from most of the rain.

Though it was still dark and somewhat stormy, Marco lifted the anchor, untied the ropes from the dock, and hoisted the small sail atop the boat. With a swift lurch, the craft began to drift into the navy horizon. With the towering palace fading in the distance, the children witnessed a group of Florian's men emerge from the same back door they had come from.

"I think they've spotted us," said Ben worriedly.

"If we keep on through the night," said Marco, "we'll maintain our lead. All that matters is that we get you to that Gate first."

Huddled together to keep warm in spite of the cold raindrops that bit their faces, Oliver, Ben, and Ellie looked toward the palace. As they had been asleep for the journey into the ornate building, they now witnessed its beauty for the first time with their own eyes. Lamps illuminated the pink walls in the dark of night, casting distinct shadows that made the place look ominous and spectacular. At its base, a larger vessel set off from the wharf and headed on an identical course as their tiny sailboat, though quite far behind. All the children could do was wait and hope that they would reach their destination before the Prince's craft could catch up to them. The motion of the sailboat in the choppy waves lulled them slowly to sleep.

CHAPTER TWENTY-EIGHT
The Door in the Cave

The daylong rainstorm had finally stopped. The palace was long gone, and the children awakened to a view of a vast ocean, reflecting soft lavenders in the early light of the sun. To their left was a thick jungle of mangroves with a series of faded mountains beyond it. A sprinkling of distant lights indicated settlements and cities even farther away. A look behind them revealed the Prince's vessel, closer than it had been upon their last inspection.

The children realized they had already passed the island town where they had met Lady Juniper, which meant they were incredibly close to the forest where they had first encountered Tazmo as they had emerged from the cave.

Tazmo pointed to a small outcropping, while Marco steered the boat toward it. When they had tied up the boat, the entirety of the party disembarked except for

Marco.

"I can go no further," said Marco. "I must return to my home, and perhaps I can lure Florian's men away if I act quickly."

Realizing this was a necessary step in their journey, the children thanked the man who had been of such great help to them. They hoped their paths might cross again someday, but knew this to be unlikely as they might soon be re-entering their own world—perhaps for good.

Marco pushed the boat off and turned the sail. It filled with wind and carried the children's protector away slowly. It was at this moment that they remembered that Florian's ship was gaining on them. With a final wave to Marco, the children followed Tazmo and disappeared into the thick jungle quickly.

The four moved in silence as Tazmo led the children back toward the entrance to the cave. A flock of wild parrots squawked overhead and landed in a tree. In no time at all, they had arrived.

"Well," Tazmo said softly. "I suppose this is goodbye."

Ellie began to cry and wrapped her tiny arms around the beast's massive legs.

"You saved my life," said Tazmo. "I'm truly indebted to you three."

Now they were all crying and, one-by-one, exchanged hugs.

When they had finished saying their goodbyes, Tazmo stood and waved as the children walked into the mouth of the cave. Oliver produced the flashlight from

within his backpack to illuminate their way through the rocky crevices. To his surprise, it worked.

At this moment, they heard a loud rustling in the forest. Looking toward it, the children realized that Prince Florian and his men had spotted them. Florian led them, holding a large fiery torch.

"Go!" shouted Tazmo, pushing the children into the darkness. With a final nod, he crouched on all fours and ran off out of sight. The children took a final glance in the direction he had disappeared and then turned quickly to continue on toward the Gate.

The journey into the cave seemed quicker to the children than their first unexpected trek through it several days prior. The sound of dozens of pairs of quick footsteps echoed behind them, growing ever louder as the children trudged deeper into the ground. After a short while, the flashlight shone upon the humble wooden doorframe that stood in the middle of the cave.

Oliver took the key from his pocket. The three emeralds encrusted in its hilt glistened under the beam of the flashlight. The boy approached the door with the key in his outstretched hand. "Well," he said. "Let's pray this works!"

As the child inserted the bronze key, the sound of a light jingling began to fill his ears. He turned the key and the door latched open, allowing a stream of an overhead hallway light into the cave. At this same moment, Oliver turned to see the glow of flames bouncing off the stone walls of the cave just behind them. The Prince had reached them.

"Quick!" said the boy as his two friends hurried

through the portal ahead of him and back into the second story hallway of the old Florida house. Oliver looked back. Florian was now within sight, just a few feet away, and his torch cast menacing shadows across his face. With a grunt, Florian tossed the torch toward the door. Oliver jumped through the portal as flames began to inch their way up the sides of the wooden doorframe.

When he emerged in the hallway, Oliver slammed the door shut behind them. Strangely, the key they had used to enter the door the first time was gone. The faintest smell of smoke filled the room, and the children looked to the door once more, waiting for it to open.

But the door remained shut.

After a few seconds that seemed like minutes, Oliver walked slowly back to the door and tried the handle. The door creaked open, revealing a dark space. Widening the opening, Oliver observed a small, dusty bedroom. A faint light snuck in through a crack in a plywood-covered window. Oliver looked puzzled, relieved, and slightly disappointed. The jingling had ceased once more.

"What was it that Lady Juniper said to us about magic?" said Ben.

"It's *unpredictable*," Ellie chimed in.

"I suppose this is what she meant," her brother replied as they started down the rickety old steps to the first floor of the house.

"Do you think we'll ever get to return and see all of our new, dear friends like Tazmo and Marco and Lady Juniper?" the girl wondered. "Now that we're home, I do miss them quite a bit."

"We can only hope," said Oliver. And so hope they did.

As they gathered their bicycles from the foggy, overgrown lawn, the children watched the sun rise gradually from beyond the railroad tracks at the end of Azalea Drive. They walked the bikes slowly up the incline of the hill and back down the other side. The streets were quiet and a humid mist hung in the air—the everyday enchantments of their own regular world.

When the land flattened out, the children hopped onto their bikes and pedaled across the big road and then turned on to a smaller one. They were at the end of their own street now, and they imagined what they might tell their families about their several-day hiatus.

As they recollected the occurrences of the past few days, they pedaled by a large banyan tree that occupied an overgrown lot, its signature hanging roots mangled with shrubs and bushes. The three friends were too busy reminiscing on their stories of the Kingdom to hear the sound that emanated from that very spot—*the faint sound of jingling.*

Kingdom of Florida
The Lamplight Society

Written by
Taylor Thomas Smythe

Illustrated by
Alice Waller

CHAPTER ONE
Annie Finds a Friend

Annie was only ten years old, but her family had already moved seven times. First, it was the old farmhouse in the Kansas countryside, which she was too young to remember well. Then it was the two-bedroom apartment downtown where she took her first steps. They continued their grand tour across the midwest, dancing through Iowa, Illinois, and Indiana—each for nearly a year. After that came the lengthier stint in Nashville, followed by eleven months in a tiny town on a mountain outside of Atlanta.

If they were trying to escape the winter cold, their latest choice was the right one; Florida didn't have much in the way of *cold*—unless one counted the three days in the middle of December when a cool front blew through or the accelerated, chilly winds on an overcast pre-hurricane day.

But this particular day was far from cold. In fact, it was warm and pleasant as the moving truck pulled onto a shady, tree-lined street in the early summer.

ANNIE

The neighborhood seemed charming enough to Annie as she peered through the glass of the passenger-side window while her mother craned to read addresses. Several groups of young children played in the driveways and front yards, stopping to wave at the passing truck and the silver station wagon that followed closely behind. Annie's father drove the car which slowed to a stop as the moving truck dipped into the driveway of a quaint single-story house in the middle of the street.

"We're here," said Annie's mother with a sigh of relief, turning off the truck.

Annie looked at the house through the bug-smattered windshield. The front wall was arced with sulfur stains from a well-water sprinkler, and the overgrown bougainvillea bushes nearly covered the entire front door. *It's not much to look at,* thought Annie. *That'll make it harder to get attached and easier to leave.*

She and her mother hopped down from their seats and onto the pavement. The house looked even shabbier without the windshield to mediate the view. Before Annie could remark on her underwhelming opinion of the house, her mother spoke up:

"Annie, dear," she said. "Why don't you go and make some new friends while your father and I wait for the movers." She then motioned toward a group of children playing with wooden swords a couple of houses down from them, but she could sense Annie's reluctance. "The sooner we know our neighbors, the sooner this place will feel like home."

What's "home" supposed to feel like anyway? Annie thought. Her mother nudged her gently toward the sidewalk and Annie finally complied. She sauntered slowly toward the children, a slight wavering in her gait. It wasn't that she felt nervous, for she was an expert in striking up conversations with strangers. She hesitated because she knew the cycle: move to a new place, start a friendship early on, and—just when she started to get close to somebody—pack up and start all over again.

But those thoughts vanished when a voice shouted: "Wanna play with us?" It was a girl's voice. Annie turned toward the girl whose small, freckled face flashed an endearing smile as she waved.

"Well?" said a boy who appeared beside the girl.

"Um," Annie fumbled over her words. "What are you playing?"

"Princes and princesses!" said the little girl eagerly.

"Ellie," said the boy. "Don't be rude. Remember what mom and dad said; you're supposed to introduce yourself when you meet a stranger."

"I thought they said we weren't s'posed to talk to strangers," the girl said earnestly.

"Well, you're doing a poor job either way," said the boy. Annie smiled at the banter and the boy extended his hand. "I'm Ben."

"Hello, Ben," she replied as she shook the boy's hand. "It's nice to meet you. My name is Annie."

"Nice to meet you, too," said Ben. "And that's just my little sister Ellie." He gestured toward the freckled girl. "She's nine."

"Nine-and-a-*half*!" Ellie retorted, her tiny hands on her hips.

"Is that moving truck for you?" Ben inquired.

"Yeah," Annie said. "We're just moving in down the street."

"Where'd you move from?" asked Ben.

"Everywhere, I guess," said Annie, brushing a lock of her dark hair behind her ear. She elaborated: "We move a lot for my dad's job. I've gotten used to moving every year or two."

"That sounds kind of miserable," said Ben with a sympathetic grin.

"Yeah," Annie shook her head, then lowered it a little. "It's not so bad if you just avoid getting too attached."

"Well," Ben said. "Maybe you'll end up staying in Florida longer than you think."

Annie was about to respond with a snarky comment when Ellie chimed in again: "So, are you going to play princes and princesses with us or not?"

Annie laughed. "Sure," she said. "I'll play with you."

"Here," said Ellie handing her one of the blunt wooden swords. "You can have my sword. We were just getting to the part where we snuck into the castle by hiding inside of a giant, wooden alligator—"

"Ellie," Ben tried to interrupt.

"—and then Oliver found the other key to the door—"

"Ellie!" Ben said, louder this time.

"What?" she asked innocently.

"You're going to overwhelm our new friend with all of your, um, *enthusiasm*," her brother chided. "How about we stick to princes and princesses?"

Friend, thought Annie. *I like the sound of that.*

"But it's all real," said Ellie. Ben raised his eyebrows—the universal signal for "not another word; or else." Ellie sulked a little and bent to gather a pair of stuffed animals from the grass.

Annie turned to Ben. "Your sister has quite the imagination," she said, nodding toward Ellie.

"Yeah," said Ben, who seemed dodgy all of a sudden. "She loves to talk about the Kingdom—um, *a* kingdom—that she thinks we—I mean *she*—discovered in an old house." Annie gave him a strange look. "But it must have all been a dream, of course," he added quickly.

"Right," said Annie, unsure why her new friend was acting abnormally all of a sudden. Then, remembering something Ellie said, Annie asked the boy: "Who's Oliver?"

Before either of the siblings could answer, a voice from behind Annie spoke up: "I am." Annie turned to face a smiling boy with dark skin and brown eyes. A pair of round glasses rested on his nose.

"What's your name?" Oliver asked.

"Annie," she replied.

"She just moved in down the street," added Ben.

"And she's going to be a princess with me," Ellie chimed in. "You wanna be a prince, Oliver?"

"As long as I'm the good kind of prince," Oliver replied, grabbing another one of the wooden swords. "Hey, I've got an idea: why don't we show Annie around the neighborhood a little?"

"I should probably stay close by," said Annie. "Otherwise my parents might get worried."

"We can go to the secret jungle," said Ellie to their new friend, who wasn't sure what the girl meant.

"It's an empty lot a few houses down," Ben clarified to Annie. "It's all overgrown with trees and vines, so we call it a jungle."

"Sounds cool," Annie said after thinking it over for a moment. "Lead the way!"

The four children started down the sidewalk, toy swords in hand. They passed by Annie's new house as a truck parked along the street. Four big men in matching tee shirts filed out and met Annie's father at the door. Annie watched as her father pointed toward the truck and the men began to unload the cardboard boxes full of their belongings, but this scene quickly passed out of view as the children continued their walk.

"So Annie," said Ben. "What are some of your favorite places you've lived?"

"Well," she began. "I honestly haven't really stayed in one place long enough to have favorites. I wish we could just commit to one city—or even one state—for more than a couple years. But my parents don't really care too much about what I *wish*."

"I'm sure they care," said Oliver. "And look on the bright side; at least you *have* your parents."

"Oh, I'm sorry," Annie started. "I didn't know—"

"It's fine," Oliver said hurriedly, though his lowered head communicated a different story. "I live with my grandfather now."

"Did you know your mom and dad?" the girl asked.

"I was really young," replied Oliver. "I don't remember much about them. I *do* remember an occasional visit from my grandmother growing up, and I remember that we didn't ever travel. But it's been a long time since..." His voice trailed off as they continued down the sidewalk.

"Since they passed," Ben completed the sentence in a whisper. The children continued on in silence for several moments.

Presently, they reached the empty lot where a row of thick fronds hung over the sidewalk, tangly weeds sprouting through its cracks. Oliver led the way, hacking a branch with his wooden sword. The other three filed behind and were soon hidden from the street.

"It really *is* like a jungle in here," Annie remarked from the rear of the pack, carefully pushing a thorny vine out of her way. "It would be easy to get lost in here."

Oliver slowed his walk and turned to face the others. "You just gave me an idea," he said. "How about a quick game of hide-and-seek?"

"Yes!" said Ellie, clapping her hands with glee.

"But what if our parents come looking for us—" Ben began to protest until Annie interrupted him.

"Let's play!" she said.

"Splendid," said Oliver. "I'll be 'it' since I thought of the idea. The rest of you go find a hiding place on the property while I count out thirty seconds with my eyes closed." Before anyone else could chime in, Oliver shut his eyes and began to count off out loud. "One, two, three—"

The other children quickly split off in different directions, disappearing into the thicket.

"—eight, nine, ten, eleven—"

Annie spotted a massive banyan tree and headed toward its thick, gangly roots. Rounding one side of it, she discovered that Ben had already crouched into a perfect, child-sized hollow in the thick roots. He motioned for her to keep moving past him and she looked frantically for another spot nearby.

"—twenty-one, twenty-two, twenty-three—"

On the other side of the enormous tree, Annie saw what looked like an even larger hollow, but it was mostly obscured by a blanket of thick yellow and green vines.

"—twenty-six, twenty-seven—"

As she clawed at the vines to make a space for her body to fit through, she began to hear the faint sound of ringing in her ears. It was a shimmering chime, and it grew louder as she moved deeper into the darkness of the hollow.

"—twenty-nine, thirty!"

Oliver opened his eyes and spun himself around,

listening for the faintest rustling that might give away the hiding place of one his friends. Hearing a crunch, Oliver turned and ran toward a small, bushy hibiscus tree. A dainty laugh gave Ellie away and Oliver quickly tagged her and enlisted her help to find the others.

Eventually, they came upon the banyan tree and discovered Ben's hiding place.

"That was a good one, Ben," said Oliver as he helped his friend out of the hole. "Now to find our new friend Annie."

Ben put his finger over his mouth to tell the others to keep silent, then pointed toward the other side of the tree where he had seen Annie run a few minutes prior. The children scrambled through the crunchy leaves to look for her. But, though they searched high and low, the children could not find Annie anywhere.

Annie, it seemed, had disappeared.

CHAPTER TWO
The Banyan Gate

The overgrown vacant lot was relatively small; in fact, they could easily view the tops of the houses on either side of it—so the children knew that Annie could not have gone far. Finally, after several minutes passed, Oliver shouted out: "Okay, Annie! You win! You can come out now!"

They waited for her response.

Silence.

Oliver shouted again.

Stillness.

Then, faintly, a sound began to fill the ears of the children. Ellie heard it first—standing closest to the vine-covered hollow of the banyan tree—but it came to Oliver and Ben soon after. They recognized the familiar sound of ringing, for they had heard it before.

"Quick," said Oliver. "Help me with these vines."

The three children set down their wooden swords and pulled on the thick vines and, one-by-one, cleared the way into the hollow. With the vines removed, the children now saw that the hollow was actually a door-way of sorts—a small, thick archway made out of crum-bling red bricks nestled inside the contours of the great banyan tree.

The shade of the huge tree made it difficult to see through to the other side of the passage (if there even was an *other* side), so the children moved in closer. The shimmering sound grew louder in their ears and Oliver gave a knowing look to his neighbors. They recognized the sound from a prior adventure—one in which the same noise preceded a trip through a magic doorway to another world. On that journey, the children learned that there were other similar portals hidden through-out their world. *Could this be one of the Gates?* Oliver thought.

Without another word, the children proceeded into the darkness of the brick archway. They contin-ued walking for several feet, and Oliver wondered when they might reach the other side of the tree. The air around them grew thicker and more humid. After a few more moments, the ringing and the darkness fad-ed as the children stepped out of the tree and through a dense thicket of vines and thin branches. Several of the branches had been freshly snapped, creating a makeshift path, so Oliver led Ellie and Ben until they reached a clearing.

The houses adjacent to the vacant lot were no lon-ger visible and the trees seemed taller as the three chil-dren surveyed their surroundings. There was no sign of Annie.

Ellie broke the silence: "Are we... back? In the King-dom, I mean."

"It would appear so," said Ben, looking around at the vast jungle. "But how?"

THE BANYAN GATE

Oliver moved closer to inspect the mouth of the passage from which they had just issued. They were clearly no longer in their own neighborhood, but the brick archway and the banyan tree looked identical to their counterparts from the vacant lot. "I think this is one of the other Gates that Lady Juniper told us about," he said. Lady Juniper was a wise and beloved old woman who once assisted the children in finding their way home from the Kingdom through a magic door in an old house. According to Juniper, the number of these portals—or Gates, as she referred to them—was once great but had dwindled down to merely a few in recent years; the remainder were either sealed off, hidden, or destroyed.

"Curious," Ben said. "I wonder why we didn't need a special key like the last time we entered the Kingdom."

"Perhaps the Gates come in all shapes and sizes," said Ellie. "Juniper did say some of them were quite old."

Just then, they heard a rustling in the bushes nearby. A tiny brown chipmunk emerged and inched its way into the clearing, sniffing in every direction. It burrowed its head into a small hole for a moment then returned to following the trail of a scent that led down an overgrown path.

"Perhaps that creature has found Annie's scent," said Oliver. "We should follow to see where it leads."

The others agreed and they began to walk behind the creature, keeping a safe distance so as not to spook their newfound guide. The path was only wide enough for one person, so the children assumed a single-file line with Ben taking up the rear.

The trail serpentined around thick cypress trees and clumps of low-lying ferns, and the children had to take care to avoid tripping on the knotty roots that grew across the path. Vines and dangling moss brushed across the tops of their heads and the children nearly lost sight of their critter guide as they turned to bat away a swarm of buzzing flies. But they trudged on.

As they rounded a corner, Oliver stopped. The chipmunk had scurried away and Oliver did not see which direction it had gone, but the children soon dismissed this as they were now in another small glade. Ellie's eyes widened as she saw something familiar in the center of the clearing: a wooden sword.

"It's Annie's sword," she said excitedly, running toward the toy. "We're headed in the right direction!"

Oliver and Ben followed closely behind. As Ellie knelt to pick up the sword, Oliver let out a yell: "Ellie, wait!"

But his cry was too late. Before Ellie could lift the wooden sword from the ground, the three children found a large net rising around them. Within seconds, the net had engulfed them and a series of ropes and pulleys attached to the nearby trees yanked them into the air. The net hung several feet off the ground, the three children piled on top of each other with their limbs poking through gaps between the thick ropes.

"Sorry," Ellie said finally.

"Now what are we supposed to do?" asked Ben, his face squashed in the net.

"Let's just stay calm," said Oliver. "We need to think of a plan."

As on their last journey to the Kingdom, the children had not prepared for a trek into the jungle, so they had few personal items that could assist them in crafting an escape. The net spun slowly with the lopsided distribution of the children inside. Oliver used this time to observe their surroundings but did not notice any obvious way to improve their situation.

"I hope Annie is okay," said Ben, who had already developed a fondness for their new neighbor.

"I do, too," Ellie replied. "This Kingdom can be a dangerous place. I hope she hasn't run into any trouble."

"It seems we're bound for trouble," said Oliver, shifting out of one awkward position and into another. "I'm sure someone will appear soon enough to check on their trap."

The children waited and thought, suspended above the forest floor. It was early in the afternoon when the children first began their game of hide-and-seek, but now they watched the golden orange rays of the sun setting through cracks in the jungle canopy.

As it grew darker and the net continued to spin slowly, the children heard a noise: the muffled crunch of footsteps coming in their direction. All three children craned their necks in the direction of the steps, but it was too dark to discern the source of the sound.

The steps grew louder and closer, and now the children could tell that they came from more than one individual; it sounded as if there were a dozen or more feet stepping through the fallen leaves and twigs. Next, they perceived the sawing sound of one object grating against another, which Oliver realized was a thick, serrated knife rubbing against a tightly-bound rope. *Snap!* Before they could react, the children felt the net around them grow loose as they tumbled onto the vegetation below.

Brushing off the bark and dirt, the children looked up and into the trees just beyond the small clearing. The trees were cloaked in shadows and the moon cast a dappled glow on the figures that began to slowly emerge. The faces of the figures were obscured, but the three children caught the glint of moonlight bouncing off the weapons they pointed toward them; each held a long wooden stick strapped with a worn metal tip that formed a crude, sharpened spear. Ben looked in either direction for a way they might escape, but more of the figures appeared, sealing off any chance of running.

They were surrounded.

CHAPTER THREE
A Tale of Two Reunions

As the figures stepped further toward the children and into the moonlight, they could now be seen more fully. The captors were all men and each wore little more than a loincloth and a large wooden mask. Their masks were painted with patterns of dots and lines, while a tuft of dry straw protruded from the top of each, emulating a shock of stiff, upright hair. Tiny oval openings were cut to allow the men to see through the masks, and the sight rather frightened little Ellie.

One of the men stepped forward and extended his spear toward Oliver. As the sharp point drew nearer to his chest, Oliver gave a yelp: "Hey! Watch it!"

The man seemed startled by the boy's cry but did not lower his weapon. While the rest of the masked men continued to step toward them, Ben pulled his little sister closer to comfort her. The circle of captors was now so tight that the men stood almost shoulder-to-shoulder.

Finally, the first man spoke a single word

gruffly: "Up!"

The children quickly obeyed, wanting to avoid any further complications. They huddled closely together, while a pair of the masked men approached each of them and bound their hands with thin ropes. When this was complete, the men returned to their places in the circle.

"Follow!" The first man spoke and then stepped back, revealing another man behind him who approached the circle with a glowing lantern in hand. The children moved toward him and he turned and began to walk into the jungle. As the one with the light led the way, the rest of the men gathered at either end of the children to prevent them from running away, and they began their trek into the dark of the forest.

Oliver, Ben, and Ellie kept close to each other to avoid the tips of the spears that pointed from the behind, and they were too afraid to think of how they might get away from their masked captors.

"It'll be okay," said Ben to his sister softly. "Let's just do our best to keep calm." The boy was feeling anything but calm inside but hoped to put Ellie at ease with his words.

The party trudged through thick patches of ferns and wove their way beside a narrow, babbling stream. Two of the men at the front of the pack turned and began to speak to one another, but the light splashing of the water muffled their words so that the children could not hear their conversation.

After some time, they emerged from a dense patch of the forest and rounded a corner. Directly ahead of them on the path hung a large blanket of dark, woven cloth, strung between two thin pine trees with a rope.

A MASKED MAN

An assortment of sheets of different patterns and materials hung in a similar way along the trees to either side of it, forming a sort of wall. The man with the lantern approached the blanket and pulled it aside, opening a path through the wall.

As the children were ushered in by the masked men, the three discovered that this was an encampment. The fabric that dangled between the trees created a large circular boundary that obscured the camp within—a camp which consisted of several tents and structures of varying sizes and shapes, all constructed from branches and similar sheets of cloth. In the center of the camp was a shallow pit of fire surrounded by stones.

Oliver scanned the camp for any sign of their lost friend Annie. At the far end of the courtyard was a large tent. A series of smaller tents lined the inside of the cloth wall. *No sign of Annie*, he thought before he felt a pair of rough hands pushing him toward the fire pit from behind.

The masked men brought the children to the edge of the fire—a spot where they could feel its warmth on their faces and the cool of the forest at their backs. Oliver watched as one of the men approached the large tent, lifted the flap, and went inside. Moments later, the masked man emerged along with a figure in a dark, hooded cape. The boy could not make out the face of the figure but observed a motion of his hands toward one of the smaller tents. A couple of the masked men ducked into the smaller tent and disappeared.

A few moments passed. The flap of the small tent opened and the two men stepped out slowly. Between them was a child with long dark strands of hair hanging over her face and thin ropes lashed around her wrists. When they reached the fire, the girl lifted her head and finally saw the three children who stood beside her.

"Annie!" exclaimed Ellie. Ben and Oliver each breathed a sigh of relief at the sight of their friend.

"Are you okay?" Ben asked the girl.

Annie nodded affirmatively. "Yeah," she said. "I'm fine."

"Quiet!" Said one of the masked men.

While the four children stood in silence around the fire, one of the masked men again approached the hooded figure who stood just outside the glow of the flames. After a brief exchange, the masked man again moved toward the fire. Oliver watched with alarm as the man reached into a leather pouch at his side and withdrew a small, shining knife. He continued to walk toward the boy.

When he was face-to-face with the boy, the masked man gripped the sharp knife tightly. With a swift motion, he slid the blade through the space between the boy's hands and severed the ropes that bound him. As Oliver breathed more easily, the man repeated this action for the other three children, removing the cords from their wrists one-by-one. The masked men then stepped away from the children and stood further from the fire.

The hooded figure had remained motionless throughout this time but now began to saunter slowly toward the fire pit. It was still difficult for Oliver to discern the face of this figure, but the gradual, shifting glow allowed enough light to recognize that he was a bearded man.

The man stood at the opposite side of the flames, his head and hood hanging low. Finally, he spoke: "Do you know where you are?"

The children looked at each other. "I believe we're

in the Kingdom, sir," Oliver answered timidly.

The man nodded slowly. "Yes," he said. "And you've traveled far, little ones."

"Who are you?" Ellie asked, still uneasy. Something about his voice seemed familiar to her, but the man made no answer nor motion to reveal his face.

"Why have you brought us here?" Ben added. "And what do you want with us?"

The man waited a moment and then replied, "I mean you no harm."

"No harm?" interjected Annie. "You people just dragged us through the jungle!" She motioned to the masked men who stood silently a few paces away.

"One can never be too careful," said the man. Turning toward the other three, he continued: "I promise my intention is to protect you, children; it always has been." As the man said these words, the children watched as he slowly removed the dark hood that obscured his face. Oliver, Ellie, and Ben immediately recognized the familiar face from their previous journey into the Kingdom. Before them stood their old friend and protector: Marco.

"Marco!" Ellie exclaimed, full of relief and delight at the sight of their old friend.

"It's good to see you again," said Marco to Ellie and the boys. Before he could make his way around the fire pit, the three children rushed over to embrace the man. On their previous adventure into the Kingdom, Marco had helped protect the children from harm and find their way back home. They did not expect to see the man again nor to return to the Kingdom at all, so they were overjoyed that both occurrences now coincided.

Annie watched the happy reunion from the other side of the flames, still unsure about the intentions of the hooded man and the vast jungle she had wandered into by some strange magic. "Excuse me," she spoke up. "Could someone explain to me what's going on?"

Marco and the other children turned their attention to the girl. "It's alright," said Ellie. "He's an old friend."

"But where are we exactly?" Annie asked. "What is this *Kingdom* and how is it that you've all been here before?"

Realizing that there was much to discuss, Marco gestured toward the large tent. "Perhaps we should convene in my quarters," he said. "I will explain everything—*where* you are and *why* you're here."

CHAPTER FOUR
The Lamplight Society

The flames in the fire pit danced in the cool night, reaching undulating golden tentacles up toward the starlit sky. The four children followed Marco as he led them across the clearing to his large tent. A pair of the masked men accompanied them from behind and took their places at either side of the tent's entrance, parting the way for Marco—their apparent leader—to enter. The children filed behind and felt the cold outside air dissipate as the flap closed behind them.

The tent seemed even more magnificent and expansive inside. An assortment of lanterns hung from wooden beams around the perimeter of the room, illuminating it with a warm, bright light. At the back of the room was a sleeping area partially obscured by folding screens. Near the front of the tent, Marco motioned to a pair of fading sofas. A clay oven nearby filled the space with a cozy heat. The children took their seats and their host offered them tea from a cast-iron pot which he now removed from the fire.

"I apologize that the men had to bring you all here in such an unwelcoming manner," he began as he poured the steaming beverage into small cups on a table in front of them. "These days, we have to take every precaution."

"We understand," said Ellie. "These are dangerous times."

"Indeed," said Marco. Annie's confounded expression reminded him that she still lacked important context as to the nature of the Kingdom and its present dangers. "For the girl's sake, I suppose I need to explain a little about this place."

"Much appreciated," she replied. "And my name is Annie."

"It's a pleasure to meet you," said Marco. Then he leaned back in his seat and began: "I presume you've already gathered that this is no ordinary land. In fact, you're in another world now—the Kingdom, as we call it. You can think of this land as a sort of mirror to your own world. It has a great many similarities, to be sure; but a few key differences, as well." He stopped, realizing that Annie was still trying to fathom the idea of the existence of a secret world. "Do you remember how you arrived in the jungle?"

Annie thought for a moment. "I think so," she said. "We were playing a game in an old lot near our new house, and I found a spot to hide in a huge old tree. I thought it was just a shallow hollow, but I kept walking and discovered that it was a deeper sort of tunnel. Next thing I knew, I was in the middle of the jungle—not a house in sight—and a bunch of those men in masks appeared and led me here."

"That tunnel in the tree," Marco said. "That was one of *las Puertas*—the Gates."

MARCO

"What are the Gates?" inquired the girl.

Ben spoke up: "The Gates are like doorways between our world and this world."

"Yes, that's right," Marco nodded. "In the early days of our Kingdom, there were a great many places where our people could pass between the worlds. They were difficult to find—pockets of magic hidden in all sorts of natural spaces—so we built the Gates to help identify where these places existed. Of course, constructing the Gates took a great deal of craft and magic itself."

"Now there aren't many Gates left," said Ellie to their new friend. "Isn't that right, Marco?"

"That's correct," said Marco. "Most of them have either been destroyed, sealed shut, or they are heavily guarded by the wicked Prince Florian." The children shuddered at the mere mention of his name.

"Who is Prince Florian?" asked Annie. "And why is he such a bad man?"

Marco took a deep breath and then sighed. "Florian did something very bad," he said. "He poisoned the entire royal family—his own family—just to take over the throne."

"That's dreadful," said the girl with disdain.

"That alone would be dreadful enough," Oliver agreed. "But it gets worse."

"How could it?" wondered Annie.

"Tell her about the Triumvirate," said the boy to their host.

He nodded in agreement. "Many generations in the past," Marco began again, "the people of the Kingdom appointed three benevolent rulers—King Palafox, King Coronado, and King Mangonia. These three rulers were known as the Triumvirate; they were kind and gracious and loved by all of their people. Whenever one of them grew old, he would appoint a son or daughter of his own family line to take his place on the throne. This pattern continued for several generations, and the Kingdom flourished. Until..."

"Florian," Annie interjected. "I think I see where this is going."

"Yes," said Marco. "Florian's father—a descendant of the line of Coronado—had grown old. When it came time for him to select an heir, Florian presumed that he would be the chosen one. He was, after all, the oldest of many siblings."

"But he didn't pick Florian, did he?" the curious girl suggested.

"No," said Ben. "He picked his younger brother!"

"Florian was furious," continued Marco. "On the night of his brother's coronation banquet, the Prince poisoned all those in attendance—the royal family members from all *three* lines of the Triumvirate."

"My goodness!" said Annie with a gasp. "Did he really poison every single one?"

"The people thought so at first," Marco replied. He set his tea down on the table in front of him and leaned forward in his seat. "Florian knew of at least one member of the royal family who had already left the Kingdom before the unfortunate event, and there may have been more. But he will not rest until he has cut off every possibility of those heirs returning to the Kingdom—and he will use any means necessary."

Blowing softly on her cup of tea, Annie asked, "So that's why you have to be so cautious?"

"Yes," said Marco. "My people recently discovered the Gate in the old banyan tree—the one that led the four of you back here. Florian doesn't know about it yet, but we fear the Prince may find it soon with the use of some dark magic or spies."

"The Gates," said Oliver. "They're the only way one of these possible heirs can come back here from our world?"

"I'm afraid so," Marco said as he lowered his head. "And time is running out. We've already heard word that the Prince has destroyed even more of the Gates; in fact, this is the only one that we know of that he hasn't yet found."

"Who exactly do you mean when you say 'we'?" Ben wondered aloud.

"That's an excellent question," replied Marco. "I'm referring to a secret circle known as The Lamplight Society." At this, he withdrew a thin gold chain from around his neck upon which was attached a circular medallion with the symbol of an old-fashioned lamp emitting stylized beams of light. Oliver, Ben, and Ellie recognized the necklace, as their older friend had shown it to them once before.

"I remember the symbol from our last visit," said Oliver.

"The same symbol hung above the home of Lady Juniper," added Ellie. "Is she part of The Society, too?"

"Yes," said Marco. "Lady Juniper helped found The Society many years ago. Since then, many others have joined—like me and some of your old friends, Bevelle and Henry."

"Oh, I do miss all of them so very much," Ellie said. "Juniper, Bevelle, and Henry were all so good and kind to us."

"I haven't seen Juniper in several weeks," said Marco. "That was before Florian raided her village on the river and burned it to the ground."

"Oh, how dreadful!" exclaimed Ellie.

"Thankfully," continued Marco, "she escaped with her life, a few old documents, and her little pet Kiwi. She's been on the run ever since, trying to recruit more allies and find a way to stop the evil Prince, I presume. But I've no idea as to her whereabouts."

Returning their attention to the prior topic of their conversation, Annie asked, "So what is The Lamplight Society?"

"The Lamplight Society is made up of those of us who hope for the return of the Triumvirate," Marco said soberly. "We have sworn to find and protect the long-lost heirs to the thrones—to light the way for their return—and to overthrow the wicked Prince Florian. It is certainly no easy task. The good news, though, is that the Prince is more afraid than he's ever been; after the three of you—small children—found your way into his heavily-guarded palace, he has made even greater strides to destroy the Gates and any mention of the heirs."

They had conversed for some time and it was now getting quite late. Ellie, the youngest of the group, let out a huge yawn. "Weren't you going to tell us *why* we're here, Marco?" As she said this her eyes blinked droopily.

"You have all had quite the adventure today," said Marco, noticing the sleepy nods of the four children. "I will have the men prepare you all a place to sleep for the night, and we can talk about that in the morning." He rose and walked to the entrance to the tent, whispering to one of the masked guards just outside. When he returned to the sitting area, he discovered that the four children had already fallen fast asleep, hunched and crumpled over each other and the thick, cushioned arms of the sofas. With a soft smile, Marco covered each with a woolen blanket, turned out the lights, and retired to his own bedchamber at the back of the tent.

The chirps of crickets and katydids serenaded the entire party into a deep and peaceful slumber.

CHAPTER FIVE
Byron the Bunglejumper

Early the next morning before the sun was up, Oliver drifted slowly out of a vivid dream. He blinked his eyes and tried to orient himself. The round lenses of his glasses were foggy and beads of sweat clung to his forehead. Oliver wiped off his spectacles with a blanket and remembered that he had fallen asleep in Marco's huge tent. He took care not to wake his host or his friends, carefully shifting the weight of Ben's sleeping head off his shoulder. When he was finally free of the confines of blankets and bodies, the boy crept almost invisibly across the darkness of the tent toward its entrance.

Lifting the flap, Oliver peered through the gap. The dying fire at the center of the camp cast a dim glow on two of the masked men that slept at either side of the entrance. *It's curious that they sleep with those masks on,* thought Oliver. *But I think I can pass without waking them.* Then, as quietly as he could, the boy hoisted the canvas a bit more and stepped out into the camp.

The camp was eerily silent—the air filled with only

the occasional crackling of the remaining blackened logs on the fire. Oliver made a quick visual sweep of the camp, which did not detect any signs of motion, so he surmised that everyone else was still fast asleep. He then turned and approached the wall of fabric that surrounded the camp and shimmied through a gap into the jungle beyond.

The morning dew dampened the sound of his crunchy steps across the forest floor, but Oliver still walked slowly to avoid being heard. When his eyes adjusted to the starlit dawn, slivers of cool-toned light revealed a sort of path before him. Oliver kept walking.

The boy trudged aimlessly, as if still not fully awake. He did not have a specific destination in mind; he merely wanted to clear his head after the night's dreams left him feeling strange and unsettled.

Oliver paused. *What was that?* He wondered as he heard a faint sound. *It sounds close.* The boy turned to determine the direction from which it emanated and then stopped to listen again.

Is that... crying? A sudden wave of compassion compelled him to walk toward the source of the tears. The sniveling continued. Oliver pushed aside a few branches of a sapling and followed the sound into a small grove of orange trees, where a little girl with dark hair sat hunched and crying. Sensing a presence as Oliver approached, she removed her hands from her face. It was Annie.

"What's wrong, Annie?" asked Oliver as he sat down beside her.

"Oh, it's not important," she replied with a snot-filled sniff. Oliver reached into a pocket and produced a handkerchief which he handed to the girl.

"Sure it is," said the boy. "Did you have a bad dream,

too?"

"Not exactly," Annie said. "I just feel so far from home. This place is strange and dangerous, and I just thought I would finally have a house that I could truly call home—not for a year or two, but the sort where you make friends and plant gardens and stay awhile. But now we're here and that all just seems so far away."

"It's alright to miss your home," said Oliver. "The Kingdom isn't so bad. Anyway, we'll be on our way back to the Gate and into our world soon enough. We can go home today if you like. I'm sure Marco and his men will lead us back."

The sun had begun to rise as they spoke, shifting the dim cool light to warmer, brighter pinks and purples.

"Marco said that there's a reason we're here—that he would tell us why we're here," Annie said. "Do you think we're meant to stay in the Kingdom for long?"

"Whatever the reason, I'm sure you'll have the choice to go home instead." Oliver said this to assure the girl but was not certain he believed it to be true. *If this Kingdom has a way to draw us in like it has done on two occasions thus far, it most certainly has a purpose in bringing us here,* thought Oliver. But the boy kept this thought to himself.

"Your dream," said Annie. "What was it about?"

Oliver closed his eyes. "All I remember," he began, "is that I saw my family—my whole family—but they were standing far away. I could recognize my mother, Vera, and her mother—my grandmother, Coral—and my grandfather, of course. But the rest of them were just faceless figures. I started to walk toward them to get a closer look and, with each step, they moved farther and farther away from me. Finally, I started running and they began to vanish and fade slowly. When I reached

224

out my hand to try and touch them before they could disappear, my arm grew long and stretched across the space between us. I was inches from my family. Then they were gone. And I woke up."

Annie was silent and waited until Oliver opened his eyes. "You miss them," she said finally. "It's okay to miss them—normal, even. And besides, maybe family is about more than who your parents are."

"I barely knew them," said Oliver. "I wish I could find a way—"

A sharp howl interrupted the boy, and the children turned toward the sound. It came from further in the forest, not far from their current place in the orange grove.

"What was that?" said Annie as she grabbed Oliver's arm.

"I don't know," he said, shaking. A second howl resounded, louder than the first. The children stood and listened as it continued, a drawn-out cry.

"It sounds like some sort of animal," Annie said.

"It sure does," agreed Oliver. "And I think it's hurt." The boy started toward the noise, which began to sound more like wailing.

"Wait," said Annie. "What if it's dangerous? It sounds like a pretty big creature."

"There's only one way to find out," Oliver said as he started into the jungle to find the source of the howling. Annie hesitated, then ran to catch up to her new friend.

The two children quickly left the orange grove and wove their way down the path, guided by the natural contours of the forest's growth. Sunrise had fully arrived by now, making it much easier for them to see the path ahead. The pair padded along the dewy earth, the howls growing louder with every turn.

Finally, they reached another small clearing. The howling had stopped and Oliver noticed that, strangely, the clearing was darker than the forest paths behind them. Annie and the boy looked around in every direction, but the mysterious creature was nowhere to be found. Then came a slow, quiet growl from above. The children cautiously craned their necks.

There above the children was an enormous mass of thick, striped fur and feathers tangled in one of the masked men's nets. The animal appeared to be nearly the size of an elephant but had the face of a lion. It whimpered when it spotted the children.

"Please," it spoke in a helpless tone. "Please help me. I've gone and fallen into a trap and I haven't the strength or cunning to get myself out."

Annie, surprised at the sight of a talking animal, hesitantly replied: "If we can help you at all, how can we be sure you won't turn and devour us?"

"That would be ridiculous," said the beast, "for bunglejumpers do not eat children."

"What's a bunglejumper?" asked Oliver.

"It's what I am," the creature replied. "We have the fearsome features of a lion—though on a scale several times larger, as you can see—and a pair of great feathered wings by which we can normally travel great distances by air. However, at the moment I'm somewhat immobilized by this horrid net and can't gather the strength by which to fly, much less to escape from this prison."

"And how do we know you won't eat us?" Oliver repeated Annie's earlier unanswered question.

"That's easy, silly child," the beast said. "Bunglejumpers are not meat-eaters. Children are made of meat and therefore I do not eat them."

"What if you're lying to us?" Annie questioned.

"You have my word I'm telling the truth," it said. "How about we make an arrangement: if you help to free me from this trap, I promise that I will refrain from eating you *and* I shall owe each of you one flight upon my back at your request."

Oliver and Annie thought over the beast's remarks and believed that the powers of flight could be useful at some point in the future. The two whispered so that the captive could not hear.

"We will help you," said Oliver at last. "But first, we'd like to know: do you have a name?"

"Thank you, thank you!" The creature replied eagerly. "And yes—I go by the name of Byron."

"Byron," Annie repeated. "It's a pleasure to meet you, Byron the Bunglejumper. Now, let's see if we can find a way to get you out of that net."

The two children scanned the clearing for a solution to Byron's predicament. Annie noticed a thick rope lashed to a tree behind them. She ran to it and began to pull and pry at the knot. With Oliver's help, they quickly undid the knot and—*Whip-whip! Woosh! Thud!* The weight of the beast toppled to the forest floor and shook the ground beneath them.

When he lifted himself from the ground, Byron the Bunglejumper stood nearly three times as tall as the children—not including his wings, which extended even higher. The winged lion's mane was made of soft, beautiful feathers that encircled his regal face. Byron rubbed a bruise on his thick foreleg and then turned to the children. "Thank you," he said in earnest. "I have hung suspended in that trap all night and was afraid I might never be free."

"It was the least we could do for a creature in need,"

said Oliver.

"Don't forget, I owe you each a flight atop my wings," Byron reminded them. "Would you like to hop up on my back and use one of these favors now?"

"Actually," said the boy, "I think we'll save that for another time. For now, we had better get back to the camp; Marco will be wondering where we've gone."

"Well, alright," replied Byron. "Should you need my services, you need only to shout my name, as we bunglejumpers have impeccable abilities to hear from many miles away."

"Thank you," said Annie.

The two stepped closer and embraced the legs of the colossal beast, sinking into his thick fur. Then the creature took a few steps back and began to flap its wings slowly. As the flapping turned into a flutter, Byron lifted off the ground. The wind from his wings blew Annie's hair across her face and into her mouth, and Oliver had to grab his glasses to keep them from blowing away. They watched as the majestic beast ascended through the canopy and disappeared into the morning sky above. When Byron was out of sight, the children began their walk back to the camp to reunite with their friends and discover what quest Marco might have in store for them.

CHAPTER SIX
Marco Enlightens the Children

The journey back to the camp was a brief and pleasant one. When Annie and Oliver arrived, their friends were already awake and the camp was crawling with dozens of men in painted wooden masks. Ben and Ellie sat near the fire in the center of the camp, where Marco dished out a freshly-cooked bowlful of steaming breakfast mush for each of them. He offered some to the new arrivals as they joined the siblings on a wide log.

Annie recounted the discovery of their new friend the bunglejumper while Ellie and Ben listened with rapt attention and wonder. Before long, they all finished breakfast and turned their attention to Marco.

"I hope you've all eaten your fill," he began. "We don't have much out here away from the villages, but we try to make the most of what we find in the jungle."

"Why are you way out here, anyway?" asked Ellie. "And where is *here?*"

"When we found the Gate in the banyan tree," answered the man, "we knew that we would need to protect it in the event that Prince Florian found out of its existence. These men and I keep watch nearby. Right now, this is the only means we have by which to pass between our worlds." There was a gravity in his voice as he spoke and lowered his head.

"Marco," said Ben. "Last night you said that you would tell us why we're here. But we're only here because we were looking for Annie. She hid inside the big tree and we followed her back to the Kingdom."

"That's *how* you came to be here," Marco said. "But it's not *why* you're here."

All four children looked puzzled but waited for the man to elaborate.

Marco continued: "I do not believe it is an accident that you found your way into our Kingdom—on this occasion or the time before it. You see, the Kingdom is in dire need of aid but our own people have all but given up hope. I *know* the Triumvirate can be restored, but we are running out of time and allies."

"What does that have to do with us?" Annie asked. "We're just children."

"Exactly right," said Marco. "You're small. Easily overlooked."

"But last time we were here the Prince was watching us with his Seers," said Oliver. "How do you know he hasn't already seen us again?"

"Our intelligence tells us that Florian is on the move," Marco said. "If he's out amidst the Kingdom, it will be some time before he returns to the palace and can utilize their magic. The Prince doesn't know you're here yet, which means you'll have the upper hand. And, if you recall, the Seers can only see *what* you're doing; they cannot see *where* you are. On your last visit, you entered through a Gate that was *known* to Florian—remember how he held the key in his vault? Thankfully, he has not stumbled across our Gate in the banyan tree yet, so he won't be looking for you."

"How exactly do you think *we* can help?" Annie wondered. She hoped that it would be simple and easy so that they could return to their neighborhood quickly.

Marco replied: "Well, as I mentioned, we believe there are heirs that could return to take the throne, but we've been unable to identify who they are, where they might be now, or if enough of them even exist to restore the Triumvirate."

"You and Lady Juniper both mentioned an heir who left the Kingdom before Florian took over," said Oliver.

"Yes," said Marco. "She left many, many years ago. With Lady Juniper missing and such limited access between worlds, though, I don't have much more information than that."

"So you want us to find the heirs," said Ben. "How?" The other children nodded as if they had the same question and turned to Marco for his answer:

"In the old days, before Prince Florian usurped the throne, the records of the royal family lines were kept up in great detail in a large book—The Royal Book of the Blood. This volume was said to contain the family trees of all the descendants of King Palafox, King Mangonia, and King Coronado. However, all record-keeping ceased when Florian took the throne, for he didn't want to have any cause for the people to remember the time before he was ruler."

"This book," said Oliver. "Can it tell us who the lost heirs are?"

"It's the only lead we have at this point," Marco replied. "I myself have never set my eyes upon the book, but I can only hope its contents will give us something useful to help us in our quest to restore the Triumvirate."

"Where's the book now?" Ellie wondered.

"That's a challenge," he said, "and it won't be an easy one: this Book of the Blood is kept in The Royal Library. It's a tower that was built on a tiny island in the middle of the great lake in the center of our Kingdom—Grand Lake. The central, secluded location allowed for any of the royal family members to use the library as a retreat, where they would take leave from their palaces to study, read, or simply spend a holiday."

"A library," said Annie, her eyes lighting up for the first time since they entered the Kingdom. "I've always enjoyed reading." In fact, the girl made a habit of reading books quite often because they allowed her to return to familiar characters—characters that seemed more constant than the transient friendships she experienced with neighbors and school classmates through her family's constant uprooting.

"I'm afraid you won't be reading for pleasure on this visit," Marco said to the girl. "The Prince has made the library nearly impenetrable—at least through its main entrance. He's barricaded every window and door on the main level, and keeps a company of his conquistadors guarding it at all times."

"There's another way in, right?" Ben asked.

"The library was built on top of a network of caves and tunnels," continued Marco. "Legends say they were once used by pirates as a hiding place for gold and treasure. They're a bit unsteady, and most of them have been filled in by now, but I think they could provide a way in."

"But?" Ben suspected there was more.

"*But* the bottom of the lake is largely uncharted territory; any number of undiscovered and dangerous creatures could dwell in its depths. And you'll need to find another way out; after all, you can't let a book get sopping wet."

Ben took a deep breath; he did not like this answer.

"You're coming with us, then, aren't you?" wondered Ellie.

"I'm afraid not, little one," Marco answered. "I must stay here to guard the Gate. Besides, I would draw too much attention—the Prince has his spies watching for me. But I have full confidence in you. You once infiltrated the Prince's secret vault and escaped unscathed, after all."

The children weighed their options and thought about all that Marco had just told them. As much as Annie wanted to return home, she knew the people of the Kingdom were in dire need. The other three children would do anything to help the friends that had once shown them such gracious hospitality. But there was no denying that the road ahead would be a dangerous one; even if they managed to acquire The Royal Book of the Blood, they would still need to use its records to track down the heirs to the three thrones.

After much deliberation, the four children agreed to embark on the quest to find the book. Marco was delighted and began to gather some supplies for them to take on their journey. Returning to his tent, their host drew them a crude map on a piece of parchment and shared further instructions on how they might infiltrate the highly-secure library.

CHAPTER SEVEN
The Flight of the Bunglejumper

With their packs strapped to their backs and their feet fitted with makeshift boots, the children were well-equipped for a trek across the Kingdom. As they were about to depart from the camp, Marco had a sudden thought.

"Almost forgot," he said as he ran back into his tent. A moment later he returned with his hand clenched into a fist. "Which one of you is oldest?"

"I'm ten," said Annie, raising her hand. She looked at the others.

Oliver's hand shot up next. "I guess that'd be me," he said. "I'm eleven." Annie lowered her hand slowly.

"Hold out your hand," Marco said. The boy obeyed, and the man held his fist over the child's outstretched hand. As he opened it, a tiny metallic item fell into Oliver's palm; it was a small, golden ring. As the boy examined it, he noticed that the ring was weathered and rough. Turning it over revealed a familiar inscription of a lantern emitting rays of light.

"This looks just like the ring we once found in that old house," said the boy. "Where did you get it?"

"I found it when I was out hunting one day," replied Marco. "The great white bird must've swallowed it—you know, thought it was edible. Anyway, the pelt makes a great display in my quarters now, and I've already got myself the symbol of the Society around my neck. That ring should come in handy for you—to show any potential allies that you're on our side."

Oliver gave a knowing look to Ben and Ellie, then slipped the ring deep into his pocket so that he wouldn't lose it.

"It's up to you, now, to light the way for the new Triumvirate," said the man. "Once you've secured The Book of the Blood, you'll need to use its records to find the heirs and convince them to take their rightful places. It certainly will not be an easy task." He paused for a moment, then added: "Welcome to The Lamplight Society."

With that, the party said their goodbyes to the hospitable man and began their journey into the jungle. Ben held Marco's hand-drawn map and guided them in the direction of Grand Lake. In the first hours of their journey, they passed soothing streams of crystal-clear water and knotty tree trunks covered in moss and vines. Occasionally the path would narrow and the children would squeeze past thick branches by turning and shimmying sideways until the trail widened.

Presently, the four children emerged from such a thicket. Ellie, at the head of the pack, called to those in the back: "I think we have a problem."

As the other three arrived at her side, Ellie pointed ahead. The path came to an end. In its place was a long, flat marshy plain that extended as far as they could see.

"Marco didn't say anything about this," said Oliver.

Ben studied the map. "We've taken the proper route," he said finally. "Perhaps we'll simply have to trudge through it. It can't be all that deep, can it?"

Annie was already testing the depth of the murky, still water. As she stuck her foot into the marsh, Oliver noticed a large ripple just beyond the girl.

"What was that?" Oliver asked.

"What was *wha—*" Annie began but was cut short as she turned her attention to the place where she stepped. Something slimy slithered past her leg and she jumped back to the dry land. When she returned her gaze to the water, Annie watched a long, scaly snake coil and then disappear beneath the surface.

"On second thought," said Ben, "I think we'd better find another way to pass this marsh."

"But look at it," Annie said. "It extends for miles. It could take us days to find another way—if there even *is* another way."

The children looked around and tried to think of another way they might cross the snake-infested marsh-land. Another muddy snake slid along the water's edge and hid among the reeds and cattails. Then Oliver perked up.

"I think I've got an idea," he said. "Annie, help me call out."

"Call out for what?" Annie wondered aloud.

"The bunglejumper," said Oliver. "Byron the Bun-glejumper!"

"What's a bunglejumper?" Ellie asked.

"The creature we told you about just this morning," said Annie, now remembering the favor the creature had granted them in return for their kindness. "He's the friendly beast we rescued, and he promised to give us each a flight upon his back."

Before Ben or Ellie could ask any more questions, Oliver began to shout: "Byron! Byron! Byron the Bunglejumper!"

He waited and listened.

"Perhaps he can't hear you," said Ben. "We are several hours out from the camp now, remember?"

"Bunglejumpers have incredible hearing," Oliver said as if he possessed expert knowledge of the creatures. He yelled again: "Byron!"

By this time, several more of the water serpents appeared at the edge of the marsh. Ben grew uncomfortable and took a few steps away. "I sure hope he hears you soon," said the boy. "All this yelling seems to be drawing the attention of those frightening creatures in the water."

"He'll hear," assured Oliver. "Help me out!"

Annie and Ellie quickly joined Oliver in shouting: "Byron the Bunglejumper! Byron the Bunglejumper! Byron the Bunglejumper!"

Before they could finish the last call, they discerned a faint *whooshing* above them. The sound was amplified as the treetops rustled in the wind. A shadow fell over the children and they looked up to find an enormous winged lion descending through the canopy.

Byron alighted on the mushy grass and gave a graceful bow. "Hello again, old friends," the beast said gently. "And hello, new friends." He gestured a paw toward Ellie and Ben, whose mouths were agape at the sight of the massive creature. To these, he said: "You look as though you've never seen a bunglejumper before!"

"That's because we *haven't* ever seen one before," the girl said with a giggle. "You are truly magnificent."

In fact, the bunglejumper was one of the most

BYRON THE BUNGLEJUMPER

glorious creatures to inhabit the Kingdom—or any land, for that matter—and he now preened the feathers of his wings as the late morning light cast a glow over the gargantuan specimen. The stripes across Byron's back were reminiscent of those of a tiger, except that his were iridescent and sparkled in the sun.

"I suppose, my little friends, that one of you wishes to redeem one of the flights I owe?"

Oliver approached Byron and nodded. "Yes, actually. I wish you to carry us across this expansive marsh to the edge of Grand Lake."

"That sounds reasonable," said the bunglejumper. "I think that I can fit the four of you on my back, seeing as you are all so small. However, you will need to hold on to my fur; the motion of the flapping of my wings tends to give first-timers quite a jolt."

While he said this, the majestic creature crouched as low to the ground as possible. Even in this position, the children had to grasp at tufts of Byron's hair to climb atop the creature's striped back. After a few moments, though, all four children sat securely between his wings and took hold of his fur.

"Here we go!" Byron shouted as he began to beat his feathered wings. The children added minimal weight, so it took no time for the bunglejumper to ascend above the jungle. In seconds, they were soaring above the marshland.

Oliver looked below and watched as the marsh quickly gave way to a thick forest. Then, just beyond that, a rocky mountain range. When they reached the other side of the mountains, the boy saw before them a huge lake. It appeared to be nestled within a ring of mountains and hills. In the exact center of the enormous lake was a tiny island from which sprouted a single tall, stone tower. *The library*, thought Oliver.

Before he could take a second look at the structure, Oliver found the beast was now descending. Byron landed in a small clearing and helped the children climb off his back. Pointing with his forepaw, he said: "There's Grand Lake, straight ahead." Indeed, they were only steps from the lake's edge. "I'll need to land here—far away from the island—otherwise my gargantuan qualities may draw the attention of the guards."

"Byron," said Ben. "Can bunglejumpers swim underwater?"

"Good gracious!" Byron gasped. "I'd never think of doing such a thing. Bunglejumpers are cats, after all, and cats *hate* water. But if you're thinking about taking a dive, I hope you'll be careful. And whatever happens: don't listen to the singing."

"The singing?" Ben repeated. "What do you mean—"

Byron cut the boy's words short. "Well, it's time for me to be going now."

"Thank you ever so much," said Ellie, hugging the creature's thick legs. She had a fondness for all the kind and friendly beasts they encountered on their journeys in the Kingdom, and she hated to say goodbye.

"You're welcome," said Byron. "I am a beast of my word, and it was my pleasure to fulfill the request of the good sir Oliver. Do not forget," he said toward Annie, "that I still owe you a flight, should you find need of it."

"Thank you," said Annie. "I won't forget!"

The children bid goodbye to Byron and watched the bunglejumper lift off the ground and sail into the clouds. Then, returning their attention to the quest at hand, the four friends proceeded on to the shore of Grand Lake.

CHAPTER EIGHT
Annie Finds a Way

Grand Lake was the largest body of water in the entire Kingdom. From his vantage point at the edge of the shore, it extended so far into the horizon that Oliver would've mistaken it for an ocean if he didn't know better. The island that housed The Royal Library stood before them with several hundred meters of deep water between.

"How do you suppose we're going to cross the lake?" Ben wondered.

"I find it odd," said Annie, "that your friend Marco would send us on a quest to an island without giving us specific instructions about how to get to it."

"If he sent us, then he knows there's a way," Ellie said cheerfully, though Annie's cynicism was not appeased.

"Ellie's right," said Oliver. "How about we search the area near the shore to see if we can find a way to cross Grand Lake."

The other children agreed and the party began to

scan the beach. Oliver and Ellie headed up one side of the uneven shoreline while Annie and Ben headed in the opposite direction. Annie kept her head down as they dipped in and out of tree patches. *I can't believe I'm doing this*, she thought. *I should have gone back home when I had the chance.*

They searched for several minutes, each pair of children trudging further apart, but found nothing to help them get across the lake.

"Perhaps we should head back and see if Oliver and Ellie found anything yet," suggested Ben.

As much as she wanted to leave the Kingdom and go home, Annie did not want to return to her friends empty-handed. "Let's keep looking," she said. "Just a few more minutes."

Ben agreed and the two continued up the coast. The boy was about to nag Annie again when he realized she had stopped walking. The girl craned her neck and squinted her eyes as if glimpsing something far off. She then pointed.

"Look," Annie said to Ben. "Just beyond those trees. What do you see?"

Ben followed her gaze. His eyes alighted on a wooden post sticking out of the water just near the shore. "Is that—?"

"A dock!" Annie exclaimed. "And I think I see a boat, too."

The pair turned and shouted back toward Oliver and Ellie, barely visible just beyond the place where they had started. They took off running toward Annie's voice and, in no time, the four children arrived at the dock.

Sure enough, moored to the derelict dock was a small rowboat. Annie jumped into it and discovered a pair of oars.

"It's perfect," said Oliver. "This should get us across the lake easily enough."

As the children gathered into the craft, Annie untied the rope and pushed off from the dock. The two boys took the oars and began to row.

"What do you think Byron meant?" Ben asked the others in between strokes.

"About what?" Annie wondered.

"He said, 'don't listen to the singing' right before he left us," the boy recalled. "I haven't heard any singing since we've arrived at the lake."

No sooner had Ben said this than a shrill chorus of wispy voices filled his ears. Frightened, the boy looked around but saw nothing but the expanse of water around them.

"Did you hear that?" Ben asked.

"Hear what?" Oliver said. "I don't hear anythi—"

Another breathy chorus resounded, this time audible to Oliver.

"I hear it now," he said. "It's the most beautiful song I've ever heard."

The ethereal singing continued in the ears of the boys, but the two girls could hear nothing.

"What are you two talking about?" Annie asked. "There isn't anybody singing. We're the only people out here."

Ellie could not hear the choruses either and she looked in every direction to try and figure out what the boys meant. Glancing between the ripples in the water, she caught a glimpse of a face. The face was fair and belonged to a beautiful maiden whose body appeared to be covered in scintillating scales. Leaning further toward it, Ellie perceived several more of the beautiful shimmering maidens, swimming beneath the rowboat. Their mouths opened and closed as if they were speaking or singing, but Ellie could not hear any sound.

The girl nearly fell over the edge of the boat due to a sudden jolt. The boys abruptly began to paddle in the opposite direction—back toward the shore of the lake.

"What are you doing?" asked Annie.

"It's beautiful," said Ben, almost as if in a trance.

"Irresistibly," added Oliver. "Have you ever heard anything like it?"

Annie was dumbfounded; she could hear no singing.

"They want us to go back to the shore," continued Oliver. "They said so in their song." He then hummed along to the song he heard in his head.

"You're going the wrong way," said Annie. "Turn us back around so we can get to the island."

The boys continued rowing toward the dock.

"Look, Annie," said Ellie, pointing at the women in the water. "I think these lovely maidens have caught Oliver and Ben in some sort of spell."

The other girl observed and nodded. "That must be what Byron meant," she said. "How do you suppose we stop them?"

The girls thought for a moment. Then Ellie perked up. "Perhaps we try singing," she said. "Maybe if we sing, we'll overpower those clever creatures."

"It's worth a try," replied Annie.

Then Ellie began singing quietly: "Row, row, row your boat, gently 'cross the lake. Merrily, merrily, merrily to the island you will take."

For a brief moment, the boys stopped rowing toward the dock. Then, hearing the voices of the creatures below, they continued again.

"It's no use," said Ellie. "Those sirens are too strong."

"I think it worked momentarily," said Annie. "Let's sing again together, only louder this time."

The girls agreed and began to repeat the song that Ellie had contrived:

"Row, row, row your boat, gently 'cross the lake. Merrily, merrily, merrily to the island you will take."

As they continued to sing, the boys switched the direction of their paddling and began to row toward the island. The girls' voices were growing weak and gruff by the time they approached the land, but they kept singing. The sirens beneath them continued their choruses, too, but were no match for the overpowering voices of two little girls.

When they were close enough, Annie and Ellie lowered their voices slightly, as most of the maidens had given up and swum away and the girls did not want to attract the attention of the men who guarded the library. Using the rope from the dock, Annie lashed the rowboat to a tree and tied a firm knot. The entire party disembarked from the boat and climbed onto the thickly-covered shore.

"What happened out there?" Oliver asked, finally coming to his senses.

"Those dainty voices you heard," said Annie, "were sirens."

"Sirens?" Ben repeated.

"Don't you remember," said his little sister Ellie, "the sirens from Greek mythology? They would lure sailors with their enchanting songs and cause them to wreck their ships. They're rather frightening in real life."

"It's a good thing you two can sing louder," laughed Ben to the girls.

The children, in good spirits, turned to look up

toward the towering Royal Library that stood atop the island. Almost every door and window was boarded up, except for a series of beautiful stained glass windows around the top of the tower. The children stood far enough away to be out of sight from the guards that lined the perimeter of the building.

"Now," said Oliver, "we need to find the entrance to those tunnels Marco told us about."

As the boy said this, Ellie noticed a large colorful turtle sunning itself on a rock. Remembering that most of the creatures in the Kingdom could talk, the girl approached the turtle to ask for directions.

"Excuse me, Mr. Turtle," she said. "Do you happen to know the way into the tunnels that run beneath this island?"

The turtle slowly turned its head to the girl and replied with little haste: "It's *Miss* Turtle, actually. And I've sat on this rock for hundreds of years, so I know all about the secret tunnels. You're very fortunate, actually, as you've tied your boat at the exact spot. Simply dive into the lake and you'll find the entrance to the tunnels right away. Follow it up until you reach the pocket of air and you'll be inside the old network of tunnels. Now, run along as you're blocking my sun."

Ellie apologized to the turtle for calling her by the wrong name and thanked her for the assistance. The children proceeded to grab their packs from the boat— which Marco had coated in oils to make waterproof— and they waded into the water.

"What about the sirens?" said Oliver.

"If you hear them," said Annie, "cover your ears. It sounds like it ought to be a short swim, though, and they seem to have left us alone for now."

Then the children, one-by-one, disappeared beneath

the surface of the lake. Annie led the way and quickly identified the submerged entrance to the tunnels. The four children each held their breath as they swam down into the dark tunnel, then began the journey back up toward the air pocket.

With a gasp, Annie emerged from the water and looked around. The other three children followed closely behind. They found that they were now in a large cave that was carved from the coral-packed rock of the island. As the children stepped out of the water and onto the dry ground, they looked around the cavern to determine which way to go next. From an unknown source came a faint glow which illuminated the chambers enough for the children to see.

Then Oliver's eyes alighted on something leaned against the carved rock wall that frightened the boy so that he stopped in his tracks: an old dusty skeleton!

CHAPTER NINE
The Royal Book of the Blood

The rest of the children saw the pile of bones, too.

"I have a bad feeling about this," said Ben with a nervous gulp.

Ellie pointed elsewhere in the chamber. "There's more," she said, covering her mouth in horror.

Sure enough, the walls of the chamber were filled with hollowed-out recesses; a skeleton lay in each—adorned with bracelets and other dusty jewelry—and the children shuddered at the sight. The sound of a slow, steady drip echoed off the rocks.

"I think this is some sort of catacomb," said Annie. "I wonder if they knew about this when they built the library."

"I wonder, too," said Oliver. "But I'd rather not spend any more time in here; this place gives me the creeps."

The boy quickly identified a tunnel that appeared to lead out of the grim chamber, and his three friends followed closely behind. This shaft wound back and forth but eventually led the children to a cramped hall with a narrow stone staircase against the wall. Having no other apparent path to take, Oliver continued to guide the group up the ancient stairs in a single-file line.

When the children were nearly out of breath halfway up the flight of stairs, they stopped to look ahead. The stairway terminated in a small wooden door, so the children garnered a second wind and pushed on until they reached it.

The door had no lock, so the boy tried the latch. The door did not open.

"Perhaps it's just stuck," suggested Annie. "Give it a push."

Oliver followed her instructions and threw his weight at the door. He heard a slight, faint *creak!* But the door still did not open.

"Here, let us help," said Ben. There was barely enough space for them to fit across the top of the steps, so they wiggled to keep their balance. Then, in unison, the children rammed the ancient door. This caused the door to open just a few inches, but not enough for any of them to be able to pass. They tried once more, this time with a little more force, and the children were able to swing the old heavy door open wide enough to fit through.

On the other side of the door, Annie stood with her mouth agape. Before her was one of the most beautiful sights she had ever seen: rows and rows of enormous old, hand-bound books. Along every wall was an ornately-etched bookcase filled to the brim with stacks of leather-bound volumes. Aisles of free-standing shelves created a maze in which one could easily get lost amidst the vast and long-untouched collection.

Dusty beams of colorful light danced about the

warm library and Oliver looked up at the stained-glass windows at the very top of the vaulted room. He had seen the windows from outside, but they were immeasurably more beautiful from within—illuminated and intricate depictions of scenes from the Kingdom's history, he surmised. The boy noticed that one of the huge windows had been smashed, leaving a large hole through which he could see the sky.

"It's wonderful," said Annie, still captivated by the beauty of the old books.

"Yes," said Ben. "And it's enormous. How are we going to find The Royal Book of the Blood in such a large collection?"

The others pondered his question, but then Annie spoke up again. "If this Royal Library is like any of the libraries I've been to, there should be some sort of order or organization to it all. Perhaps the book is in a section with other reference books."

As she said this, the girl disappeared into the maze of bookshelves and the others scurried after her. Annie quickly scanned the spines of books as they passed to look for any common theme by which she could identify a common order to the stacks.

"These are all old books of law," Annie said, rounding a corner. "And these," she said as she began a new stack, "are about agriculture and mining."

They continued on in this way for a few more shelves until Annie suggested that they split up to work more efficiently. This they did, with each child starting in a different section of the room.

Oliver found himself scanning one of the taller shelves built into the wall. He climbed onto a wooden ladder to read some of the titles on the higher ledges. One dusty cover caught his eye. With one hand grasping the ladder, Oliver used his free hand to reach out for the small book, which was almost out of reach. Finally, his fingers touched the old volume and he was able to pull it free. Brushing off the layer of dust, he discovered an embossed image on the book's front cover. Positioned in the center of the book, the silver-inlaid illustration depicted a weeping willow tree and, as Oliver discovered upon closer inspection, faded lettering that made up a title: *Guardians of the Willow.*

Oliver was about to flip open the cover to find out what the book was about when he heard a shout that echoed across the room.

"I think I found it!" Ellie exclaimed. "Over here!"

Oliver returned the old book to the shelf with reluctance and quickly descended the ladder. Navigating around the multitude of nearly-identical shelving sections, the boy finally reached the place where Ellie and the others were standing.

They crowded around a marble pedestal upon which rested a massive book. It was nearly two feet on its longest edge and featured a thick, dark leather binding. Gold lettering on the maroon-colored cover confirmed that this was indeed The Royal Book of the Blood.

"Great work, Ellie," said Ben to his little sister. "Now let's see if this book was worth the trouble it took to get into this place."

Oliver lifted the book's cover. It was not as heavy as he imagined, but still a considerably hefty tome. On the inside, the boy found a table of contents. Scanning for the names of the three kings of old, his finger stopped on a line that read: *Line of King Palafox, Page Twenty.* The boy flipped through pages full of ornate calligraphy and colorful drawings and maps until he found a family tree.

"Well, what does it say?" Annie asked, leaning over his shoulder.

Oliver followed the family tree to its most recent branch. "It says King Juno was the last heir of the Line of Palafox." He looked at the details next to the name and continued: "According to this record, he never married and he never had any children before his passing—and that was many years before Prince Florian usurped the throne."

The children's spirits fell a little at this revelation that there was no known heir to King Palafox. Then Ellie chimed in: "Perhaps there's still more to be learned about the other kings. After all, even one or two heirs may be enough to dethrone Prince Florian."

"Let's keep reading," said Annie. "Which family is next, Oliver?"

"The Line of Mangonia," said the boy as he consulted the table of contents a second time and then flipped further into the book. The other children watched as he went back and forth between a few pages before letting out a frustrated sigh.

"The page is missing," said Oliver. "The family tree for the Line of King Mangonia—it's been ripped out of the book!" He showed the others the place where the page should have been and the fragment of ripped parchment that still clung fastened into the binding.

"That's just our luck," said Ben cynically. "I'm beginning to think this may have been a fruitless effort on our part."

"Now, now," said Ellie. "We can't give up yet! There's one more line, isn't there?"

Oliver nodded and found the page number for the *Line of King Coronado*. To his relief, this page was intact and contained a robust genealogy. He found the most recent generation, where his finger stopped on a familiar name: Florian.

"What does it say?" asked Ellie eagerly.

"After Prince Florian is Ronaldo. Then their sister Fawn," Oliver read off the names of King Fernando's other children. "Boone and Banyan—twins. And Gardenio."

"Are any of them still alive?" asked Ben. "Or do they have any children of their own?"

Somberly, Oliver lowered his head and said, "I'm afraid not. All except one was present at the unfortunate incident where Florian made himself the sole ruler. The book says that, due to complications with his birth, Gardenio passed at a very early age."

After a moment of silence, Annie spoke up. "So that's it? There are no heirs—except for maybe in the Line of Mangonia, but we haven't got that page. Does this mean we return home now?"

"We can't just leave," said Ellie. "Our friends need our help! Annie, you don't know Prince Florian—what he's capable of. The Kingdom *needs* us to find the heirs."

"Ellie's right," said Ben. "Marco seemed confident that there were more heirs, but maybe we just have to keep searching. Perhaps there are heirs that weren't recorded in the book? You know—to protect them from the Prince."

"That may be true," said Annie. "But how are we supposed to find them when we don't have any information—?"

"Look at this!" Oliver cut her off before she could finish her thought. The three children huddled around the boy and the book. "In the notes for Florian's youngest brother, Gardenio, it lists his nurse on record: Lady Penelope of Melba."

"Is that supposed to mean something?" Annie said.

"It's interesting because it stands out," said Oliver. "She's the only person mentioned in any of these family trees that isn't actually part of the family."

"Do you think it's a clue?" Ellie wondered.

"I don't think it's an accident," replied Oliver. "And right now, we haven't got any other leads. Marco is counting on us—along with the rest of The Lamplight Society."

Annie thought it was a stretch, but realized she couldn't abandon her friends—no matter how badly she wanted to get back to her family's new home. The girl looked at the page of the book again.

"So how are we supposed to find this woman?" Annie asked finally.

"In Melba," said Oliver. "If we can get to this place called Melba, maybe we'll be able to track down Lady Penelope."

"I don't know about any of you," began Annie, "but I have never heard of a place called Melba."

"And we still haven't figured out how we're going to get out of this library with that book intact," said Ben. "We'd better keep it with us in case there are more clues inside."

Oliver thought for a moment then remembered something. "Byron! He still owes Annie a flight. Perhaps he'll know how to get to Melba."

"How will he get to us?" Ellie asked. "Or for that matter, how will he hear us? And won't he attract the attention of the guards?"

Oliver pointed up toward the ceiling. The others craned their necks and saw the solution: the hole where one of the stained-glass windows had broken through. "I don't see another option at the moment," he said.

None of the others protested. Immediately, the children began to call out, hoping that the bunglejumper would hear them once more. Their little voices echoed up off the stone walls.

Within a few moments, a shadow enveloped the space where the window once was. The sound of flapping wings grew louder as the massive furry beast proceeded through the hole and descended down into the library tower. Byron's padded paws landed softly on the ground and he smiled when he saw the children.

"Well, I certainly didn't think I would be seeing you again so soon," said the friendly beast. "How may I be of service?"

Annie stepped forward. "I'd like to use my favor now. Can you please fly us to a place called Melba?"

"Melba?" Byron repeated. "Certainly! Why it's only a short trip toward the coast. Hop on my back and we can be there in no time!"

The children smiled, relieved, and climbed onto the bunglejumper's back. Oliver tucked the huge Book of the Blood under his arm and held it tightly as they lifted off from the library floor. The piles and stacks of books faded away as they approached the colorful glass panels at the top of the tower. Emerging from the dim, dusty structure, the children found their eyes adjusting to the brightness of the cloudy sky and, in an instant, they were far from Grand Lake and the little island at its center.

CHAPTER TEN
The Raven

At the base of the island on Grand Lake, a black raven perched atop an avocado tree. Around the bird's neck was a gold necklace from which hung a single, elegant ruby. Hearing the faint echoes of children's yells emanating from the top of the library tower, the bird ceased preening its oily feathers and turned its attention toward the sound. When a giant winged lion appeared and then disappeared into the old building, the dark raven was intrigued and waited for it to re-emerge.

Presently, the mighty bunglejumper reappeared with four small children atop its back. With its sharp eyesight, the bird noticed that one of the children carried a large, old book. *Stolen from the Royal Library, no doubt,* thought the raven. Taking a second look, the bird read the gold lettering on the book's dark cover as it caught a glint of sunlight: The Royal Book of the Blood.

"Thieves!" said the bird to herself. "Dirty, sneaky thieves!"

Within seconds, the children and the winged lion

were gone, headed toward the ocean.

"They will not get away with this unscathed," the sly creature said, again to herself.

Then the unnaturally large bird leaped from her perch and began to fly away from the island in a different direction than the bunglejumper. With great haste, the creature winged over the expansive lake and ascended over the edge of the mountain range that surrounded it. The raven dipped into a craggy ravine, where the tall mountains and thick trees covered the area in shadows.

As the black bird descended, it began to soar on a warm pocket of air. It would have been difficult for a common person or bird to see clearly past the trees to the forest floor below, but this raven possessed a keen sense of sight. It was this ability—in addition to her natural powers of flight—that made the raven an excellent and formidable spy.

A metallic glint caught one of the bird's dark red eyes—just what she was looking for. She slowed her pace and dove through a hole in the canopy, coming to rest on the high, moss-covered branch of an oak tree. The tree was at the edge of a large clearing. In the glade's center stood a curious sight: a small, free-standing wooden door frame.

The door itself was barely visible, covered in creeping vines and colorful lichen. What made the sight strange to the bird was the fact that there were no walls attached to the frame. Just a single, solitary door that stood aging in this forgotten corner of the world.

Presently, a small band of dark figures emerged from the thicket. The armored men at the front of the pack rode atop jet-black stallions, carrying torches and long sharp pikes—no doubt the items that had caught the bird's eyes. Several more horsemen followed, encircling

MALVERNE

the old door.

At the center of the pack was a man who carried no spear, but sat confidently on the back of a large, black stag. The creature's impressive antlers were coated with silver tips that had been polished so that they appeared as sharp as the other men's weapons. The stag's rider wore a thick coat over a loose linen shirt, while an ill-fitting crown sat intermingled with the man's thick dark hair.

The large raven instantly recognized the man she'd been looking for: *Prince Florian.*

The Prince now dismounted from the large animal and sauntered slowly toward the ancient door. He turned the handle but found that the door was locked. Reaching into one of his coat pockets, Florian retrieved a large, rusty key and inserted it into the lock. *Click.* Prince Florian then tried the handle again and opened the door ever-so-slightly. A sliver of blinding daylight seeped through the gap for just a moment. Then, satisfied, the Prince closed and locked the door once more.

Next, the raven watched as Florian placed the rusty key on a large, flat rock and then gave a hand signal to one of his men. This man produced a small, sharpened axe and approached the stone. With a single swift motion, the axe fell on the old key, breaking it into exactly two pieces with a burst of sparks.

When the man with the axe had again mounted his horse, another man handed Florian a torch. The flickering flames cast menacing shadows across his face as he returned to the old, locked door. Without any hesitation, he placed the torch at the door's base. The winding vines and dry wood quickly caught fire and, as the Prince stepped back, the whole door was swiftly engulfed.

Sensing that the Prince's work there was nearly done, the raven gave a *caw!* and fluttered down to the man. The Prince recognized the sound and put out an arm on which the bird could land.

"You bring news, my loyal one?" Prince Florian asked the creature as she latched onto his arm.

"Yes, my lord," said the bird. "I bring terrible news."

"What is it, Malverne?" Florian inquired sternly. "Tell me with haste."

"Children," said Malverne the raven. "Children in the Kingdom!"

"What interest do I have in children?" The Prince was irritated now, and the flaming door cast a reddish glow across his face.

"Not just any children," said the bird. "*The* children—that, some short time ago, infiltrated your very own palace—they have returned!"

"How?"

"I do not know how they came to be in the Kingdom again, my lord," she replied. "But there is something else of note."

"What is it?" Florian asked curtly.

"One of the children carried with him a certain Royal Book of the Blood," Malverne said cautiously, afraid to incur the Prince's wrath at delivering such horrible news. "I watched from below as he and his friends escaped from the Royal Library atop a winged beast, headed east toward the ocean with the stolen book in tow."

Florian was silent as he absorbed this new information and his blood began to boil. "Thank you, Malverne," he said at last. "They can only be here for one purpose—one of the rebels must have them searching for a lost heir in the hope that they can dethrone me. I myself know of only one who could regain the throne, but I do not know whether others still live. In any case, these children returned to the Kingdom in some way, which means they have discovered another of these magical Gates. Malverne—my unwavering and trust-worthy spy—you must use your compatriots throughout the land to locate this passage. We must destroy that Gate before they can use it to bring an unworthy heir back to the Kingdom."

The raven gave a nod of understanding to the Prince and fluttered off, disappearing through the thick forest canopy. Florian had confidence that his spy would com-plete her mission with haste.

Remounting his mighty stag, Prince Florian turned to his soldiers and gave them instructions: "The raven will locate *la Puerta* soon enough. Now, we will return to my palace and discover what those children are up to." With this, the riders took off into the dark jungle, leaving the flaming remains of the old door to crumble into a pile of blackened ash.

CHAPTER ELEVEN
Journey to Melba

The wind was strong so high up in the air and the four neighbors clung tightly to their friend the bungle-jumper as he soared over trees and plains at a swift and expeditious pace. Oliver kept The Book of the Blood tightly under one arm while he held the other fast to Byron's coat. Sitting at the rear of the group on the creature's furry back, Ben thought of the ways his parents might object to his flying without a seatbelt. He held a little more tightly to the soft fur and checked to make sure his sister, seated directly in front of him, was doing the same.

Ellie was enamored with the shifting shades of greens and yellows that flew past them below. She caught the occasional glimpse of a large creature ducking into or out of the forest and imagined that one of these might be their old snifflack ally Tazmo. A flock of small green birds disrupted this thought, passing just below Byron's four legs.

"Wild parrots!" Byron practically shouted, turning

his head a little so the children could hear him over their squawks.

"They're beautiful," exclaimed Ellie.

"Must be their season for migrating," the bunglejumper said. "They fly in from the islands at a certain time of year."

The children observed as the parrots flapped in a synchronized formation and then landed in a scattered cluster atop a large, bushy tree. In a few moments, the flock was out of view and Byron began to descend closer to the treetops.

"Melba, straight ahead," he said. "Coming in for the landing. Hold on tight."

Ben grew nervous as they neared the ground but seemed to continue at the same quick pace. Byron now began to flap his wings more vigorously, jolting the children forward. There was very little space to land ahead, but the beast kept on his course. The bunglejumper dipped beneath the trees at last and sailed straight through a tangle of vines and branches that snagged his fur. Tiny twigs scratched at the children's hair and cheeks as they neared the ground, but their place between Byron's wings created a protective shield.

When at last the kindly beast hit the forest floor, the children took a deep breath. Byron the Bunglejumper was covered in sticky sap, while a mass of tiny leaves adhered to his face.

"Everyone alright," he said, turning back to his four young passengers.

They nodded and affirmed they were unharmed as they climbed down off his back. Then Annie let out a chuckle.

"What's so funny?" Byron inquired.

"I'm sorry," she said, now pointing at his face, "but

it appears as if you've got a new mustache!"

Indeed, a string of long, thin leaves just above Byron's mouth resembled crudely constructed facial hair. The other children, now seeing what Annie observed, began to chuckle as well. The creature then used a paw to wipe off the foliage and sap.

"Now, where were we?" Byron said when he finished with his cleaning. "Ah, yes, Melba. The little town is just beyond these trees." He gestured ahead with his forepaw. "This is as far as I go," he continued. "Most people tremble at the sight of a bunglejumper, for they are not aware that, though we appear as fearsome animals, we do not eat other creatures. Therefore, I dare not show myself in the town for the risk that the people might rally against me."

"We understand, Byron," said Oliver. "And we thank you very much for your incredible and timely assistance."

"It was only fair," replied Byron, "for you and dear Annie saved my life. This was the least I could do for you. Perhaps we shall one day meet again. But for now, I bid you goodbye."

The children once again said their farewells to the friendly creature and, after they had helped pick a few more twigs out of his fur, Byron flapped his wings and ascended through the treetops. The friends stood in awe for a few moments as the regal beast disappeared, but then they continued on toward the town.

Oliver led the way through the treeline and the party found that they now stood atop a small hill. From this vantage point, they could see the entire town before them.

Melba was a quaint, seaside town, bustling with activity at the present late-afternoon hour. In the distance, the children could see a semicircular layout of wooden docks and piers that formed a bay, where ships of all shapes and sizes came and went. Narrow, cobblestone streets wound from the docks to the children's present position, bordered by a variety of shops and residences that seemed squeezed into every possible space.

The refreshing scent of the salty sea traveled on the cool breeze as the children descended the hill and entered the crowded streets of the town. People brushed past them on either side, shoppers and sellers meandering toward their next transaction. Some of these characters carried wares atop their backs, with pots, pans, or birdcages clanging as they walked along the uneven ground.

The place reminded Oliver of the town in which they met Lady Juniper, except on a grander and more permanent scale. The streets were wider here, too, and the buildings were taller. The boy did his best to hide the large book under his arm but found this difficult as the volume was nearly half his size.

As they passed by the open doors of a fragrant bakery, Oliver said: "How do you suppose we're going to find this Lady Penelope in such a large town?"

The children continued walking as they thought of a solution.

"Perhaps we could simply ask for directions," suggested Annie.

The others agreed that this was a good idea, and they searched for someone to ask. Ellie spotted an older woman peddling beautiful bouquets of flowers. The woman made eye-contact with the girl and walked toward them.

"Care to buy a flower?" The woman asked, holding out a fragrant blossom.

Ellie inhaled the sweet scent, then replied: "Actually, we've traveled from far away and haven't got any money. But would you happen to know where we might find a Lady Penelope?"

The old woman thought for a moment but did not appear to recognize the name. "Hm," she said. "Can't say that I do."

"Are you sure?" Annie chimed in. "We really need to find her. She once served as a nurse for the royal family."

"Ah!" The flower saleswoman said. "You mean Penny! Why yes, she lives up on the street along the port—best views of the bay in town. It's a small wooden house painted a lovely peach color. You can't miss it."

Heeding the woman's instructions, the children thanked her and headed down the winding road to the docks. The entire town was built over a hilly area, so the streets alternated between a variety of elevations, creating for an interesting and almost haphazard look to the town. Trudging up a long stretch of one of these hills, the children stopped for a few moments to catch their breaths. From this point, they could see they were much closer to the port. The four children followed the street the rest of the way down and rounded a corner to the docks.

This thoroughfare bordered the pier, with a long stretch of narrow, tall rowhouses along one side, which all faced the bay. Fading terra cotta barrel tiles covered the row of roofs and the majority of these residences were built of brick and stone, with intricate details in the masonry around their door frames.

One house stood out near the center of the row, squished between the brick buildings: it was small, crafted with wood plank siding, and covered in a peachy pastel paint.

"That must be Lady Penelope's house," Ellie commented as the house caught her eye.

The children proceeded to the diminutive and humble home that seemed to pre-date the rest of the structures around it by several decades. Oliver stepped forward and gave a knock on the door. Within seconds, they heard the sound of thick-heeled shoes stomping down a staircase toward the door.

When the door opened, they were greeted by a tall, thin woman with fair skin. She wore a linen blouse with buttons fastened all the way up to her neck and a long skirt that rested precisely at the level of her ankles. Her reddish hair was pulled into a tight bun atop her head.

"Good afternoon," she said. "What is the reason for your call?"

"Good afternoon, ma'am," replied Oliver. "We're looking for a woman called Lady Penelope and we were told she lives at this residence."

The woman's eyes narrowed with suspicion. "And why is that you're looking for her?"

"It's a bit of a long story," said Ellie. "The short of it is that we need her help."

"Help?"

"Yes," Ben said. "We think she can help us to find a true heir to the throne."

At this, the woman gasped and leaned closer to the children. "Quiet," she said in a whisper, anxiously scanning the street to see if they had been followed. "You must come inside. Quickly now!"

CHAPTER TWELVE
Lady Penelope

The tall woman opened the door wider as the children filed into the small foyer. She then ushered them toward a sitting room sofa and closed the door quickly, taking care to fasten every lock and latch as the children took their seats.

When the door was secure, the woman drew the blinds closed and then sat in a floral-upholstered armchair opposite the children.

"Now," she said, "let us speak in hushed tones, for the enemy has spies in every corner of this Kingdom."

"Are you Lady Penelope?" Annie asked softly.

"Many people called me by that name long ago," she answered as if deep in thought or memory. "But here in my hometown, most know me as Penny." She leaned in and inquired, "Who sent you here to find me?"

"Well, no one sent us to you exactly, Miss Penelope," began Ben. "But we're on a quest and we were given instructions by a man named Marco."

"Marco?" Penelope repeated curtly, crossing her

arms and looking away. "And what gives Marco the right to send you on some foolish quest?"

"He's a member of The Lamplight Society," Ellie added, unsure why the woman had reacted so strongly to hearing the man's name.

"The Lamplight Society," repeated Lady Penelope, leaning back in her chair. "I should've known *she* was behind this."

"Who?" Annie asked.

"Juniper," answered the woman. "She wouldn't keep me out of her delusional plans, no matter how much I persisted."

"You know Lady Juniper?" Oliver asked.

"I haven't spoken to her in years," she replied. "But yes, I knew her well. Never mind her now, though—why is it that you've come here? And who are you?"

"Well, I'm Oliver," began the child. "And this is Ben, Ellie, and Annie. And like we were saying, it wasn't exactly a *person* that sent us to you. We discovered your name written on a page of this book."

At this, the boy produced the large Book of the Blood which had, up until this point, been leaning against the side of the sofa, obscured from Penelope's vision. She inspected the leather-bound book and its fading titular lettering.

"Where did you get this?" Lady Penelope said as she opened the cover and began to flip through the brittle pages.

"We snuck into the Royal Library on Grand Lake," said Annie enthusiastically. "It was easy to find our way in—once we got past those foul sirens."

"Marco instructed us to find the heirs to the Triumvirate's three thrones," said Ben. "He hoped that this book would be able to tell us who—and where—they are, but it turned out to be quite lacking in usefulness."

"Except for your name—right there," said Oliver, pointing to the page as Penelope reached Coronado's family tree.

"I see," Lady Penelope said slowly, her eyes fixed on the hand-scribed page.

"Is it true that you were a nurse for the royal family?" Annie asked.

"It is true," she replied. "I lived in a chamber in the palace and attended to all of the children of King Fernando and Queen Iris."

"Even Prince Florian?" Ben inquired.

The woman hesitated for a moment, then replied: "Yes. Even Florian. I watched him grow up from a kind and beautiful young man into—into—" Penelope turned her face away from the children to hide her tears, then choked out the ending to her sentence: "—into a monster."

At this moment, the four children heard a loud *thud*! It seemed to come from the floor above, and the children turned their gazes to the ceiling.

"What was that sound?" Ben asked.

"Don't mind that," Lady Penelope replied dismissively. Then, returning to the topic at hand, she continued: "Now, where were we?"

"You were telling us about how close you were to Florian and his brothers and sister," said Ellie. "Can you tell us if any of them survived or had any children of their own?"

"I'm afraid I can't," Penelope said sharply as she rose from the armchair without looking the girl in the eye. "What's written in that book is all there is."

There was another loud noise upstairs, startling the children once more.

"Please," said Oliver, unfazed by the curious commotion. "There's got to be something more that you know."

The woman now stood by the window and peered through a small gap in the curtains. She said nothing, but wrung her hands nervously. Then: a third *thud!* The woman looked flustered now and glanced toward the ceiling as the noise continued to grow louder.

"What aren't you telling us?" Annie asked firmly, now rising from her seat and approaching the woman. "We've come all this way—from another world where our families are waiting for us to return—and we just want some answers. Why are you hiding? Why won't you help us?"

The rumbling upstairs had grown even louder, as if heavy furniture were now being dragged across the wooden floors. Lady Penelope's face now nearly matched the color of her hair as she turned and yelled toward the ceiling: "Toro! Quiet! Come down here right this instant!"

This sudden outburst startled the children, but the sounds above them ceased. A few seconds later, they heard the slow padding of bare feet down the stairs in the foyer. Then, a small boy entered the room, standing in the doorway. His hair was dark and he looked to be just a year or two younger than Oliver.

"Toro!" Penelope said again. "What have I told you about being mindful of your volume when we have company in the house?"

"I'm sorry," sulked the boy. "I tried to be quiet, but I lost one of my toys and had to look in every place." He looked down as he opened his hands, revealing a carved wooden toy that resembled a figure with a crown on its head. "I found him," the boy said, bringing the figure over to Penelope.

As the woman inspected the toy prince, her countenance softened and she stooped so that she could look the boy in the eye. "I'm very glad you found him," said Lady Penelope. "Mother has guests in the house now, though, so run along back upstairs." As the boy turned back toward the stairs, she added: "And try to be a bit quieter this time."

When the boy was gone, Lady Penelope again sat down in the armchair and took a deep breath. "My son, Toro," she said. "He's not used to seeing visitors at the house." Then the woman took another deep breath and continued: "You'll have to forgive me. I only desire to protect my son from the evil and darkness that is out there in the Kingdom, and do not wish to get involved in Juniper's rebellion. I hoped this day would never come, but now I fear that I can hide no longer. I must break my silence and tell you the truth."

She now had the full attention of the four children on her couch and they waited anxiously for her to continue. She paused, as if determining how to begin, then recounted the following tale:

"As I shared with you earlier, I served for many years as an attendant to the royal family of the line of Coronado. When I began as a young girl, Prince Florian was but a boy near my own age, and I cared for him and his siblings while the King and Queen attended to their royal duties. It was I who ensured the children were bathed, dressed, and fed each day. I even helped with their schooling. Florian was crafty, even when he was young, and would often use his royal position to avoid the consequences of small pranks and petty thefts. Most of his antics were relatively harmless, but he felt no remorse for his actions. I could see the darkness growing in him and it frightened me to think what he would become if his power were greater.

"When King Fernando began to grow old and ill, we knew it would only be a matter of time before he appointed one of his children as heir to the throne. Everyone suspected that Florian would be named heir apparent, as he was the oldest of Fernando's children, but those who knew him well sensed that this would be a grave mistake. Though Florian's duplicity toward his father made the old man doubt these claims, King Fernando ultimately heeded the advice of one who saw the boy's dark potential, and he selected his son Ronaldo as his heir instead."

Here the woman stopped and her face became downcast.

"Who was it that warned the King about Florian?" Annie inquired.

Penelope looked up at her and replied: "It was me. I warned Fernando about what could happen if Florian became king. But it seemed as if fate was determined to have the young man become ruler, after all."

"I believe we've all heard what happened next," said Oliver. "What Florian did."

"There's more," said Lady Penelope. "More that no one knows—except for me."

The children urged the woman to continue with her story and she quickly obliged:

"Florian, who believed he was entitled to his father's throne, became furious and plotted to take it for himself. He procured a vial of poison and, at the royal coronation banquet, surreptitiously added a drop to the goblets of each of the royal family members—the men, women, and children from all three lines, including his own mother who was pregnant with her sixth child. She intended to name the child Gardenio—a family name.

"Her highness drank the poison and quickly began to feel ill. Rushing to an antechamber to try and catch her breath, I found the Queen sprawled across a bench and gasping for air. Before I knew what was happening, she had begun to give birth. I was the only person around, and quite untrained in the arts of childbirth, but I stood by as she pushed with her last moments of life.

"In the midst of the chaos and tragedy that Florian had caused, I returned to him in the banquet hall and delivered the news that his mother had passed away in childbirth and that his baby brother Gardenio had perished along with her."

"It's truly tragic," said Ellie, fighting back tears. "What an awful man."

"It is tragic," affirmed Lady Penelope. "But not entirely true."

The four children, whose eyes were all puffy with tears now, perked up.

"How do you mean?" Oliver gasped.

"Well," continued Penelope. "Only half of what I told the Prince was true. His mother *did* perish as a result of the poisoned drink. But, unbeknownst to Florian, I did not tell him the truth about his baby brother."

"Do you mean to say that Gardenio survived?" Ben's eyes grew wide as he realized what the woman had just revealed.

"I do, indeed," said Penelope. "Before I delivered the news to the Prince, the child was hidden and spirited away to a place where he could be kept safe."

Oliver was overjoyed. "That's wonderful news! Can you take us to him?"

Lady Penelope thought for a moment, then replied:

"I'm afraid I've already risked too much in telling you this secret. Not even old Juniper knew of this. I must stay here with my own family."

Annie was especially touched by the woman's commitment to her child, and she began to think that perhaps her own parents had made similarly difficult choices for her own good. Then she asked: "If you won't take us, will you at least tell us how to find him?"

"Yes," replied Penelope. "Of course, I can do that, and—oh!"

The woman looked surprised.

"What is it, Lady Penelope?" Annie asked.

"I've just remembered something," she said. "Something that may be of additional help to you on your quest."

The children were intrigued and waited for the woman to continue.

"Many years ago, Juniper entrusted to me a sealed envelope and told me to keep it hidden and to never open it until the proper time came."

"Well this seems like a proper time as any to open a secret envelope from Lady Juniper," said Oliver. "Where is it?"

"That's the part I *can't* remember," Penelope said, looking flustered. She turned to the children. "I'll have to scour through some of my old things and try to remember where I've misplaced it. Anyhow, it's getting rather late now and the streets will be dark before you know it. Do you children have a place for the night?"

"Actually, we haven't got a place to stay," said Ellie.

"Or any money, for that matter," added her older brother.

"That's alright," said Lady Penelope. "You can stay the night in our house. I'm sure Toro will enjoy the company of some other children near his age for a change. Now, let me prepare a place for the four of you to sleep."

All agreed and, with that, the woman disappeared into a hallway. Moments later, she returned with stacks of thick blankets and extra-fluffy pillows. As she arranged makeshift beds for the four children, little Toro ran around the room pretending to fly while the guests giggled at the tiny boy. Then Penelope prepared them all a hearty dinner, which they ate ravenously while crowding around a small painted table, before heading off to sleep.

CHAPTER THIRTEEN
The Secret of the Sealed Envelope

Ellie was the first to awaken early the next morning. The others continued to sleep soundly on the old wooden floorboards of the sitting room, bundled in fuzzy woolen blankets that made only the children's faces visible. The little girl tiptoed over to the front window, a thick quilt around her shoulders, and tugged ever-so-slightly on the curtains to look through the panes at the rising sun.

The town began to come alive as she peered out across the street to the bay, where a string of sailors loaded crates and barrels on to a massive galleon. It was the largest vessel in the port, surrounded by a number of smaller ships moored up and down the dock that carried a diverse arrangement of goods—bananas, sugarcane, fresh fish, and spices.

"Here," said a hushed voice behind Ellie, startling her.

The girl turned to see the Lady Penelope, holding out a gold coin.

"The fruit is always best when it comes right off the boat," Penelope said in a whisper. "Go and grab us some and I'll fix us a nice breakfast."

Ellie took the doubloon, folded the quilt, and slipped on her shoes, then quietly and carefully stepped out the front door without a sound.

The sea breeze was refreshing and brisk, so Ellie walked with little haste down to the docks. Several burly sailors of all shades and sizes passed and eyed her with curiosity, smelling of salt, sweat, and coconuts. The weathered planks beneath the girl creaked as she walked. Ellie crouched down to inspect the stability of the dock. The sloppy sound of sloshing waves beneath the dock accelerated and came splashing up through the gaps between the wood, soaking the front of the girl's clothes with a misty spray.

A tiny man just up the dock, who had watched the entire event unfold, laughed at the spectacle and then hollered to the girl: "Careful! Wouldn't want to ruin a pretty dress like that, now, would you?"

The girl tried to ignore the man—who wore an eye patch over his left eye—but he spoke again as she passed.

"Looking for something special? The port is no place for a little girl like yourself."

She turned and walked toward him.

"Actually, I'm just here for some fresh fruit."

"Ah!" The man said. "Looking for fresh fruit but you got a salty shower, too!" He bellowed once more.

The girl began to walk away again when the man apologized.

"I'm sorry," he said. "I didn't mean to hurt the poor girl's feelings." He waited for the girl to face him and then continued: "You have to admit, it was a bit of a humorous sight, no?" Then, seeing that the girl did not find his jokes funny, he said, "I apologize. But I do know where you can find the freshest fruit in all of Port Melba. You see that sloop at the end of the way?"

The man pointed and the girl nodded.

"Head straight there and ask the nice little lad—cabin boy—to give you a bushel of bananas," he said. "He'll give you the pick o' the litter for half the price of any other swindler out here."

Ellie thanked the little man and followed his instructions. The cabin boy produced a large branch covered in newly-yellowed bananas, for which the girl handed him the gold doubloon from Lady Penelope. Then, her arms stretched fully around the bushel, Ellie returned to the small peach house.

When she opened the door, Ellie detected the rich, savory scent of biscuits baking in the kitchen. Oliver, Ben, and Annie were all awake and stirring as Ellie passed them with the pack of bananas. Lady Penelope was impressed by the size of it and promptly hung the bushel by a hook above the sink.

A few minutes later, breakfast was served. Toro came downstairs groggily and the children again sat around the small table to enjoy the delicious spread—golden biscuits spread with butter, savory cuts of smoked salmon, and an assortment of tropical fruits to accompany Ellie's hand-picked bananas. A juicy blend of grapefruit and rosemary washed it all down.

As they finished, Lady Penelope spoke: "You will be pleased to know that I remembered where I hid the sealed envelope from Juniper."

"Where?" Oliver said. "Can we see it?"

"Actually," she replied, "it isn't here in the house. In fact, I wanted to be sure that it would be safe, so I placed it in a secure lockbox in the old bank in town.

It's among other valuable items and heirlooms that have been there for even longer, which I'm sure is the reason it slipped my mind."

"Do you have any idea what the envelope contains?" Annie asked.

"I'm afraid not," replied Penelope. "Of course, it's very like Juniper to give a person something important along with very few instructions. My sense was that it related to the royal family in some way, though I can't recall the specific words she used—it was such a long time ago."

The children cleared their plates and piled them next to the sink while Penelope put away the leftovers.

Over the sound of forks and knives scraping against ceramic plates, the hostess said, "I'll finish cleaning all this. You four get ready and then head down to the bank—someone's got to keep an eye on Toro at the house, and all six of us would certainly draw too much attention. This key will open Box Twenty-Nine, where the items are stored." At this, she produced a very small key from inside a pocket of her apron which she handed to Oliver.

The boy turned it over in his hand, noticing that the box number was etched into the top of the key.

"Now," Penelope continued, "it's really quite simple to find your way to the bank. Once you're out this door, you'll round your way up the next street and follow the path all the way up to the center of the town—you might have passed it on your way in last night. There's only one bank in town, so if you get lost just ask one of the merchants."

"What do we do when we get there?" Ben asked, trying to make sure he remembered all of the instructions thus far.

"Just tell the attendant that you've got to check on Box Twenty-Nine and they'll take you straight back into the room with the lockboxes. Simple!"

The children readied themselves for the walk and set out into the town. It was just as lively as the prior evening when they had arrived, but the soft morning light cast a radiant glow over everything. Colorful linen garments on clotheslines became billowing flags up above while a morning mist surrounded their ankles. A man pulled a cart full of oranges, clacking over the uneven cobblestone roads, while the children ascended the hill and wove through the man-made maze of a street. The people here seemed friendly with their faces full of sun and freckles.

Oliver walked behind Annie as they shuffled through the bustling marketplace. He leaned toward her and spoke quietly as they walked. "I had that dream again," he told her.

"The one about your family?"

"Yes," he said. "Only this time I couldn't see any of their faces—not even my mother's."

"Do you think it means something?" Annie asked.

"I don't know," said Oliver. "Strange that it's only happened since we've come back to the Kingdom, though. But it's probably just a nightmare."

Oliver changed the subject of the conversation and they continued through the crowded thoroughfare. Presently, the path widened as the children rounded a corner. The area formed a sort of circular plaza with a large, several-tiered fountain in its center. Just beyond the streaming, gurgling fountain, Annie noticed the sign for the bank. She pointed and the children hurried across the park and scampered up the wide steps.

The interior of the bank was in stark contrast to

the plaza outside; the shouting of merchants was now exchanged for a severe silence, interrupted only by the sound of well-shined shoes stepping across the polished tile floors—but even the sounds of footsteps melted away, though, into the lofty, vast ceiling above them.

Oliver spotted an attendant and approached him hesitantly, feeling for the key in his pocket. "Excuse me," the boy said. "We're here to check on Box Twenty-Nine."

The attendant glared down at him and then pulled on the breast of his dark blue jacket to tighten it. "And do you have the key to this box?" The attendant asked stiffly.

"Yes, sir," said Oliver, reaching into his pocket and producing the tiny object. "It's here."

The surly man took the key and inspected it thoroughly as if doubting its authenticity. Then, with a sniff, he said, "Follow me." Quickly, the man pivoted and began a brisk walk toward a large door at the other side of the room. The children hurried after him, catching up just as he signaled a pair of additional attendants to open the doors.

The room was dark and lit dimly by a series of oil lamps hung from the stone walls. Small bronze doors lined the chamber and, as in the vast foyer from which they had just come, this room extended several stories up. Ladders attached to tracks allowed access to lockboxes and safes above ground-level.

The attendant checked the number on the key again and looked up as he walked. Finally, he stopped in front of one of the ladders and dragged it to the side, where it locked into place. He turned to Oliver and the other children and handed back the key.

"Box Twenty-Nine," he said with a gesture toward

the ladder. Oliver followed the motion upward toward one of the bronze doors three levels up, where the number *Twenty-Nine* was inscribed on a plaque.

"Thank you," Oliver said. "That will be all."

The man hesitated, but then gave a slight bow before disappearing back toward the lobby. When he was out of sight, Oliver began to climb the ladder. He quickly reached the level of the lockbox, inserted the small key, and opened the vault.

"What's in there?" Ellie shouted from below. "Do you see the envelope?"

Oliver ruffled through a number of items that included metallic necklaces and earrings, a few large jewels, a couple of old brown books, and a bag of doubloons. Finally, shifting some of the items around, Oliver discovered a small, thick envelope. He pulled it out of the lockbox and held it for the others to see.

"Found it," he said, closing and locking the box before climbing the ladder once more. He flipped the envelope over, revealing a red wax seal with letter *J* stamped into it.

"Juniper," suggested Ellie.

"Let's open it!" Annie said.

"Not here," said Ben. "We don't know who could be watching. I suggest we take it back to Lady Penelope's house so we can make sure no one else is around."

The children agreed and left the bank. They arrived back at the house in no time and piled back around the kitchen table, where they nominated Lady Penelope to open and read the contents of the envelope. This she did slowly and ceremoniously, using an ornate letter opener to break the wax seal. Inside the envelope was a piece of folded parchment, which Penelope presently unfolded.

As the woman read the contents of the paper, she gasped.

"What is it?" asked the children in unison. "What does it say?"

"I think," answered Lady Penelope looking up at them, "that this means there may yet be another heir!"

CHAPTER FOURTEEN
Difficult Decisions

Lady Penelope placed the unfolded document on the table so the children could get a better look at it, flattening out the creases.

"It looks to be a certificate of marriage," said Penelope, inspecting the paper closely as if to determine its authenticity.

"But for who?" Ben asked.

"King Juno, it seems," answered Penelope.

The children exchanged confused glances at one another, and then Annie asked: "Who is that? And why would Juniper give us his marriage certificate?"

"Wait a second," said Oliver as he walked quickly into the sitting room.

He returned with The Book of the Blood in his hands and set it on the table with a *thud!* Then the boy flipped to the family tree of the lineage of King Palafox.

"I thought that name sounded familiar," he said as his finger settled on a name at the end of the genealogy.

LADY PENELOPE

"Remember? King Juno was the last of his line—the book said he never married or had any children."

"Then how is it that we have a copy of his marriage certic—certif—?" Ellie stumbled over the word.

"*Certificate*," her brother corrected.

"Ellie brings up a good question," said Annie. "I wonder if he was trying to hide something. Who does it say he was married to?"

Lady Penelope read from the parchment: "Her name was Palmyra. There isn't any other information about who she was."

"King Juno married a woman named Palmyra and wanted to keep it a secret," Oliver thought through the scenario in his head and then turned to Penelope. "So, do you think they had a child—an heir to his throne?"

"Any heir of King Juno would have been of the same generation as Florian's father," answered the woman. "So, if Juno had a child, he or she would be old and gray by now—if they're even still alive. Unless..." She trailed off in thought.

"Unless *what?*" Ellie asked.

"Unless Juno's child *also* had a child of their own," Ben finished Penelope's thought.

"It's certainly a possibility," Penelope nodded. "But we haven't got a name or a way to find this hypothetical heir."

As she said this, Oliver inspected the marriage certificate. He was curious and flipped it over to see if there were any other markings that might give a hint to its origins. As he did this, he noticed faint lettering, as if from a pencil, along the edge of the certificate's back side.

"What's this?" The boy asked, prompting the others to lean in closer.

"I think it's an address," said Annie, recognizing the

format. "It's a little hard to make out." She read it out loud:

1000 Lake Boulevard, Unit #2
Lake Worth, Florida

"Does that mean anything to any of you?"

"That's got to be an address in our world," said Ben. "In fact, I think that's a town near to ours."

"Curious," said Oliver softly.

"Curious, indeed," echoed Penelope. "It seems you may have a choice to make: return to your world to seek out this mysterious secret heir to the throne of Palafox or call upon Florian's brother Gardenio—who has lived in hiding for almost twenty years. His home is quite far off the beaten path and it could take a day or more to get there and back again."

"Penelope's right," said Ben. "It's only a matter of time before Florian knows we're here and finds us—or the Gate we used to pass into the Kingdom. We can't afford to lose any more time."

The children were sobered by this thought and sat in silence for some time until Annie spoke up: "We could split up."

Ben looked to Oliver and shook his head slowly, then said to Annie, "It's too risky. We can barely keep out of danger with the four of us together!"

Oliver stroked his chin, deep in thought, then replied: "Annie's right. The whole Kingdom is counting on us to find and restore the Triumvirate. We need to find as many of the heirs as possible; if we settle for just one, our efforts will have been in vain. We all know how powerful the Prince's magic can be—we've seen him use it to find us before—and we know he'll use it again if it means finding us or sealing off the last of the Gates. If we don't split up, we may not be able to restore the three thrones. The only choice we have is who will find Gardenio and who will return to our world."

Ben tried to think of a rebuttal to his friend's speech, but realized that Oliver spoke the truth.

Annie, who had been listening and thinking intently, spoke up: "I'll go to find Gardenio. Who's with me?"

"What happened to you wanting to get back home so badly?" Oliver inquired. "You've been anxious about it for our entire journey."

"Yesterday, Lady Penelope helped me realize," she replied, "that sometimes home is more than just a place; it's something you've got to fight for. Our home will still be there when we finish here—along with my parents. But this place is home, too—to so many wonderful people and beasts—and they need our help. Besides, I just moved in and I don't know the neighborhoods as well as you, so I wouldn't be much help back in our world anyhow."

Oliver smiled, glad for his new friend's change of heart, and replied, "Alright, Annie. You can lead the journey to Gardenio and I'll take the group back to our world to follow that address. I think I'm the most familiar with the town, as I've lived there the longest of any of us. Ellie and Ben—what'll it be?"

"Ellie," said Ben. "I think you should stick with Oliver. He'll keep you safe. I'd be scared out of my mind if I knew you were out here so far from home without me." He then leaned closer to Oliver and whispered in his ear: "Take care of her, okay?"

"Guess that means you're coming with me," said Annie to Ben. The boy smiled nervously in response, then nodded in agreement.

Lady Penelope, sensing that the group had come to a consensus, chimed in: "Well, that settles it then. I shall pack some rations for both parties and draw up instructions to guide Annie and Ben to the place where Gardenio can be found. Will the other two of you be able to find your way back to your Gate again?"

Oliver nodded affirmatively, explaining that he felt confident he could find the way back. Then the entire group got up from the table and began to prepare for the long journeys ahead. Oliver folded the marriage certificate and placed it in his pocket with the signet ring from Marco, while the others helped pack up their bedding and belongings. Each of the children exchanged hugs with little Toro and then Lady Penelope as they walked out onto the front steps of the house. Penelope waved as the four children strolled together up the street at a brisk pace and disappeared around a corner.

CHAPTER FIFTEEN
Prince Florian Calls on The Seers

Far down the coast in the southeast regions of the Kingdom, Prince Florian returned to the palace at last. Castillo Rosa was an imposing structure of great beauty and architectural detail. The building was several stories high, its profile consisting of a large middle-section and two lower sections at the sides. Domed turrets jutted out of the central area with flags waving in the wind, making the palace appear even taller. What made the building distinct were its peach-pink stucco walls, an abundance of arched windows and colonnades, and the burnt-orange barrel tiles that covered the roof.

Florian's caravan processed down the palmetto-lined path that led to the palace gates, where they were ushered in by a number of men in bucket-like morion helmets who helped them dismount from their dark beasts. The Prince was then escorted through winding hallways, past a peaceful garden courtyard, and through a pair of large doors into his throne room.

Shimmering, gilded patterns of palms and plants

covered the walls from floor to ceiling, while a large arched glass window let in a generous amount of natural light. A throne, carved of wood and covered in gold, sat near the center of the space, illuminated by the window's light.

As he stepped quickly toward his gold-plated throne, the Prince called to an attendant: "Fetch me the Seers." The attendant disappeared through a small hidden door at the side of the room as Florian sat. A handful of menservants assumed their positions at either side of the throne and began to fan their master with oversized palm fronds.

Presently, the tiny door reopened. The attendant led a train of seven darkly-garbed men and women toward a place in front of the Prince's throne. They wore tall collars that obscured their mouths and their eyes were a cloudy gray, as if they carried within them a thick morning fog. At the back of this group was a small boy dressed in a drab smock and wearing nothing on his feet. Around his neck was a gold necklace from which a single emerald hung. The boy had no hair upon his head as his scalp had been recently shorn.

The seven Seers assumed a semi-circular formation, while the hairless child stood in front of them. None of them spoke as they awaited Prince Florian's instruction.

"My Seers," he began. "I have often consulted you about a great many important matters, for you see all. Though I know your secret magic has limits in your ability to determine an individual's location, I now ask you to tell me one thing: *what* are those children from the outside world doing at this very moment?"

At this request, the Seers closed their eyes. One by one, their heads began to writhe slowly as they turned their necks around in every direction, brows furrowed,

as a person might do if they surveyed their own surroundings—though they kept their eyes tightly shut.
The boy stood motionless with his head down, waiting.
Then, after a short time, the seven snapped their heads
forward in unison and each slowly lifted his or her arm
to point a single finger at the small boy.

The child trembled slightly, then raised his face toward the Prince and said, "Four children walk together
on uneven ground."

The oracle was cryptic, as they so often were, and
the Prince clenched his fist. "What are they doing in
my Kingdom?"

"The children are on a great quest," replied the
boy—the Mouthpiece of the Seers.

"Tell me," said Florian. "What is this quest?"

The Mouthpiece squirmed, a bit uneasy, for he felt
a bond with the children upon their last journey into
the Kingdom. He was obliged to tell the truth, too, not
because of a fear of the Seers—they could neither speak
nor fully understand the magic they conjured—but because of the magical emerald that he wore around his
neck: the Gem of Truth. If the boy told a lie, the stone
would turn the color of blood.

"What is the quest of these children?" Florian demanded again.

"The Seers cannot read every thought," said the
Mouthpiece. "But they do see the shared desire of these
four young children: to find the heirs to the Triumvirate and overthrow his Excellency the Prince." The boy,
sensing the Prince's anger rising, defiantly added under
his breath, "And I certainly hope they succeed."

At this, Florian was furious. He leaped from his
throne and, in the same swift motion, slapped the child
across the face. As the boy recoiled and grasped at his

stinging cheek, Florian glared down at him: "The Gem of Truth remains its brilliant green. You speak truly— and will be punished for your insolence."

The Prince returned to his throne, still fuming. He then made a gesture to the attendant, who led the Seers back through the small door. The Mouthpiece lingered in front of the throne, glaring at the Prince, before slowly following the others. As the Mouthpiece and Seers disappeared and the door closed behind them, Prince Florian sat, tense and deep in thought, determining his next move.

CHAPTER SIXTEEN
Two Roads Diverge in a Wood

The children reached the outskirts of Melba again, at last, their legs already growing tired from the varying elevation of the roads in the winding town. Merchants and sailors vanished from view and earshot, giving way to the tropical sounds of the jungle. As they looked back to survey the village from atop the hill, they could see the ocean glistening beyond, an undulating turquoise ripple.

The group turned and continued on into the forest, passing through the place where Byron had landed the prior day. Crowded vines and branches made it difficult to navigate, but Ellie quickly pointed out a narrow path through the trees. The path was old and overgrown, as if the jungle itself had forgotten this route; after all, the people of Melba did most of their travel by boat and had little use for forest paths. The children pressed on.

Deeper in the forest, the air was thick. A light mist meandered about the children's ankles and an eerie silence filled the place, broken only by four sets of light footsteps on the leafy ground. Eventually, the party came to a split in the path, where the trail diverged in several different directions.

"Well," said Oliver. "I believe this is where we part ways."

Annie looked at the drawing of a map that Lady Penelope had given her and confirmed that this was correct: "Are you sure this is a good idea?"

Oliver nodded and replied, "It may not be a good idea, but I think it's the best we've got right now." He turned to Ben, holding out the large Book of the Blood: "Here, you might need this. And don't worry; I'll make sure Ellie's safe."

Ben took the book then exchanged a long hug with his little sister, who added to Oliver's assurances: "I'll be okay, Ben. We'll be back in no time."

"I know," he said. "I just feel a responsibility to make sure you don't get lost."

"Remember," replied Ellie. "I won't actually be far from home at all!"

The children laughed a little and then finished their goodbyes.

Annie said, "Once we've each completed our tasks and found the lost heirs, we'll meet back at the Banyan Gate."

"What if that address doesn't lead us to an heir?" Ellie asked.

"Whatever happens," said Oliver, "we will all return to the Gate by tomorrow morning. We can't risk being separated for longer than that—the Prince could strike at any time and cut off our way to pass between the worlds."

The mere suggestion was enough to increase their collective blood pressure, but the others knew Oliver was right. They could waste no time.

Ellie gave one more hug to her brother and then shared a quick embrace with Annie before following Oliver off down one of the paths. Ben and Annie watched and waved as they disappeared into the trees. When their friends were out of sight, Annie referred to the map again and pointed down another path.

The journey was easy at first. Annie and Ben followed the lightly-trodden path as it wound in and out of thickets and beside quiet waters. Brightly-colored macaws ogled them from their perch up in a gnarly tree while Annie admired their crimson bodies and blue-green gradient wings.

When they had traveled for several hours, the children began to grow thirsty. Ben reached for a canteen in his pack and discovered that it was nearly empty. Upon further inspection, the boy discovered that there was a small crack in the clay, whereby its last drops of water now escaped.

"Oh, great," said Ben. "Our water's nearly gone!"

Annie inspected the canteen. "That's not good," she said. "We'd better keep our eye out for a fresh stream. If only we'd known sooner—we passed a narrow river a couple hours ago."

The two children were discouraged, but kept up their pace for the next hour while they searched for a source of water near to the path. They could neither see nor hear any streams nearby, and this began to make Ben anxious.

Then Annie held out her arm in front of Ben and stopped moving. "Do you hear that?" She asked, craning her neck toward the jungle expanse at one side of the path. It was the faint but unmistakable sound of a rushing waterfall.

Ben heard it now, too, and the children rushed through the bramble and branches toward it. The churning grew louder as they neared it until Annie finally pulled back a blanket of vines to reveal a large, circular pond. A large cascade gushed fresh, cool water from a rock formation. The children knelt beside the pond and began to cup their hands to drink of the water.

As they drank, Annie thought she noticed a movement near the waterfall. She stood to get a better view and saw motion again. She tapped Ben on the shoulder and nodded for him to look in the same direction. This time it was clear that there was someone—or something—there, behind the waterfall.

The children made their way around the edge of the pond. The rocks were slippery, but formed a sort of path toward the waterfall. When they were close enough to feel its misty spray, Annie and Ben peered behind the wall of water. A small creature—smaller, even, than the children—tucked itself away in the back of the rocky space. The shadows made it difficult to see, so the children moved closer.

"Don't come any closer," shouted the small creature.

The children paused, startled by the loud voice. "We're sorry," said Annie. "We don't mean to hurt you. We saw something moving and we wanted to know what it was."

"It was *me*," the creature replied shortly. The children could now tell that the creature seemed to be a small woman, with a mess of tangled, dusty hair atop her head.

"And who are you?" Ben asked now.

"That's none of your business," she replied. The children looked at each other, unsure of what to do next. Then the small woman spoke again: "What are you doing at this pond?"

"That's none of *your* business," retorted Annie with a smirk.

The creature seemed flustered, then stepped forward into the light. "It is my business," said the woman, "as this pond belongs to me."

Ben and Annie could now see that the woman was covered in a greenish, leathery skin. She resembled a small human in shape, but some of her features seemed borrowed from a reptile or frog. The woman was wrapped in a garment of furs stitched together, the hems loose and crude.

"Our apologies," said Ben. "We had no idea this pond belonged to anyone."

"I see," said the creature, inspecting the children more closely.

She looked harmless to Annie, so the girl said, "I'm Annie, and this is my friend, Ben. We ran out of water and became very thirsty, so we found it a great blessing to stumble upon the sound of this waterfall pouring into a cool, clear pond."

"We've still got a long way to go yet," continued Ben. "And we wouldn't stand a chance of making it through these dark woods without hydration."

The creature stroked her chin with small pointed nails as she listened to the children. "You travel through the dark woods, you say?"

"Yes," said Annie. "We're following this map to find—" Here she stopped, remembering the secrecy of their mission. Ben glared at her.

"To find what?" inquired the creature.

"To find someone important," Annie said at last. "It's crucial to the fate of the Kingdom and to stopping

Prince Florian."

The creature's countenance changed suddenly from suspicion to amicability. "Then you are friends," said she, "for any enemy of that wicked Prince is a friend of mine. That man is no good; he once drove my family out of our homes near the palace and now we wander these woods without a permanent home of our own."

"That's terrible," said Annie, relieved that they had found another ally. "Why would he do such a thing?"

"I think it's because we reminded him of the old rulers," said the creature, "for in another age our people were friends of the royal families—before he stole the throne and wiped them out. But that is in the past. At present, you shall need a guide to help you through these dark woods, for they can play tricks on the minds of those who do not know the way."

The children agreed to accept her help. Then Ben asked, "I'm sorry, but what's your name? I don't think you mentioned it."

"I am Mugwig," she said with a smile. "I am the Princess of the Pond—I declared this title for myself—and I am at your service."

The children chortled a bit at the curious character as she led them out from behind the waterfall and back toward the path. She hobbled along briskly for such a small creature, and Ben and Annie did their best to keep up. Soon, they were far away from the waterfall and traveling deep into a darker and eerier part of the woods.

CHAPTER SEVENTEEN
Return to the Banyan Gate

Meanwhile, Oliver and Ellie moved swiftly through the jungle. The two children had kept a good pace, stopping at intervals to rest, so that they now drew nearer to the location of the Gate in the huge, old gnarly tree, which the children had come to refer to simply as *The Banyan Gate.*

As they came from a different direction this time, the children were able to altogether avoid the rugged mountains and the snake-infested marshes to make a direct line back to the passage through which they had entered the Kingdom. The distance between Melba and the Banyan Gate was considerably shorter than the journey of their friends, so Oliver and Ellie made the trek in just a few hours.

"Do you think we should stop to see Marco?" Ellie wondered aloud as they sat down for a brief period of rest.

"I would love to see our old friend again," said Oliver. "But we can't waste any time. Remember the whole reason we split up—the Prince could be on our trail and searching for us at this very moment."

"His camp is not far from here," said Ellie, trying to sway her friend again as she took a drink of water.

"It's too risky," said Oliver, his mind made up. "We're nearly at the Gate and we shouldn't veer off the path now. We should keep moving."

At this, the boy stood up and fastened his pack to his back. Reaching out one hand, he helped Ellie to her feet and the two continued on down the path toward the Gate.

Oliver remembered that the area around the base of the banyan tree was covered in thick bushes and branches, so he nearly overlooked the spot as they came upon a clearing. It was Ellie who pointed out the large tree—the only one of its size in this part of the forest.

The two orbited the tree for a moment as they searched for the entrance to the Banyan Gate. On the opposite side of the tree, they found an area that presented more clear access to the tree—snapped vines and branches from their previous passage. Oliver and Ellie looked closer and found the edge of the old brick archway that seemed to lead into darkness. Then the sound filled their ears once more—the shimmering that always preceded a trip between worlds.

"You go first," said Ellie to Oliver.

The boy led the way as he stepped into the murky tunnel, one hand holding Ellie's forearm so that they wouldn't get lost or separated in the expanse. With each step, the ringing became more pronounced. At one point, the children were engulfed in complete darkness, unable to see light at either end of the passage.

Then, as they continued their slow walk, Oliver caught a glimpse of the other side of the passage—bright afternoon sun illuminating translucent green vines and fronds that covered the archway. The boy parted the foliage to reveal their secret hiding place in the abandoned empty lot and allowed Ellie to pass through before him. When they were both safely out of the tunnel and had taken a few steps away from the tree, they noticed that the ringing faded and was now nearly indiscernible.

The children, being occupied with the magic of the Banyan Gate, had failed to notice a large black bird with a ruby necklace that perched in the branches of the banyan tree inside the Kingdom. The bird—who went by the name of Malverne—waited and watched them. Then Malverne focused intently as the two children brushed aside the greenery at the base of the tree and disappeared through the brick archway.

"Good fortune," said the bird to herself. "Florian will be pleased."

With that, Malverne ascended from the tree and winged away through the canopy in the direction of the royal palace.

CHAPTER EIGHTEEN
The Woods Play a Trick

Annie looked down at Lady Penelope's hand-drawn map. They were getting closer to their destination—closer to finding Prince Florian's only living brother Gardenio. The girl looked up, then glanced at the parchment again.

"According to the map," she said, "we should soon see an old tree that looks like a three-pronged trident."

Annie, Ben, and their new little friend Mugwig all scanned the forest path ahead of them to look for this oddly-shaped tree, but saw only pine trees and winding oaks. The children kept moving, slowly trudging through the eerie jungle.

The sun sank faster as they walked, now casting golden rays through the translucent leaves above while the low-lying foliage became cloaked in the first hints of shadow. Darkness crept over the forest floor, making it more difficult for the three travelers to see their own steps. Only a faint orange glow allowed the party to continue without a light of their own.

In the dimness of the setting sun, Ben squinted at something straight ahead of them on the path and then pointed: "Is that the three-pronged tree?"

Annie and Mugwig strained in the same direction.

"I think that's it," replied Annie as she quickened her steps.

Mugwig lagged behind and warned, "Careful out here in the dark woods. One can get lost if she doesn't keep her eyes fixed on the path."

The children ignored Mugwig's ramblings as they ran toward the rotting, three-pronged tree ahead. It towered above them in the distance, its graying, leafless trunk rubbed smooth by centuries of rains and salty wind.

Mugwig called again, louder: "Children! Careful in the dark woods. Remember these woods play tricks if you don't tread with care."

The two children, at last, turned to listen to the creature's words.

"What do you mean, exactly?" Ben asked, ever cautious.

"The tree," she replied as she pointed. "Things are not always as they seem in these woods. When the sun goes down, the trees play tricks on the mind. It is best to keep one's eyes on the path ahead."

As Mugwig said these words, Annie looked back toward the tree, but found the tree had disappeared.

"What happened to the old tree?" Annie said, flustered and confused.

"It was right there a moment ago," said Ben. "It seems to have disappeared while we looked away!"

Mugwig sighed softly and then retorted: "It's like I said."

Just then, Annie shouted out: "There's the tree

again!"

Indeed, there was an identical tree, though this time in a different place in the forest.

"How is it that the tree has changed its place?" Ben wondered aloud. "It certainly can't have taken up its roots and walked away."

"The darkness plays tricks on the mind," Mugwig muttered again.

Ben and Annie darted toward the tree, keeping their eyes locked on it. As they approached the tree with their hands outstretched to touch it, however, the tree vanished before their very eyes. Dumbfounded, the children searched around them to see if the tree had moved again.

Once more, the children witnessed the same three-pronged trunk standing in yet another part of the jungle. Annie and Ben again ran to touch it, but the dried-out tree was gone. They carried on in this manner for some time while Mugwig followed far behind, staying on the path where they had first seen the original tree.

This time, the tree appeared deeper in the woods, far removed from the path. Annie led Ben through the thicket, snapping tiny branches and bramble to get to the tree. Before they could touch the tree though, the children came to a large log across the path. The two climbed atop the thick branch together and then jumped down to the ground on the other side of it.

Immediately, the two children found their feet sinking into a layer of sand and sediment. When Annie tried to lift her feet to step back toward the log, she discovered that it was stuck fast. Ben attempted the same but to no avail. The three-pronged tree had disappeared.

"What is this?" Ben asked frantically. "Why can't we

move our legs?"

"I think it's quicksand," replied Annie, only slightly more calm and collected. Then she remembered their guide: "Mugwig! Help!"

She continued to shout, hoping the creature would hear them. Moments later, they heard the huffing and puffing of the tiny green woman barreling down the path as fast as her little legs could carry her. Then she appeared at the top of the log.

"Tricks!" Mugwig said when she saw the children's predicament. "Quicksand! Tricksand!"

"Can you help us get our legs free?" Ben asked her.

"Give me your hands and I will try," she said, reaching out her scaly hands to the boy. Ben handed Mugwig the large Book of the Blood, which she placed on the log. Then, mustering all her strength, she tugged at the child's arm to pull him out, but found that this did not unstick the boy at all. She pulled again with similar results. By this time, both children sunk even lower, so that the sand was now up to the level of their knees.

"Oh dear," said Mugwig. "I'm afraid I'm far too small for this."

Both children squirmed and struggled, reaching out for branches and vines to use to pull themselves out of the mire. The more they writhed, though, the quicker they sank into the gritty sinking sand.

"What can we do, Mugwig?" Annie asked as the sand now nearly covered her lower half.

"I'm afraid I don't know," she replied to the scared little girl. "We must think quicker than the quicksand, though, or the children shall be gone before long."

They resolved to stay still to slow the sinking while they desperately grasped for a way out, but inside the helpless children were completely terrified of their impending fate.

CHAPTER NINETEEN
Further into the Sinking Sand

Annie and Ben were now submerged up to their ribs in quicksand while Mugwig paced across the large fallen log in an attempt to think of a solution. The sun was gone; now the moon's bluish glow cast an ominous coolness across the forest.

"Help!" Annie cried out to anyone who could hear. "Anyone out there? Help!"

Ben and Mugwig joined in, hoping that they might be heard by someone passing through the forest. Their cries echoed off the gnarly trees and into the shadows. It was unlikely that anyone was traveling in that part of the wood at night, but they continued shouting.

"There's no one out there," said Ben at last. "We should never have run off to chase that strange, phantom tree."

"And I should have gone back home when I had the chance," added Annie. "We may never make it back there now."

"Children mustn't give up yet," said Mugwig. "Keep

shouting!"

They resumed their calls for help. The children were now covered up to their necks in the quicksand, with only their forearms above the mire, and the situation was growing bleaker by the minute.

Then, they heard a rustle in the bushes beyond them. The three travelers ceased their cries to listen more closely. Ben and Annie craned their necks to look in the direction of the sound as a figure emerged from the thicket.

The figure was a woman. She wore a rough grayish cape with a hood over her head, and her thick blonde hair spilled out of it as she moved swiftly through the fronds. Dressed in a practical ankle-length working skirt and a simple linen blouse, she bore a rucksack and a look of surprise as she came upon the scene.

"Dear me," she exclaimed with a soft voice and look of genuine concern as the sand now covered the children's mouths. Then, holding out her walking stick, she said, "Here, children! One at a time—grab hold!"

As Ben was the closest to the woman, he reached out for the staff first. With his hands gripping tightly, the woman pulled. Her strength was greater than that of the diminutive Mugwig, and found that the boy was soon rising out of the deadly quicksand. With a few more heaves, Ben was free of the sand and climbed onto solid ground.

The quicksand now drew Annie in over her head and, within seconds, only her hair and hands were visible.

"Quick!" Ben shouted to the mysterious woman. "She'll be unable to breathe if we don't get her out of there fast!"

The lady again stuck out her walking staff over the

pit of sinking sand. Annie flailed her hands, unable to see, and finally grabbed hold of the stick. When she had done this, the woman began to pull. Since she was deeper in the sand than the boy, the woman found it more difficult to gain any traction as she tried to free the girl. Ben grabbed another part of the staff to help, and the two of them tugged with all their might.

Slowly, Annie's head became visible again, and she gasped for air. Her face was covered in sticky grains of sand. Ben and the woman pulled again and again, each time lifting Annie further out of the mire. Finally, she was free and breathed deeply as she felt the solid forest floor with her hands.

Both children panted for air as they stood and tried to brush the remaining sand off their clothes. When they realized the futility of this task, Annie and Ben turned to the hooded blonde woman who now adjusted the straps on her pack.

"Thank you, miss," said Ben with a bow. "You saved our lives."

"And at just the right time, too," added Annie.

"I heard your cries and knew that there was danger," said the woman, removing her hood. "I came as fast as I could." As she said this, she gently placed a hand to her stomach, catching her breath.

"What is your name?" Annie asked the kind woman.

"Juliana," she replied. "And what are your names?"

"I'm Annie," the girl said.

"And my name's Ben," answered the boy.

Mugwig, who now hobbled over from the safety of the log, said, "I am Mugwig, Princess of the Pond."

"I'm pleased to make your acquaintance," Juliana said as she nodded to each of them in turn. Her countenance was fair and kind. "It strikes me as curious that you three small travelers have wandered into the jungle in the dark of night, though. Surely you must be on some sort of noble quest."

"Well, actually," began Ben, lifting the Book of the Blood off the log, "it is something like a quest. It's a bit of a long story and we had hoped to make it further before it grew dark."

The woman looked at the book and the children thoughtfully, then said, "You seem quite determined to fulfill your mission. But it is not safe for children (or a princess) to be out here in these dark woods at night. Will you allow me to invite you to my home for a warm supper and a hot cup of tea? I was just headed back from a hunt when I heard your cries, and my husband will be wondering what's become of me."

The children and their little guide, famished and thirsty from the day's journey, agreed to Juliana's offer with haste. Then, in the light of the moon, the woman took up her wooden staff and led the party deeper into the dark woods. A peal of thunder pierced the quiet night, followed by the gradual sweep of rain across the jungle treetops, but the four trudged on through the muddied wood.

CHAPTER TWENTY
The Message of the Raven

Malverne the raven flew as fast her oily wings could carry her, soaring over miles of jungle and rivers and into a rainstorm until she came to the coast. Following the strip of beach south, the bird eventually came upon the royal palace. Malverne approached one of the tall, pink towers that protruded from the central structure of Castillo Rosa and flew toward a small balcony at its top. She alighted on a glistening wet brass railing and began to peck at it rhythmically, creating a metallic resonation akin to a gong or bell.

Within a few moments, the glass-paned doors of the balcony opened, revealing a half-dressed Prince Florian. He emerged from the chamber, which was a portion of his private living quarters, and the rain fell lightly on his head and shoulders.

"You have returned at last, my dear," said Florian as he walked toward the bird and stroked her smooth black feathers in the rain. "I trust you bring word of the children and their means of passing in and out of

THE PRINCE AND THE RAVEN

my Kingdom?"

"Yes, Prince Florian," replied Malverne. "*La Puerta*—I have seen the Gate."

"So it is true then?" Prince Florian asked as he turned and braced himself against the balcony railing. The gray clouds swirled above the misty rain.

"It is an ancient Gate," said the bird, "forged of bricks in days of old and now wrapped in the root and cloak of a mighty banyan tree. This is the manner in which two of the children left the Kingdom just hours ago, and I believe they mean to return."

"*Two* children, you say?"

"Yes, your Excellency. A boy and a girl. I do not know where the other children are."

"These two intend to bring back an heir," said the Prince. "You remember the exact place where this Gate rests?"

"Of course, my lord," replied the bird.

"We must go to it and destroy it before these children can return," said Florian as he turned to walk back inside the tower, where a pair of servants stood.

"And what of the other two children, my Prince?"

"Their affairs inside the Kingdom do not concern me at this time," replied the Prince as one of his servants dried him with a towel and slipped a loose-fitting linen tunic over Florian's head. "Whatever they are up to, it can wait until we've taken care of that Gate. I will not allow an heir to return to this Kingdom and take away the throne that I've fought so many years to protect." Then he turned to the other attendant: "Take my faithful servant Malverne to General Pompadour so she may tell him the location of the Gate. Tell him to ready the men; we ride before the next hour strikes."

The servant nodded, walked briskly to the edge of

the balcony, then held out an arm upon which the raven made her perch. Then they hurried out the chamber door and down the spiral staircase of the tower toward the lower levels where the garrison was staged.

Before long, the platoon was ready to embark. The large front gates of the palace opened and a stream of soldiers on black horses issued forth. The steeds splashed through shallow puddles as they galloped swiftly along the glistening coral street toward the jungle. Several of the men carried torches and others carried silver-tipped spears. Prince Florian rode atop his black stag near the front of the pack while the General followed closely behind.

Florian wiped the rain out of his eyes and pressed on with pure grit and determination. He would be the first one to the ancient Banyan Gate and he had every intention of destroying it. Nothing could stand in his way now.

Especially not a few naive children, he thought.

CHAPTER TWENTY-ONE
Oliver and Ellie Ride the Southbound Bus

Upon their return to their own neighborhood, the first thing Oliver and Ellie did was leave notes at all three of the families' houses to indicate they were "with the neighbors." It was summer, in which the children often spent several days and nights at the houses of their friends without their parents or guardians worrying. The note would buy the children a little more time while they tried to track down the lost heirs—inside and outside the Kingdom.

When this was finished, the two made their way on foot toward a bus stop in the next neighborhood, for they could not risk being seen by one of the adults now that they had delivered their letters. The gilded sun shined large and low as it sank beyond the highway, and it cast one side of their faces in shadows as the children passed an open stretch of soccer fields.

The children were the only ones waiting for the bus at that hour. It arrived within a few minutes, emptying passengers onto the sidewalk to scatter in every direction as they returned to their homes from a long day's work. Oliver slipped a few coins to the driver for two tickets and then proceeded to lead Ellie to a row of empty seats near the middle of the bus. The vehicle lurched forward as it pulled away from the curb and continued its southbound journey.

The route took the children along a main road, lined with local restaurants, bars, and neon signs that flickered on as the sun disappeared. Ellie watched, her hand against the glass, as cars sped and swerved around their hulking ride.

With every stop, a handful of passengers departed. Finally, it was Oliver and Ellie's turn to disembark.

"Lake Worth! This stop!" The driver shouted as she looked into the large rear view mirror.

The children scrambled toward the front, thanked the driver, and hopped onto the pavement. When the bus was gone, Oliver removed the folded parchment from his pocket.

"We need to find Lake Boulevard," he said to Ellie, referring back to the penciled note on the paper just to be sure.

The two looked around. They stood right in front of a town hall building. Across the street were a bustling coffee shop and a bank.

"There!" Ellie pointed at a street sign at the intersection just ahead that matched the name of the street they were looking for.

"Oh," said Oliver as he started walking toward it. "That was easier than I thought it would be. Now we're looking for an address of *1000 Lake Boulevard*, so that should hopefully be just a short way down the road."

The children turned at Lake Boulevard and continued on, keeping a close eye on the addresses of the shops and buildings. It was an older commercial street, once a bustling town center but now a ramshackle time capsule. Most of the buildings were only a couple of floors tall. The street-level storefronts were dark at this hour, but lights in tiny windows above them indicated the presence of upstairs apartment dwellers.

Presently, Oliver and Ellie came upon the address. It was a larger building that spanned half the block, covered in aging stucco and two shades of off-white paint. The children approached a door at the side of the building but found it locked. They then looped around to another wall of the apartment building and discovered a clearer entrance. A small glass case to its left contained a directory of the apartments. Oliver scanned it quickly.

"Unit #2," he said as he pointed toward the second line. "There's no name listed."

"So nobody lives there?" Ellie asked.

"Maybe," replied Oliver. "Or perhaps someone lives there and doesn't want to be found. But there's only one way to find out." As he said this, Oliver pulled the door open and proceeded inside.

The children found themselves in a narrow hallway with a dirty white staircase ahead of them. Only one of the fluorescent lights above seemed to be operational, so the hall was dark. There was a door on either side of the hallway so the two children checked the numbers. Finding that these were odd numbers, Oliver proposed they move upstairs to check for the even-numbered apartments.

A dog barked from some unseen place, followed by a woman yelling from within another apartment. Oliver and Ellie ascended the creaky stairs and these noises faded away, leaving them with an eerie silence as they reached the second floor.

Only one of the doors on this level was marked: *Unit #2.* Ellie and Oliver quickly spotted the number and approached it cautiously. The boy put his ear up to the door to see if he could discern any sounds of life or movement.

Silence.

Ellie reached out her little hand and gave a series of light knocks on the door.

Oliver leaned in again, but heard nothing.

Ellie knocked a second time, but still there was no movement inside the apartment.

"Looks like there's no one living here, after all," said Oliver. He started for the stairs again, but Ellie stopped him.

"We've come all this way!" Ellie said. "Let's try again—they always say the third time's the charm!"

Oliver conceded and allowed the girl to knock again.

This time, they heard a stirring on the other side of the door.

"Hello?" Ellie yelled loudly. "Is anyone home?"

They heard it again. Slow footsteps. Weight shifting on hardwood floors.

"There's someone there," said the girl to Oliver quietly. Then she knocked again a few more times.

A low voice interrupted the knocks: "Go away!"

Ellie stopped: "We just want to talk for a few minutes."

"Go. Away!"

Oliver took a deep breath then said, "Please! We've taken quite a long journey to get here, it'll only be a minute."

There was no response this time.

Ellie added, "We think you may be able to help us

find someone—someone *important.*"

Again, there was no reply.

Frustrated and defeated, Oliver said, "It's about the Kingdom. We think you can help."

This time, there was another stirring behind the door, followed by the turning of the deadbolt. The mysterious resident of the apartment opened the door just a crack. The top half of a face appeared behind the lock chain, sizing the children up.

Then the voice spoke: "Who are you and how did you find me?"

CHAPTER TWENTY-TWO
In the Farmhouse of Juliana and Dean

The rain beat heavily on the thick leaves above the travelers, and the sounds of birds and insects echoed around them. Annie, Ben, and Mugwig kept close to the woman called Juliana as she led them through the cold jungle. To protect the Book of the Blood from the rain, Ben covered it with a thick blanket and clutched it close to his chest.

The trees were farther apart now, allowing the children to see beyond the forest to an open plain. When they came to the edge of the treeline, they stood before a series of long fields with crops of tall vegetables planted in rows. In the center of the field was a small wooden farmhouse with a rusty tin roof. Juliana moved toward a narrow, muddy red road that led from the trees up to the house. The children and Mugwig followed quickly as the rain drenched them with greater force in the open air.

Approaching the house, Annie noticed a warm glow emanating from the windows. The silhouette of a man appeared in one of the panes, peering at the incoming travelers. Then he was gone.

A few seconds later, the front door opened just as they arrived. The man from the window now stood in the doorway, motioning for them to hurry inside. When they had all entered the warm farmhouse, he quickly shut the door behind them and handed them a pile of towels and blankets with which to dry off.

The man gave his wife, Juliana, a look of concern.

"They're alright," she said to him quietly, squeezing her wet hair with a cloth.

Annie and Ben looked around at the tiny house as they rubbed the towels over their clothes. The room was filled with bespoke wooden furniture, including a small carved dining table, an empty bassinet, a series of bookshelves, and a pair of nearly-identical armchairs upholstered in worn burlap. A single door led to another room—presumably the place where Juliana and her husband slept.

"Here," Juliana said to their guests, motioning toward the far corner of the room where a kettle hung above a brick fireplace. "The fire will help you get warm and dry."

The children and Mugwig followed her and sat atop a large rug on the floor. The children kept a comfortable distance, while Mugwig put her hands quite close to the flames.

"I'm cold-blooded," the creature said casually. "I'll warm up faster this way."

Juliana and her husband chuckled, then the woman spoke: "Dear guests, I'd like you to meet my husband. This is Dean."

The man held out his hand to each of the guests and smiled warmly. Dean and his wife both appeared young and youthful. *They can't be more than twenty years old*, thought Annie.

"Pleased to meet you," said the girl.

Ben nodded in agreement: "And we have your wife to thank for saving our lives. We were nearly lost in the quicksand when she arrived—just in time."

"Juliana is known for both her kindness *and* her timeliness," said Dean with a smirk to his wife. "And any friend of hers is a friend of mine. You are welcome here."

The children thanked the couple again.

"Well," said Juliana, "I promised these poor, wet travelers that they'd have a nice warm supper."

"And it's nearly ready," said Dean. "We've got plenty to go around. Any luck with the hunt?"

Juliana shook her head and reached into her satchel that hung by the front door: "Only a few mushrooms."

"That's alright," said her husband, taking the mushrooms. "I love mushroom soup."

Dean began to slice the mushrooms with a small knife on a chopping block. While he did this, he asked the guests, "So, what were you three doing out in the jungle at night in the first place?"

"They tell me it's some sort of quest," said Juliana.

"Is that right?" Dean asked.

"Yes," said Ben. "We were following a map drawn by a friend when we got lost in the woods."

"I warned them," chimed Mugwig to herself. "Dangerous woods and tricksand!"

"A map," repeated the man as he scooped a handful of the mushrooms and walked across the room to toss them into the pot on the fire. He gave it a stir and the savory aroma filled the air. "And where was this map supposed to lead you?"

"Well," began Annie. "It's supposed to lead us to a

person—we hope."

Juliana could tell the children were trying not to give too much of their mission away. "You're safe here," she said. "You can trust us. We're not going to hurt you."

Ben looked at Annie, who gave him a nod.

"Are you sure?" he whispered.

"They saved our lives," Annie replied. "Maybe they can help us."

Ben thought about it for a moment, then walked over to the door. He carefully unwrapped a thick, wet blanket and revealed the old Book of the Blood. Setting it on the table, Ben flipped through several pages quickly as the others crowded around. Mugwig jumped up onto a chair to get a closer look.

"What is this large book?" Dean asked.

"This," said Ben as he pointed to the page, "is who we're looking for." His finger rested on the name of Gardenio in the family tree of King Coronado.

Dean gave it a contemplative look and furrowed his brow: "And did you say you were following a map?"

"Oh, yes," Ben said and fished in his pockets. He pulled out the damp, folded map from Lady Penelope and opened it. "This is where we were going when we got lost," he said to Dean, handing him the hand-drawn instructions.

Dean studied it for a moment and then showed it to his wife. Both wore expressions of surprise and confusion.

"Is something wrong?" Annie asked the couple.

"I don't know," said Dean. "But it looks like this map leads here—to our home."

The children's mouths were agape. They didn't understand what the man was getting at.

"The person you're looking for," Dean said as he took a gulp to clear his throat. "I think it's *me*."

CHAPTER TWENTY-THREE
The Heir of Coronado

The children and Mugwig sat and stood around the little table with their mouths agape. The furious sound of the rain on the tin roof continued. Annie and Ben couldn't believe what they had heard, and the boy thought there must be some sort of mistake.

"You?" he asked. "I think you misunderstood—we're looking for Gardenio, the royal heir of the line of Coronado." He again pointed at the page in the large Book of the Blood.

"Curious," replied Dean. "This map—though it's crudely drawn, it's still quite precise— appears to pinpoint this very house—*our* house—and you've just pointed out my name on this page."

"You told us your name is Dean," said Annie. "Right?"

"Dean is more of a nickname," Juliana interjected.

"She's right," said the man. "It's short for my birth name: Gardenio—though I haven't answered to that name in many years."

"So let me get this straight," Ben said. "You think *you* are the heir of King Coronado?"

"I am most certainly *not* an heir to a King," said Dean, "but that is definitely my real name on the page and my house on the map. I'm as confused as you are."

"Our host is of royal blood, you say?" Mugwig said. "I, too, am royalty. I am the Princess of the Pond."

The children smiled at their little friend then turned their attention back to the couple.

Juliana now inquired of the children, "Why is it that you're searching for this so-called heir of Coronado? And what is this ancient book that has my husband's name inscribed in it? Surely this must be some sort of coincidence, as it says here that the Gardenio of this family tree is deceased."

"It's quite a long story," said Ben.

"Then we shall hear it over supper," said Juliana as she returned to the steaming kettle and lifted it from the fire.

Everyone took his or her seat while the hostess handed out dishes and slowly poured a ladle of soup into each bowl. The warm, steamy smell made Annie remember how hungry she had grown over the course of their long journey. Mugwig did not use a spoon, but slurped the steaming liquid rather loudly. The rest of the people at the table chuckled at the amusing sight.

At this point, everyone else began to eat the soup and Annie and Ben attempted to explain their mission in greater detail, taking turns to fill in any gaps. They told of the old Gates, the wicked acts of Prince Florian, and the quest to find and reunite the lost and scattered heirs of the Triumvirate using the old Book of the Blood. Dean and Juliana listened intently as the children relayed the story of Lady Penelope's secret rescue of baby Gardenio. When they finished, the room was silent—except for the rain on the roof and the scraping of Mugwig's spoon at the bottom of her bowl.

"So you think that I'm this lost prince who was hidden away as a child?" Dean asked the children.

"It's certainly likely," responded Ben. "Given the circumstances we've just relayed."

"Dean, er, Gardenio," said Annie, turning to the man. "What do you remember of your childhood? Or your parents?"

"I never knew my real parents," he said. "I was raised by a generous family in the country, and I helped and lived on their farm until Juliana and I were wed almost a year ago."

"See," said Annie. "It makes sense now, doesn't it? You never knew your parents because they passed away when you were born. Lady Penelope brought you to safety to protect you from your older brother."

"Florian," said Dean. "I never met him."

"Yes," Ben affirmed. "Come to think of it, you look just like him."

"You've seen the Prince?" Juliana asked with surprise.

"Only once before," he replied. "My friends and I infiltrated his palace and barely escaped—he was hot on our tail and followed us back to the door to our world. He was quite frightening."

Dean seemed to drift deep into his thoughts, staring into the fire. Then he spoke up: "You've come here to recruit me to fight against him then, haven't you?"

"Only the true heirs can take his place on the throne," said Annie. "It needs to be as many of the three as we can find—so far, you're the only one we've located. So, yes, Dean—we need you."

"And what of the other heirs?"

"Our friends are searching in our world," Ben said. "Lady Penelope gave us information about another, which we can only hope is as accurate as her map and her story about you."

The man and his wife looked at each other, and then the man turned back to the children. "I cannot leave my home," said Dean somberly.

"What do you mean?" Annie asked. "The palace *is* your home. The throne *is* your home."

"No," he replied. "Not anymore. My home is with my wife—and our child."

The children were taken aback, as they had not seen or heard another child in the little house.

"Child?" The girl asked. "What child?"

Juliana put her hand over her abdomen and smiled: "I will give birth only a few short weeks from now." The folds of her many-layered garments had largely obscured her figure, but the children could now see clearly that Juliana was quite pregnant.

Dean now put his arm around her and gave her a light kiss on the side of her head. "My family means everything to me," he said to the children. "I can't risk losing my family a second time."

"But your family is still out there," said Annie, getting frustrated. "Your brother. Your heritage as a member of the royal family. They need you. The Kingdom *needs* you. Only you can do this!"

"I never knew my parents," the man told her. "I don't want my child to grow up with that same void. Besides, you can't stop Florian with only one heir. In order to truly put an end to his tyrannical reign, you need to restore the Triumvirate—you need all *three* heirs, isn't that right?"

The girl nodded slowly and lowered her head. She and Ben were discouraged by the man's resistance.

"We've traveled days to find you," said Ben. "And what about the Kingdom? Won't you do it for the good of the Kingdom?"

Dean contemplated this and said, "If you and your friends can find the other two heirs, you have my word that I will join you. But until that time, I must stay here and be with my wife. It would be far too dangerous if Florian knew I was still out there—still alive."

This gave the children a glimmer of hope, though they still felt a bit discouraged that they were unable to convince him to accompany them back to the Banyan Gate.

"You are welcome to sleep here tonight and wait out the rain," said Juliana.

"Thank you," said Annie, "but we can't waste any more time. Ben and I must return to the Gate as quickly as possible to meet our friends by morning."

The children and Mugwig cleaned up their dishes and gathered their belongings. They exchanged goodbyes with their generous hosts as they opened the front door. The storm outside had grown stronger, and the rain now fell at a windy slant.

"Be careful," said Juliana to Annie, looking out at the fearsome gusts.

"We'll try," said the girl with a smile.

Then, the children and their creaturely companion walked down the front steps and sprinted across the muddy road toward the dark, wet forest. Annie looked back over her shoulder to watch Juliana and Dean standing in the open doorway waving goodbye.

We'll see you again, Gardenio, the girl thought to herself. *I know we will.*

CHAPTER TWENTY-FOUR
The Heir of Palafox

Oliver and Ellie stood in the dark, narrow hallway outside Unit #2. The pair of leery eyes behind the cracked-open door sized them up as if determining whether they presented any danger.

The obscured figure repeated the question again: "Who are you and how did you find me here?"

Oliver and Ellie exchanged a glance, then the boy answered: "We mean you no harm."

"You've already put me in enough danger by being here," the voice said again. "Leave!"

"But we *have* to talk to you," Ellie pleaded. "We think you may be able to help us!"

The voice made no reply while the eyes continued to glare at them.

"Please," said Oliver. Then he had a thought: "We're with the Lamplight Society."

At this, the eyes fluttered, and then narrowed again. "Anyone could say that," the voice said. "Prove it!"

"But how?" Ellie said. "Can't you just take us at our

word?"

"Prove it!"

The pressure flustered the children, but then Oliver remembered something. The boy reached into his pocket and felt around for a small object—the engraved ring from Marco. He withdrew his fingers and held out his hand toward the figure peering from behind the door.

"Here," said Oliver, holding out the tiny ring for the mysterious person to see more clearly. "We're not here to hurt you. Is this enough proof?"

Suddenly, the door slammed shut. A few seconds later, the children heard the jingling of the lock chain being released, then the door swung open wider than before. A young woman stood in the darkened doorway and motioned as she said, "Come inside. Quickly now!"

The children cautiously obeyed, bearing in mind the gravity of their quest. Once they were inside, the woman hastily shut the door, fastened the locks, and ushered them down a hallway and into the living room.

Furnished mostly with second-hand articles, the space had a distinctive personality about it. Hand-drawn pictures of jungles and watercolor paintings depicting tumultuous oceans hung around the walls of the room, framed by dried-out tropical flowers. The windows were covered with thick drapes to block both light and peering eyes, and an earthy smell filled the air. The three sat down on a pair of mismatched couches.

"Who gave you that?" The woman said as she pointed to the ring still in Oliver's hand. She was young—not more than thirty-years old—and her freckled, tawny complexion was accentuated by a mass of thick, black hair tied back in a long, curly ponytail. The lady was clad in all black.

"His name was Marco," said the boy. He tucked the

ring back into his pocket.

The woman didn't seem to recognize the name: "Is he the one who gave you this address?"

"No," replied Oliver.

"Then who told you where I was?"

"Well, Lady Penelope gave us the envelope," began Ellie. "But I suppose it was first given to her by Lady Juniper."

"Juniper?" The woman repeated. "You've seen her?"

"Yes," said Ellie. "But not this time. The last time was over a month ago. Why? Do you know her?"

"I knew her well," said the woman softly.

"Then you know about the Kingdom, too," said Oliver.

The young woman lowered her head. "Yes, I know about the Kingdom and I knew Juniper. But it's been years since I've seen her." The woman seemed to drift off into a thought, but then caught herself: "I'm sorry. How rude of me! My name is Jasmine."

She held out her hand to the two children who promptly introduced themselves.

"Now, what is it that's brought you here?" Jasmine inquired.

"Show her the certi—certic—certificate," said Ellie, stumbling over the word.

Oliver again reached into his pocket and this time withdrew the marriage certificate. He presented it to Jasmine: "We were hoping you could tell us more about King Juno and his secret wife Palmyra."

The woman held the certificate closer to examine its authenticity.

"Do you know if they had any children or grandchildren?" Ellie asked. "Maybe they have an heir—"

"Yes," interrupted Jasmine. "They had children. And a grandchild."

Oliver and Ellie perked up.

JASMINE

"Do you know where we can find them?" Oliver asked.

Jasmine smiled: "Right here."

Ellie scrunched her face, confused. "What? Right here in this apartment?"

"I mean *me*, silly," she clarified. "I'm King Juno's granddaughter. And his only living heir."

"You?" Ellie exclaimed. "Wonderful!"

"You're the heir to the line of Palafox?" Oliver said. "This is fantastic news. And you must know why we came to find you then?"

Jasmine nodded and spoke softly: "Yes. I know why: You need me to come with you—back to the Kingdom."

"Will you?" Ellie asked eagerly.

"When do you intend to return?" Jasmine asked. "And have you found all of the other heirs, then?"

"Our friends are still in the Kingdom," said Ellie. "They've gone to find another one of the heirs and we intend to meet up with them before the morning—inside the Kingdom."

"We need to leave right away," said Oliver.

Jasmine thought for a moment then said, "Alright. I knew this day would come. Have we got time for one stop before we return?"

"I'm afraid we can't waste another minute," Oliver replied. "Prince Florian may already be on our tail—I've got a nervous kind of feeling and I can't bear the thought of us being apart from our friends if something were to happen. Besides, we've got a bus to catch—if you're ready to go?"

The woman nodded and then hurried into another room to pack some belongings and put on a pair of boots. A few moments later, she returned.

"Alright," said Jasmine. "Let's go save the Kingdom."

CHAPTER TWENTY-FIVE
Strange Sounds in the Night

The rain continued its constant downpour, slowing Annie, Ben, and Mugwig's journey back toward the Banyan Gate. Ben allowed Mugwig to ride on his shoulders so they could move faster than the creature's little legs could carry her. Keeping a consistent pace, though, the children made considerable progress toward their destination.

It was darker now, as well, for the rain veiled the jungle from the waning moonlight. Annie and Ben listened to Mugwig this time, and she helped them navigate through the confusing woods without falling into any pits of quicksand.

At one point, Annie thought she saw several pairs of glowing eyes moving in the trees beyond them and she wondered whether these were real threats or just figments of her imagination brought on by the magic of the forest. She resolved not to think about it for long, for both options were particularly unsettling. *Just get to the Gate*, she thought instead. *Almost there. Almost home.*

"How much farther?" Ben asked Mugwig, practically shouting to be heard above the rain.

"Not far," she replied from atop his shoulders. "If what you told me is correct, we are not far."

So the party pressed on through the dark, damp forest. A variety of growls and squawks could be heard from afar, muddled into nondescript warbles by the torrential deluge.

A couple of hours later, Annie gestured to a point in the distance off to their right: "That looks like the marsh where we saw all of those snakes."

Ben recognized the terrain as well: "We're close."

The three travelers pressed through a patch of thick bramble at a point where the path seemed to disappear. Snapping tiny, spindly branches, Ben and Mugwig led the way. Once on the other side of the thicket, Annie found her sleeves covered in sap and leaves.

"I know it's darker now," said Ben, "but I think the Banyan Gate should be just through the next clearing."

Annie followed him in that general direction until Mugwig signaled suddenly for the children to stop walking.

"What is it?" The girl whispered.

"Did you hear that?" Mugwig asked.

"All I hear is rain," said Ben.

Mugwig's large pointy ears wriggled, trying to detect the noise again. She turned to the right and stared into the blackness of the jungle at night.

"What do you hear?" Ben asked the creature.

"I'm not sure," said Mugwig. "Something moving. Or someone."

"Someone coming?" Annie inquired. "Who's coming?"

Now the sound grew loud enough that the children could hear it as well.

Annie and Ben looked at each other, but neither

suggested what both were thinking: *Prince Florian. He's found the Gate.*

The children could now see lights growing in that part of the jungle, moving fast. Ben quickly motioned for them to keep toward the Banyan Gate. Within a few moments, they could see the large old tree ahead of them, but the sound of steps now grew even louder. Mugwig leaped from Ben's shoulders on to the ground and led the two children to duck for cover behind a patch of thick palmetto fronds.

Just as they did this, they watched a group of people enter the clearing. Dozens of masked men stepped into the glade. They scattered, revealing their leader: Marco.

"It's just Marco and his masked men," said Ben, relieved. As he began to rise from the bush, Mugwig yanked him back down into hiding.

"Wait!" She whispered.

Ben looked at the creature, confused: "What? But he's our friend—"

He started to rise again, but she held his arm.

"That's not what I heard," said Mugwig with a serious tone.

Annie and Ben turned to watch as Marco commanded his men to form a perimeter around the huge tree. Then, they heard it, too—the sound of dozens of pairs of hooves galloping from the east. The masked men stood their ground as the torch-bearing horsemen entered the large clearing. Filling the space, they parted to allow a black stag to walk toward Marco.

Ben recognized the man immediately. "Prince Florian," he muttered to the others. "We're too late."

"I don't see Oliver or Ellie," said Annie. "Do you?"

"No," said the boy, shaking. "And Marco's men are way outnumbered. I have a bad feeling about this."

CHAPTER TWENTY-SIX
Faceoff

It was still raining. The children and Mugwig watched from their hiding place as Prince Florian's stag sauntered slowly toward Marco. His right-hand man, General Pompadour, stayed close beside him atop a dark horse as Florian dismounted, while Malverne—the ruthless raven—perched on the General's shoulder. A pair of the masked men stepped between the Prince and Marco until their leader motioned them away.

"I know why you're here," said Marco. "And I must ask you kindly to leave."

The Prince smirked and walked closer.

"Ah, my dear Marco," Florian replied. "When will you learn to stop being so foolish—so *blinded* by your noble aspirations?"

Marco made no reply.

"You know why I'm here, you say. Then you know what I intend to do."

"I do," Marco said confidently. "But I will not allow it."

"You know these trees belong to me."

PRINCE FLORIAN ATOP HIS STAG

Marco hesitated, and said softly: "No, Florian."

"What's that?" Now Florian was only inches from the man's face.

"I said, *no*, Florian. These trees do *not* belong to you. Nor does the crown atop your delusional head." Marco spat at the ground in front of the Prince's feet.

Florian's blood began to pulse quicker and his General drew a glistening sword, but the Prince motioned for him to keep his distance. Malverne let out a *caw!*

"What's *she* doing here?" Marco nodded toward the raven.

"She's with me," said Florian dismissively. "You're bold, Marco. Brash and bold. But you know the law—what happens to those who profane my name."

"Your very existence is a profanity," retorted Marco. "I know what you've done—to your own family."

"Rumors and slanderous lies—all of them," said the Prince.

"Say what you will," Marco replied. "But I know the truth."

"What truth?"

Marco took a deep breath, calculating his next move. "*The* truth," he said, "that your reign is coming to an end. Your worst fears are about to come to pass—the return of three heirs who will take back the thrones."

"What, you mean the errands of those petty children?" The man laughed. "It's my intention to make sure they never return to my Kingdom—I have only to destroy this dying tree."

Florian pointed toward the massive banyan tree, its long roots wrapped in tangled knots above the ground. The brick archway that formed the Gate was visible, squeezed as if the tree had grown both around it and through it at the same time.

"Long live the Triumvirate," Marco said under his breath.

"I didn't catch that," said Florian, leaning toward him.

Marco repeated it louder: "Long. Live. The Triumvirate!" At this, he pulled a thick sword from his belt, which Florian met with a blade of his own. As their swords locked, the men around them took up arms as well. The masked men ran at the horsemen, brandishing crude, handmade weapons and, suddenly, the clearing was aflutter with motion. Bolts of lightning flashed in the sky above.

Annie and Ben watched in suspense as the skirmish ensued. Helpless, they crouched lower to stay out of the battle and out of sight. Then Annie had an idea. *Byron,* she thought. *Our friend the bunglejumper. Perhaps he can hear us and come to help.*

"Help me call out," said the girl to Ben.

"What?"

"Byron! He heard us from miles away before—we can call for his help!"

"But the Prince's men," began Ben. "They'll hear us!"

"Not above the clashing of their weapons," Annie said. "Come on!" At this, she cupped her hands around her mouth and began to call out: "Byron! Byron, please! Can you hear us?"

Ben joined in, and Mugwig soon followed. They continued to shout, far enough away from the battle so as to be indistinguishable from the clamor.

When there was no sign of the great beast, they ceased their cries. Turning back toward the battle, Annie was frightened by a figure that appeared right in front of the bush. One of the soldiers, mounted atop a horse, had heard the yelling and was headed right toward them. He held a sharpened spear in one hand and a blazing torch in the other, which cast eerie shadows across the children's faces as they crouched lower.

"Who's there?" The soldier said as he fished his spear around in the bushes. Then his eyes met Annie's.

We're caught! Annie thought as she froze in fear. She closed her eyes and waited for the man to make his next move. But before the man could take any action, the girl heard a loud *whooshing* sound from above. She opened her eyes.

Byron the Bunglejumper swooped down and tore the man from the horse, disappearing back above the trees. Seconds later, the beast returned—but the soldier was gone.

"Byron!" Annie shouted. "He's come to help us!"

Again the mighty beast glided down, this time removing several of Florian's conquistadors from their mounts. Annie and Ben cheered as their allies gained the upper hand. The soldiers began to flee into the jungle at the sight of the flying beast, and soon there were only a few of them left. The masked men chased them with wooden shields and spears flailing.

The sly Malverne watched while Byron slowly tackled a number of Florian's remaining soldiers off their horses and lifted them away through the treetops. The raven fluttered away from the shoulder of the General and onto a low-hanging branch of the banyan. She waited for the bunglejumper to reappear from the canopy and then flew toward him as quickly as she could. Aiming for his head, the bird latched onto Byron's fur with her sharp talons and began to peck.

Annie and Ben watched this scene unfold from behind the bushes. Byron was turned away from them, so they could no longer see the bird. But then, after a few moments, the raven flapped away, leaving Byron alone. The hulking beast hunched over and covered his face with his huge paws and slowly inched away from the battle. The children gasped and Annie ran toward Byron despite Ben's admonitions for her to stay hidden.

The girl placed her hand on the soft, iridescent fur of the giant winged lion. She could feel that he was crying. As she reached the other side of his huge body, she spoke gently to his face: "What's wrong, Byron? Are you alright?"

The beast kept his face hidden behind his paws. "I'm afraid I can't see a thing."

"Oh, dear," said Annie. "That's awful!"

"That wretched raven," said the bunglejumper. "She did this to me. I'm sorry I was so little help—I was too late!"

"There, there," said the girl, continuing to calm him with soft strokes of his feathery mane. "You helped a great deal! The men are nearly gone. Now, hide yourself in these bushes so they can't hurt you anymore. Follow the sound of my voice."

Annie then led Byron away from the glade and into a thick patch of gnarly, mossy oak trees. The sounds of fighting and yelling grew quiet as they walked in the drizzling rain.

"Here," the girl said to the beast. "You'll be safe here. But I've got to return to my friends, now. I'll see you again."

"Thank you, dear Annie," said Byron as the two embraced. He could not see that the girl was crying, but he could feel her warm tears soaking his paw. Then she dashed back into the jungle toward the clearing and the beast began a slow, cautious path through the trees and away from the battle.

Florian and Marco continued their swordfight at the base of the great banyan tree. Aside from Ben and Mugwig who watched from the bushes and the General who stood at a distance from the fight, they were the only two men left in the clearing. The Prince taunted his opponent and smiled as if he gained some delight at the prospect of ridding his Kingdom of one of his most formidable adversaries. Both were adept in their swordsmanship, so it was difficult to predict which man might ultimately win the duel.

Then, with a single crafty move, Florian disarmed Marco and pushed him to the ground. The man's sword flew out of his hand and into a thorny bush. The Prince smiled and held his blade to the helpless man's throat. Through the rain, Marco could hear the faint, tell-tale ringing of the Gate—the shimmering.

"Long live Florian," the Prince said. "Say it!"

Marco was silent.

"Say it!"

"Never," said Marco.

"Fine then," said Florian.

"Are you going to kill me now?" Marco asked.

Florian thought for a moment, then replied: "I'm no murderer." He then stepped over to General Pompadour and held out his sword. The General took the weapon and handed the Prince a flaming torch in its stead.

Marco watched in horror as Prince Florian approached the Banyan Gate, torch in hand. Annie had returned to the bushes by this time and joined Ben and Mugwig as they observed the disheartening sight.

"There will be no more Gates," Florian said. "And there will be no more Triumvirate. Long live Florian."

With that, the children watched from their hiding place as the evil Prince slowly lowered the torch to the base of the great banyan tree then stepped away.

CHAPTER TWENTY-SEVEN
A Race Against Time

The city bus was nearly empty; its only passengers were Oliver, Ellie, and Jasmine as the vehicle sped through the thinning traffic of Dixie Highway in the night. They were traveling along the same route the children had taken to get to Lake Worth, only this time they were headed north.

As they had a bit of time until they would return to the stop in their neighborhood, the children settled into their seats and began to question Jasmine.

"So," began Oliver, "have you always lived in this world?"

"No," replied Jasmine. "I was born in the Kingdom. We lived far away from my grandfather's palace, down in the southwestern everglade regions—remember, my father's very existence was a secret. Not even *I* knew that we were royalty at the time. I was young when we left the Kingdom—around your age, in fact—and I didn't fully understand it."

"Why did you leave?" Ellie asked.

"Because it became dangerous," the woman replied. "After Florian took over, it wasn't safe for us there any-more."

"Is that why you're so secretive and tense now?" Oliver asked.

The young woman turned from looking out the window and replied, "I'm the only heir of my family line and that's a danger in itself; I think we both know what Prince Florian is capable of."

"But no one knew this address except for Lady Juniper," said Ellie.

"And Florian seems a little more occupied with shutting Gates than traveling through them," added Oliver.

Jasmine continued: "If you—two children—could find me, then it would only be a matter of time before the Prince sent someone after me. My grandparents' marriage was a secret but that wicked man would do anything to trace even a hint of an heir. And then he'd snuff it out. I'm not safe—not even here in this world. None of us are."

The children were silent, frightened. The bus now passed a familiar intersection, which Oliver knew meant they were only a few more minutes from their stop.

"You said you knew Juniper a long time ago," the boy said. "How did you meet her?"

"Well," said Jasmine, "I was much younger then—it must have been over a decade ago—when Juniper came to me. It was right after my father passed, because I remember she was at the funeral and I'd never seen her before. She was good and kind, and she told me about the Triumvirate and the Prince and who I really was. That's when I joined."

"Joined what?" Ellie asked.

"The Lamplight Society," the woman replied. "Juniper recruited me."

"Oh, yes," said Ellie. "Marco told us all about it—and gave us that ring!"

Oliver took out the shiny gold ring once more and held it between two of his fingers. The engraved lamp symbol glistened in the overhead fluorescent lighting of the bus.

"May I see it?" Jasmine asked, holding out her hand toward the ring.

"Sure," said Oliver. He placed it in her outstretched palm.

Jasmine squinted her eyes and drew the ring very close to inspect it, then stared back at the boy for a moment with curiosity: "Where did you get this?"

"Marco gave it to us," said Ellie matter-of-factly. "Like we told you before."

"Actually," said Oliver, thinking back. "I think it may be the same ring that I found in an old house some time ago—right before we entered the Kingdom the first time. It looks identical, at least."

"An old house," said Jasmine. "What old house?"

"I can't remember the exact address," Oliver said, straining to remember, "but I think it was on Azalea Drive. Over in Flamingo Park."

Jasmine smiled. "I thought the ring looked familiar," she said. "The house on Azalea Drive—that was where we met in secret. Juniper and I and the other members of the Lamplight Society held council there. We called it a safe house."

"Then you knew about the Gate upstairs?" Oliver inquired.

"Yes," she replied. "We intended to keep that portal safe so that we could return when the time was right. But—"

"But Prince Florian burned it down," said Ellie, recalling their narrow escape from the man's pursuit during their prior adventure in the Kingdom.

"That's right," affirmed Jasmine.

At this point, the bus came to a stop. Oliver looked out the window and saw that they were now back at their neighborhood. The three disembarked and the bus sped away, leaving them on the dark street. A street light flickered above them, then burnt out, making it even darker.

The boy led Jasmine and Ellie down the familiar sidewalks. They wound throughout the neighborhood until they arrived at the overgrown abandoned lot—*the secret jungle*—where they had discovered the magic Banyan Gate.

"The Gate's just through these trees," said Oliver as he pushed a bunch of thick branches aside.

The moon cast a faint glow and haphazard shadows on the party as they made their way toward the mighty banyan tree. Ellie could hear the sounds of crickets and croaking frogs all around her, then the distant screech of a neighborhood cat.

Finally, the three arrived at the base of the great banyan. Oliver ushered them to the back side of the tree, where the roots and vines created a sort of blanket that covered the entrance to the Gate itself. Ellie ran over to help her neighbor push the vines out of the way. Very little moonlight shone so far back into the overgrown lot, so they had trouble finding the brick archway of the Gate. Jasmine handed Oliver a flashlight from her pack, and the two children felt around underneath the vines. Then Ellie turned to Oliver and Jasmine.

"I don't understand," said Ellie. "I can't seem to find the brick archway."

"What do you mean?" Jasmine asked, stepping closer to see for herself in the silence of the night.

"It's not here," the boy said quietly.

"Not here?" Ellie repeated.

Then a wave of horror swept over Oliver as he realized what had happened: "Oh, no! This is horrible. It's gone."

"The bricks?" Ellie asked, still unsure what her friend was trying to say.

"The Gate!" Oliver said, louder this time. "It's gone, Ellie!"

"Are you sure this is the right tree?" Jasmine asked, trying to calm the boy down.

"I'm positive," he replied. "The Prince got to it before we did. Now the Gate is gone—the *last* Gate!"

"What about Ben?" Ellie asked, whimpering. "And Annie! How will they come back here—come back home?"

Oliver looked at her and shook his head: "They may never come back home now."

All three were silent. Their friends were trapped inside the Kingdom, and the three of *them* were trapped in the outside world. If they could not return, then the Triumvirate would never be reunited and there was no chance of saving the Kingdom. They would be separated from their friends forever.

The Prince had won.

CHAPTER TWENTY-EIGHT
The Heir of Mangonia

Oliver and Ellie sat down against the tree and began to cry while Jasmine paced in front of them.

"This is all my fault," said Oliver. "I pushed the idea for us to split up. I should have never suggested that."

"And poor Annie," Ellie said. "She only just moved into the neighborhood and now she can't return to her family."

"What are we to do?" Oliver cried.

Jasmine watched with empathy, then sat down between them to comfort the children.

"We'll think of something," said Jasmine. "We can't give up hope yet."

"What hope is there?" Oliver said with a snivel.

"I don't know," she replied. "But there's got to be another way back into the Kingdom. I don't know what it is—but there *has* to be a way!"

Then Jasmine paused for a moment and looked at the boy. She recalled the golden ring and their conversation right before they had got off the bus.

"Have you got an idea?" Ellie asked, wiping her runny nose on her sleeve.

"Perhaps," she said. "I just remembered something: Now that we've got some time, I think we need to take a short trip."

"A trip *where?*" Oliver asked.

"To the house on Azalea Drive," said Jasmine with a smile.

"What are we going to do?" Ellie wondered.

"Just trust me," the woman said, helping the children to their feet. "I have to show you. Follow me. It's not far from here."

Jasmine, who had visited the house many times, led the way through the grid of streets and sidewalks and over into Flamingo Park. The neighborhood was quiet and still, so they trudged silently over the hill of the coastal ridge and back down to the other side. Just ahead of them was a pair of train tracks.

When they were nearly to the tracks, the party turned toward the old, abandoned two-story house at 505 Azalea Drive. Its windows were covered with plywood and the paint was chipped and dirty. The three adventurers waded through the overgrown front yard toward the entrance.

The front door was unlocked, so they quietly and carefully stepped inside. Jasmine used her flashlight to lead the way to the living room.

"The old Gate is upstairs," said Oliver, pointing toward the rickety steps.

"I know," replied the woman. "But we're not here for the Gate."

Jasmine felt along the wall and flicked on a single light. The glow illuminated the space adjacent to them where a large, wooden table stood. Around it were six mismatched chairs. The table and chairs were covered by a thin white sheet, which Jasmine promptly removed. A cloud of dust particles filled the room and made the beam of her flashlight look almost solid.

The table was constructed out of what looked like mahogany and stained in a rich, dark cherry color. Oliver recalled the table from their previous visits to the old house but now looked closer to see intricately carved characters and symbols around its edges that he hadn't noticed before. While he and Ellie studied the scenes and patterns in the wood, Jasmine approached the chair at the head of the table and pulled it out from its place.

The children watched as the woman bent down and felt her hands along the bottom edge of the table. Eventually, she paused for a moment, then pulled a lever to reveal a small hidden drawer. Oliver and Ellie could not see what was inside, but they could hear the sound of rustling pages and jingling coins.

Before the children could ask the woman what she was looking for, Jasmine spoke up as she continued to rifle through the contents of the drawer: "When you found the Book of the Blood, what did it say about the line of King Mangonia?"

Oliver thought back to the moment in the library: "Nothing—the page was missing."

"And so you knew *nothing* about his descendants?"

"Not that I can recall," said Oliver. "Lady Penelope told us about Gardenio—the heir of Coronado—and she gave us your address. Juniper once said there was an heir who left the Kingdom and could come back—but now we know she obviously meant you. I'm starting to think there *is* no heir of King Mangonia."

Here Jasmine stopped shuffling in the drawer and

lifted out an old, thick, piece of paper. Its edges were uneven on one side, as if it had been ripped.

"How did you get to the Kingdom—the first time?" Jasmine asked, looking at the parchment.

"Through the Gate upstairs," answered Ellie.

"But what led you here—to this house?"

Oliver thought back, scratching his chin. "It was that enchanted map," he said finally. "The one we found in my mother's old things in the garage."

Jasmine looked up from the piece of paper: "How did your mother end up with an enchanted map?"

"I don't know," Oliver said shaking his head. "She passed away when I was very young. Why are you asking all these questions—?"

"What was her name?" Jasmine moved closer.

"My mother? Her name was Vera—what does this have to do with anything?"

Jasmine ignored the boy's questions and continued to ask her own: "And her parents—who were they?"

The boy was becoming flustered, but answered, "My grandpa Jesse and my grandmother—Coral. Listen, Jasmine. I don't know why you're asking these questions all of a sudden. Why are we here in this old house again? Do you know something—a way to save our friends from the Kingdom?"

"Yes," said Jasmine. "I know something."

The woman placed the large, ripped page on the table. The children walked over to try and read its contents. It was a drawing of a family tree—just like the ones from the other lines in the Book of the Blood. In fact, it appeared to be the missing page from the line of Mangonia!

Oliver's eyes stared at King Mangonia's name and made their way down to the later generations—to see if it listed an heir who was still living. Two names caught his eye as he scanned the page.

The boy read them out loud: "Coral and Vera." He looked up at Jasmine. "My grandmother and my mother—but that would mean…"

Oliver didn't need to complete the sentence to know it was the truth.

"Yes, Oliver," Jasmine said slowly. "*You* are the heir of Mangonia."

Kingdom of Florida
The Place Beyond the Sea

Written by
Taylor Thomas Smythe

Illustrated by
Alice Waller

CHAPTER ONE
Fire and Water

The jungle is on fire!

It was the first thing Annie thought as she opened her eyes. The blaze cast a searing warmth all around her, a blur of glowing tangerine tongues whipping into clarity while raindrops fell on her fair cheeks.

The second thing she thought was, *What happened?*

The dark-haired girl sat up, her legs nestled in a cluster of moss and dirt. Wiping the dust and ash off her clothes, Annie looked around.

She was in a clearing in the woods—she recalled as much. But every tree and bush in the glade was now enveloped in flames, which leaped and grew despite the onslaught of the constant rain. The girl coughed in the thick smoke and stood to her feet to get a better view of the scene before her.

A giant banyan tree stood at the center of the expansive clearing. Annie remembered that this was the reason she had come to the clearing in the first place—to protect an ancient passageway that was built into the base of the massive, gnarly tree. It was this passage that brought the girl into the mysterious jungle just a few days prior. But now the tree was merely a decrepit shadow of its former glory—a shell of scorched wood and a pile of broken, black bricks.

The girl ran to the massive tree and scanned for any hint of the magic passageway. There was no sign of a way through the tree anymore, nor the shimmering sound that always accompanied such a portal.

No! Annie thought in despair. *Our only way home— gone!*

The girl frantically scanned the fiery clearing for any trace of her companions—a young boy named Ben; a small, green creature called Mugwig; or Marco, the brave warrior who fought valiantly to protect the Banyan Gate. There were no signs of any of the three or their enemies—only ash and flame and the downpour of rain.

As she circled the clearing, Annie's foot stepped on something small and metallic. It was a medallion of some sort, tied to a thin gold chain. The girl stooped to pick it up, wiping off the dirt. The chain was unclasped and dirty, but Annie could still recognize the piece from a few days prior due to the symbol engraved on its surface—a lamp emitting rays of light.

Marco's necklace. Annie placed the medallion around her neck, fastened the clasp, and tucked it under her clothes. *Marco! Where are you?*

Annie worried about what might have happened to her friend and guide. He was the one who had sent the children on their dangerous quest in the first place; he had also tried to protect their only way home—the portal in that great banyan tree—from the evil Prince Florian.

The only signs of the Prince were the scattered hoof and foot marks left by his men and their horses. This slightly relieved Annie's worrying, but she still wondered what had happened to her friends. Had Florian taken them? Did they somehow find a way through the Gate before it burned down? Or perhaps they escaped into the jungle?

Just then, Annie heard the faint sound of coughing. It came from a patch of thick bushes at the edge of the clearing. The girl cautiously ran toward the sound, dodging blackened branches and leaping over half-burnt tree trunks. Then the coughing stopped. Annie waited until it started again so that she could follow it. She noticed that the flames were beginning to die down a little out there, further from the scorched banyan tree. Then the cough continued and she waded through the thick underbrush toward the source.

Annie parted a patch of large monstera leaves to reveal her little creature friend: Mugwig. The tiny woman's greenish skin was covered in soot and sand, and her typically-mangled hair was even messier than usual. But she was alive.

"Child," she said softly, turning to Annie. "Are you alright?"

"I'm fine," said Annie. "But look at you! You're a mess. Are you hurt?"

The little woman stirred and winced as she sat up with a little help from the girl. "Just feeling a bit tossed around, that's all," she said. With her scaly claws, she dusted off her furry garments and stood up. At her full height, Mugwig was no taller than Annie's waist.

"What happened?" Annie asked the creature.

"Don't know." Mugwig shook her head. "Didn't see past the bushes. Just the two men in a swordfight then the one carrying the flame."

Annie recalled the same moments—how she watched the Prince disarm Marco and then place a torch to the roots of the old tree. *But what happened next?* She couldn't remember.

"Where's the boy?" Mugwig now asked.

"I haven't found him," said Annie anxiously. "Or Marco."

"They can't have gone far," the creature said in an attempt to encourage the girl.

"But what if *he* took them?"

"Who, child?"

"Prince Florian," said Annie. "What if he took Ben and Marco?"

The creature wriggled her large pointy ears and lowered her head as if pondering how to reply. Then she looked back at Annie: "Best not to assume the worst until we've tried everything else. Now, where else could they be?"

Annie wiped a few beads of sweat and rain from her forehead: "They could be out there, somewhere in the jungle." At this, the girl turned back toward the fiery clearing. She squinted her eyes a little then scanned the jungle around them. "They could be long gone now, and we'll never be able to find them with all this rain covering their tracks."

Mugwig held up a finger. "There's always a way," she said with a smile. "Let's go back to the last place you saw them."

Annie agreed and helped Mugwig navigate through the scorched foliage, back toward the place where the party had been hidden from the Prince's view. When they arrived at the place, Mugwig crouched down and stuck her nose to the earth. She began to sniff in much the same manner as a well-trained tracking dog. Annie watched the creature's actions with both curiosity and skepticism.

"Hard to smell," said Mugwig, her face still in the ashy, wet dirt.

"It's the fire and rain," said Annie. "They've covered everything."

Mugwig kept sniffing while Annie watched. The flames around them were dying down now, finally bested by the persistent precipitation. Unfortunately, the onslaught of rain also now turned most of the forest floor to mud.

While Annie waited for her friend to sniff out Marco or Ben's scent, she listened to the calming sound of the rain on the jungle's thick canopy overhead. The pattering had a soothing property—nature's own white noise. Annie closed her eyes as drops descended across her face. Then she heard a rustling in the distance.

Annie opened her eyes and turned toward the sound. Far off, she could see a pair of horsemen moving toward the clearing—toward her and Mugwig.

The girl tapped on Mugwig's shoulder: "Can you sniff any faster?"

Mugwig glared at the girl and replied, "Patience, child!"

"Well, hurry it up," Annie said. "Someone's coming."

The creature returned to her investigation and crawled a little further into the jungle. Annie looked back toward the approaching horsemen. The rain obscured their faces, but the girl recognized the distinctive armor of Florian's conquistadors.

"Got anything yet?" Annie tapped her fingers on her arm as she turned back to Mugwig.

There was no reply. But then the creature ceased her search and looked at Annie: "Got something! This way!"

The two eagerly began to follow a muddy trail into the forest. Annie could see that the horsemen were getting closer. They would most certainly see them.

"Smell is stronger here," said Mugwig, sticking her nose to the humid air.

Annie followed as they came to a stop next to a patch of ferns. She knelt to look beyond the plants and, pushing the fronds aside, discovered one of her friends.

"Ben!" Annie said excitedly as she recognized the boy.

But there was no reply. His eyes were shut and his breathing was slow, and a giant old book—*The Book of the Blood*—was tucked underneath one of his limp arms.

"Looks like he passed out or something," said Annie, turning to look over her shoulder at the approaching soldiers. "Help me!"

The two stepped into the ferns and Annie grabbed the boy under his arms, holding *The Book of the Blood* in place with a free hand. Mugwig quickly followed suit and took Ben's feet in her claws. Annie nodded to a huge fallen log and they slowly dragged the sleeping boy toward it.

The horsemen were now close enough to the clearing that Annie could hear the whinnying of their steeds. It was only a matter of moments before they noticed them. With a forceful thrust, the girl threw the boy's body behind the tree and dove next to him herself. Mugwig scurried between them.

"Did you hear something?" Shouted one of the horsemen. Annie and Mugwig could not see either of the men now, but they could hear their voices only a few meters from the log.

"I think it came from over there," said the other.

They're coming right toward us! Annie thought.

Then they heard the sound of the two horses and their armor-clad riders trotting in their direction, clinking louder with each step. They were so close now that Annie could discern the *ping* of each raindrop ricocheting off the riders' morion helmets.

Then there was stillness and rain as the riders listened.

Annie held her breath as the rain continued to fall.

They're going to find us, she thought. *It's over.*

CHAPTER TWO
The Two Horsemen

As the girl held her breath and crouched behind the fallen tree, the two horsemen scanned the scorched, wet jungle. With one arm, Annie held Mugwig close; with the other, she tightly grasped Ben's limp hand. One of the horses snorted loudly and scuffed at the ground with a hoof.

Annie looked at Ben, passed out in a bed of ferns. *This would be a bad time for you to wake up,* she thought.

The following seconds felt like hours, and Mugwig and Annie breathed slowly and quietly to avoid detection.

"It must've been the rain," said one of the men as the pattering continued.

"Or another wild animal," suggested the other.

Annie listened as the men yanked on the reins of their horses and slowly turned them back toward the clearing.

Then Ben let out a loud gasp for air.

Frantically, Annie clamped her hand over the waking boy's mouth and placed a forefinger over her own. She listened as the horses stopped moving for a moment. Then they began to saunter back toward the fallen tree.

"You hear it this time?" The horseman's voice was closer than before.

One of the men dismounted and crunched through the bramble toward the log.

Not good, thought Annie.

Ben could hear the men now, too, and he listened intently for the muddy footsteps. The children could see a gloved hand reaching over the top of the log now.

If he climbs over the log, we're done, thought the girl. She closed her eyes tightly, as if her own lack of sight might prevent them from being seen.

The loud call of some exotic bird resonated through the jungle. Annie opened her eyes. The hand was gone.

"It's over there now," said the closer voice, stepping away from the log.

"Let's get back to *la Puerta*," replied the other. "Might be those little children."

"It's doubtful," said the first voice. "They'd be fools to come back here again. But you know what to do if they show up here again."

"*Sí*," the second man replied.

As they finished this exchange, the two horsemen once again led their horses away from the fallen log and toward the large clearing. After a few moments, when they were out of earshot, Annie removed her hand from Ben's mouth and the trio took deep breaths.

"Good to see you awake again," said Mugwig with a smile.

"Thanks, Mugwig," the boy replied softly. Then he nodded toward the horsemen: "Who were they?"

"Some of Florian's men," replied Annie. "Sounds like they've come back to guard the old banyan tree—to catch us if we try to return."

The boy looked frightened as he squinted at the horsemen across the glade: "We'll never be able to pass them to get back to our Gate. They've got spears and swords!"

"You're right," said Annie as she lowered her head. "We won't be passing them. But it won't matter now; the Gate is gone, Ben."

He was confused: "Gone? What do you mean 'gone'?"

"Prince Florian," she said. "He destroyed it with fire."

"I don't believe it," he replied. "That was our only way home! Oliver and Ellie are home and we're trapped here—I never should have let her out of my sight!"

The boy was getting worked up and began to cry. Annie put a hand on his shoulder.

"We can't change that now," she said. "There's got to be another way to get back."

"There isn't," the boy said shortly. "That was the last Gate!"

Annie was silent. *Ben's right.*

"Did you see what happened?" Annie asked the boy. "All I remember is watching Florian use a torch to set fire to the tree. I looked away for a second then blacked out."

"Yeah, I saw it," he said. "I guess it all makes sense. I saw the same thing—Florian with the fire. The masked men chased the Prince's soldiers away into the jungle. Then, as the flames engulfed the trunk of the tree, there was some sort of *wave* that moved across the clearing—a force that pushed the jungle. It sent everyone flying. That's all I remember—flying through the air, then black."

Annie considered the boy's story: "The wave—that force—must have had something to do with the magic in the Gate. Like some sort of release of its power."

"Strange magic," Mugwig chimed in. "Strange, indeed."

"Where's Marco?" Ben asked, remembering their brave friend.

"I don't know," said Annie. "He and Florian were near the tree when I blacked out—that was the last I saw of him." She showed him the medallion around her neck: "He left this behind."

"I hope he's okay," said Ben. "Do you think Florian got him?"

"We can't know for certain," the girl replied. "And it'll be impossible to look for him now that those men are watching the area."

The rain continued as the children observed the horsemen and waited for an idea about what they might do next. Then Ben heard a twig snap behind them.

The children and Mugwig turned but could not see what—or who—had made the noise. Mugwig's large pointy ears twitched as she tried to figure out from which direction the sound had come. The rain made it difficult, but finally, she seemed to have settled on a source. The creature pointed toward a large, gnarly tree in the distance and looked at the children with wide eyes.

Annie gave a quiet nod to Ben and the two slowly began to inch toward the gnarly tree, while Mugwig stayed behind the old log. The girl picked up a long, sturdy stick from the ground as they walked, and held it like a baseball bat—ready to swing at any enemy who might be spying on them. Rain trickling down their faces, the two children pressed on toward the large tree, wondering what they would find behind it.

With a sweeping hand-motion, Annie instructed Ben to go around one side of the tree while she would take the other. Then she counted down on her fingers, mouthing the numbers.

3. 2. 1!

The children leaped around the edge of the tree to discover a small figure wrapped tightly in a thick, rain-soaked overcoat. The spy wore a hood, and there was a scarf wrapped around the bottom half of the figure's face.

"Why are you spying on us?" Annie demanded, pointing the stick at the mysterious figure.

"Not spying," replied the muffled voice.

A woman's voice, thought Annie.

"Then who are you?" Ben asked. "And what are you doing out here?"

The hooded woman turned to the boy and removed the covering from the top of her head, revealing a shock of tousled gray hair wrapped in a loose bun.

"I'm here to help," she said as she started to unwrap the scarf from her face.

Ben thought he recognized the gray hair and the woman's figure and stature. His suspicions were confirmed as the old woman finally removed the scarf. She was an old friend.

"Lady Juniper!" Ben gasped.

The woman flashed a kind smile: "Hello, Benjamin. It's good to see you again."

CHAPTER THREE
The Family Tree

It was dark in the old, boarded-up house in Flamingo Park; any stray moonbeams that might have illuminated the interior were obscured by its crumbling window coverings. The property sat adjacent to a railway, and a freight train barrelled by quietly under the starlight. Though the house on Azalea Drive was usually abandoned, on this particular night it had three guests.

A light turned on in the dining room. A woman and two children crowded around an intricately-carved wooden table upon which sat a large, ripped page from an old book. The page contained a detailed family tree with names written in an ornate calligraphy. One of the children—a dark-haired boy named Oliver—stood over it, his eyes glued to two names near the bottom of the page. He adjusted his glasses and read the names again.

Coral and Vera, he repeated in his head to make sure there was no mistake. *My grandmother Coral and my mother Vera.* The boy shook his head slowly in disbelief.

"It's true, Oliver," said the woman named Jasmine.

"Those are your family names. This is *your* family tree."

Ellie, the other child, fair and freckled, spoke up: "You mean *Oliver* is the person we've been looking for all this time? That he's actually one of the three kings?"

Jasmine nodded to the girl, her long, voluminous curls jumping up and down as she did. "That's correct," she said. "Oliver is the last remaining heir to the throne of King Mangonia."

The boy was speechless. He couldn't bring himself to voice any of the countless thoughts that were swirling through his head. *Why didn't my family tell me? Why was this piece of vital information withheld from me? Is it true? What happened to my family?*

Then he zeroed in on another thought: *Even if it is true, I'm not ready for this. I can't be king.*

"I can't be king," Oliver muttered the thought aloud.

"What?" Jasmine asked, leaning closer.

"I'm just a child," the boy clarified. "How am I supposed to be a king?"

"It's in your blood, Oliver," said Jasmine, her large brown eyes now meeting his. "Both of us were born into this."

"You've been preparing for it your whole life," said Oliver. "But this is all so new to me. I just can't imagine leaving my friends and my grandpa to live in the Kingdom forever. I'm not ready."

Jasmine exhaled slowly and placed a hand on the boy's shoulder. "Whether we're ready or not," she said, "we have to fulfill our destiny as rulers of the Kingdom. People are counting on us. You've seen what Florian is capable of."

"Even if I were ready to be a king," said Oliver, "the Kingdom will never get its rulers back because we have no way to get there now. Have you forgotten how the

Banyan Gate was destroyed? We can only succeed if we reunite all *three* of the heirs and that's never going to happen now."

"They need us," Jasmine said firmly. "And if we were meant to do this—meant to be the rulers that overthrow Florian—then there *has* to be another way to get back."

Ellie chimed in: "But didn't Marco say that was the last of the Gates?"

"Yes," replied Oliver. "He said it was the last *known* Gate. And if Marco doesn't know of another, then I can't imagine anyone else who would."

"But maybe Jasmine is right," said Ellie. "There has to be another way. We *have* to find a way—not just for the Kingdom, but to bring Ben back. And our dear, new neighbor Annie. Oh, I miss them so! And I'm sure they're worried sick, trapped in the jungle with that awful Prince hunting for them, no doubt."

The three stood in silence as they thought about how they might continue.

Then Oliver asked Jasmine, "Is there anyone here in our world who can help us?"

The woman shook her head: "It's been months since I've had contact with anyone who knows the Kingdom—*years* since I've seen anyone other than Juniper. I'm not sure if there's anyone left here who can help us."

The two children began to despair.

"Then my brother is gone forever," said Ellie through tears. She sat down on the wood floor and put her face in her hands. "Oh, this is just horrible!"

Oliver moved to console his friend, while Jasmine remained standing near the table.

"It's alright, Ellie," said the boy. "We'll find them. We'll find a way."

Jasmine turned her attention from the sulking children back to the torn page that rested on the dining room table. Another name caught her eye. She looked closer.

"Wait a minute," she said with surprise as an idea formed in her mind.

"What is it?" Oliver asked.

"I just had an idea," Jasmine replied. "I think I know of someone who might be able to help us."

"I thought you just said there's no one who could help," replied Ellie, wiping tears from her cheeks.

"I've just remembered someone," said the woman, picking up the ripped page of the family tree. "Some-one who Oliver knows very well."

"Who?" Oliver asked.

Jasmine handed him the page and he looked it over, confused. The woman pointed to a name near the bottom and said, "Your grandfather!"

CHAPTER FOUR
The Return of Lady Juniper

The rain slowed to a drizzle as the dawn crept over the wet treetops. Annie and Mugwig watched as Ben embraced the little old woman who had just revealed herself.

Lady Juniper, thought Annie. She'd heard the name before but never met the woman—until now. The lady was not much taller than the children and she wore a kind smile that instantly put the girl at ease.

The woman exchanged brief introductions with Annie and Mugwig. Then Ben attempted to bring Lady Juniper up to speed on their quest and their plight.

"Thank goodness you've arrived," he said. "So much has happened since the last time we saw you, and I'm afraid things have become quite dire."

"Well," said Juniper. "I've come to help. But let us steal away somewhere out of sight of the Prince's conquistadors. I have only just arrived at the camp, and it's not far."

"You mean Marco's camp?" Annie asked. "Is he

there now?"

Juniper sighed then smiled at the girl: "It is the camp of Marco and the masked men, but none of them have seen him since last night."

Ben was worried: "Do you think Prince Florian has got him?"

"I do not know," replied the old woman gravely. "But come with me, for you three could use some food and a place to lay your head for a spell. Let us move away from here before the sun rises." Noticing the weathered tome in Ben's grasp, Juniper added, "I'll take that off your hands for safekeeping—it's quite old and should be protected."

Ben gladly handed the heavy *Book of the Blood* to her and, with that, Lady Juniper turned and began to lead the party deeper into the jungle. Annie caught glimpses of a purple sky through the gaps in the canopy above, and she watched it gradually lighten to blue as the travelers approached the camp.

Only a few days prior, Annie and Ben had stayed the night in this very camp, though on that occasion they were accompanied by the friends who were now missing—Oliver, Ellie, and Marco. Annie recognized the camp by its distinctive boundary wall, which was constructed of large sheets of fabric and cloth strung between trees. The material was dyed in dark greens and browns to camouflage the encampment from the prying eyes of the enemy.

The party now approached one segment of the semi-permeable wall. It was promptly flapped open by a man in a painted wooden mask, allowing them to pass through. Once inside the camp, Juniper led the group past a central firepit and into a large tent, which the children recognized as Marco's quarters.

Inside the tent, a blur of motion caught Annie's eye. A small creature scurried behind a trunk and then stuck out its head to survey the new guests.

"What is that?" Annie asked their hostess.

Mugwig inched toward the strange creature and crouched on all fours. Both had greenish scaly skin, but Mugwig saw that this animal could not speak. She pointed a long finger at the creature to try and touch it, but then it snapped its jaws and Mugwig pulled away quickly.

"Dangerous," said Mugwig.

"It's Kiwi!" Ben shouted and ran toward the little beast. Recognizing the boy, Kiwi cautiously emerged from his hiding place and allowed Ben to pet his head.

"Kiwi is my pet," said Juniper, nodding to the creature, which looked like a small, smooth turtle without a shell. "Don't worry, he's friendly. Just takes a bit to get used to strangers."

The girl approached to get a closer look at Kiwi, but this startled him and sent the creature back into hiding. The children giggled at his antics, then watched as he again stuck out his head.

Lady Juniper led the children over to the other side of the vast tent. As the group took their seats on a pair of small, simple couches, Juniper motioned to a few of the masked men and instructed them to bring food for the children. They disappeared through the tent flap but soon returned, each carrying a large platter of delicious fruits, meats, and breads.

"Please eat," said the woman, gesturing to the spread on the low table before them. Kiwi popped out from behind the sofa and leaped onto his master's lap, where Juniper began to stroke her pet softly.

Mugwig and the children obliged and ate their fill

of the wholesome provisions. When they were all satisfied, the children sat back on the loveseat and waited
for Juniper to speak. Kiwi jumped back down to the
ground, followed by Mugwig who began to chase the
pet around the tent.

"Now," said Juniper to Ben, "tell me your troubles,
child."

Ben began to recount the tale of their quest: "Well,
it all began when Annie helped us find our way back
into the Kingdom through that old banyan tree. Then
Marco found us and sent us out on a mission to find
the three heirs to the Triumvirate—"

"He thought *The Royal Book of the Blood* would tell
us who they were," said Annie. "But most of its family
trees were a little lacking."

"I see," said Juniper, nodding as she listened intently.

"But it did lead us to find a woman called Lady Penelope," continued Ben.

"Ah, Penny," said Juniper. "She's an old acquaintance of mine. And did she help you?"

"Yes," said Annie. "She told us two secrets; first, she
told us how Prince Florian's mother was pregnant when
he poisoned the royal family. Everyone thought she and
the baby passed away. But Penelope actually delivered
the baby—Gardenio—and took him away to be safe in
the country."

"The two of us followed Penny's instructions," continued Ben, handing Juniper a crumpled note from his
pocket—a rudimentary sketch of a map from Lady Penelope. "And then we found him: Gardenio—or *Dean*
for short."

"He agreed to help us overthrow the Prince," said
Annie. "But only if we can find the remaining heirs of

the other two lines."

"Gardenio," repeated Juniper to herself. "So there is another heir of Coronado after all." Then she broke from her thoughts and looked back at the children: "And what was the second secret?"

"It was an old envelope," said Annie. "With a mysterious address on the back of a marriage certificate. It means there's a hidden child in the line of, um, something with *fox* at the end?"

"*Palafox*," Ben corrected. Then, remembering Lady Penelope's words about the envelope's origins, he added, "But you already know that part, right Lady Juniper? You gave the envelope to Penny."

Lady Juniper nodded: "That's right. I gave it to Penny many years ago to keep safe until we were ready to reunite the Triumvirate. And I presume that your little sister and Oliver were the ones to follow its message?"

"That's right," replied Annie. "They went to follow the address back into our world. Do you know where it leads?"

"I do," she said. "That address is where the last heir of Palafox has been hiding, away from the prying eyes of Florian and his Seers. She's very special to me."

"She?" Annie asked.

"Her name is Jasmine," Juniper answered. "She has been hiding and waiting for over a decade to return to the Kingdom and take back her ancestors' throne. I suspect that your friends have found her by now."

Ben began to sulk. "It doesn't matter now," he said. "We have no way to bring them back to the Kingdom—or for us to get home, for that matter."

"Jasmine's a very capable young woman," said Lady Juniper. "She'll keep your friends safe until we can find a way for them to return."

Just then, there was a loud crash. The children looked toward the sound to find Mugwig holding fast to one of Kiwi's legs. A small nightstand and unlit lamp had fallen to the ground. Glass was everywhere.

"Mugwig is sorry," she said.

"Not to worry," said Juniper. Then she motioned to one of the masked men near the door who promptly cleaned up the mess while Mugwig and Kiwi slinked out of view.

Annie spoke up: "Even if we can find a way for our friends to travel between our world and the Kingdom again, we still haven't found the last of the three heirs—the heir of Mangonia."

Juniper's wrinkled face stretched into a smile: "But we *have* found him."

"What are you talking about?" Ben asked, his eyebrows crooked with confusion. "*Him?* But we don't know who the heir is."

"Ah, but you do," said Juniper. "And you know him very well."

CHAPTER FIVE
Hints of Lime, Ginger, and Hope

The children lounged upon the couches in the warm tent and thought for a moment about what Lady Juniper's words could mean.

Is it possible that the heir of Mangonia has been under our noses this whole time? Annie thought to herself. *Could it be...?*

She finished her thought out loud: "Oliver?"

Lady Juniper nodded. "Yes," she said. "Oliver—your dear, brave friend—is the heir of Mangonia."

"What?" Ben wondered aloud. "How can he be the heir of Mangonia? And why didn't he tell us?"

"He didn't know, silly," chided Annie.

"But I'm sure he does by now," said Lady Juniper. "Jasmine will have figured it out."

"How long have you known?" Ben inquired of the sagely woman.

"I had my suspicions when you children first arrived at my house," she replied. "Remember that old enchanted map? It looked familiar. Then I remembered that a map just like it belonged to another member of the line of Mangonia—Oliver's grandmother Coral—which I presume was passed on to her daughter Vera before you all found it in her things."

"Why didn't you say anything?" Ben continued to pry.

"I wasn't sure about it then," the woman said. "But later, when I put all of the pieces together, I knew it had to be true. I didn't tell anyone—not even dear Marco—for fear that the boy would be in danger."

The two children sat and pondered the revelation that Oliver—their simple, normal neighbor—was actually next in line to be King. Now not one but *two* of the three heirs to the Triumvirate were trapped outside the Kingdom with no apparent way to return.

Finally, Annie said, "Juniper, is there a way to bring them back?"

"Well, child," Lady Juniper began, "I have spent many of these last weeks poring over ancient scrolls and writings from the early civilization of the Kingdom. Though it is not certain to help us, I have learned something of the original construction of *las Puertas*—the Gates—that I believe may be of value."

"So you're saying there is still a way that we might get back to our friends?" Ben asked eagerly.

"Yes, dear child," said Juniper with a sparkle in her eyes. "There's always a way."

By this point in the conversation, the sun had fully risen and now cast the thin walls of the cream-colored tent in a luminous glow. Lady Juniper poured each of the children a cup of tea, and Annie wafted the aromatic steam from the steeping beverage, noticing hints of lime and ginger. She waited a few moments, then sipped delicately and found its taste to be just as

"Yes, dear child," said Juniper with a sparkle in her eyes. "There's always a way."

delightful.

"We were so sorry to hear about your village," said Ben to Lady Juniper, recalling the stilted river town she called home. "Was anyone hurt in the fires?"

Juniper took a sip of her own tea and nodded: "Everyone made it out alive, though most with little more than the clothes on our backs and what few belongings we could carry. Some made it out with even less, but we will rebuild in time."

"Why would Florian do that to such a peaceful town?" Ben asked.

"He sees me as a threat," said the old woman somberly. "I know too much about the Triumvirate—after all, I once served the royal family quite closely. And I have a feeling he found out that I helped you all get home the first time. But thankfully, I was able to salvage a few old documents from my home and procure a number of ancient scrolls from a dealer in a village near the coast. I believe they may be of help to us."

"You mentioned that you read something about the original Gates," said Annie. "Do these scrolls tell of a way to build a brand new Gate?"

"Not exactly," replied Lady Juniper. "But through these writings, I have come to believe there may be someone who still knows the secrets of their magic. Perhaps *they* know of the way to build a new Gate."

"Who is this *someone?*" Ben asked.

"The scrolls spoke of a special type of enchanter—a class of craftsmen with knowledge of old magic," Lady Juniper said. "They were the ones who built the original Gates as portals between worlds. The writings are inscribed in an ancient tongue, so there's no direct translation for what they're called, but the best word I can think of is *Carpenters.*"

"Carpenters," repeated Annie. "And you think some of these Carpenters are still alive today? I thought you said these scrolls were ancient."

"It's true, these scrolls date back centuries," replied Juniper. "But the Carpenters knew of many forms of magic. It is said that some even found ways to extend their lives for many decades—some even longer. I believe these scrolls can lead us to one who still lives."

The two children had nearly finished their tea and Juniper stood up.

"If you're up for the journey," said Juniper, "I think I can find the way to this Carpenter. But first, I think it best that you all get some rest; after all, you've been traveling all night."

Though they wanted desperately to reunite with their friends as soon as possible, neither of the children protested. They looked around, realizing that the tent had become quiet, and found Mugwig and Kiwi peacefully asleep on a shaggy rug.

Juniper smiled and said, "It seems they were tired, too."

A pair of the masked men brought pillows and thick blankets, which they spread across the sofas. The two children then nestled into their cozy makeshift beds and thanked the kind men.

"After you've rested a little," said Lady Juniper, "we shall embark on our journey to find the Carpenter. In the meantime, I will chart our course and gather supplies and rations. Have the sweetest of dreams, dear children."

With that, Juniper left the tent. Annie and Ben felt relief from the aches and stress of their past few days of travel as they quickly drifted off into a deep slumber. One thing allowed them to rest soundly for those few hours despite the plight of their dear friends: the hope that—if they located one of the Carpenters—they would see their friends again.

CHAPTER SIX
Grandpa Jesse

Oliver had lived with his grandfather since he was only a few years old but, up until the present, the boy had never thought to talk to him about the hidden Kingdom. After all, prior to Jasmine's shocking revelation that the boy and his family were descendants of one of its royal families, Oliver had no reason to believe he had any deep connection to the magical world.

Both mother and Grandma Coral knew about the Kingdom, thought Oliver, *so Grandpa Jesse has got to know something. Perhaps he knows what happened to them...*

In Oliver's early years, Grandpa Jesse had remained coy about the two women or changed the subject whenever it came up, so the boy had learned not to ask too many questions. Now in his old age, Jesse's mind was fading rapidly and he had trouble remembering even the simplest of daily details.

Sometimes the elderly have better recollections of very old memories, the boy thought hopefully. *Maybe he will know a way to travel between the worlds—to get back to our friends.*

Streaks of golden light slanted across the dusty living room through a gap in the plywood window coverings, signaling the impending arrival of morning. Jasmine, Oliver, and Ellie gathered their things—including the page torn out of *The Book of the Blood*—and quietly slinked out of the old home and across the overgrown front lawn. Under the last patches of darkness, the three traversed from Flamingo Park over to the children's own neighborhood which sat adjacent to it.

It was quite early in the morning, but Jesse was already up—Oliver could tell from a window on the side of the house that glowed with light. The three tired travelers approached the front door. Finding it locked, Oliver gave a series of short, quiet thumps on the door. The boy had his own key to the house but didn't want to frighten the old man at such an early hour.

Jesse moved slowly but surely to answer the knock and the three could hear shuffling inside. When the door opened, they were presented with a graying man of average stature. For a man of his age, Jesse still maintained a head of thick hair, white and combed back but once blonde and flowing. His smooth, pale face was freshly trimmed of any signs of stubble and his green eyes glistened in the dawn. As his expression changed from confusion to recognition of his grandson, he gave a kind smile.

"There you are, Oliver," he said gleefully. "I've been looking everywhere for you. I thought you might've been playing another one of your games, hiding in some cupboard or wardrobe."

"Hello, grandpa," Oliver replied, giving Jesse a hug. "I've been with the neighbors—you remember Ellie?" He gestured toward the little girl and Jesse nodded.

"And who's this?" Jesse asked as he turned his attention to Jasmine. "Another friend of yours?"

"I'm Jasmine," she said as she extended a hand to the old man. "It's a pleasure to finally meet you."

The wrinkly old grandfather squinted his eyes, as if trying to determine if he knew the woman, but then smiled and returned his attention to the children.

"Well, please come inside," he said finally, turning slowly to hobble toward the kitchen. "I'll fix us up some tea."

"Thank you, grandpa," said Oliver as they entered the house. "And we'd like to ask you a few questions about my mother and Grandma Coral if that's alright?"

The old man stopped halfway down the hall and turned toward Oliver. He wore a somber expression and seemed to drift deep into a thought.

"Grandpa?" Oliver asked, wondering if Jesse heard his prior request.

"Yes, Oliver," he replied. "Close that door and I'll fix us some tea."

While Jesse turned and started back toward the kitchen, Oliver looked to his friends and closed the door behind them, then whispered, "Sometimes he has trouble remembering things. Let's hope this works."

They followed Jesse into the living room, where he motioned for them to take a seat as he disappeared to prepare the tea. Oliver, Ellie, and Jasmine sat in silence for a few minutes while they heard the sound of pots and pans clinking under a cabinet and then the bubbles of percolating water. Jesse re-entered the room carrying a large tray with delicate cups and a steaming kettle, walking more slowly than usual so as not to rattle or drop the heavy load.

Jesse set the tray on the coffee table and then proceeded to pour a cup of tea for each of the guests, saving his own for last. He then placed three scoops of sugar into his tea with a small spoon and stirred it loudly.

"Now, what was it you wanted to discuss?" Jesse sipped his tea and then displayed a satisfied grin. "Three scoops. Perfect taste."

"Well, Grandpa," Oliver began, leaning closer to his grandfather. "We have some questions about Grandma Coral." He hesitated before continuing, "And I know this might be hard for you, seeing as you don't often like to talk about her since she passed."

"It's alright, Oliver," said Jesse with a smile. "My Coral's not gone."

The boy gave Jesse a curious look, unsure what he meant.

"She's just away on business," continued the old man. "Always traveling, that one."

Ah. His mind is confusing him again, thought Oliver to himself as Jasmine gave a concerned look. *He thinks she's still alive.*

"Well, then," said Oliver. "I guess you won't mind telling us about her?"

"Of course not," Jesse replied. "What is it you want to know?"

Oliver tried to think of how to start, realizing he now had a hundred questions for the old man: *Why did my family keep the Kingdom a secret? What happened to my parents? How do we stop Prince Florian? How am I supposed to rule a Kingdom? I'm only a boy.* Then, remembering the dire situation of his friends, Oliver arrived at even simpler, more basic question.

"Grandpa," he said finally. "Do you know about the Kingdom?"

CHAPTER SEVEN
Something in the Water

It was almost noon when Ben and Annie awoke, and the air in the tent was warm and dry. Lady Juniper lifted the flap at its entrance and signaled for them to follow her outside. The two children's sluggish pace got them to the doorway eventually, where they were nearly blinded by the late-morning sunlight.

"We're all ready to go," said Juniper. "Everyone feeling well-rested?"

Ben slowly blinked a few times then forced his eyes to stay widened: "Yep!"

The old woman handed him and Annie each a bespoke pack of rations and supplies, which they slung across their backs. The packs appeared to be fashioned from the same cloth as the wall around the camp—dyed and painted in greens and browns to blend in with the jungle. Lady Juniper carried a walking stick and her own smaller satchel across a shoulder.

"So where does this Carpenter live?" Annie asked as she tightened the straps on her pack.

"As it happens, the place is not far from here," replied Juniper. "We'll have to travel through the woods and into the swamplands."

Ben shuddered as he recalled the swarms of snakes that they encountered in the swamp several days prior. "But what about the s-s-snakes?" He was trembling.

"We may encounter a few of the serpents on our quest," said Juniper. "But I believe the route I have charted will keep us on a course that *should* keep them to a minimum."

The boy exhaled, deeply relieved.

"Now, where have Kiwi and Mugwig gone?" The old woman put her hands on her hips as she looked around. Near the middle of the camp, she discovered the pair of reptiles chasing each other around the unlit fire pit.

"Mugwig," shouted Annie. "Are you ready to go?"

The tiny greenish woman turned to the girl and replied, out of breath, "Mugwig is ready! A princess is *always* ready." Then she stood straight, brushed off the front of her furry garments, and joined the children. Kiwi followed closely behind and scurried up into Juniper's arms.

Two of the masked men parted the camp's fabric wall and ushered the curious party of five out onto their journey. Lady Juniper led the way while Kiwi perched on her shoulder snatching stray mosquitoes with his long tongue.

A few minutes into their journey, the trail diverged in several directions and the group came to a stop. From her satchel, the old woman produced a wooden compass with a tiny silver needle. Its markings were faded and worn, signs of a storied past. Juniper looked down at the compass then up at the paths ahead of them before pointing her staff.

"This way," she said as the children and Mugwig followed her down the trail.

On this path, the trees seemed more mangled and twisted. The children found that the ground beneath them was now less solid than before; a layer of mushy, dirty earth squished under their feet. Ben looked down at his shoes and discovered that they were caked in the grayish mud.

"I guess we've made it to the swamp," said Annie, noticing that her own shoes were soiled as well.

Mugwig waddled behind the children, her tiny, webbed feet sinking and barely visible under the thick layer of mud. At one point, it became nearly impossible for her to lift her feet out of the mire. "A little help?" She cried to the children, who were now far ahead of her.

Annie turned and recognized the creature's plight. She muddled through the loose, wet ground and grabbed Mugwig's arms. Then, with a yank, she lifted her out of the sticky mud. The girl set Mugwig on a stump to brush off the grime.

"Maybe I should carry you for a while," suggested Annie. "At least until we get back to more stable ground."

Mugwig agreed and finished wiping the mud off with a few large waxy leaves. Then, Annie hoisted her onto her back, where she sat atop the pack with her tiny legs dangling at either side of the girl's neck.

When the two caught up to the rest of the party, they found that Ben and Juniper had come to a stop.

"Are we there already?" Annie asked as she approached them.

"Nearly," said Juniper, pointing ahead. "I can see

a hut just through the trees. That must be where the Carpenter lives."

"That's wonderful," Annie said eagerly, trying to get a view of it herself. "But why have we stopped?"

As the girl came closer, she saw the reason: a large but quiet river cut across the path in front of them. The river extended indefinitely in either direction and the girl could not see a clear way across. Then Annie noticed that Ben was shaking again.

"Are you okay, Ben?" She asked as she followed his gaze to the water.

Ben couldn't say a word. The boy pointed at the brownish, slow-flowing stream. There, underneath the surface, were hundreds of slimy, scaly snakes, writhing their thick, striped bodies. Slowly Ben began to back away and Annie wondered how they would find their way across the dangerous river.

CHAPTER EIGHT
The Perils of Fording a Snake-Infested River

Ben stood at a safe distance from the snake-infested river, paralyzed by his lifelong fear of the slithering creatures, while Annie and Juniper searched for a way across. The river was not particularly wide, but the shore on the other side was too far for the travelers to make it in a single jump.

Lady Juniper suggested that she and Annie begin walking up and down the stream in opposite directions to see if there was a way across. Mugwig climbed down from the girl's shoulders to wait with Ben, who sat trembling on a log, while the others began their survey of the river bank.

It was not long before Lady Juniper called out to the children above the low rush of the river: "Here, children! I think I've found a way to ford the river!"

Annie ran back toward the woman's voice, stopping to collect Ben and Mugwig from the path on the way. Juniper continued to call out until the children and Mugwig arrived, and Kiwi let out a shrill yelp of delight when he saw them.

Lady Juniper dragged a few fallen palmetto fronds to reveal a large, rotting oak that stretched across the river. The log was thick but saturated with holes from weather and termites.

Ben studied the log, then looked beneath it at the slithering stream. "You want us to cross *that?*" He inhaled heavily then exhaled a shaky, nervous breath.

"It looks to be the only way across," said Lady Juniper, pointing further up the stream. They could see that it stretched for a significant distance with no apparent alternatives or bridges. "I shall go first to make sure it's safe."

With that, the lady gathered the edges of her skirt in one hand and made sure that Kiwi was clinging tightly to her shoulder. Then she took a large step onto the big, round stump. She walked slowly and softly but was able to cross the makeshift bridge with little incident.

Once on the other side, Juniper turned, smiled, and waved at the children to follow her lead.

Ben motioned for Annie to go first, so she followed in Juniper's footsteps while Mugwig held her hand and followed closely behind. The girl kept her eyes on her feet to avoid stepping into any of the large cavities in the rotting wood. She and Mugwig had to sidestep a few of the larger pits, but when they finally looked up Annie realized they had made it safely across the river.

That only left Ben standing on the other side of the stream. The boy crept to the edge of the river and examined the old tree trunk more closely. He still doubted the integrity of the bridge despite watching his friends and companions cross without any trouble.

"Come on, Ben," shouted Annie across the sounds of slithering and splashing. "It's safe! Don't worry. We all made it across and you will, too!"

The boy gulped then stepped up onto the log. He tried not to look down, but his gaze fell immediately to the serpents below him. He was starting to feel queasy and closed his eyes with a few deep breaths.

"You're going to be alright, Ben," Annie hollered.

Ben opened his eyes and shimmied forward on the log. It was small, slow progress as the boy continued to interrupt his short steps with brief moments of deep breathing. At one point, Ben took a larger step to over-shoot a hole in the log. When he placed his foot down, the rotten bark gave way.

Crunch!

Ben tripped forward onto the unstable log. With his heart racing, the boy landed on his hands and knees and grasped the log tightly. Ben's breathing was quick now. He gave another look over the edge of the log.

"Almost there, Benjamin," said Lady Juniper with beckoning arms.

Ben decided to remain in a crouched position and inch his way to the end of the log. It took some time, but eventually, the boy arrived on the other side. An-nie, Juniper, and Mugwig rejoiced and encouraged the boy, whose skin was pale and covered in beads of sweat.

With a few minutes of regular breathing, Ben's color returned and he nearly forgot about the harrowing ex-perience. When he was ready, the group navigated back down the stream to the path where they had first seen the Carpenter's hut.

The structure was small—a shack constructed of var-ious patches of wood and bark that were added period-ically to the facade over a long stretch of time. The hut was surrounded by several large oak trees with branches bending low to the ground like twisted tentacles. Spanish moss and vines of kudzu engulfed the little house so that the group might have assumed it was uninhabited if not for a cloud of wispy smoke emanating from a stone chimney.

Lady Juniper led the others up the path and on to the front porch of the little house where she rapped confidently on the wooden front door.

A gravelly voice from inside shouted: "Go away!"

Annie and Ben looked at Juniper to see what she would do next. The woman waited a moment, then knocked again, louder this time.

"I said go away!"

Juniper sighed, then shouted back through the door: "We're not here to hurt you; we need your help!"

"No help here," said the deep voice. "Go. Away!"

Annie, frustrated at the idea that their journey might end in failure, replied through the door, "Please! It's about our friends. We need your help. We need to find a Carpenter!"

This time there was no response from the voice in the house. The children pressed their ears to the door and heard a shifting of weight on the wood. The creaking of floorboards grew louder as the house's occupant approached the door.

When it opened, the party was greeted by a wrinkly man with a long, white beard. He attempted to widen his droopy eyes to inspect the children but, failing to recognize them, asked in a labored voice, "Who told you a Carpenter lives here?"

"Lady Juniper led us here," said Ben, gesturing to their guide.

The old man turned his attention to Juniper but did not recognize her either. He said nothing as he scrunched his face and turned back to the children and their tiny, reptilian companions.

"Well," said Annie. "Are you a Carpenter or aren't you?"

The man's miserly expression softened into a half-smile, then he replied, "I *was* a Carpenter. But that was many lifetimes ago." He lowered his head as if lost in a fond memory.

"Then perhaps you can help us," the girl continued. "You see, our friends are trapped outside this world and we need to open a new way for them to return—a new Gate."

At this, the man became somber again and breathed heavily out of his hairy nostrils.

"Las Puertas," the man muttered to himself. "Then all of our work has finally been laid to rest—and nearly all of us, too. Of what worth was our craft? Futility and toil—all of it."

The travelers exchanged confused glances.

Then Juniper spoke to the old man: "Your work was of great importance—and still is. You must know that."

The old man gave a small nod as he thought about the lady's words.

"But the question still stands," continued Juniper. "Can you help us? Can you craft a new Gate so we might reunite these lost children with their friends and family?"

Stroking his beard, the ancient man considered the question thoroughly. He did not speak for quite some time, which made the travelers uneasy. But then, finally, the man responded in his drawn-out, gravelly voice.

"It is possible to craft a new Gate," said the Carpenter. "*If* we can acquire the proper materials, it is possible. But they are rarities and spread throughout the land, and it would take some time to build even the simplest of portals."

The children's faces lit up at the possibility of saving their friends. Ben gave Annie a relieved hug.

"Where do we start?" Annie asked.

"Come inside," said the Carpenter, "and I will tell you all you need to know about the arduous and dangerous quest ahead of you."

With that, the children, Juniper, Mugwig, and Kiwi filed into the old man's tiny house to learn how they might reunite with their friends and come one step closer to saving the Kingdom.

CHAPTER NINE
Jesse the Forgetful

Old Jesse had retired from his job at the bank just a couple weeks prior, as he was no longer able to keep up with the demands of the workplace. His delusions began to alarm his employers so they suggested he take his leave. Oliver never saw his grandfather worried about this, though, which put the boy at ease.

Though his loss of employment meant that Jesse was around the house more, Oliver had never thought to ask him about the magical Kingdom before. The boy wasn't sure the man would believe him even if he told him. But now there was little doubt in Oliver's mind of his grandpa's awareness of the Kingdom—the man had married a princess, after all.

Oliver repeated his question while he sat with Ellie and Jasmine in the living room: "Do you know about the Kingdom?" The boy knew the answer but needed to hear Jesse say it.

"The Kingdom," the man said slowly. "Hmm."

The man stared into his half-empty cup of tea and

swirled it around while Jasmine and the two children waited for him to continue. After a few seconds, the man looked back up at his guests and smiled.

"Oliver!" He said jovially. "There you are!"

The boy's spirits drooped and he sighed.

He's already forgotten the question. This could be more challenging than we thought.

"And who's this new friend of yours?" Grandpa Jesse asked.

"I'm Jasmine," she said. "Remember, we met in the hall a few minutes ago?"

Jesse shook his head: "I'm terribly sorry, dear. My mind isn't what it used to be; you'll have to forgive me."

Jasmine nodded and smiled sympathetically to the old man.

"Well," said Jesse. "Shall I fix us up some tea?"

The guests exhaled deeply.

Then Oliver replied: "No thank you, Grandpa. I think we've had enough; we're just going to step outside for a little bit for some fresh air."

"Don't stay out too long," replied Grandpa Jesse.

"I won't, Grandpa," said Oliver. The boy gave his grandfather a hug and the pair said their goodbyes, then Jesse ushered the three back through the front door.

When the door closed, the children and Jasmine sat on the front steps of the porch, feeling utterly defeated and hopeless.

"Why did your grandfather keep repeating himself?" Ellie asked.

"He's getting old," said Oliver. "He has trouble remembering things, so he sometimes forgets if he's been talking to you for a while."

"I see," Ellie replied. "How will we be able to find out if he knows a way into the Kingdom if he can't even answer the simplest questions?"

"We have to keep trying," said Jasmine. "He knows about the Kingdom—I'm certain. We just have to help him remember."

Oliver was silent.

"How are we s'posed to do that?" Ellie inquired.

The young woman considered the question carefully, for it was one she was already wondering herself.

"I don't know exactly," replied Jasmine. "But I've read that memories can often have triggers."

"Triggers?" Oliver perked up.

"Yes," said Jasmine. "Something that reminds you of something else—like a smell or a sound or something that you can touch. Maybe there's some object that can help remind him of Coral or the Kingdom."

The boy thought about Jasmine's idea, then spoke: "I think I've got an idea."

"What is it?" Ellie asked.

"Something that we found in my grandfather's garage," replied Oliver. "The enchanted map!"

"You mean the one that first led us to that old house?" Ellie wondered.

"That's the one."

"What ever happened to it?"

"I've still got it," answered the boy, already standing up. "It's in a box of things in my room."

"It's worth a try," said Jasmine.

With the woman's encouragement, they promptly re-entered the house. They followed Oliver down the hall to his bedroom, where the boy quickly crouched on his hands and knees and felt underneath the bed. He withdrew a small wooden box—about the size of a shoebox—and set it on the covers of his bed.

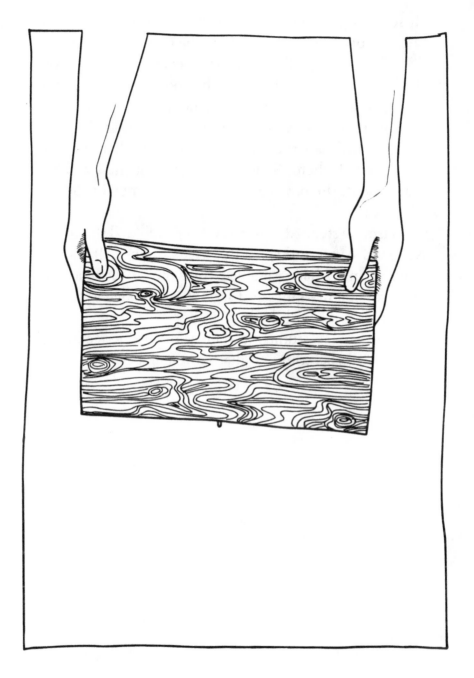

IT SEEMED TO BE FASHIONED OF
THIN, LIGHT PIECES OF PINE.

It seemed to be fashioned of thin, light pieces of pine and featured a tiny clasp, which the boy promptly lifted.

The box was filled with trinkets and objects Oliver had collected throughout his childhood: olive-green toy soldiers, a pair of marbles, birthday cards, and an assortment of tickets and newspaper clippings. But the boy shuffled past these items to find one that was hidden beneath them. When his fingers felt the wrinkled parchment, the boy tugged it free and slipped it out of the box.

Jasmine stepped closer as Oliver unfolded the thick, yellowed paper and spread it across the bed. It was an ancient map that resembled the state of Florida, but with foreign markings and scribbles sprinkled across it.

"This is it," said the boy.

The woman studied it, then said, "It's perfect. Let's hope this helps your grandfather remember."

CHAPTER TEN
The Old Map

Still in the boy's small bedroom, the group gathered around the old map of the Kingdom. The map had the signs of age and wear—wrinkles and slight rips at the edges—but otherwise seemed well-preserved.

Remembering their previous adventures, Ellie made a suggestion: "What if we just ask the map to show us another Gate?"

"What do you mean?" Jasmine asked, oblivious to the map's enchantments.

"The map is magic," the girl replied. "It can show you how to get to wherever you're going."

"So you just think of somewhere you want to go and it reveals the way—like some sort of compass?" Jasmine was intrigued.

"More like little markings," said Ellie. "They show up when you shine a light on it."

"Then," said Jasmine, "I guess it's worth a try."

Oliver agreed and said aloud: "Show us a Gate to return to the Kingdom."

When he finished saying this, he quickly moved closer to the window to allow the sunlight to illuminate the map. The three waited for the route markings to appear.

When several moments passed by with no sign of the markings, Ellie huffed and said: "That's just great! It's true then—there's no more Gates. And we'll never get Ben or Annie back now!"

"It's okay, Ellie," Oliver consoled her. "Maybe it's just not working properly today. Remember what Lady Juniper told us—*magic is unpredictable.*"

"Perhaps you aren't being specific enough," suggested Jasmine as consolation.

But Ellie wasn't satisfied. "If there was another Gate," she said, "it would show up on the map."

The boy knew she was right, but didn't want to admit that there might not be a way back into the Kingdom.

Before he could say anything back to her, though, Jasmine chimed in: "How about we stick to our plan and see if this helps your grandfather remember something?"

Oliver and Ellie agreed and the three returned to the living room, where they found Grandpa Jesse asleep in a reclining chair. The boy approached his grandfather and gently tapped on his arm to wake him up. The old man stirred and blinked his eyes a few times.

"Not now, Coral," said Jesse as his eyes closed again. "It's been the most wonderful dream."

"Grandpa," replied Oliver, shaking Jesse's arm again. "It's me—Oliver."

"Coral, dear, have you come home at last?"

Oliver sighed then put his hands on the old man's smooth face: "Grandpa Jesse! Wake up! It's your grandson Oliver."

At this, the man's eyes finally opened and met Oliver's. He smiled softly.

"Oliver! There you are," said Jesse. "Are these your friends?"

"Yes, Grandpa," replied Oliver. "You've met them—this is Ellie and that's Jasmine."

The two waved and smiled at Jesse, which he reciprocated with a nod and a grin of his own.

"We've got to ask you about something," said Oliver. Jasmine handed Oliver the old map which he began to unfold in front of his grandfather. "It's about Grandma Coral—I think this map once belonged to her. Do you recognize it?"

Oliver set the map on a small table and the old man leaned forward in his chair to get a better look.

"Yes," he said after a while. "I know this map."

"You do?" Oliver inquired hopefully.

The old man nodded: "It was ours."

"You and Coral?"

Jesse nodded again.

"Do you remember what the map is for?" Oliver asked, now hovering at his grandfather's side. "Do you remember *where* this map leads?"

"Hmm," the old man thought over the question and ran his fingers along the old parchment. He was entranced by the markings that formed the outline of a shape resembling the State of Florida. "This isn't Florida," he said, "is it?"

"Not exactly," replied the boy. "Look closer. You'll remember."

Jesse continued to study the map and its hand-drawn details. He leaned closer and caught a whiff of the map's scent—like an old book mixed with hints of salt and dirt.

Then old Jesse's eyes lit up.

"Do you remember something?" Oliver turned to look at Ellie and Jasmine with anticipation.

"I do now," said Jesse.

"What do you remember?" His grandson asked softly.

"Me and Coral," Grandpa Jesse answered. "This map was ours. It guided many of our adventures by land and by sea." The man paused and smiled to himself.

"Where did these adventures take place?" Oliver asked, sensing they were close to a breakthrough.

"All throughout the land," Jesse continued. "All throughout the Kingdom."

Oliver, Ellie, and Jasmine could hardly contain their eagerness to hear more. Jasmine nudged Oliver to keep asking questions.

"So you've been there," reiterated Oliver. "To the Kingdom, I mean?"

Grandpa Jesse nodded slowly.

"And how did you get there and back again?"

Jesse ran his fingers along the edge of the coastline and shook his head: "Coral never came back again."

His mind is slipping again! Oliver thought.

"Never came back again," repeated Jesse, this time in a quieter tone.

"But how did you pass between the worlds?" The boy was growing impatient in contending with his grandfather's memory loss.

Jesse blinked and finally looked up from the map. With a vacant smile, he asked, "Shall I fix us some tea?"

Oliver and his friends sighed collectively and the boy folded up the map.

"No, thank you, Grandpa," he said. "Thanks for

your help, though."

"Anytime, my boy."

With that, the three travelers left the house to get some fresh air and think over what plan of action they might take next.

CHAPTER ELEVEN
The Carpenter

The old Carpenter's tiny shack had barely enough room for the travelers to enter, and featured only a single chair, so most of the guests sat on the creaky floorboards around it. The Carpenter offered the chair—a surprisingly ornate piece in contrast to the sparse and utilitarian cabin—to Lady Juniper, who thanked him and obliged while the bearded man stood with the help of a simple walking stick.

"Now," began the Carpenter. "I must warn you that the construction of a new Gate is something that can take quite some time and considerable effort. Besides the actual woodworking, it requires a special elixir to activate the magic to pass between worlds. The other Carpenters and I were the keepers of this recipe, as it pertained to our secretive craft. But now I am the only one left of our kind and have become the sole possessor of the magic formula."

"Did you and the other Carpenters build all of the Gates?" Annie was curious.

412

"Not all," replied the man. "But many, scattered throughout the land. Some were merely doorways built around thin places—pockets where the fabric between worlds was already more malleable. Others needed a special dose of magic to activate their potential." The man fingered the end of his long beard as he gazed at the floor.

"Please, sir," said Ben. "Can you help us build another one?"

"It has been some time since I have utilized my abilities," said the old man. "And I'm afraid many of my skills as a craftsman have waned over the years. But yes, I believe that if I were given the proper materials, I could bring to life another Gate."

"Wonderful," the boy replied. "What do we need?"

The Carpenter stroked his beard again as if trying to remember something: "I'm afraid I can't recall the specific ingredients."

The children's hearts sank as they exchanged a worried glance. Before Annie could express her frustration, the Carpenter turned away and spoke again.

"But," the man continued as he hobbled toward a series of shelves on a far wall, "thankfully I am a bit of a hoarder and have kept the majority of recipes from throughout my unnaturally long life."

As they watched him shuffle through loose, crunchy pieces of paper on the shelf, Ben and Annie each gave a sigh of relief. Ben took a deep breath and thought again of his little sister, separated from him forever unless they could succeed in opening a new Gate. Lady Juniper stroked Kiwi, who sat across her lap in the chair, while Mugwig waited patiently.

"Ah," said the Carpenter finally, holding out a tiny fragment of paper. "Here it is."

The man quickly scanned the list of ingredients, muttering under his breath at each one. He then gave the sheet a second look as he drew his finger along a higher shelf that contained an assortment of small bottles of glass and stone. Most had tiny, handwritten paper labels wrapped around them and almost all were faded beyond deciphering. When he finished his quick inventory, the Carpenter brought the list over to the travelers.

"You're in luck," he said. "I already have many of the ingredients in my collection."

Lady Juniper, who had listened quietly to the conversation, now spoke: "And what ingredients are still needed?"

The old man squinted at the recipe: "It appears as if there are only three items needed—besides the wood for building the door and frame. The first ingredient is hair from the Regal Stag who roams and reigns over the jungles—three hairs, to be exact. The second is a leaf from the Great Willow Tree, which has long been a symbol of our Kingdom. And the final ingredient..." Here the man paused and exhaled deeply.

"What's the final ingredient?" Annie inquired.

"I'm afraid it may be more difficult," replied the Carpenter. "The third ingredient is a bit ambiguous. It requires something special—a bit of another Gate."

"But," the girl responded, "how are we to find a piece of another Gate when there aren't any Gates left?"

The old man thought for a moment and scratched his head: "That is an excellent question."

Then Lady Juniper interjected, "Perhaps we could use the remains of another Gate. One that's been destroyed might still have pieces left, right?"

"Yes, yes," said the Carpenter, waving his pointer

finger toward the old lady. "Children: how came you to be in our Kingdom?"

"The Gate in the old banyan tree," Annie answered. "But we won't be able to return to it. Prince Florian has sent soldiers to keep watch over the place in case we return."

"That's a shame," the old man said. "For it may be our only chance."

"Not quite," Ben replied, having a sudden thought.

"Whatever do you mean?" The Carpenter bent toward the little boy.

"My other friends and I," Ben began. "We first came into this world through another Gate—a door in an old house. On this side of the door, we found ourselves deep inside a dark cave."

"And what has become of this door?" The old man asked.

"While we made our escape, Florian set it on fire behind us. I've no doubt its ashes are still on the floor of the cave."

The old man excitedly waddled to another shelf and grabbed a small drawstring pouch. He handed the leather pouch to Ben, saying, "Perfect. Fill this bag with the ashes of that door—that should do the trick!"

The boy took the bag in his hands and looked back at the man: "Is that it?"

"Yes, my boy," replied the Carpenter. "Once you have the rest of these ingredients, return to me here and we shall complete the enchantment and open a new portal back to your world. Now, do you remember the three ingredients?"

Annie looked at Ben, who nodded and replied, "I think so: three hairs from the Regal Stag, a leaf from

THE CARPENTER

the Great Willow Tree, and one bag full of ashes from the old Gate in the cave."

"That's right," said the man through a nearly-toothless smile as he handed her a small cork-topped glass vial to contain the three hairs. "Do not forget."

At this, the guests rose and thanked the old man for his hospitality and helpfulness. When they were again outside, Juniper turned to the children and Mugwig as they walked down the path toward the river.

"I'm afraid it is almost time for us to part ways again," she said softly.

"But why?" Ben asked. "Aren't you going to help us find the ingredients for the magic elixir?"

"I wish I could," Juniper continued. "But it is not safe. Florian has already tried to stop me once. I fear that it would put you in too great a danger if I stay with you. And I must find out what has become of our dear friend Marco."

Annie lowered her head and placed her hand over her chest, feeling Marco's medallion around her neck. It seemed strange to her that no one—not even Juniper—knew where he was.

Neither of the children spoke, so Juniper continued, "Besides, you will have Mugwig as a guide. She seems to know her way around the jungle quite well. Don't you?"

At this, the creature smiled proudly and replied, "Yes, quite well. Mugwig knows the way to the Willow and many other paths. And I am a Princess, as well, which is also significant."

Though sad to say goodbye to Juniper, the children both laughed at Mugwig's comment.

"But come now," said Lady Juniper. "I will walk with you back across the river and then we shall say our goodbyes."

This they did and, after another series of slow crawls across the fallen log, the party was far from the snake-infested river and the old Carpenter's shack. Ben and Annie exchanged hugs with Lady Juniper and watched as the old woman disappeared with haste down a path into the jungle.

CHAPTER TWELVE
The Regal Stag

Annie, Ben, and Mugwig trudged through the moist, muddy marshland and winding forest paths. The children took turns carrying their little green friend at points where the mud was particularly thick and made quick progress back to more solid ground.

"What was the first ingredient on the old Carpenter's list?" Annie asked Ben as they wiped the grime from their shoes.

"Three hairs from the Regal Stag," the boy answered.

"How are we supposed to find a single stag out here in the massive jungle?" The girl's question was legitimate. After all, they had traveled throughout the woods for many days and the girl had yet to see such a creature.

"I'm not sure," replied Ben. "The Carpenter said that the Stag roams throughout the jungle, so perhaps he will find us?"

As they resumed their walk down the path, Mugwig interjected, "Mugwig has seen this special deer."

"You've seen the Regal Stag before?" Annie inquired,

crouching to Mugwig's level.

"Yes," said Mugwig. "Many times."

"Where is it?" Ben asked. "How do we find it?"

"The moonlight," said the creature, pointing at the cloudy, late afternoon sky.

The children both looked up.

"You mean that the Stag only comes out at night?" Annie asked.

"That's right. Only in the moonlight."

The girl continued, "And do you know what part of the jungle it appears in?"

"Anywhere," Mugwig replied. "I have seen the great deer appear in many places near this one. He roams free and wild."

Ben thought for a moment. "Well, I suppose we're going to need to wait until nightfall to find the first ingredient, then. There's only a few more hours to go. And besides, that will give us some time to chart our course to find the other two ingredients."

The rest of the party agreed and the three travelers settled into a small clearing to wait for the sun to set. As the golden hour came and went, the forest grew dark and eerie. The children started a small fire with sticks and kindling from their packs. While they ate roasted fruit from a nearby grove, Ben described the cave to Mugwig, who was able to assure the children that she could navigate to its location.

"The Great Willow is much closer to us, though," said Mugwig. "Perhaps we would do best to go there before we venture to your cave?"

"If you say so," replied the boy.

Annie agreed, then added, "I'm worried that this journey may take too long."

"What do you mean?" Ben asked. "There doesn't

seem to be any other way to open another Gate."

"I know," nodded the girl. "It's just that we're putting ourselves at risk. The more time we take to find these ingredients, the more time Prince Florian has to find us."

"You're right," replied Ben. "If he finds us then we don't stand a chance of ever seeing Ellie or Oliver again." The boy lowered his head somberly. "But I can't think of another way. Can you?"

The girl gazed into the flames, which reminded her of the previous night at the fiery clearing of the Banyan Gate.

"Byron," she muttered softly.

"What?" Ben asked, unable to hear what she said.

"Byron," Annie said again, louder. "Byron the Bunglejumper. We're not far from the place where we first met him—these are his woods. He could help us. Perhaps he could fly us above the treetops—we'd make much faster progress."

"But he was blinded after what happened the other night," replied Ben. "How could he fly us if he can't see?"

The girl turned back to the fire. "You're right," she said. "He can't see anymore. But maybe we can help him—you know, to navigate for him."

Ben thought over his friend's suggestion carefully. He had some doubts that such a plan would work. But before he could answer back, he heard the snapping of a twig just beyond the clearing.

All three travelers quickly turned toward the noise.

"What was that?" Ben asked.

Neither of his companions answered as they tried to discern the shape that stood obscured by the trees and bramble. Then they heard the crunching of dried leaves as the creature moved closer and stepped into the moonlight.

It was the Regal Stag. He was an elegant beast with an enormous set of antlers and a dappled brown coat. The Stag was larger than any other deer the children had seen before, and its gaze seemed to pierce into their very souls.

Ben and Annie felt drawn to the creature, unable to look away—and if they had been able, they might have noticed that the blazing of their fire seemed now as frozen tongues, glowing but suspended and still. The beast stood in very much the same way, unflinching and unblinking, a solemn wanderer of the night.

When the children and Mugwig finally became aware that this was the creature they sought, Annie whispered, "Three hairs!"

Ben nodded and motioned for Annie to move in the opposite direction, and the two slowly crept toward the Regal Stag from two sides. Sensing this as an attempted capture, the beast suddenly twitched its neck toward Annie and then back at Ben. The children now ran toward the deer to try and grab it, but Ben slipped and tripped on a large leaf, tumbling on top of Annie in a heap. The Stag evaded them and disappeared back into the jungle.

Annie helped the boy up as they wiped clumps of dirt from their legs and clothes. Ben stared off through the woods but could no longer see any sign of the beast.

Mugwig hobbled over to join them and inspected the ground: "The trail ends here."

The children verified that this was, in fact, true; the large deer's trail terminated at the edge of the trees, with no other scuffs or imprints of hooves to follow it.

"Well that's just great," said Annie sarcastically. "All

THE REGAL STAG WAS LARGER THAN ANY
OTHER DEER THE CHILDREN HAD SEEN BEFORE,
AND ITS GAZE SEEMED TO PIERCE
INTO THEIR VERY SOULS.

that waiting for nothing!"

"We'll try again," Ben assured her. "I think we just scared it away. Next time, we'll have to be quieter."

"What next?" Mugwig asked the children.

Ben turned to Annie: "What do you say we give your plan a shot?"

The girl smiled and nodded. Then the children cupped their hands around their mouths and began to shout:

"Byron! Byron the Bunglejumper! Can you hear us? Byron!"

CHAPTER THIRTEEN
Byron the Blind

The jungle was strangely quiet—except for the inter-mittent yells of Annie, Ben, and Mugwig. When they finally stopped calling for Byron, they waited in silence. Only the chirps of crickets and other insects filled the void. Then, they heard the tell-tale *whooshing* of large wings flying overhead.

"Byron?" Annie yelled up into the sky.

Instead of a reply, the children heard the sound of something large crashing into the upper leaves of a tree, followed by a *crack!* Several large branches fell to the ground across the clearing, followed by a massive furry being.

"Ouch," whispered Ben, running toward the crea-ture with Annie at his side. "Are you okay?"

"I'm fine," replied the beast. It was Byron. "Just a little shaken up is all. Who's there?"

"Annie and Ben," replied the girl. "Your friends. And another one of our friends called Mugwig."

The tiny Mugwig inched forward, intimidated by

Byron's largesse. "Hello," she said quickly and then took a step back to safety. Then Mugwig whispered to the children: "What is that thing?"

"He's a bunglejumper," said Ben. "A fascinating but kindly beast."

The creature lifted himself from the ground, brushing twigs from his forelegs. At his full height, Byron was nearly three times as tall as the children. He was an enormous winged lion with a striped, iridescent coat and a mane of feathers that encircled his head. As the children approached, they noticed that Byron's eyes were covered with mud and leaves.

"Oh my," said Annie. "What's that on your face?"

"I guess you could call it a mask," Byron replied, his face downcast and angled slightly away from the girl.

"What's it for?" Ben wondered.

"It's a mask to hide my hideous face," the beast answered, lowering his head. "To hide what that horrible raven did to me."

Annie approached the creature and rested a hand compassionately on his fur.

"Does it hurt?" She asked somberly.

"The pain's subsided a bit," he replied. "But I can't bear the thought of the creatures of the jungle cowering away at the sight of me. Once, I was among the most beautiful beasts of these forests and all the kindly animals would bask in my presence. Now they all run when they see my wounds."

"That's horrible," Annie acknowledged. "But this dirt you've stuck to your face is sure to cause an infection if you don't clean it properly. Perhaps we can fashion you a more sanitary covering?"

"I'd be quite grateful," Byron said with a nod.

At this, Byron crouched lower and allowed the two

children to begin scraping off the foliage and daub that covered the scars on his eyes. The bunglejumper winced as their hands grazed his day-old wounds, and when they had removed the majority of the dirt from his face, Annie poured some drinking water over the place to flush it clean. Then she reached into her pack and withdrew a long blanket, which she tore into strips. Stringing a few together, she then tied this around the beast's head like a bandage, obscuring his gruesome wounds.

"There," Annie said when she had finished. "Better?"

"Well," said Byron. "I can't exactly see if it *looks* better. But it certainly *feels* better to be clean. Now, what was the reason for your calling on me?"

The two children took turns explaining their quest—how the Banyan Gate had been destroyed and trapped their friends outside the Kingdom, and how they now had to collect the three ingredients for the Carpenter to construct a new portal between the worlds.

"We were hoping you could fly us to the Great Willow," said Annie.

"Dear sweet child," said Byron. "Did you not see what happens when I try to fly without my eyesight? With my vision impaired, I don't think I can really fly anywhere anymore—not safely, at least. The only way I got here at all was because I followed your cries."

Ben brought forth Annie's earlier idea: "Perhaps you could fly and we could give you directions?"

"We can be your eyes," added Annie confidently.

The bunglejumper considered their suggestion carefully. "If you're willing to take the risk of a bumpy landing," he said, "I'm willing to try my best to help you. It's the least I can do for my dear friends."

The children hugged the beast and thanked him for

his willingness. Even Mugwig now embraced the creature, realizing that, despite his large and fearsome appearance, Byron was a gentle friend.

"Well, we shouldn't waste any more time," said Byron, crouching lower. "Get on my back and we'll make our way to the Willow right away."

All three members of the party climbed up onto Byron's back, with Mugwig needing a little extra help from Ben and Annie. When they were all situated behind the beast's large, feathered head, the children held tightly to his fur and watched in awe as Byron began to flap his majestic wings. The flapping grew faster, kicking up wind and dust that swept around them until finally, they were levitating up through the canopy toward the night sky.

Stars twinkled in the deep blue firmament and Annie could see distant lights along the coast far away—cities and settlements. *And perhaps the royal palace where Prince Florian waits for us to be found?*

"Alright, now," said Byron. "I'm counting on you to lead the way."

The children turned to Mugwig, who was the expert on navigating the vast jungles in this part of the Kingdom. The little creature scanned the horizon with her reptilian eyes and pointed. Annie spoke instructions into Byron's ear and then he quickly careened in the direction Mugwig had indicated. The three passengers grasped Byron's fur and feathers even more firmly to avoid falling to their doom.

The air was cool and refreshing above the trees. For a moment, the children forgot about their quest and closed their eyes as the wind swept around them and whipped through Annie's long, dark hair.

Mugwig interrupted the peaceful moment with an

aggressive nudging to Annie's arm. Then she pointed down toward the stretch of jungle ahead of them. It was difficult to see in the dark from so far away, but Annie noted that the patch of trees terminated in a large, circular clearing. At the very center was what appeared to be a massive weeping willow tree.

The Great Willow, thought Annie. She then tapped softly on Byron's back to signal that they were close and gave him instructions as they descended abruptly toward the tree.

With a few sharp jolts, Byron neared the ground.

"Careful!" Ben shouted, his knuckles turning whiter as he tightened his grip.

Finally, the blind bunglejumper's paws met the moist floor of the clearing—but he was moving too fast! Byron stumbled over his own legs and fell into a heap. As this happened, all three of the travelers on his back flew off and landed in a patch of tall, soft grass.

"Everyone alright?" Byron said, unable to see where his passengers had landed.

Ben noted that his friends were moving about and didn't seem to be too scratched up, so he replied: "Yes. We're fine. We'll have to work on the landings a bit, though, for next time."

Annie and Mugwig giggled as they finished wiping bits of grass from their clothes. Byron smiled, too, and was relieved to know that his friends were unharmed. Then the party turned their attention to the enormous tree in the middle of the clearing:

The Great Willow Tree.

CHAPTER FOURTEEN
Memorabilia

As night fell on Oliver's neighborhood, he and his friends returned home to his grandfather's house. Jesse had prepared a simple but hearty supper for his guests, which they received gratefully. The dinner table was relatively quiet as they consumed their meals, but then Ellie spoke up.

"Mr. Jesse," she began, her mouth full of mashed potatoes. "How did you and Coral first meet?"

The old, beardless man scraped his fork across his plate, caught off guard, and looked up at the little girl. "It seems we've known each other forever," Jesse answered. "You know, I can't exactly recall the moment we met." He trailed off, returning his gaze to the half-eaten filet in front of him.

"You must remember *something* more about her," Oliver urged.

"About who?" Jesse asked his grandson.

"Coral," said Oliver, slightly exasperated. "Grandma Coral—what else do you remember about her?"

"I always loved her smile," replied Jesse. "You know, *your* smile reminds me so much of hers, Oliver."

At this, the boy grinned at his grandfather, who gently placed his hand on the boy's.

"Your grandmother Coral," Jesse continued. "She was—and still is—the light of my life."

As Grandpa Jesse said this he nodded his head and then resumed his meal. But Oliver had another thought sweep over him.

The light of my life. The light. The boy repeated the words in his head. Then he quickly dug his hand into his pocket.

Jasmine and Ellie watched curiously as Oliver withdrew his closed hand and placed it on the table in front of his grandfather. Then he slowly opened it, revealing the tiny gold ring that the boy had carried with him for some time.

"Do you recognize this at all, Grandpa?" Oliver held the ring closer to the old man so he could get a better view.

Jesse put down his fork and knife and inspected the small piece of jewelry. Inscribed on its surface was the symbol of a lamp emitting beams of light. The ring was worn smooth and clearly quite old.

"Where did you get that?" Grandpa Jesse asked the boy, slowly plucking it from Oliver's hand with his thumb and forefinger. He held it close to his face.

"I found it in an old house over in Flamingo Park," replied Oliver eagerly. "Do you recognize it?"

The man nodded slowly. "Yes," he said. "I do. It's the same ring that I used to marry your grandmother."

It's working! Oliver thought. *The ring is helping him remember.*

Jasmine and Ellie nodded to Oliver, urging him to

continue probing his grandfather for more information.

"And where did you get it?" Oliver asked. "Here in our world—or inside the Kingdom?"

"I found it in the Kingdom," Jesse said, still mesmerized by the ring. "It was part of a great treasure we discovered together; I later kept the ring and saved it for the right moment."

"The right moment to ask Coral to marry you," his grandson restated.

The man affirmed with a nod.

"And then you came back to our world," said Oliver. "Right?"

The man didn't answer, so Oliver continued: "How did you do it? How did you get into the Kingdom and back?"

Grandpa Jesse stopped turning the ring and placed it back in Oliver's hand. The boy waited for the old man to respond, but Jesse promptly resumed eating his dinner, which had now grown cold.

Oliver sighed and tucked the ring back into his pocket while he finished his own lukewarm supper.

We're getting closer, he thought. *We've got to keep trying.*

When they had finished their dinner, Jesse got up from the table and collected all of the plates. He then disappeared into the kitchen.

Oliver leaned over the table toward Jasmine and Ellie: "That almost worked. I think he's still got the memories, but they're tucked away."

His friends nodded, and Jasmine asked, "Is there anything else that might jog his memory? Anything else that might've belonged to your grandmother or your mother?"

Oliver shook his head: "He sold or donated their things when I was really little."

"What about the garage?" Jasmine asked. "You said you found the enchanted map in your grandpa's garage."

"You're right," Oliver said, already scooting his chair away from the table. "I almost forgot about that. Follow me!"

The three issued down the hall and into the garage.

Flipping the garage light on, Oliver led the way to a stack of boxes leaned up against the far wall. The boy pushed a couple aside and found one labeled *Memorabilia*.

"That's the one," said Ellie, remembering the day they found the old map. "The one with all of those papers and pictures of you as a baby."

"I only hope there's something more helpful in here," said Oliver. "Something that will help Grandpa Jesse remember how he traveled between this world and the Kingdom."

The three knelt around the large box while Oliver opened the flaps. They inhaled the smell of dusty papers and old books, which caused Ellie to cough. At the top of the stack was a familiar photograph of Oliver and his mother Vera. The boy picked it up softly and held it in the light.

"She was so kind," said Jasmine.

"What do you mean?" Oliver turned to the young woman sharply: "You knew my mother?"

Jasmine nodded.

"Why didn't you say so sooner?" Oliver was getting worked up. "Wait—do you know what happened to her—to all of them?"

Jasmine inhaled deeply, then replied, "I knew them—I knew Vera *and* Coral. I was just a teenager when I met them for the first time. Juniper introduced us. But I don't know what happened to them—I just know they left."

"Oliver's mother knew Lady Juniper?" Ellie asked.

"Yes," replied Jasmine. "She was part of the Lamp-light Society, too. So was Coral. They were trying to help us overthrow Prince Florian and restore the Triumvirate."

Oliver tried to make sense of all of this new information. Finally, he asked, "So Lady Juniper knew my family. Does that mean she knew I was the—the heir of Mangonia?" He was still unaccustomed to saying it.

"I don't know," said Jasmine. "Juniper's wise—perhaps wise enough even to tell your mother to keep your identity a secret from her. We knew she had a child. I put the pieces together when I met you—I presume Juniper did as well. It's like your grandfather said—you have Coral's smile."

There was silence in the garage for a few moments as the children processed all that Jasmine had shared. Then the woman gestured back to the cardboard box.

"Shall we?"

Oliver and Ellie nodded and leaned back over the box. Shuffling through more old photos and newspaper clippings, the children weren't sure what exactly they were looking for. Oliver read one of the headlines on a fragment of newsprint: *Second child missing, last seen near North Woods.*

"Missing children?" Oliver asked, handing the piece of paper to Jasmine. "Do you know what this is?"

"It was Coral's job," Jasmine began, "to identify and find more of the Gates. She knew the Kingdom better than any of us. I remember she was collecting these old newspapers—anytime there was a mysterious disappearance, Coral would investigate it to see if a portal was involved. They're all gone now, but sometimes they led her to new ways into the Kingdom."

"And the other times?" Ellie wondered.

"The rest of the times, they were more tragic tales," said Jasmine. "The people were *actually* missing—or worse."

As she said this, Oliver removed another faded newspaper clipping with a more recent date printed on it. It read: *West Palm woman missing, presumed drowned.* The boy's eyes drifted to a small black and white picture beneath the headline. It featured a familiar face—Coral.

"Oh," said Jasmine somberly. "Your grandfather must've kept those from after she—after Coral—went missing."

Oliver's breaths were short as he scanned the brief text of the clipping, his mind only allowing him to make sense of small phrases: ...*police searched for fourteen days...*; ...*no body was found...*; ...*survived by husband Jesse...*; ...*one daughter and a son-in-law...*; and ...*one grandchild...*

"I'm sorry, Oliver," Jasmine said, placing a hand on the boy's arm. "We don't have to do this now."

The boy wiped a tear from his cheek. "No," he said softly. "Let's keep looking."

Oliver set the clipping aside and the three continued to rummage through the box. Jasmine lifted out a stack of documents that were tied together with a string, revealing a small, brown book beneath it.

"What's that?" Ellie said, reaching for the book. She handed it carefully to Oliver, who flipped it over and tried to read the faded text on the front cover.

"It looks like a diary," Jasmine said, trying to decipher from the shape and size of the book. "Or a journal—I wonder who it belonged to?"

Oliver flipped the cover open and read the inside label silently. His face lit up and he turned to Ellie and Jasmine.

"This journal," he said eagerly. "It belonged to Grandpa Jesse!"

CHAPTER FIFTEEN
The Great Willow

The massive weeping willow tree looked like a huge, grassy mound in the moonlight—its branches hidden behind thick, draping strands of leaves that stretched to the foggy ground. Mugwig, Annie, and Ben stood and stared in wonder at the size of it.

"I've never seen anything like it in my entire life," said Annie, awestruck.

"Truly," said Ben. "It's beautiful."

Byron ambled slowly behind them, carefully treading across the moist and mossy earth. "Tell me," he began. "What does it look like? I've only ever heard stories and myths, but I have not seen the Great Willow with my own eyes—and perhaps I may never."

Annie stepped back to rest a hand on Byron's thick fur. "Well," she said, "it's incredibly large and tall—it appears to stretch at least twice as tall as the treeline around it."

"Yes," said Ben. "And its branches are like long strings tied with narrow leaves. Listen to the sound as they rustle in the breeze."

Here they were all quiet as a brief gust swept through the clearing. A soft swishing soothed their ears as the children and Mugwig watched the branches meander back and forth lazily in the night. When the strands of leaves again rested and the breeze ceased, Annie continued.

"It's amazing to see it in the moonlight," she said. "There's a certain glow like a halo resting on its top."

The kindly bunglejumper seemed pleased with these descriptions, so he nodded and smiled softly: "Thank you, dear children. Now, what exactly was it that you needed from this great tree?"

"The Carpenter said that we need only one leaf from the Great Willow Tree," said Annie, approaching the tree with confidence. "That should be easy enough."

The travelers followed Annie and pressed on through the fog toward the gargantuan tree. When the hanging branches were in reach, the girl extended her hand to pluck a single, thin leaf from the willow. Before she could reach it, however, something like another gust of wind—stronger than before—whisked the branches away and out of her reach. They fell back into place as she lowered her hand.

Must have been the breeze, Annie thought, and then she stuck out her hand to reach for the leaf again.

Again the branches moved quickly out of the way as if she possessed some reverse-magnetic force that repelled the tree. Scratching her head, she turned to her friends.

"What's wrong?" Ben asked.

"The tree," she said. "There's something strange about it. It won't let me reach for the leaf."

"Won't *let* you?" The boy repeated. "But it's just a

tree. Tree's don't have feelings, Annie."

"Well, there's something wrong with it, then," Annie replied. "How about you take a try?"

The boy nodded in agreement as Annie stepped back. Ben then reached for the branch himself but, to his dismay, found that the leaves scattered away in the same manner as before.

"How odd," he said. "It seems the tree doesn't like me, either."

The children then urged both Mugwig and Byron to try, but neither was able to grab a leaf before the branches swung out of the way. Dumbfounded, the travelers began to grow irritated.

"Perhaps we all try to grab a leaf at the same time," said Annie suddenly. "We can all stand on different sides of the tree and I'll signal when to go."

The others agreed with this plan and scattered around the base of the tree. When they were all in their positions bordering the tree, Annie shouted, "Go!" All four reached out their hands, claws, and paws to grab a willow branch—just one leaf—but, yet again, the strands escaped them.

"That's curious, alright," said Annie. "Mugwig and Byron—do either of you know anything about this tree?"

"Like I said," began Byron, his blindfolded gaze directed slightly away from the girl, "I have only heard stories and legends about this great tree. It has long been a symbol of our Kingdom—since even before the Triumvirate was instated."

"And there is little more that I know," said Mugwig, brushing a swath of her gnarly hair out of her face with her pointy greenish fingers. "Except that it is said the Great Willow is actually the fruit of three seeds grown together—but like the bunglejumper said, this was long before our time."

"Three seeds, you say?" Ben said. "Well, that would explain its massive size, but not the curious nature of its evasive branches."

"I suppose we'll have to wait," suggested Annie reaching for a branch unsuccessfully once more, "until another idea comes to us."

The group contemplated the matter for several minutes, some pacing back and forth. Then, when no one suggested any viable ideas, Ben sat down with a huff and crossed his arms, his back to the tree. "Well, what do we do now?"

Annie joined him on the grass and set a hand on his shoulder: "We'll find a way. We just have to be patient."

"But what about Ellie and Oliver?" Ben said, beginning to get worked up. "If we can't get one of these leaves, then the Carpenter can't build the Gate. And if he can't build the Gate, then we will never see them again."

At this, the boy burst into tears. Annie and Mugwig comforted the boy, but he continued to cry. As she slowly patted the boy's shoulder, Annie looked back at the Great Willow. She thought she saw some of its branches drift toward them and then float back.

The wind again, she thought as she turned back to the boy.

"What will my little sister do without me?" Ben continued. "I was supposed to take care of her—I *always* take care of her."

As Ben's tears began to flow even more, Annie now noticed that the tree was indeed moving on its own. But instead of whipping its branches away from them, she now saw that its branches were extending *toward* them.

"Look," she said, pointing at the branch.

For a moment, Ben stopped weeping. When he did this, the branch flopped back down like normal. Annie furrowed her brow as she wondered what was happening.

"What is it?" Ben said.

"I'm not quite sure," replied Annie. Then she had an idea: "Keep crying!"

Ben was confused, but this just made him cry even more. As Ben wiped flowing snot and moisture from his face, Annie crept toward the tree again. Its branches reached toward her. She slowly extended her hand so as not to frighten the tree with any sudden movement. Annie expected the tree to recoil as it had before but, to her surprise, the strand of leaves only came closer to her hand. Ben continued to weep.

Finally, Annie's fingers met a single leaf and she tugged lightly. The long, narrow leaf came loose from the tree with a faint *snap*.

Ben looked up through his foggy vision and, wiping the tears once more, saw what Annie held in her hand: the leaf from the Great Willow Tree.

"You've done it!" He exclaimed as he leaped to his feet and hugged the girl. "But how? How did you know how to get the leaf?"

"Once you started crying," Annie began, "that gave me the answer. The tears seemed to calm the tree—a sort of invitation to let its guard down. And then I remembered something."

"What's that?" Byron asked, standing behind them.

"This is a *weeping* willow tree," said Annie. "So it must be fond of tears and crying."

"That's brilliant," replied Ben. "Thank you, Annie. You've helped us get one step closer to a reunion with my little sister and Oliver!"

The entire party rejoiced and celebrated the acquisition of their first of the three ingredients for the Carpenter's magic recipe. Then, when they had tucked the leaf safely into one of the children's packs, Byron spoke up.

"Now, dear children," he said. "Where must we travel to next?"

"It's a cave," said Ben. "The place where my friends and I first entered the Kingdom."

"Mugwig knows the way," said the little creature.

"Then let us be off," Byron replied, lowering himself so his passengers could climb atop his striped back.

"Byron," said Ben when they had situated themselves on top of the creature.

"Yes, child?"

Ben continued: "Please *do* try for a softer landing this time."

The beast and his passengers laughed at the boy's remark, and all agreed to help Byron better navigate his landing when they reached the area near the cave. Then, with the windy flapping of his huge and noble wings, Byron soared above the Great Willow and careened in the general direction of their next destination.

CHAPTER SIXTEEN
The Journal

Oliver held his grandfather's journal in his hands. The brown book was small and worn, and it was apparent to the boy and his friends that it was very old. Carefully flipping to the first page, Oliver began to read. The ink was black and smudged at points but still legible in the dimly-lit garage:

We set out to explore the uncharted high seas...

Oliver stopped and looked up at his friends.

"Well," said Ellie. "Do you think it's something that can help us?"

She and Jasmine waited for the boy to respond. He looked back down at the book and continued to read the first lines:

We set out to explore the uncharted high seas, to perhaps claim some uninhabited island or landmass in the name of our America.

"I think it may," he replied finally. "It appears to be an account of Grandpa Jesse's travels when he was younger."

"So perhaps he'll say something about how he first went to the Kingdom," suggested Jasmine. "Or how he got back here."

"Read some of it to us," Ellie requested.

The boy obliged and continued aloud:

"*We set out to explore the uncharted high seas, to perhaps claim some uninhabited island or landmass in the name of our America. I hope in the following entries to give an account of this expedition and anything that we shall find on our way. I have nothing to lose and everything to gain. No attachments to keep me grounded ashore, no family to hurry home to, and no reason to prevent me from seeing the great, wide ocean and, perhaps, the place beyond the sea.*"

"Jesse sounds like quite the adventurer," said Jasmine when Oliver had finished reading the first paragraph.

"And it seems this was before he met my Grandma Coral," the boy said.

"Yes," replied the woman slowly, drifting into a thought. Then she added, "Perhaps we should bring it to Jesse and have him read it aloud."

"Like storytime?" Ellie asked.

"Exactly," said Jasmine. "He can read it to us and maybe it will help him remember along the way—remember how he got into the Kingdom."

"What if the way he went to the Kingdom is no longer there?" Oliver asked, closing the journal slowly.

"We won't know until we try and get Jesse to remember," Jasmine replied confidently. "Do you want to save your friends or not?"

Oliver thought about the question for a moment. He knew it was mostly rhetorical but he nodded affirmatively anyway.

"Good," the woman continued. "The whole Kingdom is counting on us to do this—to bring their new King back to the throne."

But I still don't think I'm ready to be a King—to rule an entire nation, Oliver thought. *I'm just a boy. But we have to save my friends.* With this thought, he stood up, journal in hand, and headed for the door back into the house.

"Let's go find Grandpa Jesse," he said with a nod. Jasmine and Ellie followed him inside the house, leaving the cardboard box and its remaining contents strewn across the garage floor.

The three friends found Grandpa Jesse in the living room reading in his recliner by the light of a single lamp. The man wore a pair of thin glasses at the edge of his nose, which he squinted through while trying to read a newspaper article. Oliver approached him and held out the old, dusty journal.

"Grandpa," he said. "We found this in the garage. I think it belonged to you—do you remember when you wrote this?"

The old man set his papers aside and gently extended his wrinkly hands to take the book. He rubbed some of the dust off the cover with one hand and examined it closely.

"Well, would you look at that!" Jesse said, his green eyes lighting up. "My old logbook from my travels. I thought I'd lost it long ago—Coral must've kept it without me knowing."

"This is a good sign," whispered Jasmine to the children.

"We were hoping," began Oliver, "that you could read some of it to us. You know, like a story."

Jesse was beaming. He nodded his head and said, "Yes. I'd like that very much." Then he opened the book. "Where shall we begin?"

"Perhaps the beginning," suggested Oliver.

"A very good place to start," Jesse said, smiling wide. Then he found the first entry in the journal and began to read.

"*We set out to explore the uncharted high seas...*"

As Jesse's soft voice carried on, the children and Jasmine listened closely, sitting in a semi-circle on the rug around his feet.

"I was only a young man when I wrote this, you know," said Jesse to his listeners before then he turned his attention back to the book. "*It was my hope and intention to find a certain lost city of Atlantis or maybe even the famed Bermuda Triangle. Two fabled places that have been cause for such mystery and intrigue. But, as fate would have it, I was not to find these ancient cities or geographical anomalies. It was fate's intent for me to find love.*"

Here the man paused and exhaled deeply, a soft smile once more showing on his weathered face.

"What happened next, Mr. Jesse?" Ellie asked, urging him to continue.

"It's quite a blur," he replied. "But I will continue reading: *It was only our first day of the journey when we faced the first of many challenges. We had sailed straight on course when, out of nowhere, our vessel was engulfed by a dark sky—a portent of the terrible storm.*"

Ellie shuddered and all three listeners leaned in closer with rapt attention.

"*The ship was ripped in two,*" continued Jesse. "*The crew and the two halves of the valiant vessel were scattered even more, and many disappeared into the dark blue depths—never to be seen again by my own eyes. Then, out of the bleak, cold storm I experienced two strange sensations—*"

Here the man stopped and looked at his listeners.

"I'm afraid the words are smudged a bit here," Jesse

said as he held the book for them to see. "I can't make out what it's meant to say."

Oliver held his grandfather's hand and looked straight into his eyes. "Grandpa," he said. "You wrote those words. Do you think you can remember them—remember what happened next?"

The old man returned the boy's gaze and then looked back at the open journal in his hands.

"I don't know," he said, shaking his head. "It was so long ago. I don't know if I can remember." Jesse seemed almost on the verge of tears.

"It's alright," said Jasmine, comforting the man. "How about we keep reading and see if the rest of it comes back to you?"

Jesse seemed to like this idea and slowly picked up the book. He flipped the page and continued reading.

CHAPTER SEVENTEEN
Beast of the Granada Jungle

The journey from the Great Willow Tree to the area near the cave—part of the Granada Jungle—was swift, as Byron could travel quickly above the long stretches of forest and swamp. It was still dark and there were few landmarks with which the party could identify the specific place, so Mugwig and the children helped the bunglejumper navigate into the nearest clearing.

The beast swooped more slowly this time, and the children's instructions allowed him to alight without toppling them from his back. When they had all disembarked, the children and Mugwig looked around at the clearing.

"Well, Mugwig," said Ben. "Which way do we go from here?"

The tiny reptilian woman scratched her chin and wiggled her large ears, orbiting to get a view of all possible paths.

"Um," she said slowly. "That way!" She pointed confidently toward a path with her long green finger.

"You're sure?" Annie asked.

"Mugwig is sure," she replied. "Come, children."

The children hesitantly followed while Byron stood still.

"You go on," he said. "I shall wait in this clearing until you return. It will be too difficult for me to keep up on foot and I wouldn't dare slow you down when you are in such a hurry to reunite with your friends."

Annie and Ben hugged the beast goodbye and scurried off to catch up with Mugwig, who had already disappeared around a thicket of trees. They found the tiny woman at a fork in the path, sniffing the breeze and jittering her ears. Mugwig then chose a path and the children followed her quick pace into a darker, denser part of the jungle.

The three continued on in this way for some time until they came to another split in the path.

"Are you *sure* you know where you're going, Mugwig?" Ben asked with concern.

"Mugwig was sure that she was sure," said the woman, "until she wasn't."

"So, that's a *no?*" Annie clarified her cryptic answer.

Mugwig nodded slowly.

"Great," said Ben with a heaving sigh. "Now we're running out of time *and* we're lost."

"Sorry," said the tiny green woman, sulking. "Thought I knew the way and didn't want to disappoint my friends."

Annie smiled and knelt to the level of Mugwig's eyes. "It's alright," she said, placing a hand on the woman's shoulder. "We'll find our way. There's *always* a way, remember?"

Mugwig lifted her head and smiled softly through her pointy, brownish teeth: "Yes. There's always a way!"

Then she looked around. "But which way is the way?"

Again the group surveyed their options. The paths contained no discernable landmarks or clues to sway their decision on what to do next, so Ben suggested they sit and think it over until an idea came to them. They all agreed and each of the three found a rock or stump on which to contemplate.

It was not long before Ben heard a low growl in the bushes behind his seat. Startled, he leaped from the log and nearly fell onto Annie in his attempt to get as far away from the frightening noise as possible. When they were finally able to return to their feet, Annie brushed the dirt off her clothes and squinted to see where the sound had come from.

"What is it?" Ben asked in a whisper, using Annie as a human shield in case the beast approached. Mugwig joined the huddle, trembling as well.

"I can't tell," the girl returned. A pair of sizeable eyes glowed in the moonlight; the creature was close. Its shape was hard to distinguish in the shadows of the ferns and underbrush, but Annie could tell it was large.

"Is it a bear?" Mugwig muttered, grasping Ben's leg. The boy and girl leaned their heads and tried to discern the shape of the creature.

"I don't know," replied Annie.

The beast gave another slow growl then, with a sudden rustling of the leaves, the creature emerged onto the path with a pounce, attempting to lay claim to a small bird that fluttered away.

"Goodness," said the large, furry beast. "Not again!"

Annie and Mugwig's eyes were wide with fear and confusion, but Ben stepped forward, recognizing the great creature.

"Tazmo?" Ben asked.

The hairy beast turned toward the boy and stood on its two hind legs. He had the appearance of a large bear, but with a thick circle of longer fur around his face. The creature wiggled his tiny ears and round nose and then spoke.

"Well, hello again," he said matter-of-factly. "What are you doing out here so late at night, Ben? Don't you know there are dangerous predators roaming these parts?"

The boy gave a sigh of relief when his suspicions were confirmed and smiled at the sight of his old friend: "Tazmo, it's good to see you again." Ben ran to embrace the friendly, hairy beast.

The others stood motionless and confused until they saw that the creature was good-natured. Annie asked, "Ben—do you know this creature?"

"This creature!" Tazmo laughed at the girl. "I happen to be a snifflack—a rare and exotic breed, at that."

"Oh, I'm sorry," the girl replied. "I didn't mean to come off so rude."

"Don't mention it, dear," Tazmo said. "What might your names be?"

"I'm Annie. And this is Mugwig." The girl turned to her green companion.

Mugwig extended her hand to Tazmo: "Mugwig, Princess of the Pond, at your service."

"It's a pleasure to meet you both," he replied with a dramatic nod, shaking Mugwig's pointy-fingered hand. "Now, what brings you back to these parts of the jungle at this hour? I didn't expect that I'd ever see you again, let alone in the middle of the night."

"We got lost while looking for a cave—" began Ben, "the same cave where we first met you, as a matter of fact."

"Then I'd say it's a good thing I found you," said Tazmo. "I know the place well, and it's not far from this very spot. I'll be happy to join you and show the way."

Annie, Ben, and Mugwig were delighted by this news. Tazmo quickly returned to all-fours and began to sniff at the air to determine his direction. Then he waved a paw and started off down one of the paths with the children following closely behind.

Along the way, Ben explained their quest to Tazmo, who was very curious to know what had become of both Oliver and Ellie. Tazmo assured them that he could help them until morning, when he'd need to leave to bring food back to his cubs. The travelers made only a few more twists and turns through the dark jungle before they arrived at the mossy mouth of the old cave.

"Here we are," said Tazmo.

The mouth of the cave was large and round, and it seemed to stretch infinitely deep into the earth from which it was carved. Its innards seemed even darker than Ben remembered, mostly due to the shadow of night that still hung over the forest.

Cool, drafty air issued from the passage as the travelers approached.

"Are you sure we need to go in there?" Mugwig asked, trembling.

"I'm sure," said Ben. "It's the only place we know where we can find a piece of an old Gate. Believe me, though—if we didn't *have* to do this, I'd be far away from this frightening place."

The children quickly gathered a pair of thick branches from which they fashioned two torches—one for each of them. When the torches were set ablaze, Ben and Annie quietly led the others into the cave. The lively sounds of the jungle were gradually replaced with the echoing of steps on the stony walls, and the four trudged on into the deep darkness.

CHAPTER EIGHTEEN
The Cave

The cave was humid and dank. Ben, Annie, Mugwig, and Tazmo walked closely together to avoid tripping over the rocky, uneven ground as they delved further into the earth.

"Do you remember how far you had to travel the last time you were in this cave?" Annie asked, her legs aching from their expeditions thus far.

"Not exactly," said Ben. "But I'll know the spot when I see it."

This did little to reassure the girl and their other companions, but they continued to follow the boy in hopes that he was correct.

After some time, the walls of the cavern seemed to repeat themselves—a monotonous sequence of replicating curves back and forth through the deep, cold earth. As it was still nighttime in the jungle above the ground, the children began to feel drowsy and their pace and focus slowed.

Suddenly, a noise grew from the cave beyond them.

It was the sound of a light, rushing wind sweeping through the tunnel ahead. The travelers braced themselves for the impending gust, planting their feet firmly on the cave floor. Seconds later, the wind came over them. The children closed their eyes as it rushed past and then dissipated.

When she opened her eyes, Annie was unsure if she had indeed done so, for it was still as dark as the inside of her eyelids.

Oh no! Annie thought. *Our light!*

"The torches have blown out!" Ben said, coming to the same conclusion as Annie. "How are we supposed to find the remains of our old door now?"

"Can't we just light another fire?" Tazmo asked from the rear of the pack.

"I'm afraid not," replied the boy. "I haven't got anything with which to kindle the flames in here."

Discouraged, all four of the travelers grew quiet. They could hear the steady but sporadic drip of moisture falling from stalactites overhead. Then Mugwig broke the silence.

"We keep walking, but carefully," said Mugwig's voice behind them, though neither of the children could see her.

"What do you mean?" Annie inquired.

"Mugwig has very good eyes," said the little creature. "Very good eyes for seeing when the forest is dark."

"But in the forest, you have the moon and stars to help light the way," said Ben. "Here it's pitch black!"

"Nonsense," Mugwig replied. "I'll show you. Here— can you feel me pinching your hand, Ben?"

"Ouch!" Annie squealed. When she made this sharp sound, the cave filled with a sudden, brief bluish glow, which quickly faded away.

"That was curious," Ben said.

"And that was *my* hand!" Annie said to Mugwig, irritated.

"Sorry," said Mugwig softly. "But it *was* a hand, yes?"

The children did not answer but listened as Mugwig fumbled her way to the front of the pack.

"What do you think that flash was?" The girl said, rubbing the spot on her hand where Mugwig had pinched her.

"I'm not sure," said Ben. "But Mugwig: do you think you can lead us through the tunnels or not?"

"Yes, Mugwig can do it. Form a chain. Stay together." Mugwig held out her hand and waited for Ben to find it in the dark. Ben reached for Annie's hand, who in turn grabbed one of Tazmo's paws. "Alright, let us continue."

They made surprisingly swift progress through the cave, with only a few slips and trips along the way. Then Mugwig stopped walking.

"What is it, Mugwig?" Ben asked.

"Which path to take?" Mugwig said.

"More than one path? That means we've gone too far already," the boy replied. "I don't remember the tunnel splitting off on our last journey." Ben squinted into the darkness to see if he could determine their location, but he was still unable to see anything.

"Should we turn back?" Tazmo muttered.

"Bigger problem," said Mugwig hesitantly.

"What?" Annie asked the creature. "What *bigger* problem?"

"Mugwig may have taken other paths already," she said, "and I do not know if I remember which ones."

"Mugwig, why would you do that?" Ben was furious.

"I did not know we would get lost," she replied defensively. "Mugwig is very sorry."

There was a brief lull in the conversation, then they heard the familiar sound of the light wind rushing through the cave. This time, however, it sounded distant. The gust came and went, issuing down another area of the cave network behind them.

"I have an idea," said Annie.

"We're all ears," replied Ben.

"That sound," she continued. "It rushed past us in the tunnel before we were lost. What if we simply follow the sound of that wind?"

"That should get us back on the right track," Ben agreed.

They waited until they heard the gust beginning again, and then they quickly and carefully made their way toward the noise. When the breeze passed by, the party waited in stillness until it resumed. They repeated this process a few times until they were able to feel the breeze again.

"Now," said Ben. "Keep your eyes out for a burnt old door, Mugwig. Or maybe its ashes or other fragments."

Mugwig nodded in agreement, though no one could see her. As she surveyed the cave, her eyes fell upon a lump of debris that looked darker than the dirt of the cave. And then she saw something shiny.

"There," Mugwig pointed and scurried toward it, with the rest of the party linked behind, hand-in-hand. "I think this used to be your door."

As the children and Tazmo perked up, they heard the sound of the wind rushing down the tunnel again. This time, however, it was accompanied by a deep, rumbling roar.

"What was that?" Ben asked, gripping Mugwig and Annie's hands more tightly.

No one answered; instead, they listened. All they could tell was that it was alive, it was huge, and it was moving through the cave in their direction.

CHAPTER NINETEEN
Rumble in the Deep

Annie, Ben, Tazmo, and Mugwig stood motionless in the middle of the passage. The rushing wind continued in brief but consistent gusts now, stronger and louder than before, as the growling, enigmatic creature approached.

"The wind," said Annie. "I think those are its breaths."

"Whatever *it* is," replied Ben, "it's coming right toward us. There's no way we can outrun it in the dark of the cave."

Ben's right, thought Annie. *But how will we see the way?*

"I can see it," whispered Mugwig, her pointy fingernails digging into Ben's palm.

"What is it?" Tazmo asked. "What does it look like?"

The blue glow, Annie remembered. *Perhaps the flash can happen again—and light our way out.*

"Oh!" Mugwig gasped as another large, humid breath swept over them. "It's hideous! Slimy claws, a scaly hide, and gargantuan teeth! They'll crush us in a single bite!"

"Quick," said Ben to Annie. "Hand me the pouch from my pack so we can fill it with ashes and get out of here."

Annie scavenged blindly with her hand inside the pack and her fingers found the empty pouch. She passed it carefully to Ben, who handed it to Mugwig.

As they did this, Annie tried to recall: *What had triggered the flash?*

"Can you fill it up with ashes from the door?" Ben asked.

"As much as Mugwig can fit," the green woman replied and began to scoop the ashes into the bag with her hands. "But there's something else in here, too—it's made of metal."

The large beast lumbered ominously closer.

"Metal?" Ben wondered. "It's probably just the hinges or hardware."

"No," said Mugwig. "There are gemstones attached—I can't tell their color in this darkness."

"Gemstones?" Ben thought about it for another moment. Then he remembered the last moments before this door had been burned to the ground. "The key!" He practically shouted.

At the sound of his exclamation, the whole cavern began to glow a dim blue. Annie looked to the stone walls of the cave and noticed what looked like thousands of tiny light bulbs. Ben made the mistake of looking straight in the direction of the beast and caught the briefest glimpse of its fearsome jaws—it looked as startled as Ben was in the glow. Then the light faded to darkness again and the monster continued toward them.

*The key—*thought Annie—*is the sound!*

"There's that flash again," said Tazmo. "Strange."

"Tazmo," said Annie to their friend. "Do you know any songs?"

"I'm not sure I know why that's important at a time like this," said Tazmo slowly.

"Do you or don't you?"

The growling monster was nearly upon them. Annie could feel its spittle in the smelly gusts.

"I know a few," Tazmo replied finally.

"Then sing!" Annie said. "As loud as you can!"

"If you insist..." Tazmo began to belt out an old snifflack folk tune that neither of the children recognized. As soon as his deep voice reverberated through the cavern, its walls started to glow again. The monster recoiled at the sudden sight of the bright blue light and scrunched its toothy visage, stepping back into the darkness.

"It's working," Annie remarked. "Keep singing, Tazmo!"

Tazmo obeyed. The entire cave was illuminated, and Annie could now see that the walls and ceiling of the cave were covered in tiny, bioluminescent slugs.

"Remarkable!" Annie said. "Quick—let's get out of here while we still can!"

Ben looked to their little green friend. "Mugwig—did you finish filling up that pouch?"

"Finished and full," Mugwig replied, handing him the bag. She then placed the small, metallic key in his hand. "And here's that key for safekeeping."

Tazmo continued singing for the duration of their journey back to the jungle. They were able to move much faster, as the glowing slugs produced even more light than their torches had. In no time, the four weary travelers reached the mouth of the cave and paused to catch their breaths.

When they were sufficiently rested, Ben held out the little key. It was a familiar bronze key with three green emeralds embedded in its handle. "This was the key to our Gate," he explained to Annie. "You wouldn't believe the lengths we had to go to swipe it from Prince Florian's palace." Ben tucked the key into his pocket.

Tazmo observed that the sun would soon be up in a few hours, so he agreed to help the party navigate back to Byron before he departed. "Have to get back to the cubs," he explained. "Can't let them go hungry."

The blind bunglejumper was asleep when they returned, so Annie gently tapped him awake. She, Ben, and Mugwig said farewell to Tazmo and watched him saunter off into the dark of the forest. They now had two of the three ingredients they needed for the Carpenter's magic recipe that would activate a new Gate; they only needed one more item—the three hairs from the elusive Regal Stag.

We've already tried once, thought Annie as the party climbed atop Byron once more. *Here's hoping we have better luck this time.*

And with that, they flew off into the night in search of the Regal Stag.

CHAPTER TWENTY
Jesse Remembers

"When I awoke I was caked in sand and seawater. It was the soothing, rhythmic sweep of the tide that lulled me out of my slumber. I looked around at the place where I was now made conscious and thought at first that I had been washed back to the beaches of my home—the beaches where we had set out from our journey. But it was no such place. No, this was an entirely different and wondrous place."

Jesse read the words from the water-stained pages of his old journal. His expression seemed to Jasmine and the children as if it was the first time he had heard or seen these words, but they knew it was only his old age and fading memory that made the journal's author seem like a distant and altogether different person.

"Had I stumbled upon some tropical paradise by accident—no—by fate? Surely my compatriots had not been as lucky or as fortunate, for they were nowhere to be seen. The only remnants of our perilous journey were a few splintered boards and my own salt-soaked and near-lifeless body."

The old man continued reading but he had yet to

reveal any information that might help Oliver and his friends find a way back to the Kingdom.

"When I could finally gather the strength to lift myself from the water's edge, I stumbled up the beach toward a verdant treeline. Large and leathery leaves intermingled with luscious trees of fruit, delectable to the eyes and—I presumed—the taste. I ate of one such curious fruit and found these things to be true. In fact, it tasted much like the guava fruit. But within moments, before I could even finish a few bites, I grew quickly drowsy and fell back on the sand."

Oliver and Ellie snickered softly at this moment in the story.

"What's so funny?" Jasmine asked.

"I think we know that fruit," said Ellie, giggling through a hand that she held over her mouth.

"Lady Juniper gave us some," continued Oliver, "to put us to sleep inside the Golden Alligator all that time ago."

"That sounds like a story I'll have to hear sometime," said Jasmine, turning back to the old storyteller in his recliner.

Jesse continued: *"When I awoke this time, I discerned that I was now inside some sort of tent in the jungle, for the sounds of its many inhabitants could be heard faintly around and beyond. Ropes were wrapped around my wrists and ankles to keep me from running. It was at this moment that my captor returned to the tent, brandishing a large sword. Removing a head covering, this mysterious figure revealed herself—a young woman of the utmost beauty and poise. Her dark complexion was accentuated by piercing eyes—the type of eyes that see the world with both a compassion and a fire."*

Oliver interrupted: "Was that the moment you met Grandma Coral?"

"It was," Jesse nodded with a smile, lowering the

weathered journal. "She was truly the most beautiful woman I ever laid eyes on."

Here the listeners allowed the man to pause in his story as he drifted into a daydream of Coral, while the three conferred with one another about what to do next.

"We need him to remember what happened *earlier*," whispered Jasmine. "The part of the journal that was smudged—I think it's important. I think it can tell us how he got to the Kingdom."

The children agreed.

"But he's had such a hard time remembering anything," said Oliver, discouraged. "What else can we do to help him remember?"

They thought for a moment, hoping for some spark of inspiration.

"Jasmine," began Ellie. "Didn't you say memories could be remembered with a sound or smell?"

The woman nodded. "Yes. Do you have something in mind?"

"Well," Ellie replied. "In his story, Mr. Jesse was in the ocean when that storm broke his boat."

"Go on," said Oliver.

"Perhaps if he was near the ocean he might remember," continued Ellie.

"Yes," said Jasmine, catching her drift. "If he could hear the waves crashing and smell the salty ocean breeze. Great idea, Ellie!"

At this, the children rose.

"Grandpa," said Oliver taking the old man's hand. "Would you come with us on a little drive?"

"At this hour of the night?" The man gestured to the darkened window.

"It's important," his grandson replied. "Can you

drive us?"

The man thought about the request, scratching his chin with his free hand, then answered, "I suppose I can. Where are we going?"

As they helped the man rise from his seat, Oliver took the journal and replied, "It's just a few minutes away. We're going to the beach."

They filed out of the living room and into the garage, where Grandpa Jesse started his car. Oliver took the front seat so that he could give his grandfather directions, while Jasmine and Ellie sat behind them.

It was quite late at night, so the roads were nearly empty. Thus, they arrived at the beach in about five minutes and piled out of the car. The moon was massive and full, reflecting in staggered ripples across the calm ocean ahead of them. Oliver held Jesse's hand as they made their way down to the shoreline.

All four members of the group took off their shoes so they could stick their toes in the sand and surf. Oliver now withdrew his grandfather's journal and opened it to the passage that had been blurred by water and time.

"Alright, Grandpa," he said. "How about you take a couple of steps forward into the shallows and close your eyes? Ellie and Jasmine will hold your hands to make sure you don't fall while I read from your journal, okay?"

Jesse nodded and inched further into the cool waters. He closed his eyes and listened to the calming lull of the waves and the breeze rustling the palm trees.

"*The ship was ripped in two,*" began Oliver. "*The crew and the two halves of the valiant vessel were scattered even more, and many disappeared into the dark blue depths—never to be seen again by my own eyes. Then, out of the bleak, cold storm I experienced two strange sensations–"*

Here the boy turned to his grandfather: "Anything?"

Jesse shook his head.

"Listen to the sound of the waves," said Ellie. "Smell that salty air."

The old man did this, inhaling deeply, while Oliver re-read the passage.

"Then, out of the bleak, cold storm I experienced two strange sensations–"

The old man was silent.

Oliver repeated: *"I experienced two strange sensations–"*

Jesse inhaled again, his eyes still closed.

"Two strange sensations," said Oliver once more. "What were they, Grandpa?"

All three watched and waited for him to respond.

Then, old Jesse muttered something under his breath that none of them could discern over the rippling waves.

"What did he say?" Jasmine asked the others.

He muttered again, the same sounds.

"Grandpa, what did you say? What were the two strange sensations?"

Jesse opened his eyes and turned to Oliver: "Light and sound!"

"I don't understand," the boy replied. *"What* light? What *sound?"*

"A blinding, white light," said Jesse softly.

"Like lightning?" Ellie wondered.

"Not lightning. Bright, white, and steady. A pulsing glow."

Oliver stepped closer: "And the sound?"

"The sound," said Jesse. "It was like the sound of a thousand tiny bells ringing at once. Chiming–shimmering!"

Shimmering, Oliver thought. *Like the Gates!* At this, he looked to his friends, who clearly made the same connection.

"Out there," continued Jesse, pointing toward the horizon just below the full moon. "I remember a bit of it now: we left not far from here and traveled directly east."

"Can you show us the place where you set out?" Jasmine asked.

"Yes," was his reply. "I can show you on our way home. Shall we return to the car?"

They all agreed, put their shoes back on, and hustled back up the beach into Jesse's car.

Finally, thought Oliver. *A way back to the Kingdom—a way to find our friends.*

But he could not ignore the other thought that remained in the back of his mind: *What if we can't find it? What if we can't find the way back?*

There was no choice.

We have to try. We have to!

CHAPTER TWENTY-ONE
A Ride in the Moonlight

As they drove along the moonlit coastline with the front windows down, Oliver stuck out his hand and felt the breeze through his fingers.

We're so close, he thought. *I only hope Jesse can remember enough to show us the way.*

"Are you ready?" Ellie asked the boy, leaning toward him from the back seat.

Her question snapped him out of his reverie. "Ready for what?"

"Ready to become King," she continued. "Your Grandma Coral was a princess and you're the only one left from her family line."

"I know," said Oliver. "But I can't be a King. Who's going to stay here and take care of Grandpa Jesse if I go?"

It was a valid question. The man was old, and it was only a matter of time before his forgetfulness started to affect his ability to function. Even if they found the portal out at sea, there was no guarantee they'd be able to find their way back.

"It's your destiny, Oliver," said Jasmine. "There's no one else who can take the throne of Mangonia rightfully."

"Can't *you* rule the Kingdom?" Oliver was nervous and defensive now that he realized that a return to the Kingdom could mean that he never saw his grandfather again. "Why does it have to be all three, anyway?"

"Because," the woman replied, "it's the only way for the Kingdom to exist peacefully—when all three lines of the Triumvirate have their own ruler. And we can only stand up to the Prince if we can prove that there are others to take his place."

Oliver made no reply. He knew Jasmine was right, but he wasn't ready to admit it.

They had only been driving for a few minutes when the car dipped briefly into a neighborhood, then back out onto a waterfront street. Grandpa Jesse pointed as the car slowed in front of the entrance to a now-dilapidated marina.

"That's where we set out," he said, leaning over the steering wheel. "Used to be an old, small port back in those days."

Jasmine and the children studied the scene. The place was overgrown. A broken chain-link fence surrounded the property and, beyond it, they could see a few rows of decaying wooden docks peppered with decades of bird droppings.

"How will we get out to sea?" Ellie asked, holding her palms to the glass of the rear window.

"If memory serves—" began the old man, "there may still be a few rowboats in the old shed—if it hasn't yet been cleared out. I doubt it's locked, anyway."

Old Jesse explained the course he and his crewmates had taken, then they drove back to the house.

The three passengers piled out of the car and returned to Oliver's bedroom to plot their next moves.

"Do you think the portal between worlds is still out there?" Oliver asked his friends.

"I don't know," replied Jasmine. "But it seems like it would be fairly difficult for anyone to close or destroy it so far out in the ocean."

"So we've got a good chance?" Ellie raised a hopeful gaze to the young woman.

"I'd say so," Jasmine said. "I we can find it, that is. We've got to make it even more certain, though."

"How do we do that?" Oliver wasn't sure he understood what Jasmine was getting at.

"Sometimes these magic places behave strangely or unpredictably," the woman explained. "So I suggest we do our best to replicate the circumstances of Jesse's passage through the portal—it could be as easy as bringing along some items that have belonged to him, or that he and Coral might have brought here from the Kingdom."

The children considered this and then Oliver once again removed his special wooden box from its hiding place under his bed. He flipped open the clasp, took and set the old map to the side, and dumped out the rest of its contents on the bed.

"We can use this to keep the items safe and dry," he explained. "Grandpa Jesse knew the map, so I think we should bring it." He placed the map back into the empty box and then did the same for the old journal. "And, of course, Jesse's journal. Anything else?"

Ellie remembered another: "What about the little ring with the lamp on it?"

"I'd almost forgotten," he said, reaching into his pocket. The small, golden ring glistened in the room's overhead light and the boy took one more look at it before placing it into the small chest.

"That should do the trick," said Jasmine. "Now, how about you two gather some things and then we'll have your grandfather take us back to the docks."

The children agreed and proceeded to gather a few items from around the house—including thin blankets, snacks, and bottles of water—which they stuffed into one of Oliver's backpacks. When they were ready to leave, they returned to the garage and Jesse drove the three travelers back to the abandoned docks.

The sun had not yet risen over the horizon, but they could see its imminent glow at the distant edge of the sea. Under cover of relative darkness, Jasmine and the children said goodbye to Jesse—who had already forgotten why he had driven them there—and slipped through an opening in the rusty fence. As Jesse's old car sputtered away, the travelers slinked across the overgrown lawn and into the decaying shed. Sure enough, it was unlocked, just like the old man had predicted.

Inside, they found a collection of aging rowboats. Jasmine scanned the boats quickly and chose one that was devoid of holes while Ellie grabbed a pair of oars from the far wall. Oliver placed his box and backpack into the bottom of the boat and helped Jasmine drag it out to the shore. When the children had climbed inside, Jasmine pushed the vessel off and jumped into it.

The faint glow of the impending sunrise cast eerie violet shadows across the water as Jasmine and Oliver paddled quietly away from the safety of the beach. The rhythmic lull of their rowing met the motion of the current, enabling them to glide more quickly toward the horizon.

We're coming for you, Annie and Ben, thought Oliver. *We're coming.*

CHAPTER TWENTY-TWO
A Search Before Sunrise

The majestic winged lion soared low, just above the dense jungle. A flock of green and yellow parrots fluttered by, squawking at the blind beast while Byron's passengers kept a watchful eye out for any sign of the enigmatic Regal Stag.

"The sun will be up soon," said Mugwig to the children. "A couple of hours."

"Then we've got to find the stag before then," said Ben. "Otherwise we'll have to wait until it's nighttime again for us to keep searching. We can't afford to lose any more time—we have to get back to our friends!"

As they had discovered earlier in the cave, Mugwig's eyes could see more clearly in the dark than the children's own. Even so, they had little luck in finding any trace of the mysterious and beautiful creature. Still, they continued their surveillance of the passing forest below.

Annie recalled the medallion she wore around her neck—the gold engraving of the lamp that belonged to their friend and one-time protector Marco.

"Do you think Juniper's found him by now?" She said to Ben.

"Marco?" Ben clarified and Annie nodded. "I don't know. It still seems so strange to me that he just vanished. Where has he gone? And why didn't he tell someone?"

"I hope he's alright," Annie said, clutching the thick, circular piece of jewelry. "What if Prince Florian has taken him—or worse?"

"He'll be okay," Ben assured the girl, though he couldn't be certain. "If there's one thing I know about Marco it's that he can take care of himself."

The next hour passed in relative silence as the children helped Mugwig look for any movement or tracks that might indicate the location of their quarry. Just when Ben was beginning to get nervous that they might not find the creature, their little green companion pointed and shouted.

"Look!" She said eagerly. "See?"

Both of the children looked in the direction Mugwig was pointing, but neither could see anything of note.

"What is it?" Annie asked.

"Tracks!" Mugwig replied. "Byron, fly lower—certain those are the tracks of the Regal Stag!"

Byron the Bunglejumper complied and descended carefully, bringing the flapping of his wings to a slower pace. In a few moments, they were nearer to the jungle floor. The children instructed Byron as he made another bumpy but safe landing, bringing all three passengers relief as they climbed off his furry back. A warm breeze brushed through this area of the jungle, and the children could hear a variety of distant lifeforms calling to one another with chirps and growls.

"Yes," said Mugwig, inspecting the tracks more

closely. "Most definitely the tracks we're looking for." She followed them with her eyes and saw that they led into a thicket of fruit trees.

Annie and Ben tailed her at a distance, recalling their flubs on the last encounter with the easily-frightened stag.

We can't mess this up again, thought Annie. *We've only got one shot before sunrise.*

As they pushed past the trees, Ben pulled one of the large fruits from a tree and continued walking. "It'll make a good snack for later," he explained to Annie in a whisper as he put it in his pack.

When they caught up to Mugwig she turned to them with a finger pressed against her mouth. With her other hand, she pointed just beyond them to a thin stream. There, kneeling to drink from the cool, babbling water just ahead of them, was the Regal Stag—as majestic and poised as ever.

"This time," whispered Ben, "let's try not to scare him. Annie, you go and come around from the far side of the jungle and I'll head this way." He pointed as he spoke softly. "Mugwig, you stay here in case the deer darts toward you."

Mugwig and Annie nodded to the boy that they understood, then the two children crept in opposite directions to try and sneak up on the Regal Stag from the bushes. It was difficult for them to navigate quietly in the dark, but both children managed to get to their positions without alerting the creature to their presence.

Annie peered at it from between two huge, waxy leaves. *The air feels strange*, she thought. *It feels still.* It was quiet, too—she could no longer hear the lively sounds of the jungle's many creatures. The girl looked past the stag and made eye-contact with Ben in another patch of bushes. He nodded, and both children quickly moved toward the large-antlered deer.

Annie moved quietly and quicker than Ben, reaching out her hand toward the stag's small, fuzzy tail. *Three hairs*, she remembered. *We just need three!* Her fingers were inches from the Regal Stag when the creature finally looked up from his drink and noticed that the children were upon him.

Before Annie could make contact with the stag's tail, though, he darted out of the way and made a giant leap into the air. The moment seemed to move in slow-motion as Annie watched the Regal Stag sail over the rippling stream. When the creature landed on the other side—away from the children or Mugwig—it pranced quickly into the dark forest and was gone.

"Not again!" Ben stomped his foot in the mossy dirt. "How did it get away?"

"I was so close," explained Annie, still trying to comprehend what had just happened. "I don't know how it moved so quickly—it was like I was frozen for that moment until it got away."

They stared off in the direction the stag had disappeared while Mugwig joined the children. "Fear not," she said. "We will try again!"

"But look," said Ben pointing up to a gap in the trees where a few stray orange rays of sun crept through. "Here comes the sunrise. Now we'll have to wait until the day is over again."

Annie and Mugwig lowered their heads.

"Cheer up," Mugwig continued. "Perhaps we can watch the sunrise from way up in the sky?"

The children liked this idea, so the three returned to Byron and climbed atop his back once more. He levitated through the jungle canopy just as the bright semicircular sun inched over the horizon. It was among the most beautiful sights the children had ever seen and, for a moment, they were content to remember that all hope and goodness were not lost.

CHAPTER TWENTY-THREE
Dawn

Oliver and Jasmine took a break from rowing the little old raft. Ellie offered each of them a handful of small chocolate candies, which were beginning to melt in the warmth of the rising sun.

"They still taste good," the little girl assured them as they hesitantly received the snack.

She was right, thought Oliver. *They do still taste good.*

His consumption of the tiny morsels reminded Oliver that they hadn't eaten a proper breakfast, and his stomach gave a gurgly growl as if to place a timely emphasis on the thought. The boy quickly dismissed his hungry musings as he watched Jasmine continue rowing. He picked up his oar and followed suit.

"How much farther until we reach the Gate?" Ellie inquired as she tucked the candies back into Oliver's backpack.

"I'm not sure," replied Oliver. "And I don't think it's a Gate, actually. Remember when we first went to the Kingdom? Juniper said there were some passages between the worlds that she called 'thin places'—areas where the two worlds meet naturally."

"That's right," said Jasmine in between the strokes of her paddle. "We thought most of them were gone; they're much harder to find than a Gate, anyway, since they don't look like anything special."

"If they don't look like Gates," began Ellie, "then how have so many of them been destroyed? I bet it was Prince Florian again, wasn't it?"

"Some, perhaps," Jasmine replied. "But it seems that most of them are no longer accessible because of your own world—people have built over them with shops or homes."

"So that's closed them off?" Oliver clarified.

"I'm afraid so," the woman said. "I suppose they can't close them for good—the passages probably still exist, though it would be hard to travel through a wall if you're made of flesh and blood like we are." She smiled at the children as she continued rowing.

The boat continued on toward the horizon. At first, it looked to Ellie as if they might row directly into the huge sun, but it inched higher and higher into the sky the closer they paddled. The girl looked over the edge of the boat and could catch glimpses beneath the reflective ripples. A school of colorful fish swam under the boat, and then there was a slow-moving manta ray that wiggled its long triangular body in the wake of the rowboat.

While Ellie delighted herself with watching the creatures of the sea, Oliver and Jasmine kept the vessel on course.

"She cared deeply for her family," said Jasmine to the boy, who gave her a confused look. "Your grandmother Coral," she continued. "Family was very important to her."

"Then why did she leave us?" Oliver asked. "I barely got to know her. And she left my poor grandfather all alone—why would she do a thing like that?"

"For her family," replied Jasmine. "You have to understand she left her parents and brothers and sisters in the Kingdom. They were her family, too, and she never got to say a proper goodbye to them before they passed. She couldn't just stand by and let Florian get away with what he did. Coral loved the Kingdom—it was home for her."

The boy considered the woman's words, then asked, "What about my parents?"

"Vera cared, too," said Jasmine. "I know she and your father loved each other very much—and their newborn child."

Oliver kept rowing but now stared off at the waves.

"I'm sorry," Jasmine said to him. "Are you alright, Oliver?"

"Yeah," he nodded. "I just wish I knew what happened to them—my parents, I mean."

"Coral disappeared back into the Kingdom," the woman replied. "But I never saw Vera again after I went into hiding—I figured she decided to settle down with your father and just forget the Kingdom ever existed."

"I don't know," Oliver said quietly. "Grandpa told me they passed away when I was very young, but I'm starting to doubt that's the whole story. I just wish that everything in my life wasn't some sort of huge secret. I just want some answers. What happened to—"

"Look!" Ellie interrupted with a shout.

The others followed the pointing of her tiny finger. To one side of the boat, in the distance, was a large,

"KEEP ROWING—FASTER!"

dark stormcloud. It hung ominously in the morning sky, a shadow moving slowly in their direction.

"That's not good," said Jasmine under her breath. "Let's keep rowing—faster! I think we may be close."

Oliver did his best to pick up the pace of his paddling, but the stormcloud began to move quicker. Within minutes, the wind started to pick up and the waters around the boat grew choppy. As the gusts whipped her hair across her face, Ellie watched the storm close in on them.

Then they heard the sharp cracking sound of thunder, and the three travelers watched as a thick wall of rain moved over them—first with tiny droplets on their arms and then with a torrent that engulfed them.

Jasmine and Oliver tried to paddle against the windswept waves but made little progress. They were in the middle of a dangerous storm, far from the shore, and the children quickly forgot about their quest to find a *thin place* to return to the Kingdom. Right now they had no choice but to press on—they only hoped that they would make it out alive.

CHAPTER TWENTY-FOUR
The Place Beyond the Sea

The tempest raged on and the waves swelled furious-
ly, beating the tiny rowboat back and forth amidst the
darkened ocean. It seemed to Oliver as if some wicked
force was conspiring to prevent him from ever reuniting
with his friends inside the Kingdom—or at least to make
it as difficult as possible.

"Hold on!" Jasmine shouted above the crashing
tide, tossing her oar into the center of the small vessel.
Oliver did the same, and the two children grasped the
craft's frail wooden sides. The boy decided to place his
glasses inside his small, wooden box to keep them from
getting lost or broken in the churning motion. He then
sealed and returned the box to the bottom of the boat.

The boy craned his neck as he thought he heard a
faint, familiar sound. *Was that a shimmering? The sound
of ringing?*

Before he could think on it further, an enormous
wave splashed over the side of the rowboat, drenching
the three passengers and all of their belongings.

"Where did this storm come from?" Ellie practically shouted over the thunder. "It was sunny a few moments ago!"

Neither Jasmine nor Oliver answered, for at that moment another huge wave toppled over them and filled the bottom of the boat with salty, foamy water. Oliver nearly lost his grip as he grasped at its slippery edges. As the wave recessed, it pulled one of the paddles back to sea along with it—too quickly for the boy to grab. Then the oar was gone.

"What do we do?" Oliver yelled to Jasmine.

"I think the storm is getting stronger," she answered. "We're just going to have to wait it out—" A splash interrupted her, dousing her face, then she finished her sentence: "—and hope we make it through in one piece!"

Jasmine then tried to stabilize the rowboat with the remaining oar but found this to be toilsome and futile. It was true—the thunderstorm was getting worse and the winds had picked up.

There's that sound again, thought Oliver. *Shimmering—the sound of a Gate!*

"Stay on course," shouted the boy. "We need to stay on course!"

Once again, Jasmine tried to paddle to keep them on track. The storm was so thick now, though, that none of the party could tell if this helped at all. The faint ringing sound began to grow louder.

"Do you hear that?" Ellie asked.

"Yes," said Oliver. "It's getting louder. We're almost there!"

If we can just hang on for a few more minutes, he thought, *we'll sail right into that portal—that same thin place that Grandpa Jesse first sailed through.*

The ringing grew more powerful still, now piercing

above the thunderclaps and massive billows. Jasmine and the children gripped the boat as it rocked to and fro. Another huge torrent whipped across them, flooding the boat even more. The water gushed back out as the boat tipped to one side, and Oliver watched as his small, wooden box—the trove containing the old map, the golden ring, and his grandfather's journal—began to float toward the edge of the boat. Oliver gazed in horror as the box cleared the brim and drifted into the expansive ocean. Thinking quickly, he lunged for the tiny chest.

The boy's fingers latched on to the wooden box just in time, but another strong wave tipped the boat such that Oliver lost his grip. Before he could reach for something to grab onto, the boy found himself being pulled under the violent current.

"Oliver!" Ellie screamed as she watched her friend disappear under the surface.

Jasmine stuck out the oar in hopes that the boy could grasp it, but she could no longer see where he was. Just then, a bright flash of lightning radiated around them. Curiously, though, the flash did not subside—instead, it grew brighter, searing and pulsing. Both Jasmine and Ellie had to close their eyes to keep from being blinded by the light.

By that time, the ringing had grown louder and began to irritate Ellie such that she now had to cover her ears. This was difficult to do, as she tried to maintain a grip on the slick sides of the boat and keep her eyes closed at the same time. The blinding light finally vanished, but the two kept their eyes shut.

Then came the worst moment of all: the largest wave swept them up to its height then sent them crashing down. Jasmine opened her eyes just in time to catch a glimpse of a series of sharp, craggy rocks directly in their path. The rowboat shattered into hundreds of tiny shards and sent both the woman and little Ellie in opposite directions.

Ellie clung to a stray plank as the current swept her away from the rocks. She was nearly dashed across the large, hole-ridden reef, but the waves pulled her away just in time. The little girl held tightly as she scanned the rainy horizon for her friends.

She grew worried when she could see neither Jasmine nor Oliver, but her spirits were lifted momentarily as she caught a glimpse of the young woman drifting on her own piece of the broken craft.

"Jasmine!" The little girl shouted as loud as she could and began to paddle with one arm. "Jasmine! Over here!"

The expanse between them grew smaller as the two swam toward each other. At last, Jasmine reached out and took the little girl's wet hands, pulling their two makeshift rafts together.

"You're safe," said Jasmine, though the storm continued to rage on with no sign of stopping.

"Oliver?" It was the only word Ellie could muster.

"I don't know," replied the woman. "He's gone. But we can't be far from shore—the reef means we're close!"

The two drifted and swayed, tossed about in the middle of the open sea. Ellie squinted and thought she could make out the shape of a beach or treeline, but the rain was still quite heavy.

Oh, Oliver, she thought in despair. *Where are you?*

All the little girl could do was hope and pray that her friend was still alive as the storm continued to ravage the remains of the broken rowboat and pull them wherever it pleased over the cold, dark ocean.

CHAPTER TWENTY-FIVE
Third Time's the Charm

Byron and his passengers careened over the canopy once more, heading over the jungles along the coastline. The daylight had grown more full and bright now as afternoon crept in, but the children saw curious, gray storm clouds brewing in the distance, followed by a few sharp flashes of lightning.

"Let's steer clear," said Ben to Annie. "Looks like a terrible storm."

She agreed and they instructed Byron to alter his course slightly to avoid it. Mugwig again pointed to a place, thinking she may have seen fresh tracks. The magnificent bunglejumper began to circle over that area of the jungle and Annie guided him to a landing.

"I think I'm getting the hang of this," said Byron when his paws alighted on the ground with ease. "Perhaps I'll have to keep you around as my guide, little Annie."

The girl smiled as she and her friends disembarked once more. "I wish that you could," she said, running a hand through his glittering fur. "But once we find the last of the ingredients and help the Carpenter build that Gate, we'll be heading home to our friends—in *our* world."

"Ah, yes," replied the bunglejumper. "We'll find it soon enough. But you'll promise to come and visit me, won't you?"

"I hope to," said Annie. "Often—if I can."

Byron was pleased with the girl's response. Ellie, Ben, and Mugwig once more gathered their belongings and began to explore the surrounding area.

"We shouldn't stay here for long," suggested Ben. "Or we may get caught in that horrible rainstorm."

"Just look for those tracks," said Mugwig. "Thought I saw some."

"But," said the boy, "I thought the Regal Stag only comes out at night?"

"Thought so, too," replied the little woman, crouching to inspect a set of indentations in the soft dirt. "But these are its tracks."

The children were delighted to know that, once more, they were on the trail of the creature that had already evaded them on two occasions. Ellie and Ben followed Mugwig as she sniffed at the hoof marks and began to waddle into the jungle.

The three said goodbye to the blindfolded Byron, insisting that they would call out if they again needed his assistance, then they trudged deeper into the forest while the noble beast flew away. Mugwig noted a few broken twigs and pointed down a narrow pathway that seemed to have been freshly forged. The children kept close to the little green woman and tried not to make a sound.

Before long, they again came upon the stately stag

standing stoically in the quiet thicket. The low rumble of distant thunder rolled through the forest and the air was cool.

"What do we do this time?" Annie whispered to her friends.

Mugwig placed a finger over her own mouth but did not say anything.

Then Ben reached back and removed his pack slowly. A moment later, he withdrew the small fruit that he'd procured from the tree before their last encounter with the deer.

"Maybe it's hungry?" He said quietly.

"Worth a shot," replied Annie.

Carefully, Ben set down the pack and began to step toward the Regal Stag, leading with his fruit-bearing hand. At first, the creature seemed not to notice the boy. Then, with a slight start, it turned toward him. This time, however, the Regal Stag did not run away. It stood with its eyes locked on Ben, then shifted its gaze to the juicy fruit in his hand. Ben offered it to the creature, extending his hand closer.

The deer lowered its head and began to eat the fruit straight out of Ben's hand. As it did this, the boy cautiously reached out to stroke the Regal Stag's soft neck. When, once again, the stag did not flinch, the boy turned back to his friends.

"Three hairs," Mugwig said in a mock whisper that was much louder than she intended. "From the tail."

Ben turned back to the creature. It contentedly munched at the fruit and chewed it with its large teeth, oozing pulp and juice over the boy's hand. But Ben didn't care much—his sights were now on the creature's tail.

As the creature had its head toward him, Ben realized he would have to find a way to shimmy around and reach the stag's tail without startling it. Ben tried shifting his feet a bit and found that he was able to keep his arm outstretched with the fruit and also extend his other hand nearly to the creature's end.

Almost there, he thought as his fingers came within inches of the deer's patchy tail. He reached out further. He could feel the long hairs with the tips of his forefinger.

At that moment, the deer paused from its consumption of the fruit in Ben's palm. It lifted its head and looked off into the jungle. Just as Ben was about to grab at the hairs on its tail, though, the Regal Stag started off.

"Oh, no!" Ben exclaimed under his breath.

This time, however, the creature did not disappear. It turned back toward the boy and his friends—only a few feet away—and then looked away into the forest.

"Follow it," suggested Mugwig, and the three quickly ran toward the deer.

The stag leaped gracefully ahead of them, barely making a sound, and then stopped again. When the children were again within a few feet of it, the creature hopped off again. They continued on in this manner for a few minutes until the creature disappeared from view behind a thicket of bushes.

Parting the bushes, Ben found that they were now on a long stretch of sandy beach. The sky was still dark and gray, but the Regal Stag was nowhere to be seen. As the three piled out of the jungle and onto the sand, they scanned the area to see if they could discern the stag's tracks.

"Not again!" Ben was furious. "That's the third time! The third time's supposed to be the charm! But it got away—I was so close."

Before she could console her friend, something caught Annie's attention further down the beach. It looked out of place against the light sand—a dark splotch in the distance. The girl squinted and craned her neck to try and get a better view.

"What is it?" Mugwig inquired as she followed the girl's gaze.

Annie now ran across the sand and down toward the water. As she approached, she could now see that there were two objects in the lapping waves. One was small and the other a little larger. Now only a few meters from the curiosities, Annie could see that they were people.

A child and a woman, from the looks of it. They were motionless except for the lulling of the tide that rose and fell.

Annie reached the larger body first and called back to her friends: "It's a woman! She's not moving!"

Then she proceeded to the child, whose face was turned to the side and covered in a mass of long hair and strangled in seaweed. As Annie pulled back the girl's hair she gasped in surprise at the familiar face:

"Ellie!"

CHAPTER TWENTY-SIX
Salt and Sand

Ben ran as fast as his legs could carry him across the thick sand and practically collapsed next to his sister. Ellie was soaked from head to toe and he couldn't tell if she was breathing.

"Ellie!" Ben shouted to her. "Ellie, can you hear me? Are you alright?"

The boy shook Ellie's shoulders to try and snap her out of the stupor. There was no answer. Ben wasn't ready to give up on her yet, though. As tears began to well up in his eyes, the boy shook his sister once more.

"Please, Ellie. Wake up!"

Mugwig stood at a distance while Annie placed a hand on Ben's shoulder, afraid of what might come next. But the boy continued to sway his little sister's limp, damp body back and forth to try and wake her. He did this for a few more moments until his energy began to fade.

"Ben," said Annie softly. "I'm sorry."

The boy covered his face with his hands as tears

streamed down his face. Seconds later, Ben was startled by the sound of wet coughing. Ellie choked up a mouthful of saltwater all over her brother and opened her eyes.

"Ellie!" Ben had never been more relieved. "You're okay!"

The boy helped his sister sit as she coughed up a little more ocean water. When she finally finished expelling salt-mingled saliva, she was able to smile and speak: "It worked! Oh, Ben, it worked!" Before Ellie could rejoice further, her attention turned to the other body lying on the beach: "Oh, my—Jasmine!"

Little Ellie didn't know what to do, but pressed a hand against Jasmine's arm to try and feel her pulse. Unskilled in using this technique, however, Ellie gave up and turned back to her brother and the others.

"We've got to help her," pleaded Ellie.

"Who is she?" Annie asked.

"Jasmine," answered the little freckled girl. "She's the heir of Palafox—the one we went looking for. We found her back in our world. Oh, but we've got to help her breathe or she'll be lost and it'll all be in vain!"

The children sensed the urgency of the moment but had no idea what to do next. When Mugwig stepped forward and offered to try and help, Ben and Annie quickly introduced their green friend to Ellie. Then Mugwig stood over Jasmine's cold body and began to press her hands rhythmically to restart the woman's breathing.

Ben, Annie, and Ellie held their own breaths. Finally, Jasmine gasped and began to suspire once more. She blinked her eyes, waking from a stupor, and reached out her hand when her gaze met Ellie's smiling face.

"Thank goodness you're alive," Jasmine said breathi-

491

ly, holding Ellie's palm in her own as she rose.

When everyone returned to their feet, Ben looked around and asked the two new arrivals, "How did you get back here? I thought all the Gates were gone."

"It wasn't a Gate exactly—it was a *thin place*," said Ellie. "Remember, like Lady Juniper told us about?"

The boy nodded. "How did you find it?"

"Well, it's a long story," his sister began, "but the short of it is that Oliver's grandfather—" Then she remembered that their friend had not yet washed ashore. "Oliver!"

"Did he come with you?" Annie asked, concerned.

"Yes," Ellie replied, about to cry once more. "We lost him in the storm! Now we've no way to get back out to sea *and* we've lost our friend. Oh, dear, this is just awful!"

Their grief was short-lived and momentary—for right at that time they felt a low rumble as the ground beneath them shook. While they looked around to find the cause of this uncanny tremor, the children felt it again. Then it ceased.

"Was that an earthquake?" Ellie had never experienced one before.

"I don't think so—" Jasmine was interrupted by another quake. The sand began to drift and undulate around them in the force of the vibrations, mirroring the motion of the ocean waves beside them.

The low dunes continued to rise and fall in this unusual manner as if something was stirring beneath the surface. There was a soothing sound of sand grains pouring—*like in one of those old-fashioned hourglasses from a board game*, thought Ben. Then the weary travelers heard another sound: a sharp hissing.

THE FIGURE DREW A SHINING SWORD AND
HELD IT TOWARD THE SERPENT.

Jasmine turned and saw the source of the hissing first. From within the white sands emerged a long, scaly neck. At the top of the neck was the face of an unblinking serpent—the other end was hidden underneath the dune. The enormous snake's menacing jaws looked as if they could easily consume Mugwig or one of the children in a single bite, Jasmine surmised as the creature extended its slimy, forked tongue toward her tauntingly.

"Stay behind me," said Jasmine as calmly as she could, corralling the three children and their little green friend behind her. She—the heir of Palafox—was the only thing that stood between them and the giant snake that looked ready to devour them.

The sandserpent slowly recoiled, bending back its neck as if to prepare for a quick pounce. Jasmine had no weapon or shield with which to defend herself or her little companions, so she braced herself for the imminent attack.

Just as the snake was about to lunge, however, all attention was turned to a figure at the edge of the jungle who shouted: "Hey! Over here!"

The figure was a man, his face overshadowed by a thick, hooded cloak. The children could not discern the identity of the man, but saw that he now drew a shining sword and held it toward the serpent. Unamused and hungry, though, the serpent returned its attention to Jasmine and the children and began once more to wind up for an attack.

This is it, thought Annie. *We're done for!*

CHAPTER TWENTY-SEVEN
The Sandserpent

Annie closed her eyes as the enormous sandserpent prepared to strike and Ben placed his own hand over his little sister's face. He couldn't bear for Ellie to watch something so horrible happen to her new friend.

The children braced themselves for the impending attack. But instead of the sound of sharp fangs sinking into a target, Annie heard a swift motion like the slicing of a soft vegetable with a sharpened butcher knife. The girl opened her eyes to see that the brown-cloaked figure had decapitated the huge snake—and not a moment too soon.

As the others surveyed the scene, Ben and Ellie gaped at the massive headless serpent that now lay motionless on the edge of the beach. Jasmine turned to them to make sure the children were alright, then they returned their attention to the hooded figure.

When the man had wiped off his blade and returned it to the sheath on his belt, he turned toward the party and slowly removed his hood.

"Marco!" Ellie was the first to recognize the bearded man and dove straight toward him for an embrace.

The man smiled at the girl: "Hello there, little one." Then he turned to the others. "It's good to see you're all in one piece."

"Can't say the same about him," Mugwig said as she nodded to the limp and lifeless serpent that had tried to attack them.

"You're all safe now," Marco replied. "For the time being, at least."

"Not *all* of us," Ben said, lowering his head.

"Oliver," muttered the man, noticing the boy's absence. "What has happened to him?"

"We lost him," said Jasmine, stepping forward. "Oliver and Ellie and I came back to the Kingdom through a passage out at sea, but we were caught in the storm. He was swept away before we could save him." She now lowered her head gravely.

"I'm sorry to hear that," replied Marco. Then he extended his hand to Jasmine: "I'm Marco—who are you?"

"Jasmine." She returned the greeting.

"Jasmine is one of the heirs," said Ellie. "One of the heirs you sent us to find!"

The man studied Jasmine for a moment, then replied with a smirk: "Well, I guess it's a good thing I rescued you, then."

"And for that, I'm very grateful." Jasmine smiled.

The children then introduced Mugwig to their old friend Marco, and the little green woman made a questionable attempt at a graceful bow. Then the party sat in a small circle upon the sand a little further away from the water.

"Marco," said Ben returning to the topic at hand. "We found the other heirs, too!"

At this, he and Annie explained the story of how they located Gardenio, the long-hidden youngest brother of Prince Florian and heir to the throne of Coronado. They also shared about Lady Penelope's role in protecting the child at his birth.

"That's very interesting. And amazing that she could keep that a secret for so many years." He scratched his bearded chin, then turned back to the children. "And what of the third and final heir?"

The children grew silent and somber, then Annie answered: "Oliver—he's the last heir to the throne of Mangonia. But now he's gone."

"We can't give up yet, little one," Marco urged them. "Oliver may still be out there—out at sea. We've got to find him."

"But what if we can't?" Ben was on the verge of tears once more.

"We *can't* give up on him," Marco replied. "Not yet!"

The children wanted desperately to find their lost friend—the fate of the entire Kingdom depended on it. At that moment, Annie once more felt the gold medallion around her neck.

"Oh, I almost forgot," she said as she took it off and handed it to Marco. "We found this at the old banyan tree."

The man inspected it as he slipped it over his head. "I thought I'd lost this for good; it means a great deal to me. Thank you, Annie."

The girl nodded happily but then she began to probe: "Marco, we've been wondering..."

"Yes, Annie?"

"Where have you been all this time? What *happened* to you? The last time we saw you was at the Banyan Gate when it got destroyed—when there was that *wave* that swept across the jungle."

The man took a deep breath and then exhaled. "That's a bit of a long story. But the short of it is that something *happened* when that Gate was burned down. Florian and I were close to it when that *wave*—as you called it—swept over the forest. It swept over us, too."

"Oh, my," Ellie remarked. "Were you hurt?"

"Not hurt, per se," Marco said softly as his gaze drifted away from the children. "Changed, perhaps." His silent, enigmatic musing continued for a few more seconds before he returned his attention to the children. "But that's a story for another time. Right now, though, we've got to find dear Oliver and that last ingredient to re-open the Gates. We've got to find you all a way back *home*."

CHAPTER TWENTY-EIGHT
Jasmine Follows a Juicy Lead

With the remaining hours of daylight, the children and their friends canvassed the areas near the beach in search of Oliver. Annie climbed atop some slippery rocks to get a better view of the open, turbulent sea, but failed to see any sign of the boy. Ben and Ellie, who had known Oliver the longest, were clearly the most worried. Ben didn't share his concerns aloud for fear of upsetting his little sister even more, but the boy wondered if they would ever see Oliver again.

Where are you, Oliver? The salty wind swept Annie's dark hair over her face, so she brushed it away to get a better view across the choppy water. The sky was still gray and full of dark, churning clouds, but there was no sign of little Oliver.

While the three children combed the beach for the lost boy, Marco joined Jasmine and Mugwig just beyond the treeline in an attempt to track the Regal Stag that had evaded the party three times. Mugwig pointed out the place where they had last seen the deer and the two grown-ups inspected the area for tracks.

The man crouched low. "You're sure it was here?" Perhaps it was her curious habit of referring to herself in the third person, or maybe it was the mess of tangled, twig-ridden hair atop her head, but something gave Marco doubts about Mugwig's ability to track wildlife.

"Certain," replied Mugwig with confidence. "Jumped through here and disappeared." The little green woman re-enacted a leaping motion on all fours, which made Jasmine chuckle. Mugwig waddled further into the jungle, leaving Jasmine and Marco to make sense of the creature's vague information.

"You know you really should give her a little more credit," Jasmine chided. "She's more familiar with the woods than any of us."

"You seem so certain," Marco retorted.

"Then you're a man of the woods, yourself?"

"I've spent my fair share of days and nights in these jungles," replied the man as he followed a trail of fruit juice along a bush—no doubt the drippings of the fruit Ben had fed the Regal Stag earlier that day. "Lady Juniper didn't just invite me to the Lamplight Society because of my rugged looks." He smiled back at the young woman who shook her head at his poor joke. Then she continued to follow him.

"So Juniper recruited you, too, huh?" Jasmine said as she pointed to a place where the juicy trail continued. "There."

"Thanks," said Marco as he moved toward it. "It's been nearly ten years now, I think. Juniper knew of my skills, my knowledge, and my loyalty to the Triumvirate in the early days, so she asked me to join. And you?"

"I didn't really have a choice." Jasmine said with a smile. "I guess I was sort of born into this—my *destiny* or something like that."

The pair had now completely lost sight of Mugwig but could hear her humming a tune a short distance away as they carefully followed the trail.

"So, what happened to you?"

Marco seemed confused by the question. "What do you mean?"

"At the Banyan Gate," Jasmine clarified. "What happened?"

"Some sort of wave—a release of its magic perhaps. Just like I told you all on the beach."

The woman wasn't satisfied and could tell that Marco was acting coy. "No," she said. "What *really* happened?"

Marco shrugged as he pushed away a few giant leaves. "What really happened—" he repeated, his eyes focused on the ground. "I'm not sure you would believe me if I told you."

Jasmine placed a hand on his arm, prompting Marco to turn toward her.

"Try me," she said when she had his full attention. "You don't have to treat me like one of the children—I can handle it."

Realizing he could not evade an explanation any longer, Marco inhaled deeply. Then he began: "Like I said, it's kind of hard to believe—and I'm not sure I understand it all myself—"

Before Marco could get out another word, though, they heard a rustling in the bushes.

"Mugwig?" Jasmine shouted.

"Over here!" The creature replied, but her voice was far off in a different direction than the rustling.

Marco crouched low and motioned for Jasmine to keep quiet as he approached a patch of thick trees just off the path. He felt down to the sword on his belt, prepared to use it should the sound prove to be a foe. Then, with his other hand, he pulled back the branches.

An old woman stood hunched, with her back turned to the two, examining something on the ground. When she heard the stirring of the branches, the old woman rose and turned slowly, revealing herself to be Lady Juniper.

"Well, hello there," she said with a smile. "It's good to see you've both been introduced." She turned to Jasmine. "And it's good to see you back in the Kingdom where you belong, dear."

Her tiny, reptilian pet Kiwi appeared—barking—from within the bushes and ran in circles around them. Lady Juniper offered each of her two friends a hug, then gave a stern look at Marco.

"Now, Marco. Just where have you been? I've traversed half the Kingdom looking for you!" But before the man could answer she waved a hand and said, "Never mind that. I suppose you're looking for these."

Here she pointed back to her discovery in the dirt. It was a set of deer tracks.

"As a matter of fact, we are," replied Marco, kneeling to view it more closely. "These are fresh," he continued. "Perhaps we should make camp and leave some bait for the stag once it gets darker."

The women agreed with his plan and returned to the beach to find the children while Marco set up a few makeshift tents using their sparse supplies. After reuniting with the wise old woman, the children gathered dry sticks and branches, which Juniper used to start a fire. They feasted on speckled gull eggs and roasted fruit, then waited as night fell over the jungle. Marco kept a vigilant watch for any sign of the Regal Stag throughout the night, while the children continued to wonder what had become of their dear friend Oliver.

CHAPTER TWENTY-NINE
What Happened to Oliver

The strong, stormy current carried Oliver south for some time, though he couldn't discern his direction as he drifted in and out of consciousness while floating aboard a stray plank from the wrecked rowboat. Oliver thought he could see a mass of land in the distance, but he had taken off his glasses before being swept away in the surge; the supposed land mass appeared as a series of blurry blotches on the horizon, gaining clarity as the boy drifted nearer to them and away from the storm.

At last, Oliver was close enough to see that it was indeed dry land ahead of him. The waves pulled him most of the way there. But when he could touch the ocean floor with his feet, the boy walked the remaining distance through the shallows and collapsed on the dry, warm sand, setting his tiny, wooden chest beside him. He was famished and worn out from the pulsing lull of the tempestuous ocean, so Oliver fell fast asleep.

When he finally awoke, Oliver had regained some of his strength. He recalled that he had placed his pair of glasses inside the wooden box for safe-keeping; he now opened it. To his relief, the spectacles were unharmed. He placed them on his face and then examined the other items in the box—the golden ring was tucked in a corner, the map had a bit of moisture around the edges but was mostly intact, and the journal from his grandfather's travels seemed to be in equally passable condition.

Then Oliver remembered the plight of his friends: *Ellie! Jasmine!* He rose and frantically surveyed the beach for any signs of the woman, the girl, or their shattered vessel. *Nothing. Just the vast, dark, merciless sea.*

Since he could not see any inklings of his friends on this part of the beach, Oliver took the wooden box and began to walk up the shore, hoping he might stumble upon them. *Perhaps they've washed ashore further up the beach,* he thought to himself.

As Oliver rounded a curve where the beach jutted out into the water, he had a broader view across the ocean. There was another much larger land mass in the distance, which led the boy to realize that he was now on an island. From his estimation, that mass on the horizon was the mainland—the part of the Kingdom where he and his friends had embarked on a number of adventures in prior days.

With this hunch, Oliver opened the small box and withdrew the old, enchanted map. *Where am I?* Oliver thought as he scanned the map and held it out in the sunlight. As this notion entered his mind, he noticed a red X form on a spot near the right side of the map. Looking closer, Oliver realized that this denoted a small island—one in a series of islands just off the eastern coast of the Kingdom's larger land.

So I am on an island, after all!

Then he had another idea. He looked to the map once more.

"Show me where my friends Ellie and Jasmine are." He waited.

Strangely, though, the map did not reveal a new location. Instead, the red X slowly faded away.

That's curious, thought Oliver. *Perhaps the map can only show places and not people? Or perhaps only places that it "knows"?* He decided that he wouldn't spend too much time questioning the mechanics of the magical map—for he recalled Lady Juniper's admonition that magic can often be unpredictable—but instead turned his thoughts back to his friends and the Kingdom.

If they're alright, they will be returning to the mainland to restore the Triumvirate and find Ben and Annie. I've got to find a way to join them. But how will I ever get across this vast ocean?

The expanse was enormous—far too wide for the boy to swim across. *If I attempt to swim,* he thought, *I will surely be swept away—back into the seas from which I already escaped once.* No—he would have to find another way.

Tucking the map back into the box, Oliver turned to inspect the island. Beside the beach, the island was covered in scrub and a thick jungle. The boy could not see what lay beyond the tropical vegetation, but he surmised it would be best for him to begin searching there for something to eat while he tried to come up with a solution for his predicament.

Oliver waded through waist-high palmetto bushes and scraggly succulents until he eventually found shade from the oppressive late-afternoon sun within the jungle treeline. A flurry of squawks and growls filled the boy's ears as he stepped into the forest, but these didn't frighten him. After all their adventures in the Kingdom, the boy realized that most of the creatures in the woods were harmless.

But not all of them, he thought with a shudder as he heard a louder roar in the distance. Then, with deep breaths, he continued on in search of a bite to eat, trying to forget the frightening sound.

As he rounded a little-trodden path, Oliver discovered a few large trees with long vines dangling from their upper branches. With his eyes, he followed a flurry of motion and animal noises above. Furry creatures—only a bit smaller than himself—hung and leaped from tree to tree, chanting high-pitched shrieks and *oohs* and *aahs.*

The boy recognized the familiar sound from his visits to the zoo in his hometown: *Monkeys.*

Just then, one of the lanky apes swung toward the boy on a vine and caused him to step backwards. Tripping on a vine, Oliver tumbled to the jungle floor and dropped his wooden box. The monkey immediately swung past another time, swiped the small chest with his dexterous fingers, and disappeared into the canopy above.

"Hey!" Oliver shouted as he picked himself up off the ground. "That's mine! Give it back!"

The monkey that had stolen the box looked down from a branch above and grinned widely at Oliver. The creature's obtuse expression only made the boy more infuriated, so he shouted once more: "Give that back! Please!"

Instead of obliging the boy, however, the ape tossed the box through the air—across the expanse between two trees—where another monkey caught it and climbed up even higher. This one heckled the boy with a series of irritating chuckles and then disappeared

THE MONKEY SWIPED THE SMALL CHEST AND
DISAPPEARED INTO THE CANOPY ABOVE.

behind a cluster of leaves.

Great, thought Oliver. *Now, how am I supposed to get that box back? It contains some of my most prized possessions.*

Oliver stood underneath the trees, his head craned to try and find where his box had been taken. Off in the distance, he heard another low roar. The boy then watched as the monkeys in the tree began to scurry and chatter, dropping their half-eaten fruit as they scampered into hiding. After a few seconds of quiet, the monkeys slowly emerged, realizing the frightening creature was no longer present.

This gave Oliver an idea. At the base of one of the large trees, Oliver tested a few of the thick vines. When he found one that seemed strong enough to support his weight without snapping, he began to climb his way up into the tree. He quickly reached the branches where the monkeys were lounging and tried to locate his missing box.

When he saw the monkey who had it in his hand, Oliver leaned against a thick branch and took a deep breath. Then, with all his might, the boy cupped his hands around his mouth and let out the loudest roar he could muster. The entire troop of monkeys instantly scattered, dropping everything that was in their hands. The little wooden chest came to rest at the end of the same branch that Oliver was sitting on, so he carefully shimmied his way toward it.

He tried not to look down, for the boy now realized that he was several stories up. As he approached the box, Oliver noted that it wiggled precariously on a couple thin shoots at the end of the long branch. He continued toward it with the utmost care and slowly extended his fingers until they touched an edge of the chest. The box tipped a little, about to fall—where it would most certainly shatter into a million splintery pieces. But before it could tip any further, Oliver established a firmer grip and pulled the box safely into his arms.

The monkeys began to return slowly as Oliver climbed down to the ground. They heckled at him with loud jeers, but he ignored them and continued on his search for something to eat.

It was not long before Oliver came upon a fruit tree. The boy did not recognize the shape of the fruit enough to identify its name, but the thick-skinned pink orbs that hung from its branches looked pleasing to his eye. Oliver knew that it was not wise to eat strange, unidentified food, but he was quite hungry and saw no other options, so he plucked one of the plump fruits from a low-hanging branch.

The boy inspected it. It had a sweet smell—like gardenias or citrus or basil—indeed, he discerned hints of several different scents, almost as if the fruit were changing before his very nostrils. All of the fragrances were enticing to Oliver, so he quickly bit into the ripe flesh of the pink fruit.

Its taste was even more delectable, so Oliver began to devour the fruit quickly. Soon enough, he had consumed the entire fruit and tossed its core to the ground. Still hungry, the boy reached for another. But before he could grab it, he felt his body tingling. His eyelids became heavy and Oliver lost control of his limbs, toppling to the mossy floor.

CHAPTER THIRTY
The Dream

Oliver tried to open his eyes, but all he saw was darkness.

Am I awake or am I dreaming? He couldn't be sure of which.

Finally, he was able to discern a distant speck of light ahead. Oliver began walking toward the light but, to his surprise, he could no longer feel his limbs. In fact, he had no sense of his own body at all. Even stranger, the boy now watched himself walking toward the light. He was an outside observer, hovering in place as an exact duplicate version of his own body enacted its movements.

What's happening? I must be dreaming.

As Oliver watched this other version of himself walk toward the light, the body began to contort and was obscured by a gleaming flash. When the brilliance subsided, the form no longer resembled Oliver. Instead, its appearance was that of his mother—Vera.

"Mother?" The boy was shocked at how real she

looked. *But she can't be real—she can't really be here.*

Vera did not seem to hear the boy's question, but instead continued her walk toward the light, clothed in a simple white linen sundress. Oliver followed closely behind, wondering why he was seeing this apparition of his mother.

"Mother, where are you going?"

The woman turned to him but did not answer. Instead, she stared at him. There was a hopefulness in her dark brown eyes, masked by an apparent and palpable sadness. Oliver tried to reach out and touch her, but found that he was unable to control or see his hands.

The light in the distance grew larger and stronger and now appeared as a sort of arched doorway, with its beams casting long shadows behind Vera's slow strides. Oliver watched the shadows play on the strange, solid ground. While he scrutinized her silhouette, it began to dance and twist.

When Oliver returned his attention to the woman, he no longer recognized her as his mother. Now he stood face-to-face with a specter of his grandmother Coral. But instead of the old woman he remembered from his childhood, Coral appeared as a young woman with short hair—not much older than their friend Jasmine. She was dressed in the same light sundress, which floated as she spun toward him.

By now, Oliver was thoroughly confounded and amazed.

How is this happening? Why am I seeing this?

Coral continued toward the luminous doorway. When she was a few steps from it, she turned back to Oliver and motioned for him to follow her. Though he seemed to have no control of his actions in this curious stupor, Oliver obeyed and joined his grandmother at the opening. Coral took the boy's hand and led him across the threshold behind her.

"Grandma Coral," he said. "Where are we going?"

Coral did not speak, but Oliver soon witnessed the blinding brightness transform to a verdant, misty jungle. As the woman parted a few banana leaves, the boy could now see an enormous willow tree towering over the clearing.

"Safe," whispered Coral to her grandson, pointing toward the willow.

Before Oliver could ask any further questions, though, a large black raven swooped down from the tree. It glided with haste toward the boy and his grandmother. The boy ducked out of the way, but the bird began to dive and peck at Coral violently. She did nothing to stop the raven's attacks, though and, within seconds, Coral withered away like smoke or sand and the black bird disappeared.

At that very moment, Oliver felt light-headed and his eyelids drooped. Once more, he experienced the weight of his body falling toward the ground as he drifted into slumber.

As soon as his body hit the ground, however, he awoke with a jolt. Blinking his eyes, Oliver now found himself back in the jungle beneath the tree with the pink fruit. He rubbed his head and then sat up slowly.

That was freaky—and I suppose that's why one should never eat strange fruit in the jungle!

Oliver remembered that he was still trapped on an island far from his friends on the mainland. He stood up and brushed off his clothes, then took the small wooden trinket box and started off—back toward the beach.

While he was still a good way from the water, he

heard a familiar sound: the voices of people—a crew of some ship, perhaps come to rescue him? The boy trudged past thick aloe stalks and tall grass, until he could see a small galleon just offshore. Its crew members were cooling themselves with a dip in the clear shallows of the island when a bearded, older man noticed Oliver emerging from the thicket.

"Hello, there," the man waved as he stepped ashore and dried off his feet. Upon closer inspection, the man realized Oliver was only a child. "Now, what are you doing way out here? Suppose you need a lift?"

Oliver then briefly explained his predicament—starting with the terrible storm and intentionally omitting any mention of the magic portal or the Triumvirate. "My friends," he finished. "I think they're looking for me on the mainland."

The bearded man considered the boy's story, then his gaze drifted to the small box in Oliver's hands. "What you got in the box?"

Oliver pulled it closer to his body instinctively and gave a vague response. "Some personal effects," he said. "Nothing of significant value."

The bearded man didn't seem to be convinced by the boy's quick bluff, but he held out one of his sunscorched hands, which was devoid of its ring finger. "No matter," he said with a smile. "We'll be happy to give you a ride back to the mainland. Welcome aboard!"

Oliver shook the bearded man's hand and followed him into a small rowboat which brought them to the ship. As they approached, Oliver could now see the vessel's faded moniker painted across the stern: *Emilia*. They climbed aboard and the rest of the crew quickly took their positions as they set off from the island. The old bearded man—who Oliver quickly discovered was the captain—led the boy down a small, dank corridor and into a musty cabin.

"You can wait here 'til the journey's over," said the captain. It seemed more of a command than a suggestion, but Oliver obliged. When the boy was inside the cabin, the captain closed the door and Oliver heard him throw a heavy latch across it.

Sensing that he was now locked inside this chamber, Oliver quickly ran to the door and found this to be true. He banged on the wooden door and shouted to the captain:

"Hey! Let me out of here!"

Muffled through the barrier, the captain's voice replied sternly, "When the journey's over. Quiet!"

Oliver was thoroughly disheartened and afraid.

Who is this fearsome captain? Where are they taking me? Will I ever see my friends again?

CHAPTER THIRTY-ONE
Emilia

Oliver sat on a small cot in the corner of the cabin and stared at the door in hopes that it would open. He could feel the boat lurch as it sped across the choppy sea and he realized that the Captain truly had no intent to return to the cabin until they'd reached their destination. So Oliver surveyed the space in which he was now trapped.

The room was small and damp and filled with the distinctive smell of raw fish. A wooden bucket and a dirty mop rested in one corner and a stack of rotting crates sat in another. On the far wall, Oliver noticed a series of markings. He carefully moved across the room to inspect them, wobbling with the motion of the ship atop the waves.

When he finally reached the far wall, Oliver braced himself against it and observed the markings more closely. They were tiny hatch marks, presumably etched with some sharp object to count the passage of days.

Perhaps these were carved by another prisoner, locked

away in this dark cell just like me. But who—and for how long?

As he had nothing better to do at the moment, Oliver occupied himself with counting the marks that covered the wall. This process took him quite some time, for there were several rows and columns of the little markings. But when he finally concluded, his tally was ninety-nine.

Ninety-nine! I certainly hope I am not to be kept a prisoner here for ninety-nine days! At that rate, I might never see my friends again.

Oliver returned to the cot in despair and sat with his head in his hands. The lull of the vessel's motion was beginning to make him feel sick. Then, to take his mind off the queasiness, the boy remembered he still had the wooden chest with him. He unlatched it and withdrew the small, brown book—his grandfather's journal—and began to read.

The boy began at the beginning again, but then decided to flip further ahead in the small book—past a section where several pages had been torn out. Jesse's inky writing covered every page, but some also included sketches of plants, places, or people that he'd met on his journeys. One drawing caught Oliver's eye: a black-and-white depiction of a multi-faceted gemstone.

His gaze drifted to the handwriting near the illustration: *This is my own crude depiction of one treasure we seek—the fabled Gem of Transfiguration. According to my dearest love and companion, this is one of three magical gems given to the first three Kings of this strange land. As my ink can only write in a single color—black—I am unable to properly convey its hue. By all accounts, I have surmised that this gem is a large, radiant ruby—most beautiful and ashimmer when light is cast across it.*

Oliver was intrigued by the thorough description of the item, and wondered if his grandparents ever completed their quest to find it. So, he flipped through the pages slowly, scanning for a conclusion to their search for the precious stone.

While he was doing this, Oliver noticed a faint and muffled squeaking. It was coming from beneath the old cot. The boy dipped his head underneath the bed and was startled by a small creature that scurried toward his face. Oliver let out a yelp and, yanking his head back upright and out of the creature's path, quickly realized that it was a rat. The rodent scampered across the room and tucked itself out of sight behind the crates.

Fearing there might be more rats underneath the bed, Oliver decided he would prefer not to think about it. He lifted his legs from the floor, set them on the mattress, and then leaned against the cabin wall—as far away from the grimy, frightening creatures as he could get.

The combination of the sudden fright and the back-and-forth rocking of the ship began to make Oliver feel nauseous, so he took a brief respite from reading Jesse's log. Listening closely, Oliver could hear the shouts of the crew up on the deck above him.

Perhaps we are nearing our destination, he thought.

The clamor continued and Oliver could sense that the craft was now slowing its pace. He presumed they had furled the sails and must be nearing some port.

On the mainland, I hope! I've got to find Jasmine and Ellie and the rest of our friends.

Then the boy heard the lashing of ropes and the heaving creak of the ship's timber frame being pulled against the lapping waves. Then the movement stopped—except for the ebbing of the tide—and Oliver realized the galleon had made berth.

It was several minutes before anyone came down to get him, but eventually Oliver heard the grating of the rusty latch and watched the door swing open. The bearded captain appeared and said, "We're here." With a lazy motion, he beckoned for the boy to follow him.

They quickly ascended the stairs to the deck, where Oliver was surprised the sky had grown dark. It was already night and the stars twinkled faintly above, but a variety of lamps and torches illuminated the docks. From where their galleon was stationed between several other large vessels loaded with cargo, Oliver couldn't see far beyond the area.

That changed when the boy was prodded from behind by the captain and ushered down a gangplank. Oliver, carrying his little wooden box, felt his body adjust to the absence of the ocean's motion and welcomed the presence of stationary and solid planks beneath his feet. The captain nudged him once more and they passed between two tall stacks of wooden crates. As they cleared them, Oliver now had a better view of the surrounding area, and he knew exactly where he was: the Prince's royal palace.

No! Oliver screamed inside his head. *This can't be happening!*

As the boy gaped in horror at the imposing-but-beautiful pink structure illuminated in the night, the captain muttered to him, "Keep moving. Florian's going to be happy to see you."

What do I do? Florian must know that I'm an heir—and that means he'll do anything to keep me from escaping his clutches—or worse!

Oliver wiggled and tried to run off, but the captain and a few of the crewmen held him fast, guiding him onward.

And what of my friends? Will I ever see them again?

These thoughts spun in Oliver's head as his captors led him through a large door into the palace and he watched the ocean and the docks quickly disappear from view behind him. Then everything went dark.

CHAPTER THIRTY-TWO
Around the Campfire

The night was cool and the jungle was quiet. Their camp was near enough to the beach to be able to hear the lightly-crashing surf, but the wanderers kept out of sight under the cover of the treeline. Kiwi scurried in circles around the fire while Mugwig tried to catch him; Marco stood at the edge of the camp keeping watch for the Regal Stag; the three children swapped stories from their adventures over the past several days; and, across the firepit, Jasmine and Juniper muttered quietly to each other.

"Do you think he's alright?" Jasmine whispered.

"I don't know," replied Juniper, staring at the flames. "What was the last you remember?"

"He fell out of the boat while he was trying to grab a box—it was full of things from Coral and Jesse. I should have caught him but it all happened so fast—"

"Calm yourself, dear." Juniper laid a hand on the young woman's shoulder. "It wasn't your fault. You should be proud of yourself—you helped the children return to the Kingdom, and now all the heirs are back here... somewhere." She gazed off into the night.

"What if he's not here, though?" Jasmine began. "What if he's—" She didn't need to finish the sentence. Juniper knew what she was trying to say.

"Somehow, I know Oliver's alive," Lady Juniper said. "He *has* to be."

"How will we find him?"

"Patience, child." Juniper gave Jasmine a motherly hug from the side, leaning over on the log that formed a makeshift bench. After that, the two remained quiet for some time, listening to the children's chatter.

"I wish we had some marshmallows," said Ellie. "That way we could have s'mores."

"Yum," replied Annie. "That sounds delicious."

Ben agreed, then added, "I'd like one, too. But right now, I could use some rest—we've been traveling for days!"

The children agreed that they should all try to sleep. So, nestled amidst some thick leaves and a soft padding of moss, the children fell asleep under the stars. Marco watched the three drowsy children slumber, then turned back to his post.

Jasmine walked over to his place at the edge of the camp. "Anything?"

"Not yet," he replied quietly. "But the bait is all set—a trail of fruit that should lead it right to us."

The woman looked out through the thick, moonlit forest. The jungle was silent, save for the chirping of crickets and the croaks of exotic tree frogs.

"You were going to tell me what happened," Jasmine said finally.

"Yes," replied Marco. "It was remarkable and terrifying. When that burst of light and magic happened, we were swept away to—"

Before he could continue, Lady Juniper whispered harshly from her seat: "Look!"

Marco and Jasmine turned to see her pointing at the firepit. There was something off about the flames; the tongues seemed to be churning in slow-motion, suspended in place so that their movement was almost indiscernible. A draft sent a shiver down Juniper's spine, and she stood up to look around.

"It's near," she said softly. Jasmine and Marco followed her as she stepped away from the fire and toward the beach.

When the three emerged from the trees, they stood hidden behind a patch of tall brush. From this vantage point, they could see a majestic sight: the Regal Stag asleep on the sand, his winding antlers and brown dappled coat bathed in the glow of moonlight. Jasmine nodded to the others and Marco handed her a small, rugged hunting knife. The woman slowly crept across the warm sand toward the sleeping beast.

As she drew near, Jasmine expected the creature to wake, but the deer remained asleep. Carefully, she moved toward the rear of the stag and reached for its tail. Then, with a swift motion, she cut a tuft of fur from the tail. The beast remained fast asleep and it seemed that the creature was at peace.

Jasmine waved the tuft of hair at her friends and quietly returned to their place behind the bushes.

"Well done," said Marco with a smile.

"That's the final ingredient," Lady Juniper added. "We shall return to the house of the Carpenter first thing tomorrow. Tonight, we should all get some rest."

They agreed and returned to the camp. Marco and Jasmine took turns keeping watch and, in this way, all members of the party slept soundly that night.

CHAPTER THIRTY-THREE
The Magic Elixir

When the children awoke, they were elated to discover that their friends had secured the hairs from the Regal Stag. With haste, they cleaned up their campsite, gathered their belongings, and began their journey back to the Carpenter's shack in the swamplands.

It took them most of the day to reach the hut deep in the jungle, but the children were relieved when they finally spotted the ramshackle house and the thin column of smoke issuing from its chimney. Juniper led the way and knocked on the door. This time, the Carpenter answered quickly.

"Hello, again," said the old, bearded man upon recognizing Juniper. "I didn't expect that you'd be back so soon."

"We found all of the ingredients," said Ben. "The ones you needed to finish the magical elixir and open up a new Gate!"

The old man smiled at the boy. "I knew you had the determination, but your efficiency is truly surprising.

And you're in luck! I've nearly completed the construction of the door—it's a simple design, but one I'm quite proud of. Here—come inside!"

The Carpenter opened the front door and ushered the train of guests inside. As they had gained a few members since their last visit, the tiny shack felt even more crowded, so Mugwig and Kiwi waited outside on the front porch.

Along the otherwise blank side wall of the shack, the Carpenter had built a wooden door and frame. He had taken extra care to carve a variety of patterns and symbols into its panels, but the door remained unpainted and unstained. From the powerful fragrance that filled the cabin, Juniper surmised that he had built the door with planks of cedar and pine. The man opened the door to reveal the ordinary, solid wall behind it. There was nothing magical about it—yet.

"Now," said the Carpenter removing a small cauldron from a shelf, "we need only to concoct the elixir and then it shall be quick work to activate this Gate. May I have the ingredients which you've collected?"

The guests shuffled through their belongings. Jasmine handed the Carpenter the vial full of hairs from the Regal Stag; Annie passed him the leaf from the Great Willow; and, lastly, Ben produced the bag full of ashes from the cave.

"Wonderful," exclaimed the Carpenter. "You've done well." As he inspected the items and the magic recipe more closely, he added, "So well, in fact, that we may be able to make enough of the elixir to activate *many* more Gates if we so choose."

All of the weary travelers were thrilled by this news and watched as the old man began the work of assembling the potion over his fireplace. He measured some ingredients precisely while he sprinkled others more haphazardly into the cauldron. As the pot began to bubble and steam, the Carpenter handed Annie a wooden spoon and instructed her to stir. "It'll need to simmer for a couple hours."

The children took shifts at the cauldron while the Carpenter prepared a spread of fresh fruit for his guests. Marco helped him in the kitchen and watched out the window as Mugwig and Kiwi chased each other around the overgrown front yard.

As they waited, Ellie began to wonder what had become of their dear friend Oliver. "I just miss him so much," she said to her brother. "What if we never see him again?"

"We'll find him," said Ben. "Don't worry." The boy tried to sound confident, but he was just as scared and uncertain as his little sister. He tried to think of another way to console her.

At that moment, Ben remembered the little bronze key they had found in the cave—the emerald-encrusted key that allowed them to return home on their first venture to the Kingdom. He removed it from his pocket and asked the Carpenter if he had a piece of string. The old man withdrew a length of twine from a bespoke cabinet and handed it to the boy. Ben then wrapped the string around the key a few times, tying it securely, and held up his creation—a simple, makeshift necklace.

Ben handed the necklace to Ellie. "Here," he said. "Wear this so you never forget about him—about how courageous and brave and adventurous our friend Oliver is. We'll see him again."

Ellie smiled and hugged her brother. "Thanks, Ben." She inspected the item closely—the three jewels in the key's handle glinting in the firelight—then placed it around her neck.

When the two hours had passed, the Carpenter returned to the cauldron and examined the potion's consistency. It was now thick and viscous, like molasses or sap, and dripped slowly as he lifted the spoon.

"Perfect," he said. The Carpenter removed the cauldron from the fire and allowed it to cool for a few moments.

Then, bringing the vessel over to the unfinished door, the Carpenter dipped a large paintbrush into the potion and began to spread it over the wood frame. The syrupy substance stained the boards a rich, dark brown. Though the children and their friends were eager to find out if the magic would work, the Carpenter took his time brushing the elixir onto every visible piece of the door.

When he was finished, the Carpenter set the remaining liquid aside. He referred back to the piece of parchment that contained the elixir's recipe and then began to quietly mutter a series of magic words.

As he spoke the final lines of this incantation, the Carpenter stepped back. Then, slowly, there arose a faint and familiar sound. At first, it was no louder than a hum; but then it grew into a light, airy ringing—the all-too-familiar shimmer that signaled the presence of a portal between the worlds.

Ellie's face lit up and she looked to her friends; their expressions were the same. They watched as the Carpenter reached for the door's handle and turned it slowly. The shimmering continued and grew more pronounced as he opened the Gate. Now, instead of a blank wall, those present witnessed a scene of a quaint neighborhood through the door frame. It was clear that this was the world where the children belonged.

The magic had worked. The children now had a way to return home and, with the extra potion, they would be able to open even more Gates. All that remained was to find and rescue Oliver; the children only hoped that they would not be too late.

CHAPTER THIRTY-FOUR
The Two Visitors

Oliver awoke in a dark room. The floors and walls were made of porous stone and hardened coral. There were no windows to the outside, so the boy couldn't tell what time of day it was or how much time had passed since he'd been taken into the palace. Across the room, there was a small door with a square opening covered in crossed black bars. A single flickering stream of light entered the chamber through this aperture, casting a glow from some torch or lantern in the hall.

As he rose to look through it, Oliver felt a strange, sharp force stop him in his tracks and a throbbing pressure on his wrists. Looking down, he saw that he was bound in iron shackles, chained to the wall with only a few feet of leeway to move. The boy tugged on them and, with a heavy scraping sound, found that he was indeed immobilized.

The boy's anxieties increased when he remembered the precious cargo he had brought ashore with him—the small, wooden box of family treasures.

Where's the box? Oliver frantically scanned the room in the dim, undulating orange light. When he finally spotted it across the room, the boy made another attempt to move. Dragging the weighty links as far as they would allow, Oliver reached for the box.

It was close, but just beyond the reach of his cuffed hands.

Just a few inches more.

Oliver tried once more to extend toward the chest but the chains were too strong.

Then Oliver had an idea.

Perhaps I can reach it with my legs, he thought. *For they are not bound and should be able to bring the item close enough.*

So the boy stretched out his legs and found that he was able to nudge the box closer. With a little time, the chest was within the reach of his hands.

Before he could unlatch it, however, he heard faint footsteps ascending a staircase toward the door. Oliver quickly tucked the wooden chest behind him, out of sight, as a heavy latch was lifted on the outside of the door.

The door slowly creaked open and a tiny silhouette stood in the doorway. As Oliver's eyes adjusted to the increase of light that had entered the room, he saw that his visitor was just a boy—not far from his own age, by the looks of it. He looked familiar to Oliver, but he couldn't quite place it.

The boy, dressed in a dirty, utilitarian smock, walked toward Oliver, his bare feet padding softly on the cold, hard ground. His bald head contained a few scraggly patches, as if his hair had recently been shorn with haste and little care, and he wore a piece of distinctive jewelry around his neck: a gold chain with a single, large emerald hanging across his chest.

Then Oliver remembered where he had seen this child before; this was the boy who acted as the Mouthpiece for Prince Florian's magical sorcerers—the Seven Seers. Oliver recalled seeing the Mouthpiece on his first visit to the palace, when he and his friends infiltrated the royal dwelling to secure a key to return back to their own world. On that occasion, the mysterious Mouthpiece seemed to be an ally—but that was never made certain to the children.

Oliver now saw that the Mouthpiece carried a round plate. He set it in front of the boy, who cautiously began to eat of its contents—bread, cheese, and a few slices of a lukewarm mango. As he was quite famished, Oliver consumed the food quickly while the other boy watched in silence.

When he was done, Oliver returned his attention to the Mouthpiece.

"Thank you," Oliver said. The other boy nodded, then the prisoner continued: "Do you know why I'm being kept here?"

The Mouthpiece shook his head.

"Can you tell me what's going on?"

The boy shook his head again.

Oliver was losing patience, but continued with his questioning: "Who are you?"

The Mouthpiece was silent for a moment and looked down. Then, softly, he replied, "The Mouthpiece of the Seven Seers."

"Do you have a name?"

"No name." The Mouthpiece lowered his head.

"Everyone's got a name," said Oliver. "You mean your parents didn't give you one?"

"No name," he said once more. "No parents."

530

Oliver felt sympathy for the boy. "My parents are gone, too. Since I was very young."

The boys were silent for a moment, then Oliver heard the sound of footsteps once more. The Mouthpiece looked startled and scrambled to grab the empty plate, hurrying for the door. But before he could reach the threshold, another figure appeared in the doorway; it was Prince Florian himself.

When he noticed the Mouthpiece, the Prince scoffed, "What are *you* doing here?"

The Mouthpiece stumbled over a quick reply: "Nothing."

"Nothing?" The Prince grabbed the child by the arm and discovered the plate that he was hiding behind his back. "What's this?"

"Thought the prisoner might be hungry—"

"*Thought?*" Florian released the boy's arm. "You're kept here for one job and it is not to *think*—it is to tell me what I want to know."

The boy made no response.

"Be gone." Prince Florian stepped to the side of the doorway to leave a space for the child to pass through. Hesitantly, the Mouthpiece left the room and descended the winding staircase out of sight.

When he was gone, Florian turned to Oliver.

"Finally," said the Prince as he approached the boy. "I've been wanting to meet you properly, and it seems that fate has granted me my wish."

Oliver did not respond, trembling in his place against the wall. Florian reached him and crouched to the boy's eye-level.

"So young, so youthful," said the Prince under his breath, looking over his prisoner's small frame. "If you're wondering," he continued, "I know who you are.

I wasn't sure in the darkness of that cave, but now I can see clearly—you are Coral's descendant, without a shadow of a doubt."

Oliver's heart beat faster: "Are you going to kill me?"

"I'm no murderer," Florian said in earnest.

"Then what do you want with me?"

"I believe you have something that I want." As the Prince said these words, Oliver shifted his body to further obscure the wooden box behind him.

Florian continued: "Give it to me."

"I don't know what you're—"

"The box!" The Prince interrupted. "The kind old captain told me how closely you guarded it, therefore it must hold something of value—something you wouldn't have returned to the Kingdom without."

Florian held out his hand. Oliver knew he had no choice but to hand over the chest. He slowly reached behind his back and passed the wooden box to the Prince.

Unlatching it, Florian pulled back the lid. A sly grin came across his face as he inspected its contents. It was clear that he was only interested in one item within— the old, enchanted map. He withdrew the ancient document and unfolded it slowly, setting the box on the ground.

"As I suspected," said Florian. "Your grandmother's prized possession. Crazy old woman. She would be disappointed in you."

"Don't you talk about her like that," Oliver replied sharply. "My grandmother was a good and noble woman."

When he had verified that this was indeed Coral's map, Prince Florian folded it and stood. He started for the door, but then turned back to his captive.

"*Was,*" he repeated the boy's word. "You don't know,

do you?"

"Don't know what?"

"What happened to her," replied Florian. "What happened to Coral."

"I know she's gone," said Oliver. "I can only imagine you had some part in her passing."

"Like I said, boy—I'm no murderer."

Oliver turned away. "Whatever you need to say to justify your wicked deeds."

"Don't you get it? Don't you *know?*" He looked back at the map, then back at the boy who stared back blankly. "Fine!" The Prince continued his exit and started to shut the door behind him.

"Don't I get *what?* Tell me—please!"

Florian stopped and turned back to Oliver.

"Your grandmother," Prince Florian said with a scowl. "I've learned that she is no longer moving or breathing." He paused, then continued: "But neither is she *dead.*"

Oliver's eyes grew wide and his mind began to spin as Florian slammed the door and locked it quickly behind him.

As the Prince's footsteps faded, Oliver shouted: "Wait! What do you mean? My grandmother is alive?"

There was no response. The footsteps were gone.

My grandmother is alive? Oliver let the question replay in his head, along with the hundreds of others—among them, the recollection of what he thought were his grandfather Jesse's crazed musings from the past several days. Then, as if receiving a confirmation from somewhere deep within, it became a statement—one he now knew that his grandfather had been trying to tell him all along.

Coral is alive.

Kingdom of Florida
The Fountain of Youth

Written by
Taylor Thomas Smythe

Illustrated by
Alice Waller

CHAPTER ONE
What Happened at the Banyan Gate

A Few Days Ago

Deep in the heart of the jungle, there was a magical portal. The portal was actually a brick archway built into the trunk of a large banyan tree, and this tree was a threshold—a Gate, as some called it—between two worlds: one the everyday world of normal people and the other an enchanted Kingdom ruled by an evil Prince.

Moments earlier, the tree's clearing was filled with horsemen and a tribe of masked warriors, but the men in masks had driven the others away in a flurry. Now it was dark and quiet, except for pattering rain that seeped through the jungle canopy and the glow of a single torch in the hand of a soldier. Its flickering illuminated a pair of men locked in a swordfight.

Presently, one of the men—Prince Florian—gained the upper hand with a crafty flourish of his blade, disarming the other and pushing him to the ground. The man in the dirt was cloaked in earth-toned garments. His long hair extended past his chin, now sticking with sweat to his untrimmed face, and he tried not to tremble as the handsome Prince placed his blade to the helpless man's throat.

The bearded man, who was called Marco, glanced across the clearing to a patch of bushes. He caught a faint glimpse of a pair of small children watching the scene from afar. The Banyan Gate was the only way for these children to return home to their world, and it was these children that Marco had sworn to protect.

Turning back to the Prince, Marco realized he could now hear a faint and angelic sound. It was a shimmering chime—the noise of thousands of tiny, muffled bells ringing—and it seemed to have its source in the large, gnarly tree.

The dark-haired Prince bent lower so he could look his opponent in the eye. "Long live Florian," he said, beads of rain dripping down his face. "Say it!"

Marco was silent.

"Say it!"

"Never," said Marco.

"Fine then," said Florian, rising once more.

"Are you going to kill me now?" Marco asked, almost taunting.

Florian seemed to think over the question, then replied: "I'm no murderer." He then stepped over to his faithful right-hand man—the soldier known as General Pompadour—and held out his sword. The General took the sword carefully and, with his other hand, passed the Prince a flaming torch in its stead.

Marco watched in horror as Prince Florian approached the Banyan Gate slowly, torch in hand. Its flames cast grim shadows across the man's face.

"There will be no more Gates," Florian uttered to Marco. "And there will be no more Triumvirate. Long live Florian."

What followed after that seemed to Marco to happen in slow motion. He held his breath as the evil Prince slowly lowered the torch to the base of the great banyan tree. Florian placed it amidst the roots and took a step back. Within seconds, the flames crept up the trunk and spread like fiery waves over the branches. The ancient brick archway that acted as the Gate was now obscured by the inferno. Now, even in the rain, the blaze was unstoppable and the Gate beyond saving.

The heat from the enormous fire grew stronger and Marco covered his face to shield it from the harsh warmth. As the flames grew, so, too, did the shimmering sound. It crescendoed into a throbbing, pulsing siren that concluded in a shrill, piercing screech accompanied by a sudden burst of white light.

Marco squinted his eyes, nearly blinded by the brightness which was several times more radiant than the flames around the tree. Then came a sharp and mighty wind, a wave that swept all three men off their feet. In that moment, Marco opened his eyes once more and felt his body lift from the forest floor, weightless. Like a limp scarecrow with no control of his arms or legs, he was hurled away from the banyan and sent flying across the clearing.

Then everything went dark.

The screeching and throbbing and shimmering stopped.

Marco tried to look around but was unable to control his body. He could still feel a strong wind sweeping around him, along with large billows that looked like clouds or smoke. As his eyes adjusted to the darkness,

A LARGE CAVITY IN THE GROUND—
A CIRCULAR CENOTE FILLED WITH WATER

Marco began to see dots of light, like pinholes poked through a navy sheet.

Stars! Marco realized he was surrounded on all sides by the night sky—enveloped in it, really. He managed to shift the weight of his body and turn so that he now saw a mass of dark green ahead of him. It slowly grew larger but the clouds obscured much of it.

The jungle. The green mass continued to expand now and Marco's pulse quickened when he had another realization: *I'm falling!*

Even in the darkness, however, Marco knew that he was falling more slowly than gravity typically preferred. He scanned the ground beneath him, determining whether he might fall atop some rocky mountain range where he would certainly be dashed to pieces, or perhaps a soft patch of trees that would catch him in their boughs with only a few scrapes. Either way, it would happen soon, for the earth was now close enough for the man to discern shapes and landmarks.

Presently, a patch of clouds blew away, revealing the area directly below Marco; it was a large cavity in the ground—a circular cenote filled with water that glimmered in the moonlight. The man sailed toward it quickly. The hole grew. Marco tumbled into it gradually, catching glimpses of the jungle around its edge. Vines hung loosely at the border, but Marco quickly lost sight of them as he toppled toward the lightly-rippling water at the cenote's bottom.

Finally, the man landed in the cool water in the base of the pit. When Marco came up for air, he took deep breaths and decided to float on the surface while he tried to comprehend what had just happened.

Where am I? Marco inspected the vast, natural pit. Its walls extended nearly twenty stories high. *And how did I get here?*

The man had little time to think about these questions, for now his mind turned to the question of how he might climb out of the sinkhole. With only the moonlight to illuminate the deep recess of the cenote, Marco could see no apparent ladder or staircase with which he might escape.

Just my luck, he thought. *Out of one predicament and into another.*

Marco swam toward the walls of the pit to try and find a spot of dry land. To his relief, he discovered a wide patch of stone that was raised just above the water level. When he had climbed onto the smooth, rocky land, Marco placed his hand to his chest. He felt around his neck and realized that his necklace was missing—the medallion that he wore as a symbol of his membership in the Lamplight Society.

I must have lost it on my descent. If it sunk to the bottom of this pool, I'll have to wait until the morning light to search for it.

Realizing that he could do little to help his unpleasant situation in the dark of night, Marco resolved that he would find a dry corner to sleep and try to find a way out of the hole when the sun arose. But just as the man began to clear some dirt from a smooth, flat stone, he heard a noise from above. It sounded like a scream.

Marco looked up to see another man falling through the mouth of the pit. With a splash, he disappeared underneath the dark water.

Who is this that fate has brought to join me here? Marco stepped closer to the pool's edge, trying to get a better view of the figure.

Finally, the man emerged from the pond with a gasp and spotted Marco on the shore. The two men made eye-contact and Marco recognized him instantly.

It was Prince Florian.

CHAPTER TWO
The Screeching Eel

Marco watched as Florian paddled toward the shore at the edge of the deep pit's wall. The bearded man couldn't believe his eyes.

This is all some sort of strange magic or sorcery, Marco thought. *I've never seen anything like this.*

As the Prince drew nearer, something else caught Marco's gaze: a stirring in the water. *Perhaps just the wind or Florian's wake,* he thought. But it stirred again—something alive beneath the surface of the pond. The man couldn't make out its form in the darkness, but he watched as it began to gain on Florian.

Though his expression showed fear, Marco said nothing. *For,* he thought, *if this creature were to swallow Florian whole, we'd be rid of his tyranny in an instant.*

But the Prince noticed his fear-stricken countenance: "What is it? What's frightened you so?" He turned to get a better look and caught the glint of the moonlight off a long, slippery dorsal fin, which quickly submerged. It was close, and Florian still had quite some distance until he would reach the edge.

"Don't just stand there, Marco," Florian said, paddling faster. "*Do* something!"

Marco considered the man's urgings, then his eyes wandered to a pile of rocks the size of oranges along the wall. *I could hit the creature from here...*

"Are you just going to let me perish?" Prince Florian continued his frantic strokes through the dark pond. The creature was now nearly upon him.

Still, Marco stood his ground, unable to make a move toward the stones.

The beast in the water now revealed its head, a gray and barnacle-encrusted eel with jaws that could easily swallow either of the men in a single bite—or tear them in two.

Florian deserves this fate, Marco thought. Though something in his mind fought to counter these whims, the man remained motionless.

"Please!"

The creature slowly opened its jaws.

Marco dashed toward the rocks and picked up one with each hand. Then, returning to the water's edge, he hurled the first as hard and straight as he could.

Though its target was moving, the stone nailed the beast right in the eye. The creature screeched and recoiled. Then, with much thrashing and writhing, disappeared beneath the surface once more.

This single act bought Florian enough time to complete his swim to the shore. As his hands reached for the smooth, stony ground, though, Florian turned to witness the resurfacing of the giant eel.

Marco launched the second stone with even more force. This time, it hit the eel's other eye, rendering the beast momentarily blind. It emitted a piercing shriek and then quickly submerged. The man followed a trail of small bubbles as they moved away across the water's surface and vanished into darkness.

When Prince Florian had pulled himself up onto the land, he immediately collapsed on his back, breathing heavily as his sopping clothes soaked the slick ground. His rescuer, who stood at a distance, found a large rock and took a seat to catch his own breath

As he began to consider the curious sequence of events once more, Marco turned to Florian and asked, "Do you know why we're here? Why this happened?"

Florian sat up. "I was hoping you'd be able to tell *me*. You mean the old hag didn't inform you about this?"

"Didn't inform me about *what*? That you'd destroy the last of the Gates and cause some sort of rift in space? No—Lady Juniper didn't say a thing about that." Marco lowered his head. "I doubt she even knew. Anyway, this is *your* fault."

"My fault?" Florian now stood. "How was I supposed to know this would happen?"

"I suppose you could have used your Seers," Marco retorted with a smirk.

Florian approached him, practically inches from his face. "My secret magic is not a laughing matter—and neither is our situation." The Prince took a few steps back and surveyed the expansive pit around them. "It looks like we're trapped here."

"There has to be a way out," said Marco. "There's always a way."

"The walls are too steep to climb," Florian replied. "And we're too far to reach even the lowest of those vines."

The Prince was right; there seemed to be no apparent way out of the sinkhole.

"I suggest we rest and search the cavern tomorrow in the daylight." Marco's attempt at optimism was welcome, but Florian hadn't yet forgotten his close call with the eel.

"What if that *thing* returns?" Florian stared across the now-placid pool.

"We'll rest along the wall so we're out of reach," suggested Marco. Then, realizing Florian's fear was genuine, he added, "I'll sleep between you and the water if that makes you feel better."

Florian gave a slight, hesitant nod, which Marco interpreted as a "yes," then silently meandered toward the rock wall where he began to clear an area by sweeping away small pebbles. He gathered a few clumps of thick moss that clung to the wall and fashioned a sort of cushion for his head. Then the Prince removed his wet outer garbs and laid down to sleep.

A short distance away, Marco prepared his own area to sleep. He spread the Prince's dripping robes across the rocks, along with his own coverings, to let them dry out overnight. With one last glance across the reflective pond to make sure the eel was nowhere to be seen, Marco then settled into his makeshift bed and closed his heavy eyes to sleep.

CHAPTER THREE
The Messenger

Present Day

The sun was up, but it cast eerie shadows on the jungle floor as a disheveled, old man ran through the forest. Stooping beneath a bending oak, the man's gray beard caught a smudge of sap from branches that whipped past. He didn't care, though, for he had only one purpose: *deliver the message.*

He couldn't move as fast as he did in his younger days, but he decided he wouldn't let his weak legs inhibit him from carrying out this urgent goal. *I only hope I can remember the way,* he thought as he parted a few thick palm fronds to make a path.

There ahead of him was a strange sight; it resembled a wall or fence, but it was constructed from large pieces of earth-toned fabric strung between trees. The wall created a barrier that masked a camp inside, and smoke billowed from a fire-pit beyond it.

That's it. The man was relieved that he hadn't lost

his way this time.

Approaching the cloth wall, the man was startled by two men in masks who seemed to appear out of nowhere. Their masks were carved out of wood and featured painted markings and a tuft of straw that protruded from the top like stiff hair.

"I-I'm here to see Juniper," he stuttered nervously, raising his hands as a sign of his peaceful intentions. Strangely, the man was missing a finger on his left hand.

The two masked men said nothing, but nodded and then created an opening in the textile wall, ushering the old man through it and into the camp. He thanked them as he passed and they closed the entrance behind him.

Another masked man appeared and guided the nine-fingered man past the smoky fire-pit and into a large tent. His eyes adjusted from the bright afternoon sky as he entered, and his face lit up when he recognized a slew of familiar faces crowded in some sort of important council.

"Henry!" A small, girlish voice rang out.

As the man refocused his gaze, he saw that this was Ellie, a small girl who was about nine years old, who ran to embrace him. "Hello there, m'dear. It's good to see you again."

"Oh, Henry," Ellie replied. "We've missed you!"

Just then, the girl's older brother Ben approached and gave a hug of his own.

"My, Benjamin," the old man said. "You've grown since the last time I saw you—has it really been that long since we traveled along the river together?"

"Only a couple months," replied Ben, "but it feels like years have gone by."

At this, the two children escorted Henry to the cir-

cle where the others sat. Ellie proceeded to introduce
the man to those in the circle with whom he wasn't yet
familiar, beginning with a black-haired girl.

"This is our new friend Annie," explained Ellie.
"She moved in next door to our house back in the world
where we came from." The old man politely extended a
hand to shake the girl's own. "Annie, this is Henry, the
ferry-captain who helped us escape from the Kingdom
when we were trapped here some time ago."

"Nice to meet you," replied Annie with a smile.

Next Ellie moved to a young woman with a darker
complexion and curly, long hair wrapped in a ponytail.
"This is Jasmine," said the girl. The woman was outfit-
ted in all black and a pair of tall hiking boots. Jasmine
had a hardened, weathered expression—evidence of
her exhaustive life experience—though she had not yet
reached thirty years of age. Ellie continued her explanation to Henry: "Jasmine is the heir of Palafox."

Jasmine and Henry smiled at the little girl.

"We've met," said Jasmine. "Henry was a member of
the Lamplight Society in the early days—when we used
to meet in the old house on Azalea Drive."

At this, a small green character chimed in from
behind the seats: "What's a Lamplight Society?" The
tiny reptilian woman crept into view, her hair a mess of
knots and twigs. "I'm Mugwig, Princess of the Pond,"
she said, extending her pointy claw-fingers to the ferryman.

"It's a pleasure," Henry replied, inspecting the curious creature.

Jasmine chimed in to answer Mugwig's question:
"*We* are the Lamplight Society—the ones who are going
to reunite the Triumvirate and overthrow the dreadful
Prince Florian."

"Ah, yes," said Mugwig. "Mugwig understands now."

"Then," said Ben to Henry, "you must know Marco, as well?"

"Indeed," replied Henry, acknowledging the bearded man who wore a dark hood.

Marco removed the covering and greeted Henry with a nod: "Hello, Henry." The long-haired man seemed more somber than usual.

Presently, Henry's attention turned to the final member of the circle: an old woman in patchwork garments. A small creature—called Kiwi—leaped from her lap and scurried to lick Henry's feet, then disappeared into a far corner of the tent.

"M'lady," said the visitor with a smile and a bow to the woman known as Lady Juniper.

"Oh, Henry," Juniper replied, rising to give the small man a loving squeeze. Then, stepping back, she looked the man over: "Why, you're filthy, dear! What's brought you here in such a flurry?"

"I'm afraid I bring terrible news," began Henry, finally taking a seat. Then, leaning toward Ellie and Ben, added: "It's about your dear little friend Oliver."

The children covered their mouths in shock.

"Oh, dear," said Ellie. "Do you know what's happened to him? Is he alright? Is he—*alive?*"

Henry lowered his head and his voice. "I have every reason to believe he is alive—" Here the others breathed a sigh of relief before the man resumed: "—but I'm afraid little Oliver has been captured."

"Captured?" Ben remarked. "By *who?*"

"I'll give you one guess."

The circle became silent as they all had the same realization. Finally, Annie garnered the courage to say his name out loud: "Prince Florian."

Ellie spoke up once more: "Then we've got to rescue him before it's too late!"

CHAPTER FOUR
The Search and the Swim

A thick beam of morning light shone over the edge of the cenote, illuminating the area where the two men slept. Marco, who was the first to wake, stretched his legs and gazed up at the vast cavern. In the daylight, it looked magnificent; the rippling cyan pond was mostly clear, and mangled roots and vines hung elegantly through the sinkhole's large opening far above. The man heard the sounds of jungle life in the distance and watched as a flock of green parrots soared far over the pit and disappeared.

When he found that his clothes were no longer damp, Marco dressed and began to explore the dry areas that wrapped nearly a full ring around the edge of the water. He could feel his stomach starting to churn and groan, so he hoped that there might be some source of food to be found in the pit.

If worse comes to worst, we can always hunt for eel, I suppose, he thought as he climbed over a pile of large rocks that blocked his way.

Beyond the rock mound, Marco stepped down to flatter ground. As he rested his foot on the surface, however, he felt a brittle *crunch*. Immediately, he lifted his foot and looked down. He had stepped on the dry, rotting remains of a skeleton.

Someone else who found themselves trapped in this sinkhole. Marco took deep breaths as he tried to remain optimistic about finding food and a way out of the hole.

"Have you found something?" Shouted a voice from behind. It was Florian, standing atop the rock pile as he slipped his tunic over his shoulders.

"Nothing of note," Marco shook his head and continued his slow exploration of the rocky cave walls. Florian climbed down and inspected the skeletal remains himself.

"What happened to him?" The Prince's face contorted as he looked over the bones.

Marco turned back to him: "What do *you* think?"

Florian returned the glance but said nothing. Rising, he carefully skirted around the skeleton and followed Marco along the path.

The two men took their time walking around the stony ground, moving slowly to make sure to cover every inch of the cavern. Every so often, the Prince would glance at the large expanse of water in the center of the space, still frightened from his close call with the eel the prior night. After several minutes had passed with no sign of a helpful passageway, Florian once again spoke up.

"I've never seen a sinkhole this large." The man craned his neck, looking upward. "We must be far from my palace."

Marco turned to him with a glare: "Don't defile your father's name by pretending Castillo Rosa is *your* palace; not after what you did to King Fernando—what you did to *all* of them."

"It always *will* be my palace," replied Florian, ignoring the man's references to the poisoning of the Royal Families, "for it always *has* been mine. Or have you forgotten that it's where I was raised?"

"Unfortunately, I don't think I'll ever forget," Marco retorted. "You'd do well to remember those early days, yourself—before you became the man you are now."

"I don't care to remember any of it—especially not my old man. He never cared to remember me: his eldest son." Here the Prince drifted off, speaking more to himself than to Marco. "Always too busy thinking about Ronaldo. To this day, I still don't know what he saw in my little brother. I wish I knew..."

"A little late for that now," quipped Marco.

Florian made no reply but continued past Marco, who now squinted toward the bright opening above them.

"For a cavern this deep," said Marco, "we've got to be in the mountains somewhere. Near a lake, I suppose, judging by the amount of water here." Then he had an idea: "Perhaps this chamber connects to a larger body of water. Maybe we can follow the stream out of here—we just need to figure out where the water is coming from."

The two men now looked to the vast pond that took up most of the chamber.

"It would likely be below the water level," Marco continued.

"Wait a minute," replied Florian. "You want to go back *in* there? What about that *thing* that tried to eat me?"

"Do you want to get out of here or not?" Marco turned to the Prince who remained silent. "You're welcome to wait here, but you'll end up like that poor, unfortunate soul over there." He gestured to the bones.

Florian took a nervous gulp. "How do we find the passage?"

"We swim." Marco began to remove his outer garments once more and set them in a pile on the shore. Then he picked up a small rock and handed it to Florian. "I had *your* back; do you have mine?"

The Prince took the stone and nodded his head. Marco stepped to the edge of the dry rock ledge and leaped into the clear water with a splash, covering Florian with the spray.

Marco found the water refreshing this time, and enjoyed swimming through the cool, sparkling pond. Though there were a few murky patches, he found that he was able to see quite clearly, which made his search proceed with greater efficiency than he had expected.

Florian waited nervously on the shore, pacing as he kept an eye over the water. Suddenly, he spotted a large ripple on the far side of the pond.

What was that?

He looked again, but the waves had subsided.

Perhaps it was the wind.

As he clutched the small stone tighter in his hand, he saw another ripple. This time, it was closer to where Marco swam—a part of the pond that was obscured by silt and sediment.

"Marco!" The Prince shouted, but the man could not hear him while submerged.

Not good, he thought. He readied himself to toss the stone, hoping that he could hit it if it came too close to Marco.

The waves were now only a few feet from the swimmer. At that moment, Marco came up for a breath of air and turned to the Prince, shouting: "I think I found a way!"

Florian pointed and yelled back at him: "Look out!"

Marco turned just in time to see the giant, algae-covered eel opening its enormous maw to devour him.

CHAPTER FIVE
Marco Finds a Way

Prince Florian's aim was impeccable; his small stone nailed the enormous beast once more in the eye, which wounded the creature irreparably and sent the writhing serpent away in a splash. Marco watched as the creature disappeared, then the man quickly swam back toward the Prince.

When he was upon dry land, Marco turned to Florian and gave him a quizzical look. "You saved me," he said, still in disbelief at the man's kind act. *Perhaps there's still some ounce of good in him.*

Florian didn't make eye contact. "Wouldn't you have done the same if your only way out was about to be swallowed whole by a giant eel?"

As he gathered up his things, Marco replied, "So after all those years, that's all I am to you: your *way out?*"

"For the time being," said Florian quickly. Then, changing the subject, he turned back to the man as he again removed his own outer garment and folded it up: "You said you found a way?"

Marco made a brief sigh and then replied, "Yes. On the far side of the pond there's a narrow tunnel. It's just below the level of the surface, so it won't be hard to get to. Unless..." Here the man stared out across the water, searching for ripples.

"It's not coming back this time," the Prince assured him.

Both men gathered their things and proceeded to wade into the clear water. Then, with their belongings in hand, the men paddled across the sinkhole pond toward the place that Marco had indicated. The bearded man nodded to the Prince and took a deep breath. Then he quickly dipped underneath the surface and began swimming toward the rocky wall.

Prince Florian followed as Marco dove toward a small tunnel. It appeared to be man-made—a cave carved from the rock in an age when the water-level was much lower. The walls were smooth and once covered in ornate painted designs which had now mostly eroded. Only remnants remained—Florian caught a glimpse of a stylized image of a mountain range and, beneath that, characters resembling men with pickaxes.

The submerged hall was quite long and dark, so Marco began to grow nervous as he held his breath. *How much farther?* He continued on with Florian close behind, trying to see the end of the passage.

Finally, the men discovered the end of the tunnel, which terminated in a stone staircase. They reached it and quickly bobbed to the surface, gasping for air. It was a small space, and the stairs continued up for several flights.

The two swimmers rested on one of the dry steps and rung out their wet clothes. When they had both recovered their breaths, the men dressed once more in their damp coverings. Florian observed the stairs ahead of them.

"The way out," he said as he pointed up and began to ascend the steps.

Marco seemed unsure that these stairs were the final obstacle between them and the outside world, but he hastened to follow the Prince as he climbed.

The men ascended the steps together, with Marco always a few behind Florian. They were silent for much of the journey, but discovered that the staircase continued winding up for much longer than they first anticipated.

At one point, Florian turned to his bearded companion: "Are you upset with me?"

"Pardon?" Marco replied, caught off guard by the vague question.

"You've been quiet," Florian said. "Are you angry?"

"Sure I am," answered Marco through heavy breaths as they continued climbing. "After what you did—you've trapped those poor children! Now they're stranded in the jungle all alone with no hope of ever returning to their home. And we're *somewhere*—and I've no idea how this happened, but it's all because of your delusions."

When Marco was finished with his rant, Florian said, "It was the only way."

"The only way for *what?*"

Florian continued his ascent. "The only way to keep the throne."

"The throne you *stole* like a thief!" Marco spat. "You're a mad man, Florian. I don't know how it happened, but you've changed—you're nothing like the man I once knew."

"You forget that I am the rightful ruler of this Kingdom," Florian said slyly. "After all, there has been no heir to contest the thrones, which makes me the one, *true* King of this land. I won't let a few petty children ruin that; I'll do whatever it takes."

"You're insane." Marco picked up his pace and now passed the Prince while stepping up the staircase.

At last the men came to the top of the steps. Here they found a stone landing where they stopped to rest. Beyond that stood a simple wooden door embedded in the wall of the cavern. Marco approached it and tugged on its brass handle. The door creaked open, allowing a cloud of ash and dust to float into the air around them.

With a cough, the bearded man peered inside. It was too dark to discern what lay ahead of them, so Marco looked around for a light. He discovered an unlit torch mounted next to the door. Marco removed the torch from the wall and searched for a stone with which to ignite a fire.

When he found one, Marco turned to Florian and asked, "Can I borrow your sword?" The Prince hesitated, so Marco added, "I'm not going to turn on you; I just need to use it to start a flame."

The Prince placed the blade in front of Marco, who rubbed the small flint rock against it. Within a few tries he saw sparks, which quickly ignited the torch. Florian return the sword to his belt and followed as the other man led the way through the dark doorway and into the unknown reaches beneath the mountain.

CHAPTER SIX
The Council in the Camp

The informal council in the large tent grew quiet as the day dragged on. Lady Juniper poured Henry, the recently-arrived guest, a cup of herbal tea that she'd been preparing all morning; it was still hot, much to the ferryman's delight.

"Now," said Juniper. "Are you *sure* that Florian has little Oliver?"

Henry pursed his lips and took a sip of the steaming drink. "I'm certain of it," he said. "Word that came upriver said he'd taken a dark-haired little boy with glasses and strange clothes."

"And was there anything else they said?" Ben inquired of the ferry-captain.

"As a matter of fact," replied Henry, "there was something else: they said he was found sopping wet and carrying some sort of small, wooden chest. Fished him out of the sea, I heard."

"The box!" Ellie said. "And the storm! He survived the tempest after all. Why, it *is* Oliver, indeed!"

At this, all grew silent and somber, except for Kiwi who barked at his own shadow on the floor of the tent and then chased it around while Mugwig hobbled behind.

"Why would Florian want to capture Oliver?" Ben asked.

"Maybe because he's one of the long-lost heirs," said Jasmine. "Like I am."

"But," Henry offered his own suggestion, "—and pardon my saying something that sounds so insensitive—why would the Prince keep the little one *alive* then?"

"Maybe it's a trap!" Ellie said confidently.

"The girl's right," said Lady Juniper, brushing off her skirt as she took a seat. "What if he's trying to lure us in so he can find the other heirs and *then* finish them all?"

Ben was perplexed. "Then are we just supposed to leave him in the evil Prince's dungeon?"

"We won't let that happen, dear," Juniper consoled the boy. "We'll just need to think on it some more." Here she turned to Marco, who had been strangely silent. "Marco, you know Florian better than any of us—what do you think he's up to by kidnapping a child?"

The bearded man took his time contemplating the woman's question before speaking: "I *knew* him well at one time—but I'm afraid there's not much left of the Florian I knew then." He paused and sighed as if a recollection of a distant memory had swept over him. Then he continued, "Florian's evil, but capturing a child can hardly be his goal—there's got to be something bigger at play."

"Like what?" Annie asked.

"I don't know yet," replied Marco. "Henry said the boy had a small chest; Jasmine and Ellie, you were in the storm with him—do either of you know what was inside the box?"

Jasmine thought back to the prior days: "There was his grandfather Jesse's journal from many years ago—of his adventures in the Kingdom as a young man—and a small signet ring—"

"The ring you gave us, Marco!" Ellie interjected excitedly. "The one with the lamp etched on it."

Marco smiled tenderly. "Ah yes, I remember the one. And was there anything else in this box?"

Jasmine and Ellie considered this for a moment and locked eyes.

"The map," said the girl softly.

"What map?" Marco asked.

"The one that led us into the Kingdom in the first place," Ellie explained. "We found it in Oliver's garage."

"It's a magic map," added Ben. "It can show you the way to anywhere you're looking for—at least, that's what you told us, Lady Juniper."

"That's true," Juniper nodded and turned to Marco. "I believe it belonged to Oliver's mother Vera and to her mother before her—to Coral."

Marco stood up and began to pace. When he had done this for several minutes, he stopped and said, "The map is what he wants—not Oliver."

"How can you be so sure?" Annie wondered aloud.

"Because I have been near the Prince and I believe I know what he wants," Marco replied.

"But you said he's changed since you knew him," Jasmine noted.

"That's true," he said. "Up until a few days ago, I hadn't spoken with Florian in years."

"A few days ago?" Annie scrunched her face. "You mean—?"

"—the Banyan Gate," Marco nodded. "Something happened to me—to us both—when that wave swept over the jungle."

At this point, the entire party was desperate to hear the man's story and all crowded and leaned in closer.

"Well," said Lady Juniper. "Are you going to tell us what happened, then?"

Marco nodded and began to recount the tale of his mysterious teleportation to the sinkhole, the close call with the screeching eel, and his journey through the caves with Prince Florian while the rest of his companions listened with rapt attention.

CHAPTER SEVEN
The Magical Mountain Mine

Marco and Florian continued on down the dark tunnel, with only the small torch to light their way. This chamber seemed taller and more vast than the water-filled corridor that they swam through earlier, but the walls were just as smooth. There were no signs of painted symbols on the chalky stone walls, but the Prince noted a series of cracks and seams along the rock faces.

He ran his fingers along one of the walls. "Why, it's a quarry!"

"What sort of quarry?" Marco leaned closer to examine the pale stone's substance, which glittered as he stepped near.

"Some sort of marble," replied Florian. "This must be where the builders sourced their materials for the palace. It looks as if no one's been down here in a hundred years."

Their voices echoed down the tunnel made of the rare and carefully-carved ivory stone, and the men could tell that it extended for some distance.

"Do you know the way out?" Marco questioned the Prince.

"No," he replied. "I've never been here before. But if we keep moving we're bound to find a more formal entrance—I can't imagine that the workers would've entered through that sinkhole back in the early days."

Marco agreed with Florian's suggestion and they followed the wide tunnel further. The quarry's paths seemed to lack a logical structure as they wound back and forth under the mountain for some time. But eventually the pair came to the end of the marble-walled chamber and now stood at the entrance to another.

The men approached the smaller chamber. Its entrance consisted of three wooden beams that were nailed together in a sort of crude doorway. There was no actual door, but the shaft was covered by a series of additional planks that had been hammered to obstruct the opening.

Someone wanted to keep people out of this shaft, thought Marco. *Why?*

As if reading his thoughts, Florian said, "Perhaps this tunnel guards something dangerous—or valuable."

"Either way," replied Marco, "it seems to be the only way forward."

The two men easily removed the boards with a bit of force and then Marco, who held the torch, entered first. The walls of this tunnel were rough and appeared to be a more naturally-formed cave.

Marco led the Prince down the murky path until it bent off in another direction. When they rounded the corner, they were surprised by a brilliant, colorful light; the flickering flames of the torch mingled with a plethora of large, radiant emeralds embedded in the walls of this part of the passage, which cast a greenish glow over the two men.

Florian involuntarily opened his mouth in awe, enamored by the brilliance of the valuable stones surrounding him. He moved toward one of the stones nearest to him, but stopped as Marco grabbed his shoulder.

"Careful," said Marco. "I have a strange feeling that these are no mere emeralds."

The Prince cautiously stepped back from the rocky wall and inspected the gems with both suspicion and familiarity. "They're beautiful," he said softly.

"And it looks like they go on forever," Marco added as he looked down the next curve of the tunnel. It extended as far as his eyes could see in the dim light. "Let's keep going—we've got to find a way out of here."

As they continued on underneath the glimmering, viridescent stones with Marco in the lead, Florian asked him, "When was the last time you spoke to *her*?"

Marco stopped in his tracks and turned slowly. The torch cast an eerie shadow across his face, but he was silent.

"What?" Florian said. "If you don't want to talk about it, that's fine but—"

"Ten years," Marco interrupted.

Florian smiled. "Interesting. Then perhaps you never heard about the wedding?" He looked more sly than usual in the flame's shadows.

"I heard," replied Marco curtly.

"And," said Florian, "I ask you again: are you upset with me?"

"She made her choice."

"It's no secret you hate me, Marco," continued Florian. "But I can't imagine you're simply content to live your life knowing *she* married your greatest enemy?"

"I'm content," replied Marco through gritted teeth.

As he said these words, though, something strange happened; the hue of the entire chamber began to shift from its brilliant emerald color to an ominous, blood-red. The two men ceased their conversation and swirled in amazement at the rapid change.

"What just happened?" Marco wondered aloud.

Florian replied softly, more to himself, "I thought there was something familiar about these gemstones."

"What is this place?" Marco now drew closer to the Prince. "Is this some sort of ancient enchantment?"

"If my supposition is correct," he replied, "then these stones are of the same kind as a certain Gem of Truth that I came to possess many years ago."

"Gem of Truth?"

"Yes," the Prince continued. "As long as its bearer speaks the truth, it continues to radiate a brilliant green. But when he lies, it turns blood red." The glow of the chamber began to shift back to its former verdant tone.

"I see," said Marco, realizing the Prince's hypothesis seemed plausible. "Anyway, we should keep walking."

Florian agreed and they continued on through the enchanted chamber.

"Let's play a little game," he said when they had been walking for some time. "A little game to test the nature of these magical gems."

Marco did not reply but kept walking, torch raised to guide their path through the mine.

"I'll take that as a 'yes' then," said Florian. "What is your name?"

The guide sighed.

"Come on, Marco. If fate has trapped us together in a dark cavern, the least you can do is allow me to be entertained."

Once again, Marco made no reply as he walked.

"What is your name?"

"Marco," he said reluctantly. The chamber's glow remained its natural green.

"And do you know where you're going?"

"Sure," replied Marco. Instantly, the mine was illuminated with a ruddy radiance.

"Another lie; I like this game," said Florian with a smirk. "Let's continue." He thought for a moment as the chamber faded back to green, then said, "I wonder, can this enchantment predict the future?"

"Your guess is as good as mine," Marco retorted, still plodding on through the dark.

"Gems of Truth," the Prince said as if speaking to the sparkling stones. "I shall test your magic with a statement. If it will come to pass, I presume you will keep your emerald appearance; and if it is not to be, you will glow red. So here I speak my declaration: I *will* live forever."

The stones did not change color. The Prince let out a satisfied sigh.

"I think they're broken," said Marco sharply, hoping his thought was correct.

"You know nothing of the sacred gemstones," Florian replied. "But let us continue our game. Here's a simple one: do you *hate* me?"

Still trudging forward, Marco replied, "With every fiber of my being." Once again, the cavern glowed red and Marco slowed his steps. Then, turning to the Prince, he said, "Two can play this game, Florian."

The Prince was amused: "Go right ahead."

"Did you murder the royal family?"

Florian squirmed a bit, then said, "Not exactly."

The gems remained green and Florian gave a haughty smirk.

"A clever and non-specific evasion." Marco turned his gaze from the gems back to Florian. "Do you love anyone besides yourself?"

"Yes," the Prince replied confidently.

Once again, the jewels remained their natural color.

Growing exasperated, Marco asked a third question: "Are you the rightful ruler of the Kingdom?"

Florian straightened his posture to appear more regal: "I am."

As he spoke these two words, the bejeweled chamber was illuminated with a frightening blood-red glow—more vibrant and sure than any prior. The Prince gasped and turned away from his bearded companion.

"That's what I thought." Marco turned and began to continue down the winding tunnel path while Florian stood trembling, afraid of the truth these magic gems had exposed. "Are you coming?"

The Prince ran to catch up with Marco and they rounded another corner of the dark passage. This new section of the caves was devoid of any apparent gemstones but still seemed to continue on forever. While he was growing discouraged, Marco reflected on the spark of hope that the Gems of Truth had reaffirmed: *This is all worth it—we can restore the lost heirs of the Triumvirate to their rightful places. Florian is a fraud.*

But doubts quickly scattered those thoughts; the enchanted stones had given a somewhat ambiguous response to the Prince's solicitation and now Marco wondered if their lack of change was an answer itself.

Is it true? Will Florian live forever?

Marco considered these questions as he passed through the gloomy passages. The two men continued on in silence for the next several hours as they searched for a way out of the seemingly-endless subterranean tunnels.

CHAPTER EIGHT
Concerning Ancient Magic and Parakeets

When Marco finished his brief retelling of what had transpired between him and Prince Florian, his circle of listeners remained quiet. The children seemed to be processing the strange occurrences that their friend had witnessed over the previous several days, while Henry sipped loudly on the last drops of his lukewarm tea.

"That's some story," said the ferry-captain. "Glad you made it out alive!"

"They were arduous and uncertain days," replied Marco, looking somberly at the ground.

Annie interrupted the man's thoughts: "I'm not quite sure I caught this in your story, but why does Prince Florian want Oliver's enchanted map?"

"I believe," Marco stood to address the entire group, "that Florian has only one desire in mind: to rule the Kingdom forever. And in order to *rule* forever, Florian needs—"

"—to *live* forever," Juniper interrupted.

"Exactly," replied the younger bearded man.

"Live forever?" Ellie repeated. "How does he plan on doing something like that?"

"There is only one way I can think of," explained Marco. "One ancient way."

The others in the circle waited for his reply, but Juniper beat him to it.

"I think I know where you're going with this," she said softly. "*La Fuente.*"

"Yes," Marco nodded his head. "The Fountain of Youth."

Most of the other listeners seemed confused, and Jasmine chimed in to vocalize her own uncertainties: "I heard stories of the place when I was a child growing up in the Kingdom, but I assumed they were merely legend. Are you saying the Fountain of Youth is real—that it's a real place?"

"I am," said Marco.

"You mean the Fountain of Youth that Ponce de León was searching for?" Ben wondered, thinking back to the legend that had fascinated him in school. "No one in our world was ever able to find it. Have you been there?"

"I have never been," replied Marco, "for the place is secret, hidden away somewhere in the northern reaches of the Kingdom. But it is real; I have read of it in the histories of our land. Florian was captivated by tales of the lost Fountain when we were young—obsessed with it, even—and I'm certain this is where he is going—perhaps even as we speak."

"And that's why the Prince needs the map," said Annie. "So he can use its magic to lead him to the hidden Fountain?"

Marco nodded.

"What if he *does* find it?" Ben asked him. "Is it true,

then, that he'll live and rule forever?"

"I'm afraid so."

"Even I do not know the extent of its powers," continued Juniper. "But I have been told that a single sip from its waters will allow a person to regain his youth, and I have every reason to believe that's true—after all I've seen through my years in this wondrous land."

"But if Florian lives forever," said Ellie with a slight tremble in her voice, "then we'll never be able to restore the *Trumv—Triumph—*"

"Triumvirate," Annie finished the word Ellie was fumbling over. "The three rightful kings and queens of this Kingdom—Oliver, Jasmine, and the long-lost prince Gardenio who we discovered only a few days ago—we have to let them take their places on the throne. We *have* to stop Florian."

Old Henry bobbed his head and said, "The girl's right; now more than ever, the stakes are too great for the Kingdom. Florian must be stopped."

"But how?" Ben asked to no one in particular.

"I haven't figured that part out yet," said Marco, now scratching his chin as he paced. "Unfortunately, he has the map and we don't, so we won't be able to beat him to the Fountain."

"We could follow him," said Ellie matter-of-factly.

"Follow him?" Ben retorted. "Then he'll still get there first."

"Maybe we can do it sneakily," the girl continued. "It sounds far, so he's bound to stop to rest at some point. Then we can get ahead of him."

"An ambush," said Jasmine. "We're sure to be outnumbered, but perhaps if we stay close enough we can stay a couple steps ahead and find a way to keep him from the Fountain. Perhaps a diversion would help, too."

"Juniper," Marco pointed to the wise, old woman. "Do you know any enchantments that might help?"

"I have a few in mind that might work," said Lady Juniper. "But it's going to be difficult to whip up something in such a short time and I'm not sure I can do it under such pressure."

The party was quiet as they thought about their predicament for a few more moments.

"What about Oliver?" Ellie asked, breaking the silence. "How are we going to rescue him from the palace?"

"However it happens, we'll have to do that while Florian is away," explained Marco, who had now become the lead strategist of the group. "It's going to be difficult to tackle both of these missions with so few of us, though." He turned to Lady Juniper and said somewhat reluctantly, "Perhaps it's time to call upon some of our other allies?"

Juniper nodded in agreement, then began to rise from her seat.

"Come, children," said Marco. "I think you'll want to see this."

Ellie, Annie, and Ben quickly followed Lady Juniper as she exited the tent, while the others trailed closely behind. When they were all standing in the central courtyard of the camp, Juniper produced a small wooden whistle from within the folds of her garments—it appeared to be carved from a single, thin twig with several finger-holes scattered over its surface. The elderly woman blew on the tiny instrument, creating a series of shrill, resonant sounds.

The whistling did not seem very loud to the children, but it echoed far beyond the confines of the camp. When Lady Juniper had concluded performing the airy melody, she put the whistle down and looked up at the trees.

Annie tried to figure out what the woman was looking at, but saw nothing other than the jungle. "What is she waiting for?" She asked Ben.

"I'm not sure," he replied.

Before they could continue their inquiries, however, Ellie heard a succession of faint calls from beyond the trees. "Listen," the girl said softly to her friends. The calls grew gradually louder, eventually distinguishable as warbling squawks—the tell-tale sign of an incoming flock of tropical birds.

Seconds later, a multitude of lime-green parrots appeared above the treeline and fluttered into the clearing. Their perfectly synchronized flight patterns amazed the children, who watched as the parakeets descended and alighted on objects surrounding Lady Juniper, the whistle-blower. As they hopped and preened, Ellie admired the mottled red-orange plumage that dotted their heads.

"Oh, my!" Ellie exclaimed. "The parrots—they're beautiful!"

Juniper beamed at the innocent wonder of the little girl: "Yes they are, aren't they? These lovely creatures are not just any parrots, however; these are specially trained to deliver important messages quickly."

"Can they talk?" Ellie asked as she neared one and stuck a finger out to touch it.

The parrot snapped at her finger, squawked loudly, then repeated the girl's words, "Can they talk? *Squawk!* Can they talk?"

"Guess that's a *yes*," Annie remarked with a chuckle.

"Indeed they can," Juniper acknowledged. "And

JUNIPER'S FEATHERED FRIENDS

now, my little feathered friends: we have a message for you to take to some of our allies scattered throughout the Kingdom. Can you deliver it for us?"

One of the birds, whose head was completely covered in red feathers, hopped forward: "*Squawk!* We can deliver it, *squawk!*"

Satisfied, Lady Juniper whispered to the head parrot while he listened closely. When she was finished, the birds took flight once more, amassing into a large, green whirlwind that rose above the center of the camp. Then, in perfect formation, the birds disappeared once more over the treetops and scattered in the wind to deliver their important messages.

"What do we do now?" Ben asked.

"Now," said Marco, "we wait."

As the group issued back into the large, cozy meeting tent, Jasmine walked closely to Marco near the back of the group. As she ducked under the tent flap, she turned to him: "Marco, you never told us how you and Florian escaped from the cave."

"I'll be happy to finish my story," he replied, "over a nice, hearty lunch."

The entire party agreed, as they had started to become quite hungry. Marco whispered something to one of the masked men near the entrance of the tent, who quickly disappeared. Within less than a minute's time, the masked man reappeared with a pair of others—each holding a large platter of delicacies. As the children and their friends began to eat, Marco continued where he left off in the story of his adventures with Prince Florian in the depths of the dark, mountain cave.

CHAPTER NINE
The Light at the End of the Tunnel

Florian and Marco continued on through the lengthy maze of caverns that seemed to stretch on forever. Up and down they swerved upon carved mineral steps and solid, stony surfaces through the heart of the mountain. He couldn't be sure, but Marco presumed an entire day and night had passed. At last, they came to a chamber that appeared to be a dead end.

"Did you see another way?" Marco asked as he waved the torch slowly to try and identify a route forward.

"You're in the lead," said Florian defensively. "I'm just following you. Why? Is there no other tunnel?"

"None that I can see," replied the bearded man. "But the walls of this chamber are rocky and uneven. Perhaps there is a hidden passage." Marco moved closer to the walls of the cavern and began to check every crevice methodically.

Florian sighed and felt an aching throughout his body. "I'll rest here awhile; my legs feel as if they're going to fall off."

While mildly frustrated that Florian did not desire to contribute to finding a way out, Marco appreciated a few moments to himself as he moved into the far corners of the apparent ending of the rocky tunnel.

There's still some of the old Florian in him, thought Marco, inspecting every shadowed corner. *Perhaps he could be turned—if we ever find our way out of this place.*

At the very moment he thought this, the torch-bearer stopped in his tracks and leaned lower to the ground, noticing a small, pitch-black opening in the side of the rock wall. The darkness and shadows made it difficult to see, but there was no mistaking this was a way forward.

"Over here!" Marco shouted as he scrambled to inspect the tunnel more closely.

Florian arrived at his side and looked over his shoulder. "It looks quite narrow," said the Prince. "Are you sure this is a way out?"

"I haven't seen another route in several hours," Marco replied. "It's worth a try. Or would you rather stay inside this cavern for the rest of your days?"

The Prince ignored his companion's snarky remark and gestured to the small passage. "After you."

The tunnel was narrow and its ceiling was low, so Marco had to crouch into a squat to enter it. He struggled at first, but soon found a way to make gradual progress with the torch in hand. Florian followed, muttering a string of complaints and groans as his sword clanked against the dirty ground.

The two men carried on in this way for at least an hour before Marco noticed that the tunnel's ceiling was growing lower. Switching the torch to his other hand, the men now had to crawl on their hands and knees.

Then, Florian let out a yelp.

"What is it?" Marco quickly turned and shone the light of the flames behind him.

The Prince didn't answer; instead, he pointed to the floor, which writhed and undulated as if it were alive. Thousands of tiny legs and segmented, crustaceous shells squirmed in the light, oozing between Florian's fingers. A queasy feeling washed over him and he tried to look away.

"We've got to keep going," said Marco, turning back to keep crawling. "Just try not to look down."

"I despise creeping things," Florian muttered under his breath. He attempted to keep Marco's advice but found himself taking periodic glances at the ground to make sure he avoided placing his hands near the dirty critters.

At long last, the narrow passage diverged in two separate directions. Examining both paths at the fork, Marco suggested they take the one that veered to the right. Florian did not protest, so they continued their crawl. Eventually, the cavern expanded once more and the two men were able to walk upright.

The tired men felt a sudden, cool draft brush down the passage ahead of them.

"That cool breeze can only mean one thing," Florian said, regaining a burst of energy. "We must be close to the surface!"

Marco thought the air smelled strange. "I'm not so sure that's a breeze," he said slowly, trying to discern what it could be.

As the men rounded a corner of the wider tunnel, they now saw the source of the wind—a large, slime-drenched beast. The flickering orange light of the torch cast a faint glow on its scaly hide and Marco could make out the silhouette of a series of spikes along its back.

Florian quivered at the sight of the monster. The beast blocked the entire passage—and any way forward—but it appeared to be asleep. Slobber dripped from its humongous, sharp teeth. The creature suddenly opened its huge, yellow eyes and looked directly at the trembling duo.

"Not good." Marco quickly pulled Florian by his coat and began to run back down the dark passage.

The beast produced a loud, guttural growl and slogged after them. For a creature its size, the beast moved rather quickly, which prompted Marco and the Prince to run even faster.

"Quick," said Marco in a whisper. "We can lose it in the narrower passage."

Florian agreed and the two men rounded a curve in the cave. They could see the spot in the distance where the passage became smaller, but the beast was gaining on them.

They rushed on and—just as the beast was opening its fearsome jaws to devour them—ducked into the little tunnel. They crawled quickly until the beast was out of sight. The men could hear its deep roar echo off the porous walls and Florian stopped to catch his breath.

"What a dreadful, hideous thing," said the Prince, repulsed by the frightening beast that nearly had them for a snack.

Marco did not stop moving, but instead continued back toward the fork, wielding the torch: "Let's hope the other path is devoid of heartless monsters that want to eat us."

In no time, they returned to the split in the cave and started down the other path. Much like the previous route, this area of the cavern grew wider and taller so that the men could stand upright. Marco and Florian found this route to be a smoother one, and they continued on uneventfully for several more hours.

Just when the two men were starting to give up hope, Florian shouted eagerly and pointed ahead: "Look! There's a light at the end of the tunnel!"

It was indeed true; they had at last reached a place where the path terminated and the sunlit outside world began. The two men ran quickly toward the light.

The sun was warm and radiant on the faces of the tan-skinned men. Marco lifted his hood over his head to obscure some of the blinding brightness and closed his eyes to bask in its beauty for a moment. As he did this, he heard the sound of a metal blade sliding along a leathery sheath. He opened his eyes and glanced to his side, feeling the sharp point of Florian's sword touching his back.

"So that's it?" Marco said calmly. "After you had countless chances inside the cave, you're going to kill me now—out here in broad daylight?"

"You've served your purpose," replied the Prince quickly.

"I thought you weren't a murderer?" Marco retorted.

"I'm not," said Florian, shaking slightly. "But I can't be sure that *you're* not. And I can't just let you go after all you've done to aid those poor, despicable children."

Would he do it—is Florian so far gone? Marco knew his old friend was capable of great atrocities, but he questioned whether the Prince could kill a helpless man who had just saved his life.

"Please," said Marco. "I don't want to harm you."

"Then why are you trying to stop me?" Florian pressed the blade with a bit more force on Marco's back. The bearded man winced.

"Because you know the Kingdom should only be

ruled by three—not one." Marco knew how to get Florian worked up.

"You're mistaken," the Prince spat, loosening his grip on the sword slightly. "The Kingdom is mine and I don't care who says otherwise!"

When he could feel that Florian had lessened the pressure of the sword on his back, Marco clutched the still-burning torch in his hand and swung it swiftly around toward the Prince. The flames licked part of Florian's overcoat and began to work their way up his side. Caught off guard, Florian dropped his sword, threw off the outer garment, and began to stamp out the fire.

When the flames were put out, the Prince looked up from the smoky pile of ash to see that Marco now held the sword. Trembling, Florian slowly rose while his companion placed the blade to the Prince's chin.

"You know why I have to stop you, Florian," said Marco, his face shaded by his dark hood. "And you know what I'm capable of—what I would do for the greater good—for the Kingdom."

Florian gave a nervous laugh. "You wouldn't dare."

Would I dare? Marco gripped the hilt of the sword more tightly.

Before he could think of an answer, though, Marco heard yelling and turned quickly. He kept the blade stretched toward the Prince, but scanned the horizon. In the distance—not far from them—he could see the beach, the ocean waves rising and falling underneath a stormy, gray sky. At the water's edge, he could make out the shapes of several figures: what looked like four small children crowded around a grown-up—a woman—lying on the sand, unmoving.

Could it be the children? Have they found a way back into the Kingdom after all?

Then, just beyond them, the man saw the shape resembling an enormous serpent gliding just underneath the surface of the dunes. It was headed straight for the children and they were completely unaware!

Marco quickly turned back to face the Prince, but he was gone. Florian had vanished into the jungle.

Curses! The man was faced with a choice: track down the Prince to end his reign once-and-for-all or rush to the aid of the children and their helpless friend before they were devoured by the sandserpent.

With a final glance in the direction in which Florian had run, Marco took off running down the hill toward the beach to rescue the children. He only hoped he wasn't too late.

"Hey!" Marco shouted when he cleared the final dune. "Over here!"

The huge, sandy snake diverted its attention from its prey, which Marco could now see consisted of three children, a grown woman, and a small, green person that appeared to be some sort of goblin. The bearded man drew the Prince's sword and held it up for the creature to see. Then, with as much energy as he could muster, Marco dove down the sandy dune and put an end to the vile serpent.

CHAPTER TEN
A Reluctant Ally

It was getting late and the glow of the afternoon sun hid behind the lush treetops. One of the masked men placed several small logs in the firepit at the center of the camp; in no time, the flames and smoke began to rise and reach toward the sky. Ellie, Ben, and Annie gathered around it while the grown-ups spoke in hushed tones at a distance.

I wonder what they're talking about. Annie turned toward the adults to try and read their lips.

"I'll be here when you return," said old Henry the ferry-captain as he took Lady Juniper's hand tenderly in his own.

Is she crying?

Marco noticed the girl's glance and Annie quickly spun back around.

It was nearly time for supper. Little Mugwig appeared through the flap of the cloth wall and plopped a few fish on the ground in front of the children. She then skinned them, cut them into long pieces, and crushed herbs and spices over them. Using the ends of narrow sticks, the friends silently roasted their fish fillets over the fire.

"Do you think he's okay?" Ben asked the girls. He didn't need to say Oliver's name as his capture seemed to be the only thing on any of their minds since they received Henry's news.

"I sure hope so," said Ellie softly, trying to maintain her composure. Then, in a sudden release of tears, the girl added, "Oh, poor Oliver! I miss him so much."

Annie gently patted her back. "There, there, Ellie. We all miss Oliver. But it's going to be alright, though."

"How do you know?" Ellie asked through glistening eyes.

"Because," said Annie with a sweep of her hand, "he has all of these friends who love him very much and we're not going to give up on him."

The girl's words made Ellie feel a little better, but she continued sniveling. Ben handed her a handkerchief and she blew her nose loudly, then she wiped her tears and handed it back.

"How are we going to rescue Oliver?" Ellie asked, now nearly finished with her teary release.

"I don't suppose Florian will fall for another 'Trojan Horse' plot," said Ben with a slight smile. "But I'm sure *they've* got a few ideas." He nodded toward the adults.

Marco looked frustrated.

"She's not going to be happy to see me," the children overheard the man say. "Or you, Juniper—you know that."

Juniper nodded: "I know. But who else would you have called upon?"

They were silent for a moment and the three children tried to listen for what they would say next.

"She's a very bright woman and she knew Florian better than any of us," said Juniper. Then, nodding to Marco, added, "*Almost* any of us. Besides, the birds have already left; with luck, they've already reached her. Let's just hope she actually makes it."

At last, Lady Juniper disbanded the group and joined the children around the fire, while the others scattered throughout the camp. It was now dark.

"What was that all about?" Annie asked the old woman.

"Nothing for you to worry about," Juniper replied. "Just trying to make some... preparations. Now, how is your supper?"

Annie knew that Juniper had just dodged her question without really answering it, but she decided not to press the matter. "It's delicious," she said through a mouthful of the savory meat. "Mugwig's outdone herself."

The small Princess of the Pond bowed awkwardly as a sign of thanks and then continued eating her own fish quite messily.

Then the children heard a soft *cooing* resound around the camp: a signal from the masked men who guarded the perimeter.

"Someone's coming," said Juniper in a whisper, holding up a finger to hasten the silence.

The children grew tense and looked around, unsure of which direction the interloper might appear. Jasmine and Henry joined them near the fire, also looking and listening.

After a few moments, there was a second set of *coos* in a different tone. Juniper relaxed her posture and let out a sigh of relief. "One of our allies," she said, explaining the sonic signal.

Relieved there was no imminent danger, the three children now finished the last bites of their dinner and wiped up, then turned their attention toward one of the fabric flaps that formed the wall of the camp. Several of the masked men now moved quickly toward it and stood in position.

The cloth barrier was parted and a figure in a long hooded cloak stepped through. None of the children could see the person's face as the moonlight cast murky shadows all around, but the tall, hooded figure approached the fire with purpose.

As the stranger stepped into the light of the fire and removed the hood, the children could now tell that it was a tall woman with red hair tied into a tight bun.

"Lady Penelope!" Ellie exclaimed when she recognized the woman.

"Please, child," Penelope replied almost sternly. "I've told you I prefer Penny."

The little girl acknowledged the reprimand with a smile and ran to give the woman a hug. The other children followed suit and welcomed Lady Penelope into the camp. She greeted Henry with a warm smile but seemed to hesitate when she came to Lady Juniper.

"Juniper," she said in a straightforward tone and a forced half-smile. "It's been a while." Juniper nodded, then the two hesitantly exchanged a quick and half-hearted embrace.

Continuing with her greetings, Penelope turned to Jasmine, who offered her hand in welcome. "I'm Jasmine," she said.

"Jasmine's the heir of Palafox!" Ellie added eagerly.

"You don't say?" Penelope said, looking the young woman over. "I have to say I'm quite impressed with you, children. You managed to find her after all. But do tell me: where is the fourth member of your party? *Oliver*, was it?"

The three children lowered their heads slowly. Then, a voice from behind them answered, "Florian's captured him." The voice belonged to Marco. He stepped into the light of the fire and extended a hand of greeting toward Lady Penelope.

Penelope ignored his outstretched hand and turned to Juniper: "You didn't say that *he* would be here."

"You know those parrots," Juniper replied, trying to conjure up a good excuse for her intentional omission of the important detail. "Bird brains—have to keep the messages short." She smiled but Penny was not amused.

Lady Penelope started back toward the entrance to the camp, but Juniper grabbed her by the wrist.

"Please, Penelope," said the older woman. "We could really use your help."

She stopped and turned back. "Who's *we*? You and *him*?"

"Oliver," said Juniper firmly. "The boy's in danger—and so is the entire Kingdom."

"I'm truly sorry for the boy," replied Penny. "But I don't see how that pertains to the fate of the Kingdom."

"Oliver is the heir of Mangonia," said Ben. "And he's our friend."

Surprised to learn of Oliver's royal heritage, Penelope now seemed to become more sympathetic to their pleas. "The boy is the heir, you say?"

Ben and the others all nodded affirmatively.

"And what of the present danger to the Kingdom?"

Marco stepped forward: "He has a map to the Fountain, Penny."

"*The* Fountain?" Lady Penelope's face showed her alarm.

The man nodded and briefly explained how the Prince had acquired the enchanted map from the boy. When he finished, Penelope sat down near the fire.

"That *is* quite the impending danger," she said. "If Florian drinks of the Fountain of Youth, we've little chance of ever overthrowing him. We must move quickly, for he may already have begun his journey to the ancient place."

"Thankfully," said Juniper, "we have the heirs of all three lines of the Triumvirate—except Oliver, of course. Now we just need to stop the Prince once and for all."

"All three?" Penny looked around. "Do you mean you've summoned *him*, as well?"

Lady Juniper nodded.

"I knew I never should've told you children about him," Penny said mostly to herself, but turned with a tone of frustration toward Juniper. "He was supposed to stay hidden—to be a secret—"

But before Penny could continue, she paused, hearing the familiar *cooing* sound of the masked men's signal.

"That'll be him now," said Lady Juniper. The party turned toward the entrance to the camp as the masked men flanked it once more.

CHAPTER ELEVEN
The Couple

The masked guards parted the hidden entrance to the camp, making way for the two new arrivals to enter—a man and a woman, both around twenty years of age. The couple approached the group near the fire. The woman was fair and had long, blonde hair that floated in light wisps around her as she walked. The man had short, dark hair and sun-kissed skin, evidence of his heritage and long hours worked outdoors on their humble farm.

When Ellie saw the man, she gave a start and quickly uttered to her friends, "Florian! How did he find us?"

"Relax, Ellie," said her older brother. "That isn't Florian."

Annie now recognized the couple from their prior quest to find the lost heirs: "It's his little brother—Dean! Juliana!" She ran across the camp and they exchanged embraces with gladness. "It's so good to see you again!"

"And you as well, Annie," replied Juliana.

"We came as quickly as we could," added her husband, who now turned to Ben. "Hello again, Ben. And this must be your little sister?" He crouched low, took Ellie's hand in his, and offered it a light kiss.

"That's right," she said bashfully. "My name is Ellie."

"Pleased to meet you, Ellie. I'm Dean."

"Dean?" The girl said with puzzlement. "I thought your name was supposed to be Gardon, er, Gordeen—or—"

"Gardenio," said Lady Penelope softly, casting a wistful and contemplative look at the young man.

Dean stood and appeared confused. "I'm sorry," he said. "Do we know each other?"

"It isn't likely that you remember me," said Penelope. "You were only a baby when we first met." The red-haired woman moved toward him and delicately placed a hand on his face. "My goodness, the girl was right—the likeness is truly uncanny."

Dean said nothing, waiting for the woman to snap out of her reverie.

"I'm sorry," Penny said finally. "How rude of me. I'm Penny—or Lady Penelope, as I was called more often back then. It was I who delivered you and spirited you away from the royal palace nearly twenty years ago."

Realizing that she was one of the closest things he had to a living mother—and the last person to see his actual mother alive—Dean suddenly began to cry and wrapped his arms around the woman.

"So it is true," he muttered as he released the embrace. "I owe you my life and an eternal debt of gratitude."

"Your family meant so much to me," replied Penelope. "Think nothing of it."

As the others quietly witnessed these proceedings,

the members of the circle now exchanged more formal introductions with the newcomers. Last of all came Marco, who had a similarly speechless reaction to meeting Florian's youngest brother.

"I feel as if I'm peering into some strange, magic looking glass," said Marco. "Florian and I were closer than brothers, and now I feel as if I've been transported to a time long ago. It's true—you look exactly like he did at your age."

"From everything I've been told," said Dean, "I hope I'm *nothing* like him."

"Never fear, young Gardenio," Marco replied in earnest. "I can see a kindness in your eyes—a light that no longer lives in your brother's visage. You will be a good King—a gracious ruler of the throne of Coronado."

The younger man smiled and nodded gently, then turned to his wife.

"The man's right," Juliana affirmed. "You're not bound to the same fate as your brother, dear. You will rule the people well."

Sensing a lull in the conversation, Lady Juniper now motioned for the party to return to the large meeting tent. "Now that everyone's here, we have several important matters to discuss."

All agreed and followed her into the comfortable and cozy tent. It's tall support poles made the area feel even more spacious than it actually was and all members quickly found seats in the circle. A number of hanging lanterns cast a warm glow over Juniper's wrinkly face as she began the more formal meeting.

"And now," the sage began. "The reason we have gathered you all together in such a hurry on this night is that our Kingdom now faces what is perhaps its greatest danger yet."

The gray-haired woman turned to Dean and Juliana and explained the stories of the Fountain of Youth and Florian's acquisition of the map that would lead him to it. She then informed them of little Oliver's capture and of their revelation of his and Jasmine's lineages.

"The poor child," said Juliana, placing a hand over her abdomen instinctively. "What will become of him?"

Juniper lowered her head and Marco chimed in: "It's difficult to say. Florian is wicked, but I sense there is some strand of humanity left in him—buried underneath the monstrosity."

"Still," Ellie pleaded. "Oliver's our friend and we've got to save him. We just *have* to!"

Marco nodded and reassured the girl, "We will not leave him in Florian's hand, little one. We *will* rescue him. Now it's just a matter of *how* to get to him before it's too late."

CHAPTER TWELVE
Oliver the Captive

The room was cold, small and devoid of windows. The only light that made its way into the stone-carved cell came from a flickering torch through a compact, barred opening in the door. Its square-shaped beam of firelight illuminated the face of a dark-haired, eleven-year-old boy who slept on the porous coral floor at the opposite side of the room: Oliver.

He was roused with a jolt, waking from a nightmare in which he was captured by an evil prince and chained to the wall in a dark prison cell inside of his palace.

Not a dream, he thought as he sighed and began to once again feel the sting of the heavy metal shackles around his wrists. Oliver groped around in the dark for his glasses, the chains clanking along the ground. When his fingers found them, he placed the round spectacles on his face and the blur of light across the room became more clear.

How long have I been asleep? He wondered, unable to sense the time of day without a glimpse of the sun or sky. *Must've been a day or more.*

His next thought was: *How am I going to get out of here?*

Once again he scanned the room but saw no apparent way to escape.

Even if I could find a way out, I'll never get these chains off.

Just as he began to lose hope, he remembered the one possession he had been allowed to keep upon his capture: a tiny, wooden chest—no bigger than a shoebox. Oliver had placed it behind him when he slept to keep it out of sight from any of the guards and was relieved to find that it was still there.

Moving the chest into the light, Oliver carefully opened it and inspected its contents: a weathered journal and a small, golden signet ring. Both items had been passed down to him by his grandparents: Jesse and Coral.

Grandma Coral—Florian said she's still alive somewhere! He remembered the thought that had kept him from getting a good night's sleep—whether it was actually night, the boy couldn't tell.

Florian said Coral's no longer moving and breathing, but that she isn't actually dead. What did he mean? What's happened to her? And where is she?

Oliver had lived the majority of his life believing that his grandmother had died when he was very young. Prince Florian's revelation that she was apparently still alive created quite the shock in the boy. Florian wasn't exactly known for his truth-telling, but something inside him told Oliver that this was no lie.

Grandpa Jesse knew it all along, he thought. *I thought it was just his fading memory, but he was trying to tell me that she was still alive. Somehow he knew.*

The child took Jesse's faded, brown journal in his

597

hands and began to flip through its tattered pages.

Before he could read any of the ink-scratched writing, though, a shadow came over him. A figure now stood outside the door blocking the light of the torch's flames. Oliver looked up toward it but could only make out an indistinct silhouette.

Oliver heard the jangling of thick metal keys as the figure now placed one into the lock. The boy quickly stuffed the journal back into his chest. The door creaked open slowly, revealing a woman dressed in black. Her hair, oily and matted, was the color of her garments and her shadowy complexion was framed by what appeared to be a glistening gemstone that hung delicately by a golden strand around her neck. She tucked the stone under her flowing garments so it was out of Oliver's sight and then locked her eyes on the boy.

The disheveled woman shuffled slowly over the cold ground, her sooty skirt dragging behind her. When she was only inches from Oliver, the woman crouched and cocked her head slightly, inspecting the boy. She appeared to be nearly the same age as Prince Florian.

"Florian was right," she said with an eerie grin. "Up close, you look just like them—your mother and grandmother. Same pitiful smile."

"Who are you?" Oliver shimmied backward a few inches, the chains preventing him from moving much further.

The woman bent closer toward him. She ignored his question and instead let out a brief cackle that made the boy even more uneasy.

"Who are you?"

"I know who *I* am and I know who *you* are," she said with another crazed smile that revealed a set of dirty teeth. "Little, foolish heir of Mangonia."

Oliver was afraid of the strange woman, but tried not to show it. "What does Florian want with me?"

The woman's hand moved toward the wooden box, but Oliver quickly snapped his hands to cover it. The lady recoiled, startled, then smiled once more.

"Dirty, foolish thief," she spat.

Pulling the box closer to him, Oliver replied, "I'm no thief. These were given to me and they belong to my family—along with that map the Prince took for himself. *He's* the thief!"

She cackled again and stood up, towering over him: "Florian takes what he wants."

The woman sauntered toward the door then turned back to the boy, scrutinizing him once more with her cloudy, dark eyes.

"What does he want with me?" Oliver repeated.

The lady grinned. "We shall see." Then she let out a final cackle and left the room, slamming the door shut behind her. When she had locked it once more, Oliver listened as her footsteps and the jangling keys faded away.

Once more the boy was alone in the dark prison.

That woman gives me the creeps, and there's no telling what fate she and Florian have in mind for me. I have to find a way out of here—and fast!

Oliver tried to ease his mind and think of a plan. At the same time, he wondered what had become of his dear friends and neighbors—and if he'd ever see them again.

CHAPTER THIRTEEN
Conversations After Bedtime

"That settles it, then! We shall depart at first light of dawn."

Lady Juniper dismissed the group to go and make preparations for the long and arduous journeys ahead. After much deliberation, the ragtag council had decided upon four separate groups—each with its own important mission and purpose. Little Ellie would accompany Jasmine to the Prince's palace—Castillo Rosa—where they would search for and attempt to rescue Oliver. Marco and Gardenio were to be joined by the other two children to follow Florian's caravan to the Fountain of Youth and—they hoped—find a way to stop him from drinking of its life-giving waters.

Using the leftover magic elixir from The Carpenter, Juniper and Penelope intended to traverse the jungle and open a number of Gates at strategic locations. If successful, they'd have a failsafe way to travel between the two worlds if anything went awry with the rest of their plans. "I don't like it," Penny had said defiantly.

"But if it's going to keep the Kingdom safe, I suppose it must be done."

Last of all, Henry the ferry-captain volunteered to stay at the camp with Juliana—who was much too pregnant to undergo the risks involved in the other missions. Mugwig also agreed to stay at the camp on the condition that she was allowed to watch over Juniper's faithful pet Kiwi. The old woman obliged, realizing that he would slow down her own mission considerably if she brought him along.

While most of the group disappeared to tents, Lady Penelope returned to the fire pit outside. Her moment of solitude was interrupted when Annie sat down next to her on a log.

"Oh, hello, child," said Penny, startled by the girl.

"I'm sorry. I didn't mean to frighten you."

"It's alright," Penny replied, her eyes locked on the fire.

Sensing she carried some apprehension about the coming days' quest, Annie said, "You're worried—about little Toro?" The girl recalled meeting Penelope's son on a prior adventure and wondered about his present absence.

Penny nodded.

"Where is he now?"

"He's still in Melba," replied Penny softly. "I've left him with one of our neighbors. They've got children his age." Toro was around the same age as Annie and her friends.

"Then it sounds like he's in good hands," Annie said in an attempt to be encouraging.

"I know," Penny replied. "But what if something happens to me out here in the jungle? Toro will have no one!"

Annie hesitated, then inquired, "Pardon me if this seems too intrusive, but what happened to Toro's father?"

Lady Penelope took a deep breath and did not reply.

"I'm sorry, I—" Annie stuttered.

"No," Penny assured her, placing a gentle hand on her shoulder. "It's alright. Just a little bit complicated—I'm not sure you would understand, dear."

Annie was about to insist on her own maturity and ask more questions when a voice from behind said, "It's getting late, Annie. You should get to bed."

Penny and Annie turned toward the voice; it was Marco. His eyes shifted from the girl to the woman, who promptly realigned herself to the fire.

"You're right," said Annie. "Thanks, Marco."

Marco walked away as the girl began to move toward her tent, but Annie stopped and placed her own small hand on Penny's. "It'll be alright," she said. "Juniper knows these jungles well. You'll be safe."

Lady Penelope managed to force a slight smile and nodded to the girl before she hurried away toward a small tent.

Ellie was already in her own bed when Annie entered the tent, which the masked men had prepared for each of the guests earlier that night. Annie tiptoed quietly across the room, trying not to disturb her little friend along the way. Suddenly, the girl was startled by a quiet voice from the other side of the tent.

"Is that you, Annie?" She turned. The voice was Ellie's.

"Yes," Annie replied. "It's me. I thought you were asleep."

"I tried to go to sleep already," the younger of the girls whispered.

"And what's keeping you up?"

"Oliver," Ellie said. "I can't stop thinking about how close we are to seeing him again."

Lifting back the covers, Annie slid into the child-sized bed. "We're very close, indeed," Annie said. "With luck, you'll see him in a day or two!"

"I'd like that," replied Ellie with a yawn. "Jasmine says she's got a plan, but she hasn't told me much about it yet."

"She's very capable. She'll tell you when she's ready."

Both girls smiled with their eyes closed and turned over in their beds. With another pair of yawns, Annie and Ellie sunk into a deep sleep.

CHAPTER FOURTEEN
Parting Ways

The children were awakened by the gentle nudging of their grown-up counterparts. They quickly dressed and gathered their things for their respective journeys. To Annie it still looked as dark as night outside, but she knew from the in-fading chirps of distant wildlife that the sun was rising beyond the thick trees that surrounded them.

The girl watched as Henry and Lady Juniper exchanged a long hug before they parted ways. At the opposite side of the group, Juliana gave a farewell kiss to her husband. Dean placed a soft hand on the woman's abdomen.

"I do this for our child," he said softly. "For a better Kingdom where he'll grow up without fear of my brother's evil ways."

"I know, my love," Juliana said, tears forming at the edges of her eyes. "Return to us swiftly."

"I intend to," replied the young man. They embraced and then Dean joined Marco and the children.

When all three parties were ready, the rest of them said their collective goodbyes to Henry, Juliana, and the creatures that would stay behind at the camp. Mugwig held Kiwi in her arms like a baby, but he jumped out and ran after Lady Juniper, licking at the old woman's feet. With a chuckle, Juniper crouched, pet the creature lightly, and then sent him back toward the little green woman.

The masked men parted the camp's patchwork wall and allowed the travelers to pass through. The guards handed a torch to a member of each group to light their way for the first dark hours of the day ahead.

Juniper and Penny were the first to separate from the larger pack.

"Be careful," offered Marco earnestly with a somber look to each of the women. Juniper smiled and offered the man a brief hug, while Penny simply nodded and started down the path.

Soon it came time for the remaining two groups to part ways. Ben ran to his little sister and wrapped his arms around her tightly.

"Ellie," he said, trying not to cry, "you don't have to go if you're too afraid."

"I'm not afraid," she said, her speech partially muffled by her brother's shirt as he continued to hold her. "Jasmine will take good care of me."

Finally, the boy released his sister and looked at her directly in the eyes. "Promise you'll be careful and stay close to her?"

The girl nodded.

"I need to hear you say it," Ben said, his tone still full of concern.

"I promise," replied Ellie.

Ben was slightly relieved. He gave Ellie one last

squeeze and then his party—led by Marco—trudged down a jungle path and faded gradually out of sight. This left Jasmine and Ellie alone in the dark morning woods.

"Which way is the palace?" Ellie asked the young woman.

"This way," she pointed. "If we keep a good pace, we'll be there before nightfall."

Ellie followed as Jasmine bore the torch and guided them down a winding, mossy path. The land was softer and mushier than before as they entered a part of the Kingdom fraught with a network of narrow streams.

Jasmine helped the girl step across the streams, using the spindly, above-ground roots of mangrove trees to remain dry. On a few occasions, Ellie tripped and nearly fell into the shallow waters, but the woman narrowly snatched the girl from such a soggy fate. Jasmine's reflexes were quick, as she'd been training for a moment like this for most of her life; for that, Ellie was truly grateful.

As they forded the tiny rivulets, the pair felt a wave of warmth as the sun crept into view. Its dappled shadows pounced and played on the surface of the rippling waters, casting a sparkle over the whole area.

While she was enamored with the morning's beauty, Ellie held tightly to one of the mangrove trunks. She felt a slight tickling sensation on her hand that began to move slowly down her arm. The girl turned to see what had caused this feeling and let out a shrill scream.

"What is it?" Jasmine whipped around.

"A spider!" Ellie said, watching the large, long-legged arachnid make its way along her arm.

"Careful," said the woman. "Don't make any sudden movements or it may bite."

"Is it vemon—venomous?" Ellie stuttered, nearly hyperventilating.

With wide eyes, Ellie froze as Jasmine crouched to the level of the frightening creature. It was large and featured a prominent yellow abdomen and legs with stripes of black. "I think so," Jasmine replied as she looked around for a way to remove it safely.

The spider crept slowly along the girl's tiny arm, drawing nearer to her shoulder.

"Can you get it off?" Ellie said almost frantically, still trying to control her breathing so as not to startle the creature into biting her soft flesh.

"Hold still," said Jasmine, reaching for a small stick. She poised, waited for the right moment, then struck.

The spider shrieked and shriveled, pulling its many limbs into its body, and fell into the stream. The light current carried it away as Ellie stood in shock taking heavy breaths.

"Thank you!" The girl hugged Jasmine.

"Don't mention it," the woman replied. "Ready to keep going?"

Ellie nodded. "I'm going to keep an eye out for any more of those horrid creatures."

The rest of their journey was relatively uneventful. Soon the two crossed a humble footbridge and passed by a small village.

"That's where we first met Marco," said Ellie. "And our friend Bevelle—she's the one who designed the golden alligator!"

"I've heard much about this interesting sculpture," replied Jasmine as they continued on.

"It was quite exciting," Ellie added. "We used it to sneak into the palace—the first time—and we were able to outsmart the Prince and his strange Seers. Come to

"WE'VE ARRIVED," JASMINE REPLIED AS SHE
PULLED BACK A FEW THICK BANANA LEAVES.

think of it, I've never actually seen the palace in the daylight and—" The girl paused and had a thought. "I've been meaning to ask you, Jasmine: what's our plan for getting into the palace this time? Or perhaps you'll tell me when we arrive."

"We've arrived," Jasmine replied as she pulled back a few thick banana leaves.

In the midday light, the palace gave off a rosy glow. Its tall stucco walls were painted a peach-pink and the roof sections of the huge, handsome structure were covered in rounded terra-cotta tiles—no two tiles exactly the same ruddy shade. Arched windows and jutting parapets dotted the facade while tattered flags waved from twin pinnacles.

"Castillo Rosa," Jasmine explained. "The royal palace of the line of Coronado."

"It's so gorgeous," said Ellie, her mouth agape.

"Yes, it is," said the woman. "Now, let me tell you how we're going to get inside—"

Before Jasmine could continue, they heard a heavy, wooden creaking. The two watched from the distance as the large front gates of the palace were slowly opened. Seconds later, a stream of riders on black horses issued from within. At the center of the pack, Jasmine spotted one mount that was distinct from all the rest; in fact, it was a rare, black stag with imposing, sharpened antlers with tips coated in silver. The rider atop the stag was also dressed differently than the others and he was immediately recognizable to little Ellie.

"Prince Florian!" She said with a sharp gasp.

"It's a good thing our friends left when they did," muttered Jasmine, pointing to the old map in his hands. "He's off to find the Fountain of Youth."

CHAPTER FIFTEEN
Marco's Recollections

That morning, Marco's party had set off in a north-ward direction, as legend and lore suggested the location of the Fountain to be somewhere in the far upper regions of the Kingdom.

"Until we're on Florian's tail," Marco had told his companions, "we'll continue on in this direction."

And so they did. Just like their counterparts who sought to rescue Oliver, the other group made quick progress through the jungle during the early daylight hours. Ben thought much of the area looked familiar from their first excursion into the Kingdom, but he couldn't be sure—after all, most parts of the jungle were hard to distinguish from one another in the absence of definitive landmarks.

The boy stuck close to Annie as they walked, for the deeper, darker pockets of the forest frightened him.

"I-I want to make sure you're safe," Ben fibbed with a tremor in his voice.

Annie smiled and tried to hide a chortle. "I appreciate that. And I feel very safe with three, strong protectors leading the way."

At this, Ben involuntarily straightened his posture so that his chest was puffed out and his chin was a little higher. He was completely oblivious to the fact that Annie could see right through his terror of the unknown world around them, but being near to her made him feel a little more at ease.

Marco glanced back at the two children who walked behind him and flashed a grin to Annie before turning back to the path ahead.

"Tell me more about my brother," said Dean. "Before he—um—"

"Before he changed?"

Dean nodded.

"Well," Marco began, "I suppose he always liked to get into trouble—jumping out from behind a wall to scare the nurses; snatching the keys from the groundskeeper so he'd get locked out of his quarters—harmless things, really. But there was a fire in him—a vitality that was infectious. It drew everyone in. People loved him—truly."

Marco paused and Dean waited for him to continue. "Still, he was unsure of himself—always questioning his father's love. Comparing himself to his brothers and sister. I could see that the king loved Florian as deeply as any of his children, but I felt sorry that the Prince couldn't see it himself."

Marco paused to warn the group of a thick root—a tripping hazard—as they continued through the jungle, then Gardenio asked, "How is it that you were so close to him?"

"I grew up in the palace," replied Marco. "I was not of noble birth, but I was raised on the palace grounds."

"Then you knew Lady Penelope, as well?" Dean inquired.

Marco was silent for a moment, then said, "Yes. We were all quite close in age and friendship."

"And what of my father?" Gardenio continued his interrogation. "What was he like?"

"King Fernando? He was a great man—and the closest thing to a father I've ever known."

"Do you have any children of your own?" Dean asked, then backpedaled as he realized the question might've been a little too intrusive. "I'm sorry for all the questions, I just meant—"

"It's alright," Marco consoled him, looking back to make sure Ben and Annie were still keeping up. "I wouldn't be much good as a father. But you're about to be one yourself, I hear?"

Gardenio nodded. "Juliana's expecting any day now, as a matter of fact."

They came to an area in the jungle where the vines grew thick, obscuring the way forward. Marco withdrew a blade and hacked at them as the others followed in a single file line.

"I've often wondered what it would be like to be a father," continued the younger man, "as I never had the chance to know my own, either. What am I supposed to do when I have to keep a child alive and I've had no one to show me the way?"

"I have a feeling," said Marco between chops, "that you've inherited the best of King Fernando's traits. With his kindness and grace, and Florian's one redeeming quality—his looks—" Marco smiled at Dean, "I think you'll make a fine and winsome successor, and perhaps an even better father."

Dean felt a closeness to Marco, one of the few connections between his family's past and present. With this in mind, the younger man was warm and content as they continued their steady journey.

"How much farther?" Ben shouted from the rear of the pack.

"We'll make camp soon," replied Marco. "We've got one quick stop to make, but until the sun begins to set, we should continue our hike."

The others agreed and remained in relatively good spirits as they slowly progressed through the thick, vine-draped pathway.

Suddenly, Marco stopped moving. Ben wasn't paying much attention and bumped right into Annie, who had also paused her steps, so that the two tumbled to the mossy ground in a heap. The boy clumsily untangled himself, stood up, and supported Annie as she wiped the dirt off her clothes. Marco turned sharply to the children and covered his mouth with his finger to urge them to be quiet.

In the stillness, the other members of the party looked around—searching in every direction for the source of whatever sound Marco heard. Then, faintly, Annie discerned the light pattering. It slowly grew to a more percussive and rhythmic sound then, finally, into an audible trot.

"Horses," said Marco in a whisper.

"Florian?" Ben asked with a gulp.

Their guide nodded. "Quick, get low to the ground."

They did so quickly, crouching behind the thick, ferny underbrush. In the distance, they saw what looked like a cloud of black growing at the end of a wide path not far from them. In a matter of minutes, the shadow was clearly visible as Florian's army of soldiers, brandishing sharp weapons while riding slowly on horseback. Near the middle of the group, Florian perched upon an imposing black stag with fearsome silver-gilt antlers. Also in the pack were several wooden wagons to round out the caravan.

They moved slowly to keep the wagons in tow, but when they had passed by and the sound had faded away, Marco stood and motioned for the others to follow.

"We're on the trail now," he said. "We will make camp at nightfall and stay close on Florian's heels."

"But they're on horseback!" Ben said. "How will we keep up?"

"Like I said before," replied Marco, "we've got one brief stop to make—and we're nearly there. Follow me!"

CHAPTER SIXTEEN
Beasts of the Royal Menagerie

Marco led the others in surreptitiously crossing the hoof-marked path, where they were again engulfed in thick shrubbery. When they had proceeded past the bulk of the vines and thorny bushes, they entered a sort of clearing that was flanked by a number of large, mangled oaks. Spanish moss hung in large tufts from on high, and the golden sunset seeped through the oaken branches, lending a mystical quality to that corner of the jungle.

The children watched Marco as he spun in either direction, apparently looking for something or someone.

"What is it, Marco?" Annie inquired of the man.

"Should be around here somewhere," he mumbled to himself.

Gardenio was as confused as the children and observed as Marco now knelt at the base of one of the trees which had a mark etched into its trunk. Digging through the crunchy leaves, the bearded man said, "There they are!" and returned to the others.

In his hand were two oddly-carved sticks that looked nearly identical. They were less than a foot in length and appeared to be constructed of a heavier, thicker wood than a typical twig.

Ben tried to get a better look. "What are those?"

"This is how we'll call them," replied Marco, who now began to hit the two sticks together. Their sound was resonant and rich, like a marimba or a mallet on hollow wood.

"Call who?" Annie watched as the man continued to hit them together rhythmically, wandering about the clearing.

Marco made no reply. He held the sticks at either of his sides, once again bringing a silence to the clearing.

Soon four creatures emerged slowly from beyond the group, making almost no sound as they sauntered across the crinkled leaves. They were large birds, each taller than the men, with thick grayish plumage and long narrow necks.

"Ostriches!" Annie said with delight, cautiously moving toward the beautiful beasts. "Can these creatures speak like so many of the others in the Kingdom?"

Marco shook his head. "They're well-trained, but not in the powers of speech."

"Where did they come from?" Dean inquired of the man, stroking one's feathery coat as it came near.

"As I told you before," Marco answered, "I grew up on the palace grounds. I served as an apprentice of sorts to the old groundskeeper and took a special interest in the palace menagerie. These are a few of the wondrous creatures that I was able to set loose before I left the palace for good."

The children and Dean continued to marvel at the massive ostriches while Marco withdrew a few small bits of food, which were nibbled up graciously.

"They will serve us well and can move quickly through the woods," he continued. "Are you ready?"

Ben was unsure of the bird's stability, but Marco and Dean helped him onto its back with ease. They did the same for Annie and then leaped onto their own steeds. The bearded man whispered something into the ear of his mount and the bird softly squawked a message to its friends.

"Hold on tight," said Marco just in time, as the birds began to move rapidly across the clearing and back toward the trail where they had seen the Prince.

Once he overcame his fear of the curious creatures, Ben began to rather enjoy traveling on the back of an ostrich; they moved much quicker than the party could on foot and the swift motion generated a refreshing breeze as the sun continued to set.

Shadows stretched across the path and cast gnarled shapes all around. There was now little light left in the day, and they had not yet caught up to Florian's caravan.

"Are you sure we're heading the proper direction?" Ben wondered aloud to their guide.

Marco examined the dirty path ahead of them. "I'm sure. These tracks are still fresh. We're gaining on them."

With a burst of renewed energy, the party followed the tracks a bit further until Marco held up a hand for the ostriches to stop. They obeyed the signal. The children and Dean grew tense as they could sense the caution in their leader's movements. Marco disembarked from the ostrich and pointed into the trees just ahead.

"It's Florian's men," he said in a whisper, helping the others to the ground and leading the pack a few meters back. "We'll make camp a safe distance away so as not to draw attention."

As they assembled a tent and gathered dry firewood, Dean used the kindling to light a flame. After a hearty but simple dinner, the group went to sleep. The two men took shifts throughout the night to keep watch for any of Florian's men, and to be ready and alert should his caravan resume its journey.

CHAPTER SEVENTEEN
The Note

Oliver lay on the cold stone floor, his wrists rubbed raw from his rusting shackles. He couldn't recall how many days or nights he'd been trapped there and he had grown accustomed to the meager rations provided to him by the attendants who came—he presumed—on a daily basis.

Or did they come nightly? The boy was losing his hope and his appetite. *And my mind, it seems.*

His thoughts turned to his friends—Ben, Ellie, and Annie—whom he missed very much. Though it had only been a few days since he had last seen them, the monotony of the windowless chamber made it feel to Oliver as if months had passed.

Next, he recalled his grandfather Jesse. He was the one who had given Oliver and his friends the clues they needed to get back into the Kingdom earlier that week. The man was old and his memory was fading, but most of what he disclosed was true and helpful. He had written down many stories and kept logs of his adventures in the Kingdom as a young man in his journal, which had passed on to the boy.

The journal.

Oliver removed his grandfather's tattered journal from the little wooden box that he kept near him in the cell. It's faded brown cover was simple and leathery. Oliver cycled through a few of the yellowed pages and revisited a familiar one; it featured a crude but detailed sketch of a gem in black and white. His grandfather's words described it as a ruby with magical powers of transformation.

Next, he decided to flip forward in the journal to see if he could stumble on any tidbits of information that might either help him escape from his prison or, at the very least, bring him some bit of levity.

Jesse was a decent artist and had filled the pages of his diary with sketches of the Kingdom's exotic wildlife, unique herbs and plants, and mystical locales. There was even an attempt at a map of the entire land that resembled the larger one that Prince Florian had taken from Oliver's belongings—the map that once belonged to Coral and Jesse, the boy's grandparents.

Oliver turned the journal sideways to inspect the map that spanned an entire two-page spread. It looked just like the maps of Florida that the boy was accustomed to—except for scattered symbols that indicated mountains near the center of the landmass, encircling what looked like Lake Okeechobee with a note labeling it as *Grand Lake* instead.

That's where we found the library, he recalled.

There was also a series of small islands off the southeastern coast. *I think one of those islands is where I landed after that dreadful storm that tore our boat apart,* thought Oliver. *Before I was taken aboard the* Emilia *and made a captive.*

Just then, the boy's recollections were interrupted by the sound of soft footsteps padding along the stony stairs outside the prison cell door. Oliver turned toward the door, waiting for someone to open it. But it remained shut.

"Who's there?" Oliver shouted. There was no answer; just shuffling.

Through the crack of light that spilled under the wooden door, Oliver noticed the shape and shadow of someone moving—now crouching. As he squinted to get a better look, a sudden motion startled the boy and he lurched back. A small piece of folded paper slid across the carved-coral floor, propelled by the mysterious figure outside the door. It stopped just short of Oliver, who inspected it with curiosity from a distance.

The footsteps scampered away and out of range of his hearing. Oliver leaned toward the piece of paper. He couldn't reach it with his shackled hands, so he bent out his leg and, with much struggling, nudged the note closer until it was within his grasp.

Unfolding it, Oliver shifted so he could allow the torchlight to illuminate the paper's contents. It was a note. Written quickly in a dark ink, the note looked sloppy, as if a child had been its scribe. Oliver surmised that the letter had come from the small boy who had recently been reprimanded for visiting him—the one called the Mouthpiece.

The note was simple. It read:

Dont trust the wich.

Oliver tried to ignore the spelling and grammatical errors and wondered why the child had delivered him this message. *Which witch is he referring to? The woman in black, perhaps?* Oliver already had a distrust of the woman based on his singular interaction with her, but the Mouthpiece's warning confirmed it.

It also confirmed something else that Oliver had been unsure of up until now: the Mouthpiece was an ally—a friend. Every time he had seen the small boy, it looked as if he had been taken care of very poorly— or even punished too harshly—and made to engage in strange magic rituals for the Prince's gain. Oliver felt sympathy for the boy, as well as gratitude for his role in helping give him and his friends vital information to escape from the palace on their first visit.

If I ever find a way out of Castillo Rosa, Oliver thought, *I'm bringing the Mouthpiece with me.*

With that thought, Oliver folded the Mouthpiece's note and tucked it away inside the pages of Jesse's journal to keep it out of sight of any future visitors. Then he continued reading his grandfather's words to take his mind off his worries about what had become of his friends.

CHAPTER EIGHTEEN
The Village

As it was growing dark, Ellie and Jasmine briefly retraced their steps until they arrived at the village. It was a quaint town, with homes and shops painted in soft colors and adorned with sturdy cedar beams.

"We'll need to find a place to lay our heads for the night," said Jasmine, looking in every direction.

"I know of just the place," said Ellie, dragging the woman by the hand through the cobblestone streets.

They rounded a bend and turned onto a quiet street where a two-story inn with milky windows stood before them. Ellie did a double-take to make sure she had remembered correctly, then motioned for Jasmine to follow her as she approached the establishment with haste.

The door sounded a little bell as they entered the lobby, which prompted a large bearded man to emerge from a first-floor door. As he lumbered over to the front counter, Ellie shouted almost too loudly: "Barnaby!"

The imposing man quickly smiled a jovial grin and

caught the little girl up in his arms as she skirted the counter.

"Well, hello again, my dear," said the innkeeper. "Didn't think I'd be seeing you again!"

"I always hoped we'd come back into the Kingdom," replied Ellie. Then her voice became somber. "Only, we aren't here on a pleasure visit, Barnaby. One of our friends—you remember Oliver? He's been captured by Prince Florian and we're going to rescue him."

"We?" Barnaby said as he turned to Jasmine, who had remained quiet during the exchange.

"This is my friend Jasmine," explained Ellie. "She's got a plan to get us into the palace, but first we'll need a good night's sleep."

"Good night's sleep, eh?" Barnaby said, reaching beneath the counter for a jingling set of keys. "That happens to be my specialty." He smiled and motioned for the two to follow him as he began to ascend the stairs.

The steps creaked under the weight of the massive man, and he nearly filled the entire space of the hallway. Soon, though, he unlocked a room, opened the door, and handed the keys to Jasmine.

"How much?" The woman asked Barnaby, rifling through a pouch of coins.

"My treat," he replied. "For an old friend." He tousled Ellie's hair, which made her giggle. She hugged the man once more before he started down the steps.

"Barnaby," Jasmine said quietly, unsure of who else might be housed down the hall. "Where would a weary traveler go to get a good drink in the village after dark?"

The man gave her a knowing look, sensing the woman was interested in more than a refreshing sip. "Head down the main thoroughfare and you'll come to *El Lugar*—you can't miss it."

Jasmine thanked Barnaby and followed Ellie into the room as their host lumbered away.

"Don't mention it," the man hollered back, halfway down the staircase.

The two weary travelers closed the door and removed their shoes and packs. Ellie sprawled out across a child-sized bed and took deep, relaxed breaths. Then the girl sat up and asked Jasmine, "So, what's the plan? What do we do next?"

Jasmine hesitated. "I think *you* should get some rest. *I've* got to make a little trip into the village tonight, and it may draw too much attention if I were to be seen out with a child at this hour."

"Then you've got a way for us to get into the palace?" Ellie asked.

"I've got an idea," said Jasmine. "Sometimes that's the only place you can start." She took a breath before continuing: "We'll find disguises to pose as maids and enter through the servant's entrance, but we'll need the password first. I've got a hunch that some of Florian's guards will unwind at a local spot after a long shift, so maybe I can get one of them to let it slip."

Ellie wished her luck and finally gave in, readying herself for bed while Jasmine put on a neutral coat with a hood to hide her face. "Just to be safe," she explained. The young woman tucked little Ellie under the covers and blankets and switched off a lamp. She quietly closed and locked the door behind her as she stepped out into the hall.

The woman, cloaked in the dark, slinked across the quiet street, hopping from shadow to shadow. There was an eeriness in the village—quite different from the jovial, welcoming feeling they'd experienced on their way into town. The lights in the windows were mostly gone now, and shopkeepers locked their storefronts with jangling keys before making themselves scarce. Jasmine looked around and hugged her coat close as she crossed another desolate street.

As she approached El Lugar, the establishment that Barnaby had recommended, Jasmine heard lively music and revelry. A soft, warm glow issued from the diamond-paned windows onto the dirty, silent street as a couple of conquistadors stumbled out the door in light spirits. For the brief moment, before the door swung back into place, she heard a *crash!* of glass breaking.

This could be interesting, Jasmine thought, pressing on toward the entrance to El Lugar.

The incident of the broken glass created a welcome diversion, for no one seemed to notice as the cloaked heir of Palafox surreptitiously made her way to the counter and ordered a ginger brew. The server quickly produced the icy beverage in a tall glass. Jasmine felt the foamy bubbles tingle on her face as she tossed the tender a coin and took a sip.

During her several-year absence from the Kingdom, Jasmine had forgotten the many little things she used to take for granted like cool summer days, strolls in the everglades, and a good homemade ginger brew.

Perfection, she said. *Just like I remember.*

Her wistful recollection was interrupted by a gruff man who pulled up a chair next to her and began to speak in Spanish as if they were long-time friends. They weren't. Jasmine nodded, smiled, and turned away to get a better view of the room.

She spotted a quartet of strapping, tan-skinned men sitting around a small table, laughing louder than people normally should while indoors. Though they were cloaked in the traditional garb of the town's working class, the neatly-trimmed black hair around their necks and ears told a different story; these men worked in the palace.

Conquistadors, no doubt.

Jasmine inconspicuously made her way to an empty table near the men and sat with her back to them. The woman picked up a book that had been left on the table and began to feign reading it as she listened to the conversations of the nearly-inebriated guards. She took another sip of the fizzy ginger drink, catching the tail end of a joke being told by the man directly behind her:

"And then *I* told *him*, 'That's not your wife—that's a *blackbird!*'"

All four men burst into another hearty roar, splashing their drinks a little as they tried to sip and react at the same time.

"Then what did you do?" Another asked when the laughter died down.

"Well," continued the joke-teller, "I walked straight out of that chamber before he could fire me!"

Another howl erupted, and Jasmine took this opportunity to make her move. Rising from her seat, she turned quickly, ginger brew in hand. The woman faked a trip and sent the remainder of her drink pouring over the joke-teller.

"Oh, dear," Jasmine said with imitated concern, grabbing a rag to dry off the man's shirt. "My apologies! Oh—"

The man was in too good of a spirit to be angry, but eyed Jasmine as if determining whether he recognized her: "Do I know you?"

"Why, yes," fumbled Jasmine, thinking fast. "It's me—Mercedes—from the palace."

The guard took another look, unable to recall the

woman's face due to his drowsy state. But, afraid of the embarrassment of forgetting the name and face of someone he probably met at some point in his years of service to the Prince, the man nodded and remarked unconvincingly, "Ah, yes. Mercedes!"

"It's been quite some time," Jasmine improvised. "You're still working at the servant's gate, no?"

"That's right," he said. Jasmine's heart leaped with the briefest of hopes as the man continued: "When I'm not working throne room detail, that is."

"But I'll see you tomorrow?" She was betting everything on her plan now.

It felt like minutes before the guard responded with a slow nod: "Yes, m'lady."

"Good," Jasmine replied. "But you aren't going to change the magic word on me again, now, are you?"

The man smiled and shook his head. "No, sir," he said, mixing his words, "Still '*solamente*.'"

Yes! Internally, Jasmine felt a wave of achievement. She nodded politely to the man, handed him the damp rag, and took her leave from the table slowly.

When she was back in the street, Jasmine quickened her pace back toward the inn.

One step closer to rescuing little Oliver, she thought. *One step closer to restoring the Triumvirate.*

CHAPTER NINETEEN
Solamente

The next morning, Jasmine and Ellie awoke to the scent of freshly-baked pastries wafting up the stairs and under their door. They groggily made their way down to a room on the first floor where a number of small dining tables were set.

Ellie chose one and, as they sat down, Barnaby appeared in a fruit-stained apron to pour them each an earthen mug full of tea.

"Thank you, Barnaby," said Ellie sweetly. The man nodded then disappeared.

He re-emerged a moment later with a platter of delicacies: the long-awaited and enticing pastries, slices of mangoes, clusters of red and green grapes, and an array of biscuits and jams. Jasmine and Ellie helped themselves as Barnaby returned to the kitchen.

"Good news," began Jasmine as she plopped a grape into her mouth.

Ellie nearly spilled her tea: "You discovered the password?"

"Mhm," the woman nodded then swallowed the bite. She leaned close and whispered to Ellie: "It's *sola-mente*." The word, when translated, meant *only* or *alone*. "No doubt one of the Prince's selfish jokes," she added, mostly to herself. "The '*only*' ruler." She cut her pastry with a knife.

"That's wonderful news," said Ellie. "What's next?"

"We'll embark as soon as we're finished with breakfast," Jasmine instructed.

The two quickly enjoyed the rest of their meal, thanked their host, and rummaged through an old armoire in their room upstairs to furnish their disguises. Jasmine found a pair of simple skirts and blouses that fit her and Ellie well enough and, once they had changed, the woman grabbed a couple of scarfs and wrapped one loosely around Ellie's head to obscure her face.

"It's not unusual for young girls to serve in the palace," explained Jasmine, "but we'll have to take precautions since you've infiltrated it once before. Can't risk someone recognizing you."

To complete their disguises, the two friends slipped on aprons over their skirts. When they were ready, Jasmine and Ellie locked their room and returned to the village street. At this early hour, it was bustling with activity and chatter from people and creatures of all shapes and sizes. The two travelers blended in well as they wound their way through the streets toward the palace's inconspicuous side entrance.

Once again, Ellie was in awe of the grand architecture of the peach-pink waterfront palace. As they neared the servant's entrance, the building seemed to grow larger, towering over them with its tattered flags waving in the ocean breeze.

The two stood in line behind the other servants,

who were waved in one at a time by the guards at the checkpoint.

"What was the word again?" Ellie asked. "Salami?"

"*Solamente,*" whispered Jasmine, a look of worry coming over her face.

"S-salamander," Ellie tried to repeat it.

Jasmine panicked but was called up next, leaving the little girl behind her. The guard asked her for the password and the woman replied, out of Ellie's earshot. Jasmine cast a troubled glance over her shoulder as she was ushered into the palace and disappeared into the darkness.

The guard waved Ellie forward.

"Password?" The guard said curtly, eyeing the little girl with suspicion.

Ellie took a gulp and began, "S-s-s—"

What was it again—Salamander? Salmon? Salamon—

The guard narrowed his eyes and tapped his foot impatiently. The girl thought she saw him reaching for his sword.

"Solo," she finally let out. "S-solamente!"

The guard relaxed his gaze, nodded to another guard who opened the door, and motioned for Ellie to enter. The girl took a deep breath and, relieved, entered the unseen innards of the palace.

When her eyes adjusted to the dimmer light, Ellie saw a hand reaching toward her. The hand grabbed her by the arm and tugged her behind a corner and into the shadows.

"Jasmine!" Ellie exclaimed when she identified her face.

"Keep your voice down," replied Jasmine, motioning for the girl to step further away from the corridor from which they'd just come.

"That was a close one," whispered Ellie.

"You did great," Jasmine affirmed with a smile, looking the little girl in the eyes. "And now that we're inside, we've got to find out where Oliver's being held."

"Last time we were inside the palace," began the girl, "our friend Tazmo was held in the dungeon on the lower levels. Perhaps Oliver's in there as well?"

Jasmine thought for a few moments before replying, "Perhaps. But we can't just rush down there. If we're going to find him *and* get out of here alive, we've got to try and blend in—to take on the roles for which we're dressed—and see what we can learn. We'll stick together, okay?"

Though Ellie was eager to locate Oliver and reunite with her dearest friend, she knew that Jasmine's plan was wise. They couldn't risk blowing their cover so soon.

When the two agreed upon their immediate course of action, they slipped back into the corridor and followed the single-file trail of maids and butlers as they processed to their posts. Jasmine walked in front of Ellie as they moved toward the kitchen with about a dozen other women in similar garb.

Before Ellie could enter the kitchen, though, a cleanly-groomed man put out his arm to stop her. The girl looked up at him, worried, then glanced toward Jasmine who turned to make sure Ellie was still following.

The man pointed to another doorway with his other hand. "This way," he said sharply. "Kitchen has enough hands."

Ellie considered making a dash under the man's arm to stay with Jasmine, but knew that would jeopardize their entire rescue mission. Jasmine subtly nodded, as if to say, *It's okay. Go with him.*

Reluctantly, the girl lowered her head and followed

in the direction of the man's gesture. She took one more glance over her shoulder to witness a final nod from Jasmine before the woman disappeared from view.

It's just me now, thought Ellie. On my own—solamente.

CHAPTER TWENTY
Ellie Explores the Palace

The well-groomed man led the way through a few more narrow, winding hallways and up a flight of stairs. Ellie followed closely, with a half-dozen or so other servants at her heels.

They stopped at a landing on the second floor. The head butler produced a wooden box from which he handed each of the maids an assortment of cleaning instruments. Ellie received her's last—a feather duster—and the man quickly disappeared back down the staircase. The girl took her cue from the other women as they spread out across the second level of the palace and began to find their own sections and rooms to clean.

Ellie looked over the balcony railing and down into the open-air courtyard below—the center of the palace. By this time, the large structure still cast a long enough shadow to cover the whole area, and the ambiance of trickling fountains created a soothing environment that masked the steps of the inconspicuous servants.

Next, Ellie strolled down the landing, slowing her

pace to view a series of immense portraits that lined the wall.

The Royal Family, she thought. *Kings and queens of Coronado.* The largest portrait featured Prince Florian. *Typical.*

As she had to keep moving so as not to draw attention to herself, she was unable to read the tiny inscriptions below each of the paintings. Shifting her priority back to her role, Ellie identified a couple of doors ahead—one of which was half ajar. None of the other maids had claimed it, so the girl approached the first door cautiously with her dusting instrument in hand.

No one else occupied the room at the moment, but Ellie gazed in wonder at the ornate furnishings of the large bedchamber. Every item was carved of richly-stained woods or coated with glittering flakes of gold. The bedsheets were embroidered with leaves and floral patterns, stitched with care and sewn with the finest materials.

I suppose these once belonged to the princes and princesses that lived here, Ellie thought. *It's a shame they've gone unused for so long.*

The little girl dusted dutifully as she inspected the remainder of the bedroom. When she felt satisfied with her work, Ellie returned to the hallway and continued on to the next door.

The second door was closed, so the girl knocked softly and pressed her ear to it to listen for a reply. She heard the sound of a light movement, but no one answered back.

"Hello?" Ellie said to the room's occupant on the other side of the door. "May I come in and dust?"

Again there was no reply. Wanting to fulfill her role well, Ellie tried the door handle. It was unlocked, so she

THE LARGEST PORTRAIT
FEATURED PRINCE FLORIAN.

opened it and peered inside.

The room was much smaller than the bedroom she had just dusted; in fact, it seemed to be merely a closet of sorts. Thick curtains were drawn over the window, but Ellie's eyes alighted on a small boy in the center of the narrow room shuffling a stack of loose papers and an inkwell under a simple wooden bed.

The boy, having stuffed the items out of sight, turned and stood to face Ellie with a look of surprise. When he realized it was just a girl near his own age, the child relaxed his posture.

"Oh, I'm sorry," said Ellie, entering the room. "I didn't mean to frighten you!"

The child did not respond.

"Is it alright if I do some dusting in here?"

He nodded. The child looked familiar to the girl, and he wore a necklace with a large, green gemstone. *Is this the boy who spoke for the Seers—the one from our first journey into the palace?* It certainly looked like him. *And what's happened to his hair?* His scalp was mostly bald, with a few stray hairs forgotten in a hasty trim.

"Wait a minute," Ellie said. "You helped us before—helped us escape."

He remained silent but moved to the door to shut it quietly behind Ellie.

"Do you know if my friend Oliver is here—in the palace?"

The bald boy—the Mouthpiece of the Seers—nodded.

"Oh!" Ellie said excitedly. "That's such wonderful news! And do you know where he's being kept?"

The Mouthpiece placed a finger over his mouth and another over Ellie's with a *shh!* sound. He craned his neck to listen as a set of determined footsteps moved across the hall outside, becoming louder as they approached the door. The Mouthpiece rushed back to his papers and began to scribble something down.

Before she could see what he was doing, Ellie was startled by a knock on the door behind her.

"Boy!" A woman's voice shouted angrily. "I'm coming in!"

The door swung open. A woman with greasy, black hair stepped over the threshold. Her dark, flowing gown billowed around her like a thundercloud. "You had better not be—" She stopped as she spotted Ellie. The girl was dusting a small wooden chair in the corner of the room and looked up at the woman as she entered.

"Who are you?" The woman in black scowled as she moved toward the frightened girl, who could hear the soft clinking of an unseen necklace beneath her voluminous trappings. "Who gave you permission to be in here?"

"I'm sorry—I'm just cleaning—"

The Mouthpiece stood and placed himself between the girl and the witch with one of his hands behind his back. He slipped a folded piece of paper into Ellie's apron pocket, but she kept her eyes glued on the imposing woman.

"Get out of my way!" She shouted to the Mouthpiece, pushing him aside. The witch crouched so that her eyes were on the same level as Ellie's. "Who gave you permission to be in this corner of the palace?"

Before Ellie could reply, the witch added, "It is *forbidden!*" With that, she grabbed the girl by the ear and dragged her out to the hall. Ellie winced but tried not to make a sound.

"Now," said the woman from the doorway, leaning back in to yell at the Mouthpiece, "if I catch you fraternizing with the servants *one* more time, you'll be sleeping in the dungeon for a *month!*"

She stepped outside, slammed the door, and glared at Ellie.

"And *you,*" the witch said. "Run along before you're thrown back to the street!"

Ellie didn't need to be told twice. She scampered to the nearest stairwell and climbed the steps to the next level, eager to get out of the woman's presence. The witch stormed across the hall and slammed another door.

Yikes! Ellie was shaking. *What a rude and frightening woman!*

Ellie dusted a few more rooms without incident when she remembered the paper that the Mouthpiece had slipped into her front pocket. Reaching in, she pulled out the crumpled sheet and unfolded it carefully. It was a note, written quickly in the boy's sloppy-but-legible handwriting:

Frend in southwest towar. Wich has skelton key.

Oliver! A newfound hope rushed over Ellie as she read the misspelled words. *We're coming for you, Oliver!*

Slipping the folded note back into her pocket, Ellie continued dusting to pass the time as she wondered what to do next. Soon enough, the day drew near to a close and the rosy evening sun cast a beautiful haze over the whole palace. The girl followed the other maids as they processed back downstairs and out through the servant's gate.

Ellie glanced through the crowd of similarly-dressed women until she found Jasmine. Rushing over to her, they embraced and continued walking with the crowd away from the palace.

"Are you alright?" Jasmine asked.

"I'm fantastic!" Ellie replied.

"And why is that?" Jasmine chuckled at the girl's response.

"Because," she started, reaching into her pocket, "now we know how to rescue Oliver!"

She handed the note to Jasmine who read over it quickly.

"We'll just need to locate this *skeleton key*," the woman said. "Tomorrow, when we return to the palace, we'll find the key—and we'll find Oliver."

CHAPTER TWENTY-ONE
The Caravan on the Move

Early the same morning in which Jasmine and Ellie had first infiltrated the palace, Prince Florian's caravan resumed its trek north toward the Fountain of Youth. Marco, who was on guard as the sun began to creep through the thick jungle treeline, woke Gardenio and the children gently but with haste. With some help from the two men, Ben and Annie remounted the tall ostriches and, when everyone was situated, they began to follow the well-armed caravan.

Florian's men moved swiftly over the already-forged paths through the forest. The four ostrich-mounted travelers, however, attempted to stay off the beaten roads so as not to draw too much attention. This made their journey a bit slower, but they were able to keep their sights locked on the dark horsemen ahead.

Around mid-day, the Prince's men slowed to a halt. Marco instructed the ostriches to do the same, and the party used this opportunity to eat a meager lunch.

"So how exactly are we going to stop the Prince from

drinking from the Fountain?" Ben asked their leader as he consumed a slice of mango.

"We need to get closer to him—" said Marco, "before he arrives at the Fountain."

"Closer?" Annie wondered how they could get any closer without being discovered.

"I think I know where Marco's headed with this," Dean said, turning to Marco. "You're thinking we infiltrate his ranks?"

Marco nodded affirmatively.

"But we're children," said Ben doubtfully. "They'll notice us right away."

"Yes you are," Marco replied. "That's why you two will continue to follow from a distance—it'll be safer, anyway. Dean and I will blend in perfectly with Florian's men."

This plan made the boy even more nervous. "What if something happens to you?" He spouted off his countless worries in typical Ben fashion. "Or to *us*? And how will you get into the camp?"

"Leave that to me," Marco assured him. "Once it grows darker, we'll make our move."

Though the children were still uncertain about the details of Marco's plan, all agreed that it was the most practical way forward. Prince Florian's troops resumed their progress through the jungle. The four followed along until they came to another stop as the sunlight was slowly swallowed by the starry expanses above.

As discussed, Marco and Dean put their plan into motion when the jungle had become dark enough to give them cover. Annie and Ben, both on edge, unwittingly clung to each other's hands as they watched the two grown men vanish into a patch of large-leafed shrubbery.

"What if this doesn't work?" Ben whispered, trembling.

"It has to," Annie said, trying to sound confident.

Florian had dispersed sentries to keep watch at points all around the perimeter of his encampment. Marco and Dean moved quietly through the dark underbrush until they were only feet away from one such guard. Having the element of surprise on their side, Marco quickly approached the sentry from behind, covered his mouth, and threw him to the ground. The force, combined with the weight of his clunky armor, knocked the man unconscious. The two men quietly dragged him behind a tree farther away from his post, removed the man's armor and weapons, and tied him to the trunk with a cloth around his mouth to keep him from screaming for help when he awoke.

They did this a second time with similar ease. Marco slipped into one set of armor and found that it fit perfectly. Gardenio followed suit and the men carefully slinked back to the sentries' positions before anyone could notice the absence of the actual guards.

To Marco's relief, the armor featured a metal shroud that covered his neck and the lower half of his face. *That'll keep Florian from recognizing us.*

A few hours later, the men were replaced by another pair of sentries starting their shift to allow the others to get some rest. Marco and Dean each made their way to the Prince's camp and reunited at its edge in the shadows of a large oak tree.

"What now?" Dean whispered when they were out of earshot of the rest of the camp.

Marco took a nervous glance in either direction, then replied, "Find Florian."

Gardenio nodded.

"If we find Florian," continued the bearded man, "we find the map. If we get the map, perhaps we can find the Fountain first."

It was a risky plan—both men knew it—but they were making it up as they went along. Dean agreed with Marco and the two split up to search the camp for any sign of the Prince or the enchanted map.

The men blended in easily; the camp was dotted with tents and crawling with hundreds of half-faced conquistadors who nodded out of habit as Marco passed. Finally, he noticed one tent that was larger than all the rest, glowing from a lamp lit within.

Florian's tent, he thought. *Naturally.*

The tent's entrance was flanked by two guards in identical armor.

His heart beating quickly, Marco approached and spoke with some hesitation: "I'm here to relieve you."

The sentry eyed him with suspicion but said nothing. A few seconds passed—which felt like minutes to Marco—then the guard finally nodded and stepped away from the tent. Marco tried to mask his irregular, anxious breathing as he took the guard's place with his back to the canvas tent, hoping he had chosen wisely.

Finally, he could distinguish voices from within the tent.

"How much further, sir?" Said a voice that Marco couldn't identify.

There was a long pause before a second voice replied: "We'll arrive before the sun sets tomorrow night." The voice was unmistakable to Marco.

Florian—we found him!

CHAPTER TWENTY-TWO
Eavesdropping

With an actual sentry standing at the opposite side of the entryway, Marco tried not to show signs that he was eavesdropping on the conversations within the Prince's tent.

"Are you sure about this?" Asked the voice that didn't belong to the Prince—Marco assumed it was one of his generals.

"The map cannot lie," Florian assured him sternly.

"Of course, your Excellency," the general muttered. "I just meant to say, er—do you really think it is wise to journey so far from Castillo Rosa in order to seek something so—so, um, *fantastic?*"

"What are you getting at, General?"

"The Fountain of Youth," replied the general. "It's an old wives' tale—a legend, sir."

"And?" The Prince was clearly growing more agitated.

"Don't you think it might be wiser to return to the palace and turn your attention back to the matter of locating and eradicating the rest of the scattered heirs?"

"General Pompadour," said the Prince with a fire in his tone. "I will let you know when I desire your opinion. For now, I *must* reach that Fountain, for there is no better way for me to retain my vigor and, with it, the throne that is rightfully mine. As long as I live, none can challenge me."

Beneath the fiery reprimand, Marco detected a slight tinge of fear in Florian's voice.

He's afraid to grow old, Marco thought as he continued to stand guard. *Afraid to lose what he's worked so much evil to attain.*

"I know you think it a fool's errand," Florian continued. "But I am certain of the Fountain's veracity—and of its magical properties."

"Yes, sir," replied General Pompadour doubtfully. After another brief moment of silence, he asked, "What shall happen when you reach this Fountain?"

Marco heard the sound of the old map being folded up. "When we reach it," explained Florian, "we will wait until the time is right."

"Sir?" Pompadour was unsure what Florian meant.

"This Fountain sits atop a network of ancient springs," Florian elaborated. "According to the legends surrounding it, one must wait until the waters are stirred up to drink and partake of its powers."

"*Wait?*" The general asked. "How long?"

"I'm unsure," replied Florian. "But we shall wait as long as it takes."

At this, their conversation came to an end. Marco straightened up and assisted the other sentry in lifting the tent flaps to allow General Pompadour to exit. As they returned the flaps to their closed position, Marco caught a glimpse of the Prince deep in thought.

He's worried—worried and growing weaker. Perhaps there's still a chance that he can be turned—that the old Florian is still in there somewhere.

Marco had little time to dwell on this thought, for at that moment he watched as a soldier crossed in front of him, moving somewhat hurriedly. Then another. And another. There was a flurry of activity as the camp seemed to come alive.

What's going on? Marco wondered.

Another soldier scampered by, his familiar eyes meeting Marco's own.

Dean!

Marco interpreted concern in his gaze, then the disguised Gardenio passed out of view once more.

Next, General Pompadour returned, his steps now quickened. Marco helped the sentry part the entrance to the Prince's tent once more and then listened intently to hear what had caused such a ruckus in the camp.

"What is it, General?"

"We've found something," replied the nervous general.

"Found something?"

"Some*one*," Pompadour stammered. "Two, actually."

"Following us?"

"It appears that way, sir," continued the general. "They were found just beyond the boundary of the camp."

"Well, who are these men?" Florian's temper started to flare.

"Not men, exactly," clarified Pompadour.

"Then *who?*"

Marco's heart sunk in his chest. He was afraid to hear the answer.

"Two ch-ch-"

"Spit it out, General!"

"Two *children*."

No! Marco couldn't believe his ears. *This is not good.*
Florian's men had discovered Ben and Annie.
Not good at all.

CHAPTER TWENTY-THREE
The Children

Florian's guards wrapped blindfolds around the eyes of Annie and Ben and escorted them into a small, dim tent. The boy's sweaty grip was broken from Annie's as they were commanded to sit back-to-back against a wooden support beam in the center of the tent. The guards bound the two children together around the post then exited the shelter.

When it seemed that all of the soldiers were gone, Ben whispered to Annie, "Are you hurt?"

The girl shook her head even though her friend couldn't see it: "I'm fine. You?"

"I'll manage," Ben replied shakily.

The children could hear the sounds of shuffling outside, along with the muffled shouts of generals as men were sent further into the jungle to look for any other potential enemies.

"What do we do now?" Ben wondered.

Annie wriggled her arms and found that the ropes had little give. "We wait and think of a plan."

"Do you think Marco and Dean have been found out yet?"

"I sure hope not," replied Annie. "They're our best chance of getting out of here."

Presently, a familiar metallic clinking indicated a man in armor approaching the tent. The flap opened and the children listened as the metallic steps crunched toward them.

"Please don't hurt us!" Ben trembled.

He started when the soldier's hand reached for the blindfold on his face. To his surprise, though, the conquistador lowered it, allowing the boy to see his visitor clearly.

"Dean!" The boy nearly shouted.

"Quiet!" Dean whispered as he removed the cloth over Annie's eyes as well. "We've only got a few moments, so listen closely." The children remained silent as he continued in a low whisper: "The plan has changed. We're going to find a way to get you out of here, but we need some time. Whatever you do, do *not* mention our names or you'll risk blowing our cover—"

The three were startled by the sound of another individual entering the tent. Dean turned and rose to greet the man—it was Prince Florian.

"Sir!" Dean lowered his head to avoid the Prince's piercing gaze.

"Just as I suspected," Florian said as sauntered past Dean and headed straight for the children. "You always find your way back into my domain, now, don't you?"

"Y-y-you're a fraud!" Ben stuttered clumsily in an attempt to be courageous. "This is *not* your domain and you know it."

The Prince smiled and crouched so that he was on the boy's eye-level. "Is that fool Juniper filling your head with her lies again? Or perhaps you've been spending time with my old friend Marco?"

Neither of the children replied.

"I find it amusing that they send children to do their dirty work," Florian continued. "It's a dangerous place out here in the jungle. Someone could get hurt." He glanced at the sword that hung from his belt and then back to his two captives.

"We're here to stop you!" Annie said, more confident than her friend.

"Stop me?" The Prince stood. "Stop me from doing *what?*"

"We know you have the magic map," continued Annie. "And we know where you're going. And we're going to stop you."

Florian laughed, genuinely entertained by the girl's comments. "Child," he taunted. "You must've forgotten something." He bent down once more and tugged at the taut ropes around them: "You're not going anywhere unless I say so."

The Prince turned and started toward the tent's entrance. "As a matter of fact, how about you two come along for the ride? It would be a shame for you to miss an opportunity to see the power of the fabled Fountains, after all."

With that, Dean parted the tent flap and allowed Florian to exit. The young man in disguise gave a final glance and nod to the children before following the Prince back into the camp.

"Did I hear him correctly?" Annie asked Ben when the men were gone. "Did he say *Fountains?* As in, more than one?"

"That's what I heard," agreed Ben.

"Juniper and Marco didn't say anything about another Fountain," the girl said, thinking out loud. "I wonder what it means."

"Perhaps there are more springs with other powers?" Ben suggested.

"Your guess is as good as mine," said Annie with a yawn. "Anyway, I'm sure we'll learn of it soon enough if Florian means to bring us along with him."

Ben agreed. They were silent for a few minutes until Ben said, "I sure hope Ellie is alright. I miss her so."

Annie made no reply. Ben turned and realized that she had drifted off to sleep, her head leaned against the wooden support beam.

"Sweet dreams," Ben said softly. He tried to shift his position slightly before leaning back his own head. It wasn't the most comfortable position, but Ben soon fell asleep, dreaming of how they might escape and reunite with their dear friends scattered throughout the Kingdom.

CHAPTER TWENTY-FOUR
Drawings in the Closet

The next morning, Jasmine and Ellie once again donned the uniforms of palace maids and returned to the palace.

"Keep your ears attuned," said Jasmine as they approached the servant's gate, "for any mention of where this mysterious witch might be keeping that key."

"Maybe it's in the vault," suggested Ellie. "The vault where we found this key to our Gate." She revealed the old, emerald-encrusted key that she wore around her neck, then tucked it back under her shirt.

"Florian and the witch would be foolish to keep it there," Jasmine said. "They know that's the first place you would look."

"I suppose you're right," Ellie nodded. "But if either of us finds anything today, we'll share that in secret during our break—is that right?"

"Right," replied Jasmine.

The two filed through the gate, muttering the password to the guard more confidently this time, and returned to their assigned posts in separate areas of the palace. Once again, Ellie and the rest of the housekeepers spread out through the different levels of the castle and began to clean and dust the various mostly-unoccupied rooms.

Perhaps that bald boy knows where the key is kept, Ellie thought as she dusted a detailed glass sculpture of a noble duke, slowly making her way toward the child's closet-like room. *Better keep watch for that frightening witch, though.*

The girl slinked across the landing, glancing over her shoulder with every other step. When the last of the other servants had disappeared into other rooms, Ellie gave a quiet knock on the Mouthpiece's door.

I don't hear any movement this time.

She knocked once more, a bit louder, but heard no response. Ellie turned the handle and peered inside the sparse room. There was no sign of the curious child.

The Mouthpiece had left several of his papers strewn loosely across the space, so Ellie entered and began to inspect them, shutting the door behind her. These sheets had few written words; instead, they were covered in drawings, scribbled with ink in the young child's hand.

Ellie's eyes scanned the artwork for any sign of something that might help them find the key to rescue Oliver from the southwest tower. She sifted through one stack of drawings on the edge of the bed, which featured animals in striking detail—parrots, flamingos, a raven, and a tiger.

In the middle of the stack, there was a drawing of a building that looked like a small house with a pointed tip on its roof.

Interesting, Ellie thought, removing it from the stack,

folding it, and tucking it into her apron. She had never seen a building quite like it before.

The next piece of paper had a drawing of something of great interest to Ellie: a large key with a handle in the shape of a skull.

The skeleton key! The girl carefully folded the drawing and put it into her apron pocket with the other. *So that's what it looks like. Now we've just got to find where it's being kept.*

At that moment, Ellie's pulse quickened. She heard footsteps outside the door. Quickly returning the stack of drawings to its place on the bed, the girl grabbed her feather duster and darted to the door. As she opened it, she was face to face with the imposing head butler from the prior day.

"This area is off-limits," he said without a hint of a smile.

"Sorry, sir," Ellie replied, keeping her head down.

The man's nose contorted as he sneered and inspected the young maid. Ellie held her breath for what felt like minutes. Finally, the butler gave a sigh and said, "Well, move along!"

Ellie scurried away and made herself busy wiping down trinkets on a side table. The head butler watched her for a few moments to ensure that she followed through, then he slowly turned and hurried down a spiral staircase.

That was a close one!

A short time later, Ellie was sent to take her morning break. She waited outside the kitchen entrance until Jasmine was released, and then the two snuck up to an unoccupied dining room overlooking the south terrace.

"Did you find anything?" Jasmine asked hopefully.

Ellie lowered her head somberly. "Not much," she said. Then remembering the drawing, she reached into her pocket and unfolded it. "Except for this drawing—I think it's a picture of the skeleton key that will help us rescue Oliver!"

Jasmine inspected it more closely. "Where did you get this?"

"It was in the room of that little bald child," said Ellie. She and Jasmine had recapitulated their adventures the prior evening over dinner. "He's the one who gave me the note, too." After a few moments, she asked Jasmine: "How about you?"

The young woman shook her head: "Nothing helpful—unless you count learning a new recipe for one of Florian's favorite meals?"

They both smiled and Ellie looked out the large glass windows into the terrace below. This area—to the south of the palace—was dotted with ornately-trimmed trees and hedges fashioned into mazes. At the farthest end, a series of carved-coral steps led up to an elevated terrace on which stood a familiar, enclosed pavilion with a pointed spire on its roof.

"The house from the drawing!" Ellie exclaimed in a loud whisper. She shuffled through the contents of her apron pocket.

"What?" Jasmine turned to inspect the building for herself through the brilliant panes.

"That little building," the girl explained, unfolding the Mouthpiece's drawing of the many-windowed structure. "The bald boy had this drawing of that little glass house in the same stack with this picture of the skeleton key!"

"Then perhaps that's where we should continue our search," suggested Jasmine. She squinted to try and get a better look from so far away: "It doesn't seem like a house exactly—its walls are made of dark glass. Perhaps it's some sort of shelter or garden shed."

"Whatever it is," said Ellie, "we've got to check it out. It could be the next step to saving Oliver!"

As their time away from their palace jobs was nearing its end, the two agreed to return to their posts for the present. Then, at their next break, they would reconvene in the garden to investigate the curious glass pavilion.

CHAPTER TWENTY-FIVE
The Curious Glass Pavilion

When the time came, Ellie met Jasmine in the massive garden behind a distinct topiary trimmed in the form of a flamingo—a landmark which they had decided upon in advance. Carefully, the two navigated the length of the winding garden maze, only getting lost on two occasions. There were no guards inside the walled garden, for Prince Florian preferred to have a space in which he could wander in peace. This put Jasmine at ease.

The babbling of fountains and the shade of several large trees cast a coolness on one side of the terrace, which provided Jasmine and Ellie a brief respite from the scorching late-morning sun.

"How much farther to the pavilion?" Ellie asked, out of breath.

Jasmine pointed at the thick carved stairs: "Not much. Just up those steps!"

When they were ready to continue, the travelers ascended the wide coral steps. At the top, they reached the upper terrace. It was shaded by ancient oaks, which hung like guardians over the large, glass pavilion in the center.

Ellie strained between steps and heaving breaths as the ground leveled out in front of them: "It's. Quite. Beautiful!"

"Quite, indeed," echoed Jasmine.

"What do you think it's for?" The little girl asked, now resuming a normal breathing pattern.

"I'm not sure," Jasmine responded, half her attention turned to inspecting the curious structure.

The two approached it slowly, realizing how immense the building truly was as it now towered over them. The glass panes that made up the walls were nearly opaque, covered in a greenish patina. Jasmine identified the door and moved toward it. It was unlocked.

The woman opened the door just a crack and peered inside. The sun cast a translucent, spectral glow across the interior, creating a mosaic of shimmering colors on the floor. Before she could get a better view of the space, Jasmine heard a loud fluttering and was knocked backwards out the door as a gigantic, colorful bird dove toward her then disappeared up into the eaves. The woman let out a scream, which startled Ellie, then slammed the door shut with her foot.

"What was that?" Ellie asked frantically.

"Birds!" Jasmine's heart was racing. "It's an aviary!"

"A *what?*" Ellie had never heard the word before.

"An aviary," repeated her counterpart. "It's a place where birds live."

"Why would the skeleton key be in an av—" Ellie paused, then slowly pronounced the word, "a-vi-a-ry?"

"Not sure. But if it's in there, we'll find it!"

In agreement, the two once again approached the

door. This time, they were prepared for any surprises. The two travelers cracked open the door just enough to slip through and closed it quickly behind them.

The sounds of squawking and the flapping of wings filled the expansive space. Ellie looked up in wonder at the aviary, which was filled with birds of all shapes, kinds, and colors. A few of the amazing creatures perched on carefully-placed beams and hoops that hung from the ceiling. Up in the farthest reaches of the space, the girl could see a few bird-sized openings in the glass and several gargantuan nests made of straw and sticks.

"It's like we're inside an enormous birdcage!" Ellie exclaimed.

"Exactly," echoed Jasmine. "Now, we just need to find that key."

Ellie remembered that many of the animals inside the Kingdom had powers of speech, so she called out to an oversized white dove that rested nearby: "Hello there, dove. Have you by chance seen a skeleton key that looks like this?" The girl held up the drawing.

The dove twitched and rotated its head. Ellie wasn't sure it was going to speak until it let out a *coo!* then began to reply softly: "Hello. *Coo!* Seen it. Up in the eaves. *Coo!*" The bird nodded her smooth, feathery head up toward one of the large nests. "Nest of the raven. *Coo!*"

"The key's up in the raven's nest?" Ellie clarified as she craned her neck to see.

"*Coo!* Yes, but hurry before she returns. *Coo!*"

Ellie stepped back and examined the distance between the nest and the ground. "How are we ever supposed to get all the way up there?"

"Leave that to me," said Jasmine, already moving toward one of the walls. She approached it quickly and leaped to reach one of the hanging wooden perches. The woman pulled herself up onto it and looked around for the next closest beam.

Ellie watched from below, a bit nervous but quite impressed by her friend's feats of agility. "Careful," she said over the sounds of passing peacocks.

Jasmine, the heir of Palafox, ascended like a gymnast, leaping from hoop to hoop. On a few occasions, her acrobatics frightened a preening parrot or a mockingbird, who fluttered away in a flurry.

As Jasmine neared the nest, the entire flock inside the aviary began to grow silent and their squawks turned to whispers.

"What's that all about?" Ellie asked the white dove, still perched near the ground.

"*Coo!* The raven!"

The rest of the birds began to mutter "the raven" in overlapping hoots and chirps, which made Jasmine and Ellie uneasy.

"Quickly, Jasmine," shouted the girl from the floor. "I think the raven is about to return!"

The woman took a final dive toward the nest and nearly missed it. Grabbing onto the loosely-built side, Jasmine slipped but hung on tight. Ellie gasped. Then, the courageous woman slowly inched her way up the wall of the nest and into its center.

When she was safely inside the nest, Jasmine was confronted with a confusing mass of items of all sorts. Focused on her mission, she began to dig through the pile to look for the elusive key.

"Do you see it?" Ellie hollered nervously.

Jasmine continued to rifle through the rubbish: "I'm looking!"

After a few more tense seconds, Ellie watched as Jasmine's head reappeared over the side of the nest.

"Found it!" Jasmine held out an object that looked quite similar to the one in the drawing. "The skeleton key!"

"Wonderful!" Ellie clapped her hands in delight. "Now get down from there quickly before you're caught by the raven."

Jasmine was already on her way back down to the ground, jumping across the perches like a skilled circus performer. Finally, her feet reached the floor and Ellie gave her a big hug. The woman held out the key so she could see it up close.

A raucous screeching suddenly arose above them as the birds throughout the aviary began to jump up and down in anticipation of the arrival of the infamous raven. While the two travelers moved slowly back to the door, they caught a glimpse of black feathers fluttering through one of the openings near the roof. It vanished behind the nest.

"Now!" Jasmine whispered to Ellie. They took this opportunity to push open the door, slink out, and shut it quietly behind them. As the door was closing, they heard a blood-curdling screech from the raven.

"Thieves!" The black bird screamed. "Dirty, rotten thieves!"

But Ellie and Jasmine were already moving quickly back toward the palace. They descended the steps down to the lower terrace and sprinted to the south entrance without looking back. When they were finally back inside, they ducked into a darkened pantry.

"Are you okay?" Jasmine asked the little girl.

Ellie nodded. "That raven caused me such a fright!"

"What a horrible screech she had! But at least we found what we were looking for." Jasmine withdrew the skull-emblazoned key and held it out to inspect up close. "Now all that's left is to find and rescue Oliver."

Ellie nodded and smiled in agreement, then the two crept away down the hall, hovering in shadows as they made their way toward the southwest tower.

We're coming for you, Oliver.

CHAPTER TWENTY-SIX
The Ascent

Ben and Annie were startled awake by the feeling of motion. The boy blinked his eyes and saw light. When he opened them fully, he could tell that they were now no longer in the tent where they had been bound the night before. Presently, the children were inside some sort of wheeled contraption, pulled through the jungle by horses.

"Are you okay?" Ben asked when he saw that Annie was awake as well. He attempted to reach out to her across the wagon but discovered that his wrists were wrapped tightly with a thick rope.

"I'm fine," said Annie. "You?"

The boy nodded affirmatively. "We're on the move again. I wonder how close we are to the Fountain."

"You mean *Fountains*," corrected Annie.

"Right," said Ben. "Regardless, I sure hope Dean and Marco are still on our trail. Otherwise, there will be no way for us to escape."

"They won't give up," Annie assured him. "They'll

find a way to stop Florian and get us freed."

Just then, a distant soldier yelled an indiscernible command and the wagon came to a sharp halt, sending Ben toppling over. When he managed to shimmy upright again, the wagon's canvas flap was abruptly opened and two of Florian's conquistadors reached in to grab the children. With a swift and effortless motion, Annie and Ben were pulled through the flap and thrown to the forest floor.

Annie stood up quickly. They were in the middle of the jungle and the road just ahead was rocky. A well-worn path led up a series of natural stone steps toward a higher elevation.

"We make the rest of the journey on foot," said one of the men, nudging Ben and Annie forward. They complied and were ushered through a throng of soldiers until they reached Prince Florian. The man smiled pretentiously when he saw the children.

"Good morning. I trust you slept well," said Florian. He didn't wait for a response before continuing: "According to the map, we're nearly there."

The Prince, who held the old map in one hand, motioned toward the stone steps.

"Bring my things," he barked to a handful of men. "We may be up there for some time."

His servants hurried away to prepare his belongings and supplies. The children scanned the crowd for any sign of Marco or Dean but found it difficult as all of the men wore similar armor—many with shrouds that covered much of their faces.

Where are they? Ben thought, a fresh wave of worry coming over him. He could not identify either of the men in the crowd.

A short amount of time passed and the Prince's

servants returned bearing packs of goods and supplies. Prince Florian motioned for the children to follow, which they did reluctantly with a final glance around for their friends. General Pompadour joined a small platoon of conquistadors that took up the rear as the group began to ascend the crudely-eroded steps up the hill.

The first leg of the journey was relatively quiet, with only the Prince barking out instructions about the terrain of the path ahead. Finally, the children spoke up.

"What did you do with our friend?" Annie said accusingly.

Florian laughed and continued walking. "I presume you're referring to the little child who was delivered serendipitously into my grasp—the long-hidden heir of Mangonia?"

He knows! Up until that point, the girl and her friends weren't sure the Prince was aware that Oliver was one of the very heirs whose return he sought to prevent.

"He's alive," continued the Prince, "for now. And in my custody."

"Why are you keeping him?" Ben interjected. "If you hurt him, you'll be sorry—"

"He's unharmed," Florian assured the boy.

As if his assurances could be trusted! Ben felt his blood pressure rising and his fists clench more tightly. He strained to scale a large step, so Annie supported him with her shoulder.

"The boy is a sort of failsafe. If anything should go wrong with our quest—" Florian turned back to the children, breathed deeply, then smiled. "Well, let's just hope nothing goes wrong and leave it at that."

The children weren't sure what the Prince meant

but knew it did not sound good.

"Is it true that there is more than one Fountain up there?" Ben inquired, trying to change the subject from Oliver's potential fate. "Besides the Fountain of Youth, I mean."

"I'm only interested in *that* one," the Prince replied. "It is not the only Fountain atop this hill, but it is the wellspring of power that will allow me to retain my youth and, therefore, my power and rule over the Kingdom. You troublesome children cannot stop me; in fact, I'm only bringing you along so that you can watch your dreams get crushed in front of your very eyes." He smiled back at them in his signature, menacing way before continuing up the incline.

The entire ascent was made more bearable by the abundance of drooping mango and banyan trees that bent shady branches over the rocky staircase. To one side, the steps terminated in a sharp, steep cliff that made Ben nervous as he looked down. The group moved slowly but consistently, taking periodic breaks to rest on the journey.

"You said we'd be up on the mount for some time," Annie said to the Prince, nodding toward the large bushels of supplies carried by the soldiers and servants.

"That's correct," said Florian, taking a swig of water from a stoneware canteen. "We must wait until the time is right." Then, realizing the children would likely just keep asking him questions, he decided to elaborate: "These Fountains are from another era entirely—ancient remnants of the time before the loathsome Triumvirate was formed. Bygone explorers discovered the magical properties of the natural springs and enshrined them within a man-made structure built at the top of this very mount. But, according to the legends, the powers of the Fountains can only be accessed when the springs are stirred up from deep in the ground. When the Fountain of Youth is bubbling over, I shall drink of it and be restored to my former glory forever."

The children shuddered at the thought.

"And what if this is all just a legend—" said Annie, "like you said?"

"Then I have my failsafe," Florian replied. "But I have no doubts that these Fountains possess the true power from ancient times."

Ben huffed and puffed as he navigated the rocky terrain: "If you lay *one* finger on Oliver, I'll—"

Before he could finish his sentence, Ben tripped on the stone steps and lost his balance. As his wrists were still bound, the boy couldn't reach out to grab anything to stop his fall. Tumbling toward the cliff at the edge of the steps, Ben's pulse quickened.

"Ben!" Annie screamed, turning toward the boy. She was too far away to reach him in time. She watched as he fell headfirst toward the abyss.

Then, unexpectedly, one of the Prince's soldiers moved quickly toward him. He grabbed the boy by one leg and caught him just in time. Suspended in the air, Ben couldn't see the face of his rescuer, but he heaved a huge gasp of relief.

Carefully, the soldier pulled the boy back onto the steps and set him on the solid ground. With deep breaths, Ben looked into the face of his savior and had a shock of recognition. The soldier's mask had fallen off in the shuffle, revealing a face that was familiar to the children and Prince Florian.

"What an unexpected surprise," said Florian in disbelief. "I was beginning to think you'd left these children to their own devices, Marco."

Marco felt the area around his face and realized the shroud was gone. His disguise was foiled.

Florian motioned to a guard: "Tie him up."

With a feeling of defeat, Marco held out his wrists and allowed the man to bind him.

"I suppose you'd like to join these children in watching me drink from the Fountain," continued the Prince. Without waiting for a response, he continued: "Well, you're in luck, old friend—we're nearly there."

Prince Florian gestured up the path. Ben, Annie, and Marco followed the motion of his hand and could now see an old, fading structure peeking through the gaps in the low-hanging branches.

Marco flashed a look of concern to the children.

How are we going to stop the Prince? Ben thought. *We're quickly running out of options.*

Now, they had no choice but to continue on up the path and hope that they could think of a way to stop the Prince before the springs were stirred up.

CHAPTER TWENTY-SEVEN
The Court of the Fountains

The group quickly scaled the final steps up to the top of the hill. Florian pushed aside a few large palm fronds so that they now stood in front of a stucco-covered archway. The arch was part of a larger structure that once formed a tall, colonnaded wall around the sacred fountains, but much of it had crumbled over the years of storms and creeping vines; the spindly strands still covered many of the remaining arches and wall fragments in a living shroud of green.

Through the intricately contoured threshold, the party could now see inside. At the center of the open-air courtyard were two identical rectangular pools—the Fountains—separated by a narrow walkway that bisected them. The catwalk featured steps on either side that led into the shallow, tile-covered pools, while the remainder of their perimeters were covered in a short wall that rose to about knee-height.

Prince Florian's eyes lit up when he saw the still, clear waters. "We've arrived," he muttered, moving slowly—almost reverentially—toward them.

"Which one is which?" General Pompadour followed closely behind, while the remaining soldiers kept a tight rein on their three captives.

Florian scanned the cracked tiles until his eyes landed upon an inscription: "This is the one." He pointed to the pool. "There's supposed to be a chalice with which to drink from the Fountains. Search the court, Pompadour. If we can't find it, another will likely do, but I'd rather not take any chances."

General Pompadour nodded, motioned for two of the soldiers to join him, and began to canvas the courtyard in search of the ancient goblet.

"Are you both alright?" Marco, still dressed in the stolen uniform of the conquistador, whispered to the children as they stood before the two pools.

They nodded.

"Marco," Ben whispered. "How are we going to prevent Florian from drinking of the Fountain?"

"I'm working on it," the man replied. "For now, remain calm. We may be able to buy some time as we wait for the stirring of the springs."

Prince Florian walked toward them and barked commands to the servants: "Prepare our camp here while there's still daylight. These waters are unpredictable and we need to be ready for when the moment strikes."

With a flurry of motion, the servants removed their packs and began to assemble a few small tents on the solid ground. While they did this, Marco and the children sat on the steps at the entrance to the courtyard, their hands still lashed with ropes.

Annie leaned close to Marco: "Did you know about the second Fountain?"

The bearded man shook his head. "That was a surprise to me, too. I've no idea what purpose it serves, but it must hold properties similar to the Fountain of Youth."

Pompadour's search party continued to inspect every corner of the courtyard, but they still saw no signs of the elusive chalice. Frustrated, the Prince urged them to keep looking as he waited impatiently.

"These waters may writhe and bubble at any minute," he said. "Search harder!"

One of the soldiers walked near the captives and stole a quick glance toward them. Annie thought she recognized the man's eyes.

Do my eyes deceive me, or was that—

Her thoughts were interrupted by Prince Florian, who turned to them, nearly fuming. "Help them search," he demanded sternly.

The children hesitated and looked to Marco for guidance. He remained on the step, resolute and determined to defy the Prince's orders.

"If you do not obey," Florian said through gritted teeth, "you will be thrown into the second Fountain." He pointed to the other mysterious pool, apparently the bearer of some foreboding counter-magic.

Annie stuck out her chin and said, "First, you have to tell us what it is—what the other Fountain's magic will do."

"Fine," replied the Prince.

At the far end of the courtyard, the search party continued their quest for the cup. A soldier chopped down a blanket of vines and leaves, revealing a stack of gold plates and dishes—but there was no sign of the goblet.

Florian paced as he began to tell the children and Marco about the second fountain. "Nearly everyone has heard the tale of the Fountain of Youth," he started. "But this second Fountain contains a magic of equal power—some would say even *greater* power."

At that moment, General Pompadour moved toward the raised walkway between the two pools and began to scan the clear waters of the Fountain of Youth.

"What is its name?" Ben asked the Prince.

"It is known in your tongue as the *Fountain of Maturity*," replied the Prince.

His listeners were confused by this revelation, for they weren't entirely sure what the name implied.

"There's something in the water!" Pompadour interrupted with a shout to Florian.

"The chalice?" Florian wondered eagerly.

"I can't quite make it out," said his General, leaning over the waters.

"What is the power of the second Fountain?" Annie wondered, trying to draw the Prince's attention back. "What is the magic of this so-called *Fountain of Maturity?*"

Florian, still watching and waiting to see what Pompadour had discovered, finally turned back to the children: "The Fountain of Maturity does the opposite of the Fountain of Youth—"

Pompadour extended his arm into the waters to try and reach the object on the pool's floor. It certainly looked like the goblet they were looking for.

"Instead of granting the power of eternal youth and removing one's age and fragility," continued Florian, "this mirrored Fountain makes one grow old and wise at rapid speed."

"That doesn't sound so bad," muttered Annie.

"It *isn't* so bad if you were to only take a sip," the Prince replied. "But if your entire, measly bodies were tossed into its waters, the power would be far too great—it would consume you."

As the Prince said these words, he heard the faint sound of bubbling. Florian and his captives turned their attention to the Fountain of Maturity, where General Pompadour continued to grasp for the goblet at the base of the pool. The surface of its waters began to ripple while the other Fountain remained still and calm. At first the ripples formed soothing waves, but these quickly turned to violent writhings.

"Got it!" Pompadour said as he finally grasped the submerged goblet.

"Excellent," shouted Florian, moving toward the waters. "Bring it to me!"

Before Pompadour could withdraw his arm from the turbulent waters, though, he felt a strange tingling overcome his limb. With an agonizing wail, the General rolled onto his back on the narrow catwalk between the pools. The ancient, golden chalice glinted in the fading sunlight.

The children's attention quickly shifted to the hand and arm that held the gilded cup. Pompadour's healthy, muscular arm was now gone; in its place was a shriveled, skeletal limb, devoid of flesh and muscle.

Ben screamed. Marco demanded the children close their eyes.

The General was just as shocked and, as the bubbling subsided, called to the Prince: "Help me!"

"Quickly now," Florian said to a pair of his men. "Wrap his hideous limb from view and fetch me that chalice."

The soldiers and servants followed his orders and helped Pompadour to his feet. When the golden goblet had been placed in his hands, Florian held it and gazed in wonder. He turned back to his captives and smiled once more.

"That," he said, "is what will happen to each of you if you defy me!"

Annie and Ben reopened their eyes and shuddered at the thought, shimmying closer to Marco.

We don't stand a chance against the powers of these two great Fountains, Annie thought. *What are we going to do?*

CHAPTER TWENTY-EIGHT
The Skeleton Key

Castillo Rosa was an immense palace, which made it difficult for Jasmine and Ellie to navigate the maze of hallways, corridors, and staircases on their search for the southwest tower. Eventually, though—with Jasmine's significant navigational skills—they discovered the long, winding steps that led up into the tall tower.

"You think Oliver's actually up there?" Ellie's voice echoed off the stucco and stone walls as her eyes followed the curves of the spiral staircase upward.

"Only one way to find out," replied Jasmine, leading the way.

They crept slowly, stopping every few steps to listen for any guards or persons who might be looking for them. Though this made the journey slower, the two travelers still maintained a steady pace as they ascended the tower.

While torches lined most of the staircase's walls, the upper levels featured no windows, which made it difficult to tell how much time had passed on their long

CASTILLO ROSA

ascent. At last, Jasmine and Ellie reached the top of the tower, where the steps terminated in a single wooden door. The woman peered through its barred opening and looked into the dark room.

When her eyes adjusted to the lower light, she saw a crumpled figure in the corner of the room. He appeared to be sleeping.

"Oliver?" Jasmine whispered loudly.

"Is he in there?" Ellie asked excitedly, unable to reach the height of the opening herself.

"I think so," replied the woman as she watched the body stir. "Oliver, is that you?"

"The skeleton key!" Ellie suggested.

Jasmine reached into her pocket and withdrew the pale key. She quickly inserted it into the door and turned it. The door unlatched with a *click* and swung open, creaking.

More light flooded into the cell through the doorway, illuminating the weathered form of a gaunt, bespectacled boy who sat up against the wall with chains around his wrists.

"Oliver!" Ellie shouted as she ran to embrace him. "Oh, we've been so worried about you! Did they hurt you?"

"Ellie," the boy said with a smile. "I'm alright—it's so good to see you again."

When they concluded their embrace, Oliver greeted Jasmine, who stood in the doorway to allow the children to have their moment.

"Hello again, Jasmine," said Oliver.

"I'm glad you're alright, Oliver." She smiled: "We're here to rescue you."

"I hope you've got an idea of how to get me out of these chains." The small boy held up his wrists to show them the large shackles that bound him to the wall.

"Try the key again," said Ellie. "The skeleton key!"

"If you say so," Jasmine replied, reaching for the key once more. She placed the key into a slot in the metal bindings and, sure enough, found that it released one of Oliver's wrists.

"Wonderful!" Ellie clapped. "Now the other!"

Jasmine complied and unlocked Oliver's other wrist. "Time for us to get out of here and get you on the throne where you belong!"

As the chains jangled to the ground and Oliver rose, they heard a voice from behind that startled them.

"I can help." It was a soft voice.

The three turned to see the silhouette of a boy framed by the doorway. As the torchlight flickered around him, they could see that he was small and bald.

"Oh," said Ellie with a sigh of relief. "It's just the Mouthpiece—the boy who helped us find the key!"

They moved toward the child, who placed a hand over the bejeweled necklace that hung across his chest.

"Do you know a way out?" Jasmine asked him.

"Yes," he said eagerly. "Follow me quickly! But first, hand me the skeleton key!"

Oliver, who had reached down to grab the small wooden box of his family heirlooms, now stopped and stared at the boy.

Something isn't right, he thought.

"What do you need the key for?" Jasmine hesitated.

"Just give it to me," said the bald boy firmly, holding out both of his hands. The gem around the child's neck had a fiery glint in the flickering light. "Do you want to get out of here or not?"

"Yes, of course," said Jasmine, handing the skeleton key to the boy.

"Wait—" Oliver whispered a moment too late.

As soon as the woman placed the key into the boy's hands, the little child hurried toward the door. Oliver sprinted across the room to catch up with him as the bald boy reached for the door. With a swift motion, Oliver swung his wooden box. There was a hollow *thud!* as the chest hammered across the bald boy's head and sent him tumbling to the ground. Ellie screamed. The metallic skeleton key slid across the floor and landed at Ellie's feet.

The little girl was horrified. "Oliver! What on earth did you do to him?" She picked up the key and ran over to the bald boy, who now lay face-down on the cold ground.

"That's *not* who you think it is!" Oliver replied, crouching next to the boy's lifeless body. "Help me flip the body over."

Jasmine assisted in turning the child so that he was now lying on his back: "He's got a pulse—he's fine."

Oliver pointed to the necklace that hung from the bald child's neck.

"Look!" He said. "That's not the Gem of Truth— otherwise it would be green!"

Sure enough, the stone at the end of the gold chain was a gigantic, red ruby.

"What?" Ellie was baffled. "I don't understand. If this isn't the Mouthpiece, then how is it that he looks *exactly* like him?"

"That ruby," continued Oliver. "I believe *that's* the reason."

Jasmine turned to the boy: "I'm sorry, but I'm not following you either, Oliver."

"Give me a minute." Oliver opened his wooden box and withdrew his grandfather's tattered journal.

He quickly flipped through the pages until he came to the one that featured a sketch of the familiar gemstone. "Here!"

Jasmine leaned over to read the page in the light of the flames: "*The Gem of Transfiguration?*"

"Exactly," said Oliver excitedly. "My grandpa described it as a '*large, radiant ruby*'—just like that one!" He reached for the stone, but recoiled and winced when he found it quite hot to the touch.

"So that is someone pretending to be the Mouthpiece?" Ellie now understood what her friend was trying to suggest. "Someone who has taken on his shape?"

Oliver nodded.

"But who is it—"

She stopped mid-sentence as the bald boy's body began to move.

"Quick!" Jasmine said, ushering the children toward the door. "Before he wakes up!"

"I don't think that's a *he*," said Oliver under his breath, following Jasmine's orders.

When they reached the stairs, Ellie handed the key to Jasmine and she slammed the door shut. As the woman locked it, she took a final glance inside the cell. The bald boy was now awake, but before her very eyes, Jasmine watched as the child's form contorted and shifted and grew until it was nearly her own height. The figure stood with her back to Jasmine, covered in billowing black clothes.

"The *witch!*" Jasmine whispered to the children. "Run!"

With that, the children and Jasmine took off down

the stairs as fast as their legs could carry them, leaving the shape-shifting witch trapped in the cell behind them.

They had a head start—but for how long?

CHAPTER TWENTY-NINE
Hide and Seek

Back in the heart of the jungle, far from the palace and the mystic Fountains, old Henry the ferryman had remained at the camp to watch over Juliana—who was quite pregnant—and the pair of mischievous creatures known as Mugwig and Kiwi. Over the course of the several days that their friends had been gone, they passed the time quite unremarkably. In the mornings, Henry would go fishing and bring home a couple of meager morsels. Juliana, still clinging to her pre-pregnancy mobility, made sure to take walks near the camp's perimeter every afternoon.

As for the creatures, they tried their best to keep out of trouble. Mugwig and Kiwi played their favorite game—hide-and-seek—regularly, exhausting nearly every possible hiding place within the camp. The masked men didn't mind their scampering around; in fact, they were rather entertained by the two reptilian curiosities.

On one occasion, the ferry-captain was asleep past his usual fishing time. He was rudely awoken by a pair of tiny green hands that shook his arm. When his eyes blinked open, he saw that it was Mugwig.

"Well, Mugwig, what is it? What's wrong?" He could sense concern in the creature's eyes.

"Kiwi!" Mugwig muttered. "Can't find him anywhere!"

"Well," said Henry, sitting up in his makeshift bed, "perhaps he's just playing another round of your favorite game?"

"Not a game," replied the little green woman. "Mugwig tried seeking!"

Reluctantly, Henry pulled away the covers, threw on his outer garments, and followed Mugwig out into the open-air center of the camp. Juliana sat around the fire with a few of the masked men.

"You seen Kiwi?" Henry asked her.

"Not since yesterday," replied Juliana while she placed a hand on her bloated abdomen and stirred a steaming pot with the other.

"What's for breakfast?" The ferryman inhaled the sweet aroma as he took a seat.

"One of my husband's favorites," the blonde woman answered wistfully. "Just a simple dish of boiled oats with a bit of sugar from the cane growing near the camp's edge."

Mugwig tugged at Henry's shirtsleeve: "What about Kiwi?"

"First, we eat," replied the old man steadily. "Then we will search for our little friend. He can't have gone far."

The diminutive Princess of the Pond joined the men and Juliana in partaking of the warm and steaming morning ritual, which brought a momentary peace and quiet to the camp before the usual daytime bustle.

When they had finished and wiped their bowls clean, Henry turned to Mugwig: "So tell me: where was the last place you saw little Kiwi?"

Mugwig scratched her chin with her lanky, pointy fingers and looked around her.

"Hmm," she said slowly. "Can't remember."

"That's no help," Henry muttered. Then, a little louder, he said, "I guess we'll have to search the whole camp." He shook his head and surveyed the camp once more. "Juniper'll be furious," he said under his breath.

The entire camp joined in the search for Lady Juniper's elusive pet, spreading out to look in every crevice and corner. Even Juliana followed, albeit slowly, as they searched for any sign of the squirrelly creature.

Henry kept near to the woman while they searched, lending her an arm to support her as she hobbled slowly across the large camp. The ferry-captain could feel that the woman's pulse was quickened.

"Are you alright, m'lady?"

Juliana gritted her teeth and nodded unconvincingly.

"You sure? You don't look too well."

"Probably just the flurry of activity," she said with a dismissive wave.

"Do you want to sit down?" Henry gestured to a fallen log nearby. The pregnant woman accepted this suggestion and they both took seats.

Juliana took labored breaths, which slowed after a few moments.

"Now," said Henry. "Anything you want to talk about? You look nervous—scared, I might say."

Realizing that she could no longer hide her emotions from the ferryman, Juliana burst into tears: "Oh dear—it's because I *am* scared—terribly frightened for my beloved Dean. What if something has happened to him?"

"There, there," Henry consoled her with a gentle touch. "He's with Marco—one of the most capable men around. He won't let that wicked Prince lay a finger on your husband."

This seemed to cheer Juliana only slightly, for her tears began to fade.

"It's just that I can't bear the thought of our child growing up without him," she said. "Without a father."

"A fine father he will be," the ferry-captain said confidently.

Before Juliana could reply, they heard a delightful shriek from across the camp: "Look!"

It was Mugwig.

"Tracks!" The creature shouted excitedly.

Henry rose and began to move toward Mugwig, but Juliana grabbed his arm with a surprisingly tight grip.

Turning to her, Henry asked, "Juliana? What's wrong?"

"I think it's coming," she said. Her cheeks were rosy and beads of sweat formed at the edges of her hairline.

"What?" Henry asked, though he knew exactly what she meant.

"It's coming," Juliana repeated through quick breaths. "The baby's coming!"

CHAPTER THIRTY
Waiting for the Waters to Stir

The clouds above the Court of the Fountains grew dark and heavy, ready to release at any moment. Some time had passed since the unfortunate incident with General Pompadour's arm, which was now wrapped in a makeshift cast, and Florian's remaining servants helped to prepare a meal while they waited for the waters to stir once more. The Prince set the golden chalice at his side while he ate.

Annie and Ben huddled closely to one another, their wrists still wrapped in itchy ropes. The bindings made it difficult to eat the rations that were provided them, but they slowly consumed it, fearful that this meal could be their last.

Most of the meal passed in silence, but Marco broke this abruptly to ask Florian a question: "If you could take it all back, would you?"

"I'm sorry?" Florian said, caught off guard with his mouth full.

"If you were given another chance," clarified Marco,

"would you still do everything you did—all the evil?"

"I don't see what you're getting at," replied the Prince. "What's done is done."

"I'm just asking *if* you had a second chance," Marco said.

The Prince took another bite. "No one gets a second chance," he said somberly. "You can't change what's already been done."

"You wouldn't bring back your father—your family—or all the others you've sacrificed to get here?"

"I regret nothing," Florian replied, but Marco wasn't convinced that the man actually believed it.

I know there's still a human in there somewhere, thought Marco. *There's still some glimmer of good.*

"You, on the other hand," continued the Prince. "Let's talk about *your* regrets, Marco."

The children glanced at their bearded protector, wondering what painful memories the Prince was drawing as reference.

"I've never *killed* before, Florian," said Marco confidently. "Don't pretend my domestic affairs are anything like your own."

"They're not so different and you know it." The Prince finished his dinner and glanced back toward the still waters of the two Fountains longingly. "Are you quite finished?"

Marco made no response. He consumed the final morsels of his meal and, with his wrists still bound, handed the platter to one of Florian's men. As he did so, he looked him in the eyes and recognized a familiar visage: *Dean!*

The disguised Gardenio, the lower half of his face still shrouded, collected the remaining dishes and returned them to a small tent. He returned a moment later as Florian walked to the edge of the sacred pools.

"A storm is coming," said the Prince, looking to the gloomy clouds above. He held out a hand, felt a few light raindrops, and continued, mostly to himself: "The sort of weather that precedes a significant moment—the moment in which I will finally drink of these waters and secure my eternal rule of the Kingdom. Bring me the chalice—I want to be ready the very instant this spring is stirred."

Dean took up the ancient goblet and slowly approached Prince Florian. As he drew near, a large thunderclap echoed throughout the courtyard, accompanied by a blinding flash of lightning, paralyzing everyone in fear for a split second. Then, the gradual fade of a torrential rain swept over the jungle canopy and, finally, the Court itself, drenching the Prince and the onlookers in its surprisingly frigid deluge.

Returning his attention to the sacred cup, Florian took it from the young man's hands. The Prince held it up and inspected it with reverential awe.

"Yes," he muttered. "It's almost time."

The rain poured around them and most of the servants crowded into a corner of the courtyard that was covered with a massive tree, providing some respite from the chilling drops. The three captives remained in their places on the steps, their garments completely soaked. The children shivered in the terrible cold and returned their attention to Gardenio and the Prince.

"What are you doing, just standing there?" Florian asked the young man, who now seemed to be staring—even inspecting—the Prince up close.

Finally, Dean stammered out an answer: "I'm sorry, I-I—it's just I've never seen you up close."

"I beg your pardon?" The Prince said, squinting his

eyes in the rain. "Do we know each other?"

What Dean did next surprised even Marco, who watched with his mouth agape as the young man carefully removed the shroud that covered his face, revealing the near-mirror image of Florian. The Prince made no verbal response, but instead observed the man in the soldier's uniform that now stood before him as rain dripped down both of their faces.

What is Dean doing? Marco thought frantically. *He's going to get us all killed!*

"We've never met," replied Dean finally. "But you see our resemblance—I think you know who I am."

"This is impossible," gasped Florian. "None of my family survived! What is this evil trickery?"

"This is no evil," the young man said. "I am the child borne by your mother—*our* mother, Queen Iris—as she gasped her dying breaths."

Dean, you'd better have a plan...

"Impossible," Florian repeated in a whisper.

"No," Dean shook his head. "I am Gardenio, son of King Fernando—your youngest brother."

Prince Florian stood with his mouth agape, grasping the golden chalice loosely in one hand as he shook his head in disbelief.

Annie and Ben, who watched the entire scene unfold from a short distance away, waited to see what would happen next. The dark, gray clouds above continued their deluge; the situation was bleak.

Then something else happened. Amidst the pitter-patter of the rain, the children heard the faint hints of another watery sound.

"The spring," said Annie, nudging Ben. "It's beginning to bubble!"

Ben craned his neck to view the pools more clearly:

"But which one is it?"

From their vantage point on the steps and with the downfall of the rain, it was difficult to tell. Florian and Gardenio turned toward the pools, also hearing the sound.

"Both," Marco muttered.

Prince Florian smiled.

"Excellent. Right on time."

CHAPTER THIRTY-ONE
The Ones Who See

Oliver, Ellie, and Jasmine hurried down the spiral staircase, watching over their shoulders for any sign that the witch was following them. Because of the acoustics of the smooth, stone walls, Jasmine couldn't tell if the echoing footsteps were their own or if they belonged to someone else who was close behind. *Keep moving,* she told herself.

Finally, they neared the ground floor. Ellie guided them on a detour when they reached the second floor of the palace and they came to a quiet landing on the residential wing.

"This way," said Ellie, leading them toward a closed door. "I know someone who can help us."

She approached the door of the closet and knocked softly. There was no answer, so she threw it open.

Inside, the Mouthpiece was startled from a peaceful slumber on his small bed in the corner. He rubbed his eyes and looked in awe on the three fugitives.

"Sorry to barge in," said Ellie as she hurried toward

the bald boy. "But we need your help!"

"Wait!" Oliver stopped her with his arm. "What if it's another trick?"

The girl realized that Oliver's point had some credence and took a step back: "But how will we know if he's the real *him?*"

"If he's the real Mouthpiece," explained Oliver, stepping slowly toward the boy, "he'll remember something—something specific."

"Like what?" The little girl asked impatiently.

"Do you remember the note?" Oliver asked the other boy, reaching the side of his bed. "Do you remember what the note said—the one you gave to me?"

The bald boy looked nervous. His gold-chained necklace was tucked underneath his signature smock, so Oliver couldn't tell the color if its jewel.

"Well—do you?" Ellie urged him, beginning to doubt that this was the authentic specimen.

Finally, the boy replied. "I remember," he said. "It said not to trust the witch."

"That's right," affirmed Oliver. Then, turning to his friends, he added, "It's really him!"

"Oh, wonderful!" Ellie rejoiced. "Now, do you know a way for us to get out of here?"

The child nodded slowly and pointed to the door.

"That's a good start!" Jasmine said with a smile.

The party followed the Mouthpiece out of the small room and back into the hall. Leaning over the landing, Jasmine caught a glimpse of a platoon of guards standing alert near the stairwell on the first floor.

"Better not go that way," she warned the Mouthpiece, who looked to see the guards for himself.

The boy thought for a moment, then darted off in a different direction. The others followed as he disappeared into a dark hidden door tucked in a corner alcove. The passage led to another set of stairs—this time leading them upward.

"We need to get back to the ground floor," said Ellie to their little bald guide.

"Up *then* down," the Mouthpiece said, nodding his head quickly.

Reluctantly, the travelers trusted the boy and followed him up the dark steps. Soon, they reached another long hallway with vaulted ceilings. The Mouthpiece pointed to the end of the corridor and the whole group moved in that direction.

They reached a humble, inconspicuous door; it was so small and hidden that the bald boy nearly passed it.

"In here," said the Mouthpiece as he pulled on the heavy door. It creaked open, revealing a pitch-black room. A cool draft issued from within, causing Ellie to shudder.

"What's in there?" The girl asked, peering inside.

"Way out!" The Mouthpiece spoke confidently, but the rest of the party seemed unconvinced. He started to enter before Jasmine grabbed his arm.

"Wait," she said. "Tell us what's inside—it doesn't look like there's any way out through there."

The boy sighed and nodded, so Jasmine released her grip.

"The ones who see," said the bald boy in a harsh whisper, as if the very words frightened him.

"You mean those strange people that the Prince uses to see what people are doing around the Kingdom?" Oliver recalled their observation of the Seers and their strange magic on their first adventure in the Kingdom.

The Mouthpiece nodded. "Secret tunnels," he added.

"Of course," said Ellie. "That's how they get to all

of those rooms in the palace so quickly—they have their own secret passages!"

"Yes," the Mouthpiece nodded again, more vigorously this time. "A way out!"

"Lead the way," said Jasmine, trusting that the boy had a plan.

"Hold my hand," he said as the three travelers formed a human chain behind the Mouthpiece and followed him into the dark room, shutting the heavy door after them.

They released their hands as they entered a separate, winding narrow corridor lined with dim torches. The Mouthpiece led them past a series of small doors. One was a bit larger than the rest and painted with the symbol of a giant red eye.

"What's that one?" Ellie asked curiously.

"Seers," replied the Mouthpiece as he continued walking.

Oliver stopped in front of the door. "Wait," he said.

The others turned toward him, wondering why he'd stopped.

"We need to go in there," Oliver said with certainty.

"Why?" Jasmine asked. "We don't have any time to lose!"

"There's something I need to know," replied Oliver. "Please!"

"What is it, Oliver?" Now Ellie was curious.

"Prince Florian—he said my grandmother Coral is *alive!*" Oliver explained. "I need to know if it's true—I need to know where she is and what's become of her."

"Can't tell where," the Mouthpiece said with a touch of sadness.

"He's right," said Ellie. "Remember, the Seers can only tell what a person is doing or feeling, not *where* they are."

"I know," Oliver replied. "I just need *something* to know if he was lying or not."

The group seemed to come to a consensus and the Mouthpiece reluctantly guided them into the door with the red eye.

This room was also dark, but a mysterious glow from above cast an eerie gray light around the place. When the group entered, they saw a flurry of motion. Seven figures in neutral-tinted robes stood up from their slumber on the hard floor and formed a cluster, prompted by the echoing of the intruders' footsteps.

Ellie gasped when one of the figures looked toward her, for its eyes were a light, milky gray, devoid of color. The Seers then began to arrange themselves in a semi-circle when the Mouthpiece approached them.

"Stand back," he instructed Jasmine and the children. As they took a few steps backward, the bald boy took his place at the center of the Seers.

"Now," said Oliver to the Mouthpiece when he was ready. "It's time to find out what happened to my grandmother."

CHAPTER THIRTY-TWO
The Mouthpiece Tells the Truth

The Seven Seers were tall and gaunt. Their billowing robes covered their thin frames and their mouths—for they did not speak. (*And perhaps they couldn't*, Oliver surmised.)

The small boy known as the Mouthpiece of the Seers now stood in front of the eerie men and women, his bare feet planted firmly on the cold ground waiting for the strange rite to begin. Then, one-by-one, the Seers closed their vacuous eyes and began to writhe their necks in every direction. They whipped them in a manner that seemed haphazard to the onlookers before finally pointing their chins forward with a sharp motion. Their vacant eyes opened quickly.

In unison, the seven figures gradually raised their right arms, each with a single finger extended, until they were all pointing directly at the Mouthpiece. He closed his own eyes and shivered.

"What do you see?" Ellie asked softly.

"Dark, cold," the Mouthpiece replied.

"And Coral?" Oliver wondered. "Do you see my grandma Coral?"

"Difficult to see," was the reply. "Clouded."

A lump formed in Oliver's throat. "Does that mean you can't find her? That she's—"

The Mouthpiece interrupted: "Searching. The Seers are still searching."

Jasmine looked over her shoulder. She thought she heard a sound from beyond the closed door. "How long will this take?" The woman tried to sound calm. "We haven't got much time before that witch catches up to us."

"Still searching," said the Mouthpiece while his eyes remained shut. "Still seeking."

Ellie glanced at Jasmine, worried, then back at Oliver: "She's right, Oliver. We have to go!"

Oliver shook his head slowly. "I *have* to know," he said, his eyes glued to the bald boy in the center of the room. "I have to know if she's still alive."

Once again, Jasmine thought she heard a noise— *footsteps?* Perhaps it was just her mind playing tricks on her, but they were still running out of time.

"Oliver?"

"Just a few more seconds," he said, holding up his hand.

Another sound, thought Jasmine, turning quickly. *Definitely footsteps—and they're moving fast!*

"We *have* to go!" Jasmine urged.

"I have to *know!*" Oliver moved forward toward the Mouthpiece, but Ellie grabbed her old friend's hand and began to pull him toward the door. He resisted for a moment, then reluctantly gave in and started back.

"Wait!" The Mouthpiece said suddenly.

Oliver whipped around: "Do you see her?" He ran

over to the bald boy so that he stood inches from him. "Do you see Coral?"

The Mouthpiece nodded slowly, causing the emerald around his neck to bounce lightly.

A wave of emotion came over Oliver and he stumbled over his words: "Is she—what happened—my grandmother! Is she alive?"

Once again, the Mouthpiece paused and then spoke slowly: "She is alive. Immovable and in a form that is not her own—but alive."

Oliver began to cry tears of joy and he hugged the other boy tightly.

"It's true!" Oliver sobbed. "Coral is still alive!"

The boy's celebration was short-lived, however, for a moment later he and his friends heard a menacing cackle echo throughout the chamber.

The eyes of the Mouthpiece shot open and he whispered harshly: "*She* is here!"

Ellie and Jasmine huddled in the center of the room with Oliver and the Mouthpiece as a second, louder laugh seemed to surround them. Then, from the shadows emerged a familiar woman in feathery black robes. The Gem of Transfiguration rested on her bosom, glistening blood-red in the dim gray light.

"Dirty, rotten thieves!" She spat as she stepped into the glow. "I thought I recognized you from the jungle all those days ago—vile children!"

"What are you talking about?" Ellie asked the woman as she drew nearer.

"You mean you haven't figured it out?" The dark-haired witch cackled. "The library, the book, the banyan tree, the nest—don't you get it?"

"The raven," said Jasmine softly. "She's used her magic gem to change shapes—*she* is the raven *and* the witch!"

Finally, the children understood and realized that their companion was correct. When Jasmine spoke these words, the Mouthpiece looked down at the gem around his own neck, which had begun to flicker with a faint glow of green. He clung tightly to the hands of Jasmine and the other children who stood close.

"Please," the witch said as she sauntered toward them, "call me Malverne." She smiled and crouched in front of Oliver, inspecting the bespectacled boy. Delicately, she removed his glasses and looked over his face. Oliver flinched.

"So afraid," she taunted. "So unprepared to step into your grandmother's shoes."

"You know nothing of my grandmother!" Oliver snapped.

"How wrong you are," Malverne sighed and placed the glasses back on the boy's face. "I truly can't get over the resemblance of your smile. It's uncanny."

Ellie squeezed Oliver's hand a little tighter.

"You have the exact same expression she had," continued Malverne, "before I *transformed* her!"

Oliver's jaw dropped. He couldn't believe what he was hearing. "*You* transformed her?" He practically shouted. "Where is she? What have you done with her? Tell me!"

Jasmine held the boy back as Malverne laughed: "That would spoil all the fun, boy."

The witch stepped back and cackled again.

"You will *not* get away with this," said Oliver firmly.

"I already have," Malverne retorted. "And now I get to do the same to you!" She raised her hands as if to begin an enchantment.

"And then what?" Oliver asked, interrupting her.

"Why, I rule the Kingdom aside Florian, of course," she said. "Once he drinks of the Fountain, his reign will never end."

The Mouthpiece, who had remained silent for some time, now spoke up: "You're wrong!"

Malverne's smile faded to a scowl: "You *dare* speak against me, boy?" She slapped the Mouthpiece across his face, but he glared at her resolutely.

"Florian's rule is at an end," he said. "They have *seen* it!" He nodded at the Seers but kept his hands firmly linked with his friends. The emerald around his neck glowed again, a touch brighter than before.

"Florian is unworthy to be King," continued the Mouthpiece, now taunting the witch. With each phrase he spoke, the gem grew more brilliant, casting its green light across the whole room.

"He's an evil, selfish man!" Ellie chimed in, huddled close to the boy.

"Oliver is a rightful heir," added Jasmine. "As am I—the heir of Palafox!"

"You speak lies!" Malverne shouted at them, furious.

"No," Oliver smiled confidently, noticing the gem. "We're telling the truth—see for yourself!"

As he said these words, the Gem of Truth glowed even brighter than before. It shone so radiantly that it became impossible for Malverne to look upon it without experiencing sharp pain. She shrieked and backed away slowly.

"Dirty, vile children!" The witch screamed at them, hurrying away. "We're not finished—not even in the slightest! Curse you all!" Then, with those words, she disappeared down the hall in a flurry, screeching as she went.

Oliver and his friends, relieved, took deep breaths as they realized the witch was now gone—at least for the time being.

"Well, then," Oliver said to the Mouthpiece. "How do we get out of here?"

CHAPTER THIRTY-THREE
The Power of the Fountains

The rain was cold, but it did not deter Prince Florian from walking briskly toward the walkway that separated the two Fountains as their waters roiled. The catwalk's ancient tiles were slick and slippery, so Florian slowed as he reached it.

"Don't do this, Florian!" Marco shouted.

The Prince turned to the bearded man. "I have to," he said. "I've grown old, Marco—just like you—and this is the only way—the only way to keep the one thing that's ever brought me any meaning."

"It's not the only way forward," replied Marco through the rain. "There's another way!"

"The throne," Florian shook his head. "It should have been mine from the beginning, and now I've proven it—proven that I can be King."

"You've only proven how low you'll stoop to get your way, Florian. Your father wouldn't have wanted this!"

"My father?" Florian said angrily. "My father never cared about me."

"That's not true," said Marco.

"Then why didn't he give me the *one* thing I desired?"

"Because," Marco pleaded, "he cared for you more than *you* ever did—and he knew what was best for you. What you'd become if you took the throne. Now come away from there. Please!"

Marco had descended the steps so that he came near to Gardenio at the edge of the pools while Florian stood on the walkway in front of them.

"My mind is made up," said the Prince firmly. "I'm going to drink of this Fountain and then I'm going to rid my Kingdom of you two—and those horrible children—once and for all."

Annie and Ben widened their eyes in fear, watching as Prince Florian twirled the golden chalice in his hands. Then, he began to bend toward the turbulent pool—the Fountain of Youth.

Florian carefully dipped the goblet into the waters. He withdrew it and checked to make sure the cup was full. Then, with a wistful smile, he brought the chalice to his parched lips and drank of the magical waters.

The onlookers seemed to hold their breaths as they watched and waited to see how this ancient power would affect the Prince—all except for one.

Thinking quickly, Gardenio rushed from his place at Marco's side and sprinted toward Prince Florian. The young man—Florian's only remaining brother—caught the other by surprise, wrapping his arms around him tightly. The Prince writhed to get free but was caught in Dean's strong grip.

The children gasped in horror as they watched the scene unfold. Marco couldn't move.

"Get *off* me!" Florian shouted over the gurgling

springs and pattering storm. "You're too late!"

Dean, determined to stop the Prince at any cost, wrestled with Florian for several tense seconds that felt like minutes before Marco realized his intentions.

He's trying to throw him into the Fountain of Maturity— it's the only way to reverse the other Fountain's magic. And he intends to go with him! Marco couldn't believe it.

"Gardenio!" Marco shouted. "Don't do this!"

But his cries were too late. At that moment, Florian broke free of Dean's grasp. With a sharp push, the Prince shoved his brother away—right toward the deadly Fountain of Maturity. Marco watched as Gardenio fell slowly, backward, and landed with a huge splash in the still-bubbling waters that closed in over him.

Before the children or Marco could move to try and help him, though, Prince Florian took a step on the wet walkway to pivot back toward the other Fountain. His boots met the slick tile. Suddenly, he found himself on uneasy ground. Florian struggled to steady himself and released his grip on the golden goblet, then slipped. In a mirror-image of his youngest brother's unfortunate fate, Florian tumbled backward—directly into the Fountain of Youth.

Annie and Ben arrived at the edge of the two pools, along with the limp-armed General Pompadour, but Marco held them back. The rest of the Prince's soldiers and servants maintained their distance, unsure of the fate of their fearsome master. Steam and smoke now billowed from the twin Fountains, making it even more difficult to see what was happening to the submerged men.

The rain began to die down. No one spoke. Finally, the stirring of the springs ceased and the bubbles subsided. Marco moved first toward the Fountain in which

Dean had fallen. He looked through the clearing liquid but turned his face away quickly at what he saw.

"Dean is gone," he said quietly, lowering his head in sadness.

The children followed suit, unable to speak.

Then Annie asked, "What of the Prince?"

Marco now turned carefully across the wet tile catwalk. He could discern a floating mass of Florian's garments and trappings, but couldn't tell if the man himself was still somewhere hidden within. Then there was an unexpected sound: the cry of a helpless baby.

Marco looked once more into the still waters of the Fountain of Youth, baffled. There, amidst the loose clothing, was a small baby boy—a newborn child—floating on his back atop the surface of the pool. Marco held out his arms to Pompadour.

"Please! Unbind me—quickly!"

The General swiftly sliced through the ropes on Marco's wrists without stopping to question him. Then the bearded man rushed down into the water, which came up to his waist, and grabbed the crying child. He wrapped it in the loose garments and held the baby close to his chest.

"Is that—?" Annie didn't finish the thought.

Ben nodded: "Prince Florian! The Fountain of Youth—it's made him young again!"

"I don't believe it," said Pompadour, watching as Marco brought the baby near.

"That was most unexpected," Marco muttered.

"What do we do with him now?" Annie wondered.

"I can think of a few things," said Ben sternly. "To pay him back for what he's done to our friends—and to the Kingdom!"

Marco shook his head and crouched so the children

could see the baby up close: "Look at him. He's only a baby now—he can't hurt you or your friends."

"Right now he can't," Ben agreed. "But one day he'll grow up—again—and be the same, mean old Prince Florian!"

"Maybe not," suggested Annie.

"Huh?" Ben looked at her, confused.

"Maybe he won't turn out the same," she explained. "Maybe this time Florian will grow up to be kind and generous and *good*."

Ben was still unsure, but Marco agreed with the girl. "Either way," said their protector, "he's a helpless child now and we can't just leave him out here in the jungle. But he's no longer the ruler of this Kingdom—we'd better get back to our friends and tell them the good news."

The rain had stopped by that time, and the Prince's soldiers now approached the group at the edge of the pool and granted their allegiance to Marco, who graciously accepted their companionship. Then, when they had packed their belongings and supplies, they embarked on the long journey back to their friends.

CHAPTER THIRTY-FOUR
"I've Never Delivered a Baby"

A shrill scream echoed through the jungle, startling a muster of storks from their treetop perches. Juliana let out another wail, grasping tightly to Henry's hand with her own sweaty palm.

"Hang on," said Henry as calmly as he could, though his face was now nearly as red as the woman's. "You're going to be okay!"

The ferry-captain waved a handful of the masked men over to them. They lifted the pregnant woman off the log and carried her carefully into one of the tents while Henry stopped to think over his next course of action.

At that moment, Mugwig returned and frantically tugged at Henry's shirt.

"Tracks!" She exclaimed.

"Not now, Mugwig," replied the ferryman. "Juliana is going into labor."

"What about Kiwi?"

"Kiwi will be fine," Henry said, attempting to console his small, green companion.

"And the baby?" Mugwig picked at her tangled mess of hair.

"I've seen a *lot* of strange things throughout my days," he replied through heavy breaths. "But I've *never* delivered a baby—let alone in the middle of the jungle!"

Juliana screamed once more from inside the shelter.

"Poor thing," Mugwig said as she shook her head. "What to do?"

"I'm thinking," Henry replied quietly. Then, to himself, he muttered, "If only Juniper and Penny were back."

His musings were interrupted by another distant sound: a guttural bark.

"Kiwi?" Mugwig wondered, hurrying toward the noise, which was just outside the camp's textile walls. She pushed aside the fabric barrier and wiggled her large, pointy ears to locate the bark.

As Henry arrived at her side, they heard the sound again.

"Kiwi!" Mugwig was confident this time. She pointed to the tracks that led in the direction of the sound: "This way!"

The two companions hurried into the thick brush, following the tiny prints left by Kiwi's reptilian paws.

"Are you sure these are Kiwi's?" Henry gasped for air as they stopped to listen once more.

"Mugwig is very sure!" The creature said twirling her long-nailed pointer-fingers. "Mugwig is certain!"

Then Mugwig took a few more steps and pushed aside a large leaf—larger than her own body. Through the gap, Henry and Mugwig could glimpse not only the miniature pet Kiwi but two familiar women as well.

"They're back!" Henry shouted, trampling through

the large leaves to greet Juniper and Penelope. "Thank goodness, you're back!"

Kiwi leaped off the ground and into Lady Juniper's arms, where she smothered him with her soft embrace. "Hello there, my pet," said Juniper. Then, turning to the breathless duo in the bushes, she added, "This is quite the welcome! What's got you all so frantic?"

"You need to come quickly," said Henry, attempting to regain his breath. "It's Juliana—"

"Is she alright?" Penny chimed in.

"The baby!" The bearded man gasped. "The baby is coming—now!"

Without delay, the women followed Henry and Mugwig back through the forest and into the camp. Juniper and Penny paused next to Juliana's tent and instructed Henry and the creatures to wait outside. The ferry-captain wholeheartedly complied and escorted Mugwig and Kiwi to play by the fire.

A couple of hours passed. Henry cringed every time he heard Juliana's wailings. Then, all at once, her screams ceased. The camp grew quiet as all of its inhabitants turned their ears toward the tent where the women were hidden away.

Finally, they heard the sound they were awaiting— the sound that set their hearts at ease: the first cries of a newborn baby.

Henry peered through the tent's threshold. He watched as Lady Juniper swaddled the baby in fresh, clean linen and handed the child back to its mother.

"It's a girl," Juniper said softly.

Juliana smiled at the infant through sweat and tears: "My sweet girl."

The bearded ferry-captain now came to Juniper's side and placed a gentle arm around her waist. The old lady tilted her head slightly onto Henry's shoulder and beamed peacefully.

"What is her name?" Lady Penelope inquired, crouched at the edge of the bed.

Juliana, enamored with the precious new life in her arms, stroked the girl's wispy dark hair. "Aria," she said breathily, as if the name were imbued with magic. "We always said we'd name her Aria if we had a girl."

After a moment of gazing into her child's small brown eyes, Juliana turned to Henry and the nurses.

"Where is her father?" She asked, a tinge of fear in her tone. "My sweet Gardenio—where is he?"

CHAPTER THIRTY-FIVE
What Happened Next

By the time the day was drawing to a close, Oliver, Ellie, Jasmine, and the Mouthpiece arrived at the camp. The fading sun licked up the last drops of the rainstorm's dew and disappeared beneath the jungle canopy while the masked men ignited a fresh fire.

Henry and Juniper greeted the children warmly and they all sat down for supper around the flame. Ellie took the initiative to introduce the Mouthpiece to all of her friends in the camp. The bald boy took a special liking to Kiwi but remained quiet for most of the night.

Oliver, on the other hand, was quite vocal, sharing the entire story of what happened to him over the past several days—the closing of the Banyan Gate, the revelation of his status as the heir of Mangonia, the terrible storm out at sea, and his capture and rescue. Ellie and Jasmine chimed in every once in a while to fill in some of the gaps.

Back in her tent, Juliana had fallen asleep with baby Aria in her arms, drifting into a silent dream in the cool of the night. She must have sensed the arrival of the next group of travelers, for she stirred and opened her eyes, rising just at the moment that Marco's party returned.

Peeling back the canvas flap, the blonde woman's drowsy eyes flitted from one soldier to the next, scanning the crowd of somber conquistadors for her husband. First, her eyes were drawn to the pair of children—Annie and Ben—who ran joyously to their long-separated neighbors. Then she noticed a somber General, quietly clutching his bandaged arm.

Marco came last, carrying a bundle of his own. The young woman ran to him, holding Aria close to her bosom. Juniper and Penelope appeared a few steps behind.

"Where are the others?" Juliana asked, glancing beyond Marco through the gap in the wall that was now being closed by masked guards.

Marco lowered his head: "There are no others."

Juniper placed a gentle, comforting hand on the woman's shoulder. Then, as tears began to well up in the new mother's eyes, Juliana buried her face in Lady Juniper's embrace. There were no words that could console the grieving widow, but her companions remained close while she mourned over the great loss of the one she loved so dearly.

Lady Penelope noticed the subtle movement of the object in Marco's arms.

"Is that—a child?" She wondered, leaning in.

Marco nodded slowly.

"Whose child is it?"

The bearded man took a deep breath before he gave an answer. "It's a bit difficult to explain, Penny," he said. "You may want to take a seat."

Penny followed Marco to the circle, where the children crowded around him to look at the precious baby in his arms while Juniper stood a short distance away consoling Juliana. General Pompadour stood at the opposite side, just beyond the light of the flames. Then Marco proceeded to tell the tale of what had transpired at the Court of the Fountains.

When he spoke of Dean's bravery and heroism, Juliana let out another sniveling cry which woke baby Aria. At last, the bearded man explained the strange magic rite that had transformed the evil Prince Florian—the terrible usurper of the Triumvirate's thrones—from a full-grown man into a helpless, newborn child.

"Remarkable," said Henry after a brief period of silence. "I've never seen anything so strange."

The rest of the party agreed.

"So, what happens next?" Annie asked the grownups in the circle.

"Well," said Lady Juniper from the edge of the circle. "At the moment, the Kingdom has no acting ruler."

All eyes turned to Oliver and Jasmine, who sat next to each other on a log. The bespectacled boy looked up at the young woman, then back to Juniper.

"Then I suppose it's time—" Oliver suggested. "Time for us to fulfill the roles we were born for."

"That's right," nodded Juniper.

"But Lady Juniper," Ben chimed in. "What about the babies—Aria and Florian? Which one will take the throne of Coronado?"

"They are both too young now," Juniper agreed. "Until they reach ten years of age—or in Florian's case, reach ten years a *second* time—they cannot rule. Unfortunately, the Kingdom will have to settle for a decade with two rulers instead of three. Unless another, older heir exists unbeknownst to us—though that's not likely."

She paused in thought, then smiled at Jasmine and Oliver: "But *two* will be much greater than the one we've had, for these heirs are good and kind and worthy."

All agreed with a round of cheers. Even Juliana managed to flash a wistful smile while rocking her baby back to sleep.

"Well, children," said Lady Juniper, rising from her seat. "It's quite a bit past your bedtime—" She raised her eyebrows at Oliver. "Even if you *are* the heir to the throne of Mangonia!"

The boy giggled and all of the children said goodnight.

"Tomorrow the Kingdom will rejoice," Henry said to all. "For we will crown our new and rightful rulers at long last!"

Little Ellie squeezed the ferryman tightly, then hurried along after her friends. The Mouthpiece followed Oliver and his neighbors into the large meeting tent where they all fell quickly asleep. It was the first time that the children had dreamed pleasant dreams in quite some time, and they drifted into slumber with contentment and anticipation for the coming festivities.

CHAPTER THIRTY-SIX
The Coronation

The next morning at the break of dawn, the travelers formed a caravan and made their way to Castillo Rosa. It was the closest of the Kingdom's three regional palaces; after the formal coronation ceremony, Oliver and Jasmine intended to return to the palaces of their respective royal families to rule over their own people. There they would likely repeat all of the pomp and circumstance once more, but today they would celebrate with the people of the southeastern coast—celebrate the end of a tyrant's grip over the entire land.

At the word of the royal Master of Ceremonies, the palace gates were opened wide and the caravan was ushered in. The news of Prince Florian's demise spread quickly throughout the surrounding lands and villages, and a large crowd began to gather in the expansive palace courtyard in anticipation of the conveyance of an important message regarding the Kingdom's future rule.

A pair of servants finished adjusting a sash on

Oliver's ceremonial white robes then quietly left the third-story sitting room. In the midst of the busy preparations for the impending ceremony, Oliver and his friends now found themselves alone for a brief moment. Ellie peered through the curtains at the people in the courtyard below and smiled back at her friends.

"They're all here for *you*, Oliver!" She said, returning to a set of armchairs and sofas where the other children sat.

Oliver fidgeted with the little wooden box that held his grandfather's possessions. "If only my family could see me now," he mumbled, stroking the carvings on the chest.

"They would be very proud," Ben said, placing a hand on Oliver's shoulder. "They spent their lives protecting you—all for this moment!"

The boy nodded in agreement. "You're right, Ben," he replied. "I just wish I knew how to find Grandma Coral—or whatever that witch has transformed her into."

"We'll help you look for her," added Annie with a smile. "But let's enjoy today; you're about to become a *king*, after all!"

At that moment, the doors from the hall swung open and Jasmine entered, clothed in a gilded linen dress. A collar of stones and feathers hung around her neck as she glided gracefully into the room.

"Oh, Jasmine!" Ellie said, rushing over to her. "What a beautiful dress!"

The young woman gave a twirl: "It is, isn't it? The seamstresses took extra care to model it after the fashion of my people." The linen floated back to the ground, covering her feet as she finished showing it off.

Marco entered quietly with the Master of Ceremonies and a pair of guards.

"Are you ready, Oliver?" The bearded man asked, smiling softly at the children.

The boy nodded hesitantly, then took Jasmine's hand as they approached a set of glass doors that led to the balcony. As they swung open the doors, Oliver was overwhelmed by the sound of hundreds of people cheering below. He and Jasmine waved with their free hands and gazed upon their loving subjects.

The Master of Ceremonies, one of the last remaining vestiges of Florian's leadership, hesitantly stepped up to the edge of the parapet and with one hand signaled for the people to quiet down. When they were ready to listen, he began his brief speech:

"People of the Kingdom, near and far. It is with great anticipation that you have gathered here today. Many of you have already heard the tragic tale of Florian and his demise." The man paused for a somber effect, then continued. "But today is a day for great celebration! For on this very day, it is my highest honor to announce the coronation of *two* of the rightful heirs to this Kingdom—the beginning of the restoration of the Triumvirate, the rule of three."

Here he motioned for Oliver and Jasmine to come forward, which they did swiftly.

"First, I present to you the honorable and valiant Queen Jasmine of Palafox!" The people burst into shouts of joy as a servant placed a crown of flowers and sprigs atop Jasmine's head; a real, metal crown would be given upon her arrival to her own palace on the other coast of the Kingdom at a later date. The dark-haired woman waved gracefully and blew kisses to the villagers below, then stepped aside.

"Next," shouted the Master of Ceremonies, "it is my

distinct honor and privilege to announce the crowning of the brave and generous King Oliver of Mangonia!"

A crown of leaves was placed upon his head. The boy felt a rush of emotion as the crowd's cheers surged into a deafening roar. Oliver—the little boy from Florida who grew up with no parents—could hardly believe that the moment was really happening. He turned back to his friends who stood clapping just beyond the open doors. His glasses began to fog up. Oliver wiped them with his finger then once more faced the joyous masses, waving his small hands in delight and gratitude.

When the cheering died down, Oliver heard a voice shout from below: "What about the Prince?"

The Master of Ceremonies seemed taken off guard by the question but, before he could answer, a second voice added: "What has happened to him?"

The man was about to speak when Oliver stepped forward.

"The Prince, by some strange magic and a twist of fate, has once more returned to the form of a newborn child," Oliver said loudly. "He will need someone to look after him and to protect him, so that perhaps this time he may grow up to be *good* rather than evil." Here the new King turned around and locked eyes with Marco, whose crossed arms loosened in surprise. Oliver motioned for him to step forward.

Hesitantly, Marco approached the edge of the balcony and looked out across the crowd.

"I believe," continued Oliver, "that the newborn child—once known as Prince Florian—*and* this palace should be placed into the care of the one person who knows both better than any other man: Marco."

The crowd erupted once more as Marco thanked Oliver and the two exchanged a heartfelt embrace.

"Thank you, your Highness," said Marco softly, kneeling in front of the boy.

"Please," said Oliver, motioning for the bearded man to stand. "You are a friend—you need not bow. But I do have a second favor to ask of you—if you are willing?"

"I am willing," Marco nodded.

"If you are to look over the palace of Castillo Rosa, it will give me great comfort to know that you will also keep watch over the poor, unfortunate child known as the Mouthpiece. Will you do this one thing for me?"

"I will do it," replied Marco confidently. "With great honor."

When this exchange was completed, Marco returned to his place at the back of the balcony while the Master of Ceremonies gave a few closing remarks. As a final cheer echoed throughout the courtyard, Oliver and Jasmine withdrew to the adjacent chambers with their friends to prepare for several days of feasting and merrymaking in their honor.

CHAPTER THIRTY-SEVEN
A Familiar Sound and Place

What followed the coronation ceremony was truly spectacular; dancers, twirlers, fire-breathers, fantastic beasts, and people from all across the land flowed through the streets and fields to pay their respects to the newly-crowned King and Queen. It had been decades since the last time such a celebration occurred in the Kingdom and the people were as joyous as ever.

Eventually, though, the celebrations and parades and feasting came to an end—like all such festivities often do—and the people of the Kingdom returned to their homes and their work. The palace courtyards and the garden terrace once again became quiet and sparse; but now, instead of feeling lifeless, these places seemed to be filled with a burst of expectancy—as if something wonderful or magical were about to happen at any moment. It was about this time that Oliver realized he would now have to part ways with some of his dearest friends.

"Don't cry, Ellie," Oliver said to her as he gave the

girl a big hug. "We'll see each other again before you know it." Ben and Annie stood nearby, waiting for their turn.

Ellie nodded, "I know. It's just that the Kingdom seems so far away from our little neighborhood back home."

"Then," said Oliver with a smile, "I suppose you'll just have to come and visit—call it a holiday! All of you are welcome whenever you like!" He motioned to the other children.

"Are you sure you're ready for this?" Annie asked. "Are you sure you're prepared to be King?"

"I don't think I'll ever feel ready," replied Oliver. "But this is something I *have* to do—no one else can take my place as King of Mangonia; it's in my blood."

"You're right," said Annie. "It's who you are."

"In my humble opinion," Ben spoke up, "you're going to make a great King!"

Oliver lowered his head bashfully and smiled. "Thanks, Ben. I'm going to miss you." Then nodding to the girls added, "I'm going to miss you *all*."

"I've just thought of something," said Ellie. "How are we going to get home?"

"That's a good question," said Ben. "The nearest Gate is quite some distance from here—"

He was interrupted by the sound of the door creaking open behind him. Lady Juniper walked in confidently, a small bag slung across her shoulder.

"A good question, indeed," Juniper said to Ben, smiling. "For the answer—leave that to me."

The children were baffled by the woman's sudden appearance, but if there was one thing they had learned on their many adventures, it was that Lady Juniper always had a plan.

"You may recall that Penelope and I recently underwent a quest to open a number of Gates throughout the land," she continued. "We thought that it might behoove us to save a bit of the old Carpenter's potion in the event that we needed to create an additional portal for some other purpose."

"Of course!" Ellie clapped her hands in delight. "We can create another Gate right here in the palace!"

"Exactly," said Lady Juniper, reaching into her pouch. "That'll save you some trouble if you should ever desire to visit, too, I might add." She produced the vial that contained the remainder of the Carpenter's magic elixir. "Now, let's see—" She inspected the room and wandered over to a small linen closet. Looking inside, she verified that it was unused.

"That'll do," she muttered to herself.

"Juniper," asked Annie. "Where exactly will this Gate take us—I mean, *where* inside of our world?"

"That's the fun of this enchantment!" Juniper smiled. "We can get a little creative, now that I've learned more about how it works. How about somewhere, er, familiar?"

The children nodded slowly, confused.

"I have just the place in mind," she said as she began to sprinkle a few drops of the elixir onto the closet door. "How about," she muttered the magic words under her breath, "a certain old house on Azalea Drive?"

As she said this, the door began to sparkle and glow at its edges. A shimmering sound—a faint ringing as of distant bells—filled the room and the children smiled widely. Lady Juniper opened the door and revealed a portal into a musty hallway.

"Alright, then," she said. "Time to go."

The children knew that she was right, but they

didn't want to part. Finally, with a few more tears and hugs, Oliver's three neighbors moved toward the open door and began to process through it, with Ellie taking up the rear.

"Wait," said Oliver, running to his three friends. He fished into his pocket and withdrew a small envelope, which he promptly placed into Ellie's hands. "Can you give this to my Grandpa Jesse? It's important."

Ellie nodded, then she and the other two children waved goodbye to Oliver. Then, turning away, they walked straight through the Gate and Juniper slowly shut the door behind them. The ringing faded. Ellie ran over to the door and turned the knob, letting a stream of sparkling light back into the hallway.

"We're still here," said Juniper through the crack, smiling at the girl.

Then, realizing that they would have a way to return whenever they wanted, Ellie closed the door once more and followed Annie and Ben down the rickety stairs from the second floor of the old, decrepit house.

When they were outside, the three children were greeted by a beautiful, sunny Florida day. They squinted as their eyes adjusted to the brightness, then started back toward their street.

The first stop they made was at the home of Oliver's grandfather—Jesse. The children knocked and waited on the doorstep as the old man hobbled to the door. When he recognized them, he smiled a handsome grin.

"Well, hello there," he said. "Oliver's not home right now, I'm afraid."

"Actually," replied Ellie with a smile. "Oliver is right where he belongs!"

They all chuckled. Ellie handed the man the envelope from Oliver, said their goodbyes, and continued on down the sidewalk.

Next, they arrived at Annie's house.

"Well, that was *some* adventure," the girl said. "I hope we'll be able to return to the Kingdom soon!"

"Me, too," said Ben. Then the boy awkwardly approached for a hug and—as Annie did the same—collided with the girl's nose.

"Ouch!" Annie giggled.

"Sorry!" Ben stepped back.

Ellie rolled her eyes and said, "Oh, *brother.*"

They all laughed and Annie waved goodbye, closing the door behind her.

"What do you think it meant?" Ellie asked her older brother when they were halfway across Annie's front lawn.

"What?" Ben wondered.

"The letter," she replied.

Ben stopped walking: "Ellie! You *read* it? That was for Oliver's *grandfather!*"

"I know," said Ellie, continuing down the sidewalk. "But it wasn't sealed."

They walked on in silence for a moment before Ben spoke softly, "Well?"

"Well, what?"

"The note," the boy said. "What did it say?"

"Oh, um," Ellie muttered. She scratched her chin and tried to remember the brief message. "It only had three words."

"What were they?"

"It said: '*I believe you.*' What do you think Oliver meant by that?"

Ben smiled as they reached their front door. "I think I know what Oliver has on his mind."

"What is it?"

"Oliver's going to try and find his grandmother, Coral," Ben said, looking his sister in the eyes with excitement. "And we're going to help him!"

The adventures continue...

Find out what happens next in
The Curse of Coronado!

Follow along and sign-up for updates on
www.KingdomOfFlorida.com
for news on future books in the series

If you enjoyed *Kingdom of Florida: Volume I*,
make sure to leave a review on *Amazon.com*

Thank you for reading!
- Taylor

ABOUT THE AUTHOR

Taylor Thomas Smythe is a native of West Palm Beach, Florida, which has been a source of inspiration for a variety of his creative works. He is the author of the Kingdom of Florida series and other forthcoming adventure stories. Taylor enjoys creative writing of all kinds and topics, but he especially likes to write stories about interesting places or magical worlds.